it stings so sweet

Stephanie Draven

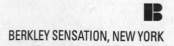

BERKLEY SENSATION, NEW YORK

THE BERKLEY PUBLISHING GROUP
Published by the Penguin Group
Penguin Group (USA) Inc.
375 Hudson Street, New York, New York 10014, USA
Penguin Group (Canada), 90 Eglinton Avenue East, Suite 700, Toronto, Ontario M4P 2Y3, Canada
(a division of Pearson Penguin Canada Inc.) • Penguin Books Ltd., 80 Strand, London WC2R 0RL,
England • Penguin Ireland, 25 St. Stephen's Green, Dublin 2, Ireland (a division of Penguin
Books Ltd.) • Penguin Group (Australia), 707 Collins Street, Melbourne, Victoria 3008, Australia
(a division of Pearson Australia Group Pty. Ltd.) • Penguin Books India Pvt. Ltd., 11 Community
Centre, Panchsheel Park, New Delhi—110 017, India • Penguin Group (NZ), 67 Apollo Drive,
Rosedale, Auckland 0632, New Zealand (a division of Pearson New Zealand Ltd.) • Penguin Books
(South Africa), Rosebank Office Park, 181 Jan Smuts Avenue, Parktown North 2193, South Africa •
Penguin China, B7 Jiaming Center, 27 East Third Ring Road North,
Chaoyang District, Beijing 100020, China

Penguin Books Ltd., Registered Offices: 80 Strand, London WC2R 0RL, England

This book is an original publication of The Berkley Publishing Group.

This is a work of fiction. Names, characters, places, and incidents either are the product of the author's
imagination or are used fictitiously, and any resemblance to actual persons, living or dead, business
establishments, events, or locales is entirely coincidental. The publisher does not have any control over
and does not assume any responsibility for author or third-party websites or their content.

IT STINGS SO SWEET

PUBLISHING HISTORY
Berkley Sensation trade paperback edition / February 2013

Berkley Sensation trade paperback edition ISBN: 978-0-425-26318-1

An application to register this book for cataloging has been submitted to the Library of Congress.

PRINTED IN THE UNITED STATES OF AMERICA

10 9 8 7 6 5 4 3

It Stings So Sweet

To my husband,
who changed everything
I thought I knew about the world.

ACKNOWLEDGMENTS

Thanks go to my husband and to my critique partners, Ann Arbaugh, Christi Barth, Sabrina Darby, Anna Genest, and Kate Quinn. Special thanks to Eden Bradley and Kate Pearce for talking me through the hard parts. And thank God for Jackie Barbosa, without whom this book would never have been completed, and she knows why. Last, but not least, I'm grateful to Megan Hart, as always, whose own ideas about erotic fiction permeate this work.

This book started out as a dream starring Jonathan Rhys Meyers dressed up in 1920s garb, guzzling cocktails at a ritzy party. And he was extremely angry. I woke up wanting to know why, and that's how *Love Me or Leave Me* came into existence.

After that, I started researching the period and my reading list was the bee's knees. I reread F. Scott Fitzgerald's *The Great Gatsby*. I devoured Joshua Zeitz's *Flapper: A Madcap Story of Sex, Style, Celebrity, and the Women Who Made America Modern*. I also consulted the article "Gotham's Daughters: Feminism in the 1920s" by Maureen Honey.

My research on sexuality in the Roaring Twenties led me to stumble over a little snippet of a vintage stag film of uncertain date called *Nudist Bar*, which has been preserved in digital format and can be found on the internet today. While entirely pornographic in nature, it was also so cheeky and charming that I couldn't help make up a story about a similar, fictional film.

Clara and Leo's picnic was inspired by Donald Ogden Stewart's "Correct Behavior on a Picnic," excerpted from the 1920s etiquette book, *Perfect Behavior; A Guide for Ladies and Gentlemen in All Social Crises*. The imagery and a few evocative phrases helped me set the stage for authenticity.

Much of Sophie's dialogue finds its source in the *Birth Control Review*, published between 1917 and 1929, just as Margaret Sanger and the American Birth Control League were intensifying their fight to pass legislation that would legalize contraception in the United States.

Credit also goes to Wikipedia for its description of an Immelmann turn, something I have not had the pleasure of witnessing firsthand. I relied heavily upon the Online Etymology Dictionary and the *Oxford English Dictionary* to wrestle my prose into period-appropriate language. I did not always succeed, as sometimes a more modern word or anachronistic idiom seemed more artful, but I am indebted to those sources and my tireless copy editor, Angelina Krahn.

Though the characters in these stories were inspired by many different archetypical people from the era, I'd be remiss not to mention Clara Bow, specifically, whose story helped inspire mine. Quotes from her and about her are sprinkled throughout this manuscript to bring the time period alive, and wherever she is now, I think she'd be tickled by the tribute.

CONTENTS

love me or leave me

CHAPTER

One

Nora

The band is playing "A Good Man Is Hard to Find," and tonight, its lyrics about heartbreak cut entirely too close to the bone. As the singer growls through the soulful song, Jonathan's cool blue eyes pierce through a wreath of smoke to accuse me, and my whole body tightens, overly aware of him.

With his lean elegance and chiseled good looks, he's the star attraction in any social gathering, but Jonathan stands out especially at this swanky party, a glass of gin dangling so casually from one hand, at odds with the formality of his coat and tails. He wears a white vest, shirt, and tie pulled too tight, but it isn't the tie that has stiffened Jonathan's neck.

He wants to leave. The way his eyes keep darting to the exits show me just how much he wants to escape the clink of glasses and the laughter of women who twist long strands of pearls between their breasts to entice him. Something green and ugly writhes in my belly at the thought that he can have his pick of the women who flirt with him; I've heard women whispering about him. With his dark hair slicked back and the lightest hint of a mustache over his full, brooding lips, he is the most striking man in this or any room.

He is also my husband, or at least he will be, until morning.

He wasn't born to this life. His father was a man who worked with his hands, and Jonathan still remembers going hungry. Even so, threading his way through the crowd, he shows no interest in the chocolate-covered cherries, caviar, or oysters on the half shell. A girl asks him to dance, but he declines in so genteel a fashion that she purses her red-painted mouth to blow him a kiss.

Jonathan is nothing if not mannerly. Distant, unknowable, but unfailingly polite.

Even now, as furious as he is with me, he gives me a gentlemanly bow of his head. "Are you enjoying the party, Mrs. Richardson?"

I grimace with bitter amusement that this might be the last night we share a name. At home, his bags are packed. By morning he'll be gone. Unless I do something about it.

Pressing my hands against the wood-paneled wall to steady myself, I lean in, trying to be heard over the tinkling piano. "Jonathan, please let me explain—"

"I've got a bit of an edge," he interrupts, affably saluting me with his glass so that I can see that he's drained it. "Perhaps we should make the rounds and get going."

His ability to remain so even-tempered makes me angry, and for a moment I'm inclined to agree that we *should* leave, even if leaving this party is the last thing we'll ever do together. But I've let myself draw too near to him. I've caught a whiff of his scent, something musky and male that combines with the alcohol on his breath to make my knees weak. "I'd like to stay a little longer, if you don't mind."

"Whatever you like," he says, agreeably.

He's always agreeable. He's never complained about my overprotective father. Nor the distance that has separated his bed from mine for the past year. Nor the silent breakfasts or awkward good-nights.

As far as I know, my mild-mannered husband has never been bothered by *anything* until this morning, when I confessed my sins.

He listened to everything I had to say, then laid his butter knife carefully at the edge of his breakfast plate and calmly announced his intention to divorce me. Now, I reach for his hand, trying to make him listen. "Jonathan, can't we talk about this?"

"This doesn't seem like the time nor the place," he says with a tight smile, deftly avoiding the closer intimacy of tangled fingers by tucking my arm in the crook of his elbow. The heat of his body through my clothes is electric and forces my eyes closed. I've wanted him from the first time I saw him—and I *had* him. All of him. Not the bottled-up bluenose he's become. Not the man who transformed himself to fit in with this crowd. Once I had *all* of him. The wild, savage beast of him.

We met at a party like this one, but he was a crasher then. I was drowning in liquor, too zozzled to dance with the flappers in my set, too drunk to stand up straight. His face was thinner, chin sharply angled, lips curled with the insolent snarl of a workingman, but his eyes were the same. Such intense blue.

I've always been a girl too much inside her own head, or so my father tells me, though it's the way he taught me to be. "Look at a thing from every angle, my little bunny," he used to say. "Always go with what you know."

But the moment I met Jonathan, a mad, instant lust took hold of me. I didn't know anything about him except that I wanted to be underneath his body. He could've undressed me in front of all the guests and I wouldn't have stopped him. To get his attention, I'd tickled him with a feather from my headdress. He let me take a puff off his cigarette. Somehow, we ended up in the buggy seat, my knees over his shoulders, my father's car bouncing on its wheels as Jonathan fucked me raw.

I remember that he ripped the front of my dress, catching the beads around my neck by accident, snapping the string, and sending them spilling everywhere. I still occasionally find one of those beads in my handbag or in the driveway, and it makes me wilt with the scorching heat of the memory every time. You see, I loved him that night. I loved all the filthy things he said to me. I loved all the ungentlemanly things he did to me. I loved the way it felt to have my dress wadded up around my waist, to feel him inside me, not even knowing his name. Not knowing that he worked for my father or that he would be the kind of man to return with flowers and a marriage proposal when he found out I was knocked up.

I'm jarred from my memories by the voice of Paul Kendrick. "Jonathan, old sport!" The moneyed banker slaps my husband on the back. "Saw your Bentley outside. A gift from the father-in-law? Nice racket if you can get it—" Paul Kendrick suddenly realizes I'm standing there. Quickly clearing his throat, he laughs too loud. "Ah, Mrs. Richardson. Pardon me. I didn't see you through the haze of smoke."

I show him a flash of teeth. I hate men like Paul Kendrick, who belittle Jonathan under the guise of friendship. Men who ignore the fact that in the time he's worked for my father, Jonathan has already earned enough money to buy his own Bentley. "I do fade into the woodwork . . ."

Kendrick snorts at my sarcasm. "You must not be paying your wife the attention she's due, Jonathan. She seems not to know how attractive she is."

"Oh, she knows," Jonathan says, and an awkward silence follows.

"I love Hollywood parties, don't you?" Kendrick asks, surveying the bootlegged bottles on the bar behind us. But Prohibition doesn't apply to people with money. People like us. Sometimes I think the temperance movement only concerns itself with the poor. "Not a bad outlay of alcohol tonight."

Jonathan doesn't say anything and I don't, either. Paul Kendrick's glance darts from me to Jonathan and back again, finally sensing the tension. He makes some excuse to go, hastily retreating across the polished wood floor to join a cadre of men debating the merits of the Scopes Monkey Trial from a few years back. I have my own beliefs when it comes to that, for I have very good reason to believe that we're really all just animals inside.

From the nearby sideboard, Jonathan chooses a decanter and fills his glass. "Is he the one?"

The words are spoken so softly, I wonder if I've imagined them. I follow his gaze to where Paul Kendrick stands and feel myself flush, but I have no right to be offended. "No. Not him. Of course not."

Jonathan adds something dark to his drink, then drops two cubes of ice into the mixture. "Who was it then? I deserve to know his name."

Nothing good can come of this, but I find myself strangely gratified that Jonathan has finally asked. That a hint of agitation has finally touched his expression. "It makes no difference who it was. It was only a kiss. I've been trying to tell you, it was a drunken . . ." I struggle for the right word. I cannot call my infidelity a lark, for it was nothing that innocent. "It was a drunken *nothing*. It meant nothing at all."

My husband's tone is light, but his eyes are anything but. "It was just the hooch, then. Is that what you're saying?"

"Yes. He was tanked."

"What about you? Were you tanked, too?"

"Yes," I admit, taking a deep, relieved breath of air. As long as my husband is asking questions, perhaps he can find a way to forgive me. "I had too much. Sometimes I lose count."

"I see." Jonathan lets my hand drop. The break in contact between us is like an arctic wind. "Kind of like the night we met. Was that a drunken nothing, too?"

When he lifts his overflowing glass to his lips, I clutch at his arm. "No. Jonathan." I know that he wants me to tell him that I love him, but I can't make myself say the words. Not even now. Especially not now, because I've never found the courage to say it before. If I let those words fall from my lips now only to watch him walk away, it will kill me. "You're my husband. What's between us isn't *nothing*."

"You're spilling my drink," he says mildly, as if he can't hear the desperation in my voice. He sets the glass down, brushing my hands, and the spilled liquid, from his jacket. Then I watch him take another glass and fill it as well, adding a splash of cherry. He hands that one to me. I take it only because I'm desperate for the brush of his fingers over mine, even if they are wet and cold.

"Drink," he says, eyes pale as ice.

My hand shakes and the cherry in my glass bobs up and down. "Jonathan, I'm sorrier than you know."

"Are you going to drink?"

I stare at the glass in my hand, the carved crystalline ridges scraping my palm, and regard it as if it holds poison. "No. Spirits have done enough damage between us."

"Then I'm leaving," he says, emptying his glass. "I'll send a driver back to fetch you."

He whirls and I catch him, heedless of the stares we draw. I can't let him go.

"What?" he snaps, savagely. His first real show of temper.

He stares, waiting for me to speak, watching as I wrestle with my tongue. "What can I do to show you how sorry I am? How can I make it up to you?"

His shoulders actually shake with anger. I worry he will say that nothing I can ever say or do will ever make up for allowing another man to kiss me. Instead, he says, "You can drink."

It's too small a request to refuse him, so I lift the cool rim of the glass he's given me, taking a swallow of something that stings sweet. This seems to satisfy him. He tugs at his tie and no longer seems like himself. No longer mild-mannered, polite, or distant. He stares at me as if he might tilt my head back and pour a drink down my throat. I wish he would. I love the feel of his strong hands tangled in my hair. "Drink it *all*, Nora."

I take two more gulps. "You want me to tell you who the man was? Is that what you want?"

He gives a bark of bitter laughter. "What I want is to punish you . . . and I want you to drink."

CHAPTER

Two

He wants to punish me. Why does the thought steal my breath, warm my blood, and quicken my pulse? It recalls to mind one late-night encounter, early in our marriage, bent over the bed. In his excitement, he'd taken the belt from his pants and slapped it against the back of my thighs. Once, twice, maybe three times. No more than that. I only remember that I yearned for him to do it harder. But the next morning he was so sheepish that I dared not raise the subject. And he never did it again. Still, the memory of it forces me to exhale sharply with a thrill of anticipation.

Unfortunately, I doubt that is the kind of play-pretend punishment my husband wants to dole out tonight. I've told him it was only a kiss, but he's unconvinced. Perhaps he's imagining me naked, in bed with another man. Even if that were true, isn't a divorce enough punishment for a single night's indiscretion? The divorce will cause a scandal but I know there are men who will overlook any black mark on my name if it means they stand a chance of inheriting my father's money.

So perhaps Jonathan has something crueler in mind.

"You want to punish me . . ." I repeat slowly, worried that the wet glass is going to slip through my hold. Just saying the words makes me feel vulnerable. "Will punishing me make you feel better about what happened?"

Jonathan crosses his arms over himself, one hand held up, fingers worrying over each other as he considers my question. "I'm not certain," he finally says. "We'll have to find out. The only thing of which I *am* certain is that if you don't do exactly what I tell you to do, I'm going to leave."

And I'll never see him again. Of this much, I'm certain, too. This, and the fact that he wants me to drink.

Lost in the unfathomable depths of his glacial eyes, I tip my head back and swallow everything in my glass. The liquid burns the back of my throat, but I don't stop until the glass is empty and I'm panting for air.

"Atta girl," he says, one eyebrow raised, and I cannot tell if it's surprise or admiration. Something changes in him. Something snaps. Unravels. His shoulders loosen; his posture becomes more languid in the way of a predator toying with his prey. A hapless waiter passes too close to us, and Jonathan blocks him. While the waiter tries to regain his balance, Jonathan grabs a mint julep from the waiter's tray and offers it to me with a leer. "Drink this, too, Nora."

So he wants me *drunk*. He must want me on the floor tomorrow morning, heaving and sick. I deserve it. Bent beyond oblivion is probably the only way to escape the pain of heartbreak anyway, so I snatch the glass from him and gulp it down, mint leaves and all.

My head already spinning, I grab the edge of the bar for balance. He wants me to drink? Then I'll drink. I turn, jostling bottles together in a frenzy, refilling my empty glass. I don't know what I'm pouring. I'll happily drink it all.

"Stop." Jonathan catches my wrist, his grip like iron. Not since the first night we met has he pressed his fingers into my flesh to the point of pain. Somehow, until this moment, I hadn't remembered how good it felt. I'm unable to fathom how I can be so aroused by him. How, even now, I want desperately to rip his clothes off.

"I'm just doing what you told me to do, Jonathan. You wanted me to drink."

He shakes his head. "I'm not trying to kill you with it. That's enough."

Booze sloshes in my belly with the poison of despair, and I fall silent.

With his chin, Jonathan motions to Mr. Kendrick. "Go ask him to dance. I want to see the two of you together."

I think I understand the reason for this strange demand. "Jonathan, I told you it wasn't him. It wasn't *him!*"

"I don't believe you, Mrs. Richardson," my husband replies, skewering me with his last name. "Even if I did believe you, it wouldn't matter. Kendrick watches your heart-shaped ass every time you walk across a room. When you turn to face him, his expression glazes over as if he were trying to guess if your nipples are pink or red or brown. He'd love to put his slobbering lips all over you, given half a chance. He'd love to fuck you if you let him, and who can blame him? So why not give him a taste of what he fantasizes about . . ."

Jonathan has never spoken to me this way before. Not even the first time. Flushed with instant fury, I want to strike him, but he still has my wrist locked in his grip. As I struggle, he grabs my other wrist for good measure and we draw a few stares.

Jonathan laughs, attempting to convince outsiders that we're just a playful couple, up to hanky-panky, but nothing about my anger is feigned. Jonathan only proposed because I was pregnant. After the miscarriage, he moved into his own bedroom. In all the months since, he's never laid a hand on me. Now he expects me to believe he actually cares whether or not someone else wants me?

"You've just been waiting for this," I hiss. "Haven't you? You've just been waiting for an excuse to leave me and I was foolish enough to give it to you."

My husband works his beautiful, angled jaw, holding something back. For a moment I think he'll retreat behind his mannerly veneer. He'll say that this isn't the time or place for ugliness. He'll spout some platitude about wishing me well and apologize for having lost his temper. He'll be a gentleman instead of a fiend.

And I'll hate him for it.

Instead, he says, "The only thing I'm waiting for is to watch you dance."

In all the time I've known him, my husband has never been petty. And yet, I much prefer this bullying to the cool distance between us. I see him, somewhere, in that temper. The real him. The one he hides from everyone. So I only say, "Be careful what you wish for."

I use the back of one hand to brush away my brimming tears, careful not to smear my mascara, knowing that there isn't a man on the dance floor who would refuse me. They all know who my father is. They want me for my fortune, but they never make me burn with lust the way my husband does. Perhaps I have only ever wanted him because he's the one thing I can't have.

So if my husband is going to leave me, maybe it's best if his last sight of me is in the arms of another man. I hope it pains him. I hope it stabs at him. Probably it will only make him feel justified in walking away.

But he doesn't walk away. Even after I make my way onto the dance floor with Mr. Kendrick and let him put his clammy hand between my shoulder blades, my husband just stands there at the edge of the party, arms folded over his chest.

As I've said, I loathe men like Paul Kendrick. Men in my father's social circle whom I've known all my life. Men who haven't ever known a day of adversity and who have no mercy or compassion for anyone who has. Paul Kendrick is, of course, a perfect dancer, executing the fancy footwork of the Charleston with utter grace while the frenetic pace requires all my concentration. With my knees bent and springy, my breasts jiggle to the music and my dance partner makes only a token effort not to notice them. He has that glazed expression that Jonathan described and I wonder if it's true that he's trying to guess the color of my nipples. They harden at his attention, much to my shame.

My beaded gown slaps against my thighs as I twist on the balls of my feet. I wonder if men are looking at my legs, catching a glimpse of my garters when I kick too high. I have never before considered that men might be appraising me this way—for my body alone. That this very moment, as furious as Jonathan is, *he* might be appraising me this way. The thought stokes a furnace in my belly and I dance harder, putting a shimmy in my shoulders.

I'm tall and leggy, but curvier than is fashionable. The straight flapper gowns don't drape the way they should on me. But Jonathan has filled me with curiosity about just how my body might appeal.

"Your husband is watching you," Paul Kendrick says, not even winded. "I don't think he's enjoying this party. Maybe you need to be born to the right kind of people to get the most out of these functions, eh?"

It's an unsubtle cut from an unsubtle man and I let my elbow jab into his ribs as he turns me. My teeth are clenched and perspiration drips down the back of my neck. I'm unutterably relieved when the song comes to an end.

"Well?" I ask, returning to Jonathan's side. "Did you see what you wanted to see?"

My husband nods, gaze intent. "I did. It wasn't him."

"Now you believe me?"

"I believe my own eyes, Nora. I know how you look at a man who kisses you."

"It's been so long since you kissed me, I somehow doubt you remember."

Jonathan blanches and I feel the momentary thrill of having pierced his armor, but he hands me another drink. This one has a pineapple on the rim. "I remember everything, Nora. Now part those treacherously beautiful lips of yours and drink up."

Pulling the fruit off the glass and rolling it between my teeth, I sway slightly to the music and the strange pleasure of finally having my husband's complete attention—even if it is the wrong kind of attention. "Mr. Kendrick doesn't believe you're enjoying yourself tonight, Jonathan."

"Oh, but I intend to," he says with an ominous note. Then, using one long finger to tap the bottom of my glass, he forces a splash of liquid into my mouth. Our eyes lock and I swallow, remembering the way he tastes. The way he smells. The way he feels inside me.

His hand brushes my jawline, holding me still like he did the time he forced his tongue in my mouth, kissing me so hard that his teeth cut my lip. In spite of everything, I want him to do it again, right here and now. He has to know it. He has to see it as I angle my face up to him in offering. "Jonathan, I'm lightheaded . . ."

"Poor little bunny," he says, using my father's nickname for me. Then he dips his head and nuzzles my ear. The warmth of his breath gets under my skin, seeping into my blood and setting it to boil. Then I feel the sharp bite of his teeth on my earlobe. "Too dizzy to do what I tell you?"

"No," I whisper, not knowing or caring what he does to me so long as I can keep him this close.

"You're going to dance with our host, next. Show me and Teddy Morgan what a vamp you can be."

Anger and inebriation make for a dangerous cocktail. I grip my husband's lapels, nails digging in. "I'm *not* a vamp."

Jonathan's eyes narrow to slits. "Then why did you step out on me? Unless you wanted me to notice. Is that it? Because I tell you, Nora, you have my interest now. Show me how much you liked playing the slut for Big Teddy Morgan and I won't look away."

"Stop it, Jonathan. Just stop it. It wasn't Ted Morgan, either. I'll tell you who kissed me—"

"But I'd rather guess," Jonathan interrupts, his hard body boxing me in. "I'd rather watch you dance with every cake-eater in the joint.

I want to see them paw you, and pinch your ass, and sneak a peek at your gams when your skirt flips up in the back."

"Why? Just to *humiliate* me?"

"Now you're on the trolley!" Both of his dark brows shoot up to accompany a mirthless smile. But when my lower lip trembles, he falters and the grim smile fades away. I see a mask of regret descend over his expression, as if he stands in shock at his own behavior. "You can stop the ride any time you like, Nora." The pressure of his fingers turns gentle. He's rueful. Embarrassed. "I'm handling this badly. I shouldn't have come to this party tonight. I just hoped to spare you the embarrassment of trying to explain things to your friends and family. I suppose it's too late for that . . ."

"We shouldn't have to explain anything to anyone, Jonathan! It was just a kiss."

This irritates him, if the flush on his face is any indication. "Quite right. I ought to be a gentleman about this."

"I don't *want* you to be a gentleman," I say, even at the risk of prolonging our argument because I've seen more passion from him in the past few hours than in a year's time. He's here with me now in a way he hasn't been since we were first married. "I'm sick to death of it!"

He glances up, gauging me. "You're playing with fire, Nora."

He is the flame, and I'm already burning. "You don't scare me, Jonathan. You never have."

A flash of something lights behind his eyes. "Are we going to play this game, then? Because if we are, this is the right song, Nora. Ted Morgan's on his way over. Are you going to dance with him?"

Everything about my husband is a provocation now. His stance, his words, everything. Maybe it's the buzz of liquor that addles my brain, but I like the word *game*. There's hope in that word. Games can be won. And I have nothing left to lose. "I'll dance with him if you stay to watch it."

"Oh, I'll be watching, Nora."

"Then I hope you choke on it."

He leans in closer, whispering in my ear. "There's a reason they call him Big Teddy. He's hung like a horse. I'm guessing if he tried to put it in your mouth, you'd be the one to choke on it." His crudeness embarrasses me and I turn my head to the side, but he makes me look at him, his face very close to mine. "What's the matter, Princess? I thought you didn't want me to be a gentleman. Am I too vulgar for you? That's what all your friends say, don't they? You've probably always feared the real Jonathan Richardson might make an appearance and send you into a fainting spell with his rough, uneducated tongue."

"I said I've never been afraid of you!"

"Well, you should be," Jonathan says, grinding his teeth.

I think he'll say more. I want him to say more. Instead, he points at Big Teddy. "Go dance the tango with Ted Morgan. Press against him. Make him hard. Make him want to fuck you so badly that he can't keep his hands to himself. Let him catch a whiff of that sexy perfume drifting up from between your legs. You're aroused just thinking about it, aren't you?"

"No."

It's a lie. I'm trembling with arousal, but it has nothing to do with Ted Morgan. It's that the crueler Jonathan is, the more I seem to like it. I don't understand, but I don't need to. I only know that the way he stares at me now makes me feel like the only woman in the room. And I am intoxicated on more than liquor.

My husband calls out to the barrel-chested tycoon. "Teddy! Take my girl off my hands for a spell, won't you? She's keen to dance tonight but I've had a bit too much of the giggle juice."

"Posilutely!" Big Teddy says, grabbing hold of my hand in one of his meaty palms and yanking me towards the dance floor. He's a fleshy middle-aged man. Jolly. Too affable to notice the way my husband's eyes burn holes in his back.

It's a twisted game we're playing. It's clear to me that Jonathan's fury isn't feigned. He's been betrayed. He wants to punish and humiliate me. The idea that another man put his mouth on me has ignited a fire in my husband. But it isn't only anger. I can read Jonathan's body the way I've never been able to read his mind. Looking at him now, I can see the sexual tension roll off his body in waves. I realize with shocking clarity that he's excited.

Jonathan *wants* me.

And maybe I *am* a vamp, because the jolt of that realization makes me damp behind my knees, at all my pulse points, and between my thighs. What's more, my nipples tighten harder, creating bumps that must be visible against the thin drape of my dress. My dance partner pretends not to notice, but when I glance down I see the enormous ridge of Big Teddy's cock swell under his pants. Under the searing glare of my husband's scrutiny, I press a little closer, trying to brush against Big Teddy with my belly and thighs as we tango.

I'm rewarded by sexual heat that arcs through this other man's body, across the dance floor to where my husband is standing. Now it's as if Jonathan and I are dancing together, this interloper between us. Teddy's hand dips lower on my back than is appropriate, but then, this is a graceful dance not meant for the likes of him.

Perhaps my brazenness has encouraged him. I feel wild and licentious, just as I did the first night I met Jonathan. And with my eyes locked on my husband, I do exactly as he instructed, taking every opportunity to rub up against Big Teddy's body.

And, god help me, I like it.

Perhaps my obvious pleasure at the feel of this man's enormous erection is proof to Jonathan that I'm a tramp—that he can't trust me to be faithful. But with every gyration, I feel as if I'm touching Jonathan, not this other man. I half want to crawl up my dance partner's body, and the shock of my desire makes me stumble.

Big Teddy catches me, taking the opportunity to draw me closer. "Had a little too much to drink tonight, Mrs. Richardson?"

The man thinks he's taking advantage. He even has the grace to be somewhat red-cheeked and ashamed of himself. But that doesn't stop him from pressing his erection against me. I feel it pulse against my leg.

"Mmm," I say, not sure I trust myself to speak.

The dance floor is crowded now and we're jostled together, so I angle my hips, grinding slightly against him. He's wide as a bat and my clitoris pounds at the pressure between my legs. I could come like this. Just rubbing against this thick prick. I am so near the edge I think anything might push me over. What would Jonathan think of that? Would it please him? Would it make him want me more? Or would it make him walk away?

Big Teddy's voice lowers, grows husky. "Between you, me, and the gatepost, what's the story, doll? Your man two-timing you and you're trying to get a little tit for tat? Or don't you get enough at home?"

There hasn't been *any* at home since I miscarried, but I say, "Some gals just can't get enough."

Teddy gives a belly laugh that vibrates all the way down my body to the molten hot spot between my thighs. "May I cut in?" Jonathan asks, tapping Big Teddy's shoulder with a good deal more force than is required.

I hadn't seen my husband approach, but I'm desperately grateful that he's here now.

Big Teddy releases me, his eyes averted as he adjusts the crease of his pants. "Quite a live wire you got there, Richardson. Has she met the star of our party? I can introduce her to Clara—"

Jonathan spins me away without letting the man finish.

My husband has always been a close dancer and I melt against him when he grabs me tight against his body. His eyes are hot. Angry. I've never seen him so furious. Rage makes him darker, sexier, more dangerous. My husband's hand glides down my back, snagging on the fastenings of my dress before resting on my ass. The gesture is lewd. Possessive. Obvious. If people hadn't been staring at us before, they are now.

The music changes to something quick and peppy, so my husband shouldn't clutch me, but he dances to a music of his own. A melody fraught with danger and tension. "It wasn't Teddy Morgan, either."

I gasp, nearly insensible with lust. "I told you it wasn't." I want him to undress me here and now. I don't care what anyone says or thinks. And the way he stares down at me, I think he means to do it. Jonathan's body is hot to the touch and, laying my head against his chest, I hear the gallop of his heartbeat, arousal and fury running side by side.

"So," Jonathan says tightly. "Ted Morgan must be as big as they say. I saw your eyes go wide. When I'm gone, I'm sure he'll come calling and shove that horse-cock inside you and make you scream with pleasure."

I should object, but my own shamelessness has robbed me of my delicate sensibilities. I wrap my arms around my husband's neck, as if to draw him down for a kiss. "He's not the one I want. I want *you*."

These aren't the words I meant to say. They are, nonetheless, a true confession, and one that I've never made to him before. "I've always wanted you, Jonathan."

My husband's lips start to curl with contempt as if ready to spit venomous words at me. But he cannot do it. Instead, his lips brush mine with a tenderness completely at odds with the rough grip of his hands. "Christ, Nora, you don't even know who I am. You should have married one of these pretentious swells. Your father would have been happier."

But would I have been? I doubt it. And since his lips are so close to mine, I capture them, trying to fill that kiss with all the things I've never been able to say.

We both taste like liquor and heartbreak.

When we finally draw apart for breath, he says, "Why do you have to be so beautiful? Do you know what you do to me? Do you have any idea?"

"No," I whisper. "I don't. I wish you would show me."

He caresses my cheek, and I press against his palm and watch him struggle for words. He's going to forgive me, I think, because I see something that looks like love in his eyes.

I'm so lost in that gaze, so hopeful, that I don't see the man approach us until it's too late. It takes me a moment to realize that someone is tapping Jonathan's shoulder, wanting to cut in. And when I look up, all the blood drains from my face.

I've known Robert Aster all my life. Dapper in a white suit, with his blond hair slicked back, he seems to have recovered nicely from what must have been an outrageous hangover after the other night.

He was always a brash boy, now grown into a big brash man, but even I didn't think he had the nerve to do *this*.

My husband startles at the interruption, but gives Robert a polite headshake, as if to say that he's done sharing his wife tonight. To Jonathan's credit, he's utterly composed . . . until he catches the expression on my face.

Jonathan said he'd be able to guess the man who kissed me. That he'd be able to tell. He isn't wrong.

Robert gets as far as, "So nice to see you tonight Nora—" before Jonathan thrusts me away, turns, and lands a heavy fist square to the other man's jaw.

The crack of flesh on flesh is so loud that the musicians lose their rhythm and the song falls apart.

Robert staggers back, but not before my husband is on him, fists flying. He isn't the only one to land a punch. The man with whom I've been unfaithful catches Jonathan below the eye, snapping his head to the side.

Several women scream and Big Teddy Morgan wades into the fray to break it up.

All this happens before I can take another breath.

"Jonathan!" I cry, grasping hold of his sleeve.

"What? What do you expect of me?" he asks, shaking his fist as if he's broken every knuckle.

I think he's waiting to see if I'll defend Robert Aster. If I'll protect him, like a woman protects her lover.

I won't.

"She doesn't want you to cause any more of a scene," Paul Kendrick says, grabbing hold of my husband's arms, trying to hold him back.

"Is that right?" my husband asks as everyone crowds round. "Is that what you want, Nora? You don't want me to create a social embarrassment?"

"Too late for that, man," Big Teddy says.

Meanwhile, Robert Aster has his legs back under him and red blood drips from a split lip onto his white suit. He looks at me, almost triumphant, as if he thinks to win me back. He snarls at my husband, "Shall we finally have a fair fight for her, Richardson?"

My husband tries to break free to attack him again, but I whisper, "It's me that you're mad at."

Jonathan's eyes bulge. "You're goddamned right I am."

And when he yanks away from the men trying to hold him, he doesn't attack Robert Aster.

Instead, he grabs me.

CHAPTER

Three

As he drags me from the dance floor, my husband is a rampaging bull. The crowds part with shrieks and shouts as he bowls over anyone in our way. He throws open the door to the parlor, then pushes me inside. He gives a jerk to the crystal handle, and the door crashes closed behind us again. Then he yanks the key out of the hole and throws it on the floor.

We are alone.

Mesmerized by this stranger who looks like my husband but rages like a beast, I take three steps back and nearly stumble in my heels. He catches me before I fall, herding me backwards. My calves hit a desk and we crash into it with such force that it hits the bookcase behind it, sending a dozen volumes spilling to the floor. Jonathan has me pinned, his body wedged between my knees, and a trill of fear makes me cry out.

Someone pounds on the door. "Richardson! Open up."

Jonathan seethes. "It had to be him. Of all of them out there. I should've known. You've always carried a torch for *him*."

Robert Aster is the man my father wanted me to marry. The man

I might've married if I hadn't met Jonathan. But I did meet Jonathan and that changed everything. "No. That was a long time ago."

Someone jiggles the door handle. I think it's Big Teddy Morgan. "Now see here, Richardson. What you do at home to your wife is your own affair, but not at my soiree. Don't make us break down the door."

Jonathan's hands are so tight around my wrists that his knuckles are white. Suddenly, he notices, and he lets me go all at once with an expression of horror. "What am I doing? What the hell am I doing? . . . *Christ*, Nora, I never wanted you to see me like this."

I've wrecked him. There are tears—actual tears—in his eyes.

"I told Robert to stay away from me," I say. "He was a fool to approach us tonight. He *wanted* a fight."

My husband has now broken out into a sweat and yanks his tie to loosen it. "I shouldn't have given him one. You've got me so balled up, Nora . . . this isn't who I want to be. This isn't ever who I wanted to be for you."

Maybe it's the alcohol talking, but I say, "I never wanted you to be anyone but who you are."

His sharp look cuts me. "You need to leave me, Nora."

"I'm not going to leave you. You may want to leave *me* but I don't want to leave you."

"You would if you had any idea what I want to do to you right now."

"Tell me," I say, breathless. "What do you want to do to me?"

Jonathan cages me in with his arms. "I want to reach between your legs and see if dancing with those men made you wet. And if you're wet, Nora . . . by god, I want to slap you. And then I want to fuck you like you're a whore."

A throb of outrageous arousal pounds through my body, drowning out every other sound. I can't have heard him right. Or, at least, I must be even drunker than I think I am, because the words make me squirm. I can't imagine what it might be like to be slapped but my whole body roars to attention at the idea of something so . . . *wrong*. "Do it."

My husband reels back. "I'm not going to hit you. I'm just trying to make you understand why you should leave me. I don't hit Janes and I'm not going to hit you."

"I want you to," I say, brazenly yanking my dress up over my hips, exposing the tops of my stockings and the lacy step-ins that leave little to the imagination.

At the sight of my wantonly splayed thighs, Jonathan groans like I've dealt him a mortal wound. "No."

"I want you to slap me," I say. "I want you to do *anything* you want to me."

I'm desperate for it. Mad for it. I think it must be guilt that drives me. I must be so desperate to earn his forgiveness that I *need* him to slap me. But what if this mad desire is much deeper? Much darker. A need for him to reach me. I'm a girl who lives inside her own head. Only this can break me out.

He cups my cheek tenderly. "I shouldn't have said such an awful thing."

A frenzy builds inside me. "Why not? Because you didn't mean it? Please, Jonathan. I want you to touch me . . . and if I'm wet . . . I want you to slap me."

I no longer hear the pounding of the door. I no longer hear anything but his breathing and the echo of my plea. My husband and I are locked eye to eye, connected in a way we haven't been since we first married. No, not even then. I am, in this moment, completely and utterly sobered. And I see him. He sees me, too, perhaps for the first time. He truly sees me.

In slow motion, he reaches for my sex, and I'm so wet that I soak the fabric separating his hand from my flesh. He groans, and the pressure of his hand nearly sends me right over the edge. When he speaks, his voice is almost a sob. "You're soaked."

Then he does it.

I feel an explosion of sharp pain as his palm slaps across my cheek. He's held back his strength, but still the blow turns my face to the side, and I wonder if the heat I feel burning is the shape of his hand-print. The sound of the slap now echoes in my mind. He's done it. He's actually slapped me across the face.

And I am dying with pleasure.

"Do it again," I whisper. I don't understand the rules of the game anymore. I only understand the fierce hunger of my own body and the certain knowledge that my husband isn't the only beast in the room.

Jonathan takes a tortured breath. "It shouldn't have even happened once."

"I wanted it to," I say, glancing up at him with molten heat. "And I want you to do it again."

He shudders. "Why?"

"Because it's going to make me come."

This makes him snap. His fingers press hard against the soaked fabric between my legs, the scent of my arousal between us. There's no hiding it, no denying it. He slaps me again and this time, I fly apart. The intense pleasure of my orgasm rocks me. My cry is high pitched as my whole body pulses with its shallow climax. Waves of release roll over me and I make incoherent sounds of pleasure.

When he pulls his hand away, I cry, "Please don't stop. I can't bear for you to stop . . ."

"I'm not going to stop. I'm going to fuck you."

I gasp with relief. I don't care that there are people outside this room who might be listening. I don't care about anything but having him inside me. Reaching for his belt, I kiss him and feel his mouth tremble under mine as if he were the one about to be ravished. Then his hand fists my hair, and his teeth are on my throat while I open his trousers and yank his underpants down.

He doesn't take them off. Instead, he pulls my underwear down to my knees, literally tearing the fabric, before throwing the sex-soaked garment on the rug. It's pure relief when he positions himself at my entrance. His isn't the first, or even the largest, cock that I've had pressed against my flesh tonight, but the feel of it nearly causes me to sob with desire.

He slams into my body, pulling back only to shove inside again. I'm so wet, so ready, that I hadn't expected any pain, but it has been more than a year since he's taken me and a startled cry tears itself from my throat as he stretches me wide. Soon that cry is replaced with throatier sounds of pleasure. He bangs me so hard against the desk that my teeth rattle and several more books fall from the shelf overhead. One of them smacks him in the shoulder and rolls off his back, but he doesn't stop pumping into me.

In the grips of some sex-starved fever, Jonathan tears at the hem of my gown to get it out of the way. I kiss his mouth, his chin, his throat . . .

And then the door crashes open. I'm dimly aware of voices. Of shocked gazes. Of people watching us. My insides squeeze with the unbearable excitement of knowing men are feasting hungry eyes on my bare legs and bouncing breasts. Even those who aren't staring would surely hear my moans and the sounds of Jonathan's body slapping against mine. Tears sting the corners of my eyes but I don't know if they're tears of shame or frustration when Jonathan stops.

"Beat it!" Jonathan shouts, throwing a murderous look at the intruders.

In the doorway, several men hover with expressions of leering astonishment. Paul Kendrick scowls with distaste and says, "I suppose it doesn't matter how much money he makes. You can't make a working man into a gentleman."

"Out of my house, Richardson," Big Teddy Morgan roars. "Or will you make us give you the bum's rush?"

Jonathan pulls out of my throbbing body, yanking me upright. Then he removes his jacket. Given the tightness of his shoulders under his white shirt, I think he means to start another brawl, but he takes the coat and spreads it over me, covering my ruined dress and shielding me from onlookers. It's a strangely gallant move, considering his mood, but it doesn't persuade the men in the doorway.

My dress is torn. My cheek still burns where he struck me. This can't look good.

Big Teddy says, "Leave your old lady here with us, Richardson. You can fetch her when you've cooled off."

"I'm not leaving her here," Jonathan says. He's ashamed, I can see. For my sake, he's ashamed. But he doesn't say anything to defend himself.

Robert Aster stands in the doorway, holding ice in a towel against his bleeding mouth and bruised jaw. "You're not worthy of her. You never were." He holds a hand out to me like a knight ready to rescue a damsel in distress. "Come with me, Nora. I'll take you home."

This shakes Jonathan. I can see it. He glances at me as if afraid to find me huddled up, damaged and broken. But I stand up to my full height, loop my hand in his arm, and say, "I'm sorry, Robert. I'm going with my husband."

Normally, we would wait for a driver to bring the car around, but tonight we walk together to where the cars are parked on the street. The night air tingles against my oversensitive body and I hug his coat jacket tight around me, overwhelmed by the scent of him. "I don't want to go home," I murmur, seized by the terror that once we get there he'll grab his suitcase and I'll never see him again.

"We're not going home," Jonathan says, his expression predatory in the moonlight. He turns me so that my back is against the Bentley, arching me slightly over the hood with a wolfish kiss that I am certain will bruise my lips. I welcome it, because I want it to last. I want his mark on me. It's too late now for either of us to have any shame.

"Into the backseat," he says, yanking the rear door open and helping me into the luxurious coachlike interior. Then he's on me, shoving me back. The breath in my lungs seems to ignite when he says, "I'm not finished. Spread your legs."

Splayed in the backseat, I can't seem to find the right angle, and

I struggle to obey. He doesn't wait. Yanking one of my thighs up over his hip, he uses his fingers to find my slick opening. I'm still so wet, so hungry for him, so desperate. I need to come again, as if the first time unleashed a bottomless appetite for him.

Thankfully, he shoves his cock back into me, driving me against the seat in a relentless assault. He fucks me and fucks me and fucks me until every muscle aches. And all the while, the fire of desire licks down my body while the car rocks beneath us. "Jonathan." I moan his name, my breath almost too fast to speak.

"Just lie there and get fucked," he barks, hitching my legs up over his shoulders.

It was like that the first time. My knees near my ears, my body open to him. And I know he doesn't want me to talk. He just wants me to lie underneath him, but I can't help but ask, "Do you remember?"

I think he hasn't heard me. He seems too intent on pounding into me, his pubic bone smashing against my sex with delicious pain in every stroke. His calm and cool exterior has melted away in fevered sweat. But he says, "I remember everything about you, Nora."

To prove it, he grabs at the front of my gown where two strands of pearls tangle between my breasts, and he yanks them off. The *pop* and *zing* of the pearls as they fly accompanies the music of my tissue-thin dress shredding open under his hands. The pleasure of the memory made new again is so intense that my insides melt in shuddering release. "Oh god, oh god, oh Jonathan!"

His sounds are more primal than mine, a masculine growl that gets louder just before he pulls himself free and spurts his seed on my belly.

It's this last part that destroys me. That he pulls out. His conscious decision not to risk another child. Nothing that he'd done to me at the party—not the way he talked to me, not making me dance with those men, not slapping me or taking me on a desk in the midst of a party—none of it shamed me like this.

He told me that he'd fuck me like I was a whore; I just hadn't believed him until now.

Mopping the semen from my belly with my chemise, I'm consumed by a feeling of degradation that forces tears to my eyes. A few sobs escape me before I stifle them with the back of my hand. Jonathan remains sprawled in the backseat, his tie discarded, head thrown back, eyes closed as if he might be asleep. After a few moments, however, I know he's not. "*Christ*," he says quietly. "I promised your father that I'd never do something like this."

"Something like what?" I ask bitterly, the scent of liquor swirling in the backseat with the scent of sex.

"Cause a social embarrassment for your family," Jonathan answers. His eyes pierce through the car window, following the glow up to the top of the building where the party we left is still in full swing. "There's no help for it now. The bastards are probably all gathered around that balcony to watch us."

I don't doubt that he's right. Paul Kendrick, Big Teddy Morgan, Robert Aster, and god knows who else are probably standing out there, cigars in hand, looking down on us. "Do you think I care about that, Jonathan? Do you think I've *ever* cared about that?"

"You *should* care," Jonathan says, and lays a surprisingly gentle hand at the back of my neck, massaging it. "You deserved a different life, Nora. One where no one would be making cracks about how you married down. If I hadn't come along—"

"You *did* come along, Jonathan, and I chose you."

"Don't feed me a line, Nora. You didn't *choose* me. You got knocked up and didn't want anyone to find out about the little bastard in your belly."

I try to hit him. "You're the bastard!"

He snatches my hand to defend himself and I'm no match for his strength. "You've a right to be angry, Nora. I know I took advantage the first night we met. But I swear to you, it wasn't because I was looking for a payday. I didn't know whose daughter you were. I just took you . . . because I wanted you."

"I wanted you, too," I say, my voice shaking with fury. "Or don't my wants count for anything?"

"*Baloney*. You didn't want me. You were young. You were drunk. You expect me to believe that you wanted someone who treats you like *this*? That you wanted me to shove you in the back of a car and use you like a little quiff? Like you're something I paid for?"

"Yes," I say defiantly, wiping my eyes with the backs of my hands.

His face crumples. "If you like it so much, then why are you crying?"

I shake my head, refusing to give him that.

"This isn't what you want, Nora. Tonight I made you—"

"I *wanted* it. Or didn't you feel me come on your hand? I liked it. I *loved* it."

His mouth opens, then snaps shut again. "Prove it."

My body quakes with renewed interest even as my emotions are dangerously close to spilling forth.

In answer to the question in my eyes, he puts a heavy hand on my head. "On your knees."

Slipping from the seats to the floor, brushing pearls out from beneath me, I find myself shaking. I know what he wants but now that he presses my cheek against his pant leg, doubts batter at my resolve. Between the open flaps of his dress pants and lowered briefs, he's only half-swollen, shining with the remnants of his orgasm and mine. I reach out for him, tentatively slipping my manicured hand around his shaft.

"There's my little society girl," he says when I hesitate. "Use your mouth."

My insides melt at that simple command and I wet my lips, wondering if they glisten the way the head of his cock does when it expands. Leaning forward, I purse my lips into a kiss, inhaling the musk that is his scent and mine. I brush my lips along the length of him, kissing the surprisingly smooth skin. "Like this?"

"No. Suck me."

My lips part to wrap around his cock, and I groan. I taste myself on him, knowing that this is the same instrument that opened and stretched me moments ago. No expertise guides me in this—only instinct—and when my tongue swirls over the pulsing vein, Jonathan swells in my mouth.

His breathing deepens in such obvious pleasure that my anger fades. He is even more beautiful when aroused, his masculinity something at once natural and dangerous. The throbbing hardness between my lips becomes my whole world, and when my clumsy efforts at suckling are rewarded with a clench of Jonathan's fist and a jerk of his hips, a thrill of triumph dizzies me. I like the roughness of his pubic hair on my lips as I breathe heavily through flared nostrils. The musk of his arousal encourages me to take him deeper. The spongy slick flesh slides deliciously in and out of my mouth.

"*Jesus Christ*," Jonathan whispers, his hand atop my head.

That's when I become aware of the way I'm humping his shin, trapping his leg between my thighs.

"*Jesus Christ*," Jonathan repeats, as if I'm torturing him upon a rack. "You're a good cocksucker . . . so beautiful . . ."

Groaning with obvious delight at this praise, I suck harder, and Jonathan convulses, hitting the back of my throat with the knob of his arousal. The unexpected choking sensation ought to intimidate me, but it's my husband who is now shaking like a leaf. A sense of power makes me cruel, and I tease him, slowing the suction, glancing up at him, my cheeks bulging with the effort to take him. I use my lips, my teeth, my tongue and fingers.

Our eyes meet and Jonathan's mouth falls open in silent ecstasy. He's going to spill his seed in my mouth, I think, and I want him to. Jonathan grips the back of my head and breathes another string of expletives. But he doesn't come. Instead, he pulls my face up, dragging me into his lap until we are nose to nose.

"Do you know how easy it would have been to blow into the back of your throat just now?" he asks, the roughness of his words undercut by the whisper in which he speaks them. "Do you?"

"Yes," I whimper, my nipples erect against the buttons of his shirt.

"I could make you swallow it, Nora. Every last drop," he says, jaw tight with restraint.

I wrap my knees around his waist and ask, "So why don't you?"

He blinks. His nostrils flare as if he needs to think through an answer. He blinks again, then says, "Because you're not a prostitute."

"Are you sure?" I ask, because the tables have somehow turned, and his need for me has made him vulnerable. I feel the hot, throbbing evidence against my own soaked pussy lips. Shamelessly, I position myself over the head of his cock . . . and sink down.

A long breath escapes him and his hands go to my hips, squeezing the flesh there.

"Are you *very* sure?" I ask, taking full advantage of the fact that Jonathan can't seem to tear his eyes away from my exposed breasts. "Because you made me dance with those men and let them grope me and you made sure to check and see if it excited me, remember?"

"Which it did," he manages to growl through clenched teeth.

"Yes." I lift up a little bit, then sink all the way back down until he's in me so deep that I imagine I can feel him in my throat. "But it excited you, too."

He can't deny it. Especially not with his stiff erection buried tightly inside me. Not with the sticky semen on my belly gluing us together. But he's not as hurried in his arousal this time. He has more self-control now. "If it excited me, it's because I told you to do it, Nora. Because we did it together. Because you came back to me after each dance and I watched them all envy me. Not because I want to be cuckolded."

The slow agonizing roll of my hips is arrested by my husband's strong hands. For balance, my hands drift up to the roof, which leaves me vulnerable to Jonathan's mouth. He dips his head, leaning forward to capture my nipple between his teeth. And he bites.

The pain is like an electric jolt straight to my womb, and I'm not sure whether to beg him to stop or beg him to do it again when his mouth drifts to my other breast. Wanton lust seizes me as both nipples harden to diamonds. He's close. I know he is. His shirt is soaked with sweat and every cord of his neck is tight with the need for release. But he holds back. "Touch yourself, Nora."

Until this moment, I thought I was shameless. But with his face so close to mine, his eyes boring into me, I can't fathom doing as he asks. A conflagration of embarrassment burns in my belly as I wonder if he knows all the nights my hand has danced between my thighs in secret. It's not something anyone ever talks about. Certainly nothing that I've ever done in front of anyone. "I—I can't."

Jonathan taunts me, biting and sucking at my other nipple until I can't breathe. His tongue is wet and insistent and the blood rushes to my sensitive areolae until I'm sure that he could lead me around by my nipples like a dog on a leash. Instead, he drags me up and down on his cock, forcing me to ride him, and when I whimper with sexual need, he becomes even more demanding. "Touch yourself, Nora."

Arching my back, aching for the release that he's denying me, I clench on him over and over again. "No, Jonathan, please . . ."

"Why not? You want me to believe that you like this. That you want me. *Me.* Well, this is who I am. A depraved monster who wants to watch you rub yourself."

His tone is hard and unmerciful, but his fingers are gentle as they tangle with mine, drawing my hand to the thicket of dark hair where we're joined. My sex is swollen, engorged, slick to the touch, and the moment he forces me to cup it, I whimper with complete surrender. Gasping at the way it lays me bare, I touch myself, flicking at the slippery, swollen button at my core.

Everything seems wet right now. My belly is wet with semen and I'm damp with a sheen of sweat. Even the windows are fogged up with our rapid breaths. Touching myself with more confidence, I rock back and forth on his erection with exquisite abandon.

"Fuck!" Jonathan says it so intensely that I think I've done something wrong. Then I realize that he's straining not to explode. He's watching my fingers in the valley between us. Those eyes of his, icy blue, have thawed into the eyes of a hungry wolf. They are eyes that cannot be denied.

Jonathan yanks my hips, controlling my motions. Then I feel the sharp slap of something on my ass cheek, and I realize it's the crack of his palm. "Faster," he pants, making me pump my hips. Another spank lands on the other ass cheek driving me to an untamed rhythm. My heart is pumping, my lungs are burning. I'm blinded by arousal, humping faster, my fingers caught between us, my orgasm near enough to drive me to insanity.

He spanks me again. Then again. "Faster!"

I cry out, but it isn't a protest. It is endless. I'm spanked again and again. And I can't make my body move fast enough. I buck up and down on him, fucking him so hard that it hurts, fingering my pussy in such a blur of motion that I no longer care what he sees. It's this edge, this edge of pain and pleasure and total abandon that I think I've been seeking my whole life.

"More," I moan, helplessly. "More, more, please, Jonathan . . ."

He can't possibly know what I want, but he does. He spanks me harder, until I'm shrieking with the blistering sting of it. Finally, mercifully, he says one simple word. "Come."

The avalanche of my orgasm makes everything inside me tumble down. I scream until it hurts my throat. I've never come so hard. Never like this. The raw spasms rock me so completely that I don't understand what he's doing until it's too late.

"No, don't stop!" I shriek, trying to hold him with my thighs. "Don't pull out!"

Jonathan's stronger than I am, though, and I'm spent. Limp. I can't stop him from pulling his cock free, jerking it roughly in his fist. Between us, it stiffens, pulses, and spurts a thick rope of semen onto my breasts and the front of his vest.

CHAPTER

Four

On the floor of the car, I curl around my heartache, idly collecting loose pearls. His voice comes through the dark, hoarse and scratchy. "I love you, Nora."

The words, spoken now, pierce me like an arrow. That he's done it again, denying me a child, tells me that these words mean nothing. Perhaps he never wanted the baby that we lost, but I had wanted that baby desperately. Now there will never be another chance.

"Nora, I *love* you," he says again, reaching down for me. "Do you hear me?"

I shrug away from his touch, tucking my knees tighter against my chest. "I heard you."

He catches my chin in his palm and angles my face up. "I have loved you from the first moment."

I stare at him for a long time. Then I ask, "Does it change anything?"

He blanches, turning to stare into the blackness of night. "No. I don't suppose it does."

"Then take me home. Just take me home."

"Mr. Richardson," the doorman says by way of greeting, making way for us in our expansive foyer.

Jonathan carries me into the house and I'm too weak to fight him. The alcohol, or the anguish, has made me cold and clammy. I feel as if I'm going to be sick. I groan when Jonathan lifts me up the first few steps, vertigo and nausea swirling inside me. He must know it, because my husband says, "Mrs. Richardson is ill. Please send up some water and Bayer tablets. Maybe some Bulgarian herb tea."

When we enter my room, Jonathan puts me down on the edge of the bed, then goes to one knee. He unbuckles my shoes, then rolls my stockings down, one at a time. When he eases his coat jacket off my shoulders, I realize that he intends to undress me completely, but I don't feel as exposed as I was in the car when I showed him everything . . . almost everything.

Now I'm closed off again; I'm far away, retreating into my own mind.

"Lift your arms," my husband says, and when I do, he gently strips what remains of my dress and chemise over my head.

I don't know what he'll do to me next. I tell myself I won't care. If he wants to take me again, I'll lie beneath him, perfectly still. Given the way I react to him, lust for him, want him even now, this is probably just a lie that I tell myself, but I'm too tired to be honest.

"Again," he says.

"What?"

"Lift your arms again," he says softly, and when I do, he slips a nightgown over my body.

Moments later, he is pulling back the covers for me, tucking me into the bed, stroking my hair softly.

A servant knocks on the door and Jonathan takes the tray, bringing it to my side. He holds the carved crystal glass to my lips. "Drink some water."

I can't bear to take even a sip. "No. No. It'll make me sick."

"Just enough to wash down the aspirin," Jonathan says, perching at the edge of my bed to coax me. I let him put the tablets on my tongue, then tip the glass back for a swallow of water that makes me grip the end table in my fight to keep it down. "You're going to hate me in the morning," he says.

This makes me laugh. Some half-deranged sound.

"I already hate you," I say, though I don't mean it. I don't mean it at all.

"That makes two of us." Warmth touches my cheek as he brushes the spot where he slapped me. "It doesn't look as if it will leave a mark."

And this makes me cry.

No mark. No memory. Nothing tangible to hold on to.

He bends over me, the bed creaking beneath him as he presses his lips softly to my forehead. It is a kiss good night, or good-bye. I cannot tell which. So I simply close my eyes.

CHAPTER

Five

At my dressing table the next morning, I use my gilded brush to tame the waves of my hair into a bob. My face is pale in the mirror, a bluish tint of exhaustion below my eyes. A warm bath in the claw-foot tub soothed the soreness in my muscles, but my head still pounds with crushing insistence. Perhaps it would have been better if I *had* been sick the night before. If I'd heaved up everything inside me instead of letting it fester.

The house is quiet but for the periodic ring of the telephone from downstairs. I've ignored it for hours, caught in a cloud of depression. My girl, Dolly, raps at the door. She has a pot of tea and she pours some for me, stopping to arrange the vase of bluebells and violets. "Your father intends to call upon you this afternoon, ma'am."

There's an edge in her voice and I don't have to guess why. My father will have heard about last night. He'll be smug, insufferable, perhaps he'll demand that Jonathan stay married to me. My father is always one to bluster and issue threats. But he can't subject Jonathan to financial ruin—at least not anymore. This time, there is nothing either of us can do to make Jonathan stay.

"Breakfast is almost ready downstairs," Dolly chirps, as if to rouse my spirits. "Fresh butter, cream, and eggs from the Saturday market."

I'm about to say that I'm not hungry, when I realize that I'm famished. Some ravenous creature inside me has been awakened, and I need to eat. Downstairs at the table, I take my place at the far end, reaching for a pear from the fruit-bowl centerpiece. Then I stare at Jonathan's empty seat. This is how it will be from now on, but I can't think of that at the moment.

"Should we wait for Mr. Richardson?" Dolly asks, hovering with a basket of biscuits.

"He's gone," I make myself say, biting into the pear, which tastes like ash. "And he's not coming back."

Dolly tilts her head in confusion. "He's upstairs, ma'am."

The bite of pear catches in my throat. I swallow with difficulty. "He's here? Here, in the house still?"

"Yes, ma'am. In his bedroom."

Launching up from my chair, I rush to the stairway, nearly catching my heel in the expensive imported rug. I have to check myself. He's *here*. Jonathan is still here. At least for a little longer. My hand turns on the smooth wooden banister and I hurry up the stairs, an effort that has me breathless by the time I reach my husband's door.

He's stripped to the waist, stooping over the suitcase on his bed. Another one is open on the chair. Just looking at him, and the preposterous good looks with which he's been blessed, the pain shoots through me and I have to steady myself on the door frame. Jonathan glances up. "What's wrong?"

"I can't seem to catch my breath," I say, because it's so obviously true. "And my head aches terribly."

"I'm sorry," Jonathan says, with a rueful sigh. "I shouldn't have made you drink all that."

"I'm sorry that I let Robert Aster kiss me, but that's not going to keep you from leaving, is it?"

"I'm not leaving," he says without looking at me.

My mouth falls open. "Then what are you doing?"

He holds up the folded shirt in his hands. "Unpacking. After last night's misconduct, it doesn't seem right to let you face the music by yourself."

So he is the agreeable gentleman again. The bloodless man who has lived in this room, apart from me, for the past year. "You're not leaving," I say, to be certain I have it right.

"I'm not leaving. Not now." Again, he averts his eyes so that I can't read anything in that striking blue gaze. "Not unless . . . not unless you want me to."

I surprise myself by saying, "That depends."

He takes some sock garters from his bag, folding them precisely. "If it's the money you're worried about, you can have it all. I won't leave the marriage with anything but what I brought to it."

"You bought this house, Jonathan. With money that you earned."

"Working for your father," he says, flatly. "It's been very profitable for me."

"You could work for someone else. Or for yourself."

He turns away to open a bureau drawer. "I'm sure I could."

I'm captivated by the beauty of his lean shoulders and the youthful arch of his spine. That I feel as if I can't reach out and touch him, that I can't press my lips to the back of his neck and draw him into a kiss . . . that even though I am his wife, I don't feel free to do any of these things, not even after last night, decides it for me. "Jonathan, I don't want you to stay if nothing is going to change."

He stiffens, hands gripping the edge of the bureau. "I can't give you what you need, Nora."

"I know I behaved like a spoiled brat. I let another man put his hands on me to get your attention. I acted like a daddy's girl who has never had to go without anything she ever wanted in her whole life—"

"No, you didn't."

"Yes, I did. When I couldn't have your attention, I let Robert Aster give me his. It was foolish. *I* was foolish. I was selfish. And you have every right to be furious—"

"Stop it," Jonathan says.

"Why won't you let me tell you how sorry I am?"

"Because all of this is my fault, not yours. And even if it weren't, I've already forgiven you."

A gasp sputters from my throat. "What?"

"You were drunk and you kissed another man. It's not the crime of the century. I forgive you. It's done, Nora. It's over. We never have to speak of it again."

"Given the scene at last night's party, I doubt that very much."

"That won't happen again."

"Maybe it should."

He turns to face me and bellows, "Goddamn it, Nora! I don't know what you want from me."

"I want you to *want* me," I cry, though it is only the smallest part of what I want from him.

"For the love of God, woman, I can't *stop* wanting you. That's the whole problem."

If this is a problem, it is one that has never occurred to me. "Then why have we been sleeping apart for the last year?"

Pure agony swims in his eyes. "I'm trying to protect you from the monster that lives inside me."

"You're no monster," I say, coming to him to give comfort.

He shrugs away. "I am. You know I am. You saw only a glimpse of that monster last night—"

"I provoked you, Jonathan."

"And some part of me was grateful that you did. You gave me just the excuse I needed to let my worst instincts run riot. Watching those men touch you, watching you dance with them, it made me need to possess you. To show them all—and you—that you're mine."

"I *am* yours," I whisper, unspeakably aroused by the way he says the word *mine*.

"You gave me an excuse to punish you, Nora. And I liked it. I *loved* it."

Am I supposed to condemn him for this? I'd be a sorry hypocrite if I did. His words only make me want to do it all again—push him to the edge of fury. The only thing that stops me is the fear of pushing him too far. "So . . . maybe . . ." My head feels as if it's filled with cotton and I have difficulty forming thoughts. Trying to capture everything I'm thinking, everything I'm feeling, I say, "I'm your *wife*, Jonathan. Maybe you don't need an excuse."

"Wife or not, I have no right to treat you that way. You stand here telling me that you're sorry, asking for my forgiveness, when I'm the one who should be on bended knee, begging for yours."

"For what? I don't know how many ways I can say it, Jonathan. You didn't do anything to me that I didn't want you to do."

He looks me directly in the eye. "I killed our child, Nora, and you know it."

This stops me. Startles me into utter silence. My limbs go rigid. I am a statue of horror. "*What*?"

"Don't pretend you don't know what I'm talking about. I can't stand it."

But I don't know what he's talking about. I haven't the faintest idea. I only know that the reminder of the baby I lost still hits me so hard that I need to sit down. I find a chair, a stool, I don't know what. I just flounder for it, and sink down. "What did you do, Jonathan?" I ask, in morbid fascination.

That he didn't want the baby, that it had trapped him into marriage, was obvious from the start. But I could imagine no scenario in which he might have taken action against me or my unborn child. I'd been wretchedly sick, that much is true, but he can't have had any control over that. What is he suggesting? Poison in my tea?

Jonathan slams the door, as if that would prevent the servants from hearing our argument. Then he turns on me like a madman. "Are you going to tell me you don't remember the last time we had sex?"

"Given the state of my ruined dress, I'm not likely to forget it."

"Not last night. Before. The *last* time."

I shake my head. I remember the night of the wedding on a bed piled high with cushions. The time in front of the fireplace, on the chaise lounge. The afternoon when we stole away from a garden party and found a place against a tree in the hedge. But all of that was before the miscarriage . . . I don't remember which time was the last time.

He crosses the room in three angry strides and grasps me by the back of the neck. "Stand up." Slow to move, I'm propelled by his strong arms into a standing position. Moments later, I find myself down, face-first, on the mattress. "Does this refresh your memory?"

It does, actually, and all of my insides turn to liquid heat.

"I took you from behind," Jonathan says, shaking me like a rag doll on the bedspread. "Like an animal. I held you down against the mattress. I struck you. With my belt."

The memory forces me to moan. It had taken two, maybe three cracks of his belt on the backs of my thighs before I begged him to put himself inside me. He'd shoved inside me, slammed his hips against me, and kept me pinned to the bed. And when I fought to push back, to take him deeper, he'd caught the nape of my neck in his teeth. I'd yelped with an orgasm that left me exhausted and deeply satisfied.

The thought that he might do the same to me now makes me weak with desire, but he's trying to make a point. "Do you remember, Nora?"

"Yes," I say, stretching my hands to push the half-packed suitcase off the bed. It falls to the floor, spilling its contents everywhere, and I twist in his arms. He has me in his grips, but I have him in mine. "I remember."

His expression collapses, lower lip trembling. "Two days later, the baby was gone."

He's tangled with me upon the bed now and I make him look at me. "That wasn't your fault, Jonathan! God, how can you even think it?"

His voice is barely a whisper. "I beat that child right out of you."

Some dark part of me nearly seizes onto this explanation. Finally, an answer to all my questions. All my late-night tearful pleas, in which I begged God to show me what I'd done wrong. In which I'd been certain that losing my child had been a punishment for all my wickedness. It took so long for me to accept that there was nothing we could, or should, have done differently. But somehow, looking at the anguish on Jonathan's face, it takes only seconds for me to accept it again now. "Women miscarry, Jonathan. It just happens."

"It doesn't *just happen*," he says.

"Yes, it does. My mother lost four pregnancies before she had me. My sister lost her first as well."

. This seems to shock him. "I didn't know . . ."

"I never wanted to tell you. I didn't want you to worry that . . . that you'd married a woman who . . . who couldn't bear you children." It's horrifically difficult to admit this to him. Still, his body is knotted in wordless pain that I'm desperate to soothe. "A few little slaps with a belt in love play did not cause a miscarriage, Jonathan. You didn't beat the child out of me!"

His features twist with grief, eyes bloodshot. "Then why did you tell your father that I did?"

I begin to wonder if Jonathan is still drunk—or perhaps I am. "My father? What are you talking about?"

"I can't blame you for running to him. He told me what you said, Nora."

By god, what had I said? Consumed with grief I had gone to my father's house after the miscarriage. But only for a few days. I'd just wanted to sit in my old room. I'd wanted familiar things around me. I can scarcely now recall, in my haze of mourning, what I'd said or done. "Jonathan, I didn't blame you for what happened, even then."

"You told your father that I put rough hands on you," he says.

"I did not!" I exclaim, hurtling up to a sitting position.

"You told him that I was too rough with you. That I hurt you. That I hurt the baby—"

"I said no such thing," I insist, and this time, there are no doubts. No madness of grief would ever make those words pass my lips. Not to my father or anyone else. "It isn't true. It just isn't true."

My husband has been carrying this for a year now and I see how reluctant he is to put it down. "Nora, you don't have to protect me. I'm a man. It's my job to protect you."

"You didn't hurt me or our baby and I never told anyone that you did. I didn't go running off to my father, or to Robert Aster, to get away from you. You're my *husband*, Jonathan."

He searches my eyes, as if he wants to believe me. "Am I truly? Because I know that you were trapped into this marriage when you got pregnant. And if I were any kind of honorable man, I'd have let you go before now."

The breath goes out of me. "You think that *you* trapped *me* into this marriage? That's what you think?"

"I remember how scared you were the day you told me that you were pregnant. But I was thrilled, Nora. I was barely making a wage. I didn't know how I was going to support a wife and child. But none of that mattered to me because your being pregnant meant that I had you. I *had* you and no one could take you away from me. I had something that would've otherwise never been in my reach."

Is he talking about me or my father's fortune? The revelations turn my world upside down. "Then my father threatened you. He told you that you'd lose your job if you didn't propose marriage to his daughter."

Jonathan laughs. It's not a joyful laugh. It's sour as lemons. He rolls to the side, eyes on the canopy over the bed, one knee bent in casual disdain. "Oh, that much is true. Your father did threaten me."

He laughs again and I don't like it. It's a sound of dark despair. "He tried to run me off. But I wouldn't go. I promised to ruin you if he wouldn't let me marry you."

I'm incredulous. "*Ruin* me?"

"I wasn't about to allow Robert Aster to raise my child. I wasn't going to let *him* have you. I was perfectly willing to trap you in this marriage. So, yes, I threatened to ruin you. There it is. Now you know the truth."

Now *I* want to laugh. He'd threatened to *ruin* me. To mire me in scandal. I find it perversely romantic, charming and quaint, and utterly demented. Curiosity overwhelms me. "And what were you going to do? Tell everyone I wasn't a virgin? Or did you plan to seduce me in such a way that I'd be caught with my skirt up over my hips, drunkenly surrendering my virtue in the parlor on a desktop?"

His ears redden, and I regret mocking him. He is so vulnerable to me right now. My hands go to his dark hair, and I devour his face in kisses. The dark brows. The impossibly sharp cheekbones. The thick, brooding lips that have given me so much pain and pleasure. "You're a fool, Jonathan. A fool," I say tenderly. "Women like me aren't trapped into marriage. My father could have sent me away into the country if I'd have been willing to go. I'd have developed some mysterious ailment and returned some months later and been courted by fifty men, all of whom would be more than willing to overlook the scandal in favor of my father's fortune."

"But you wanted to keep the child," Jonathan argues. "So you had to take me in the bargain."

This is the man who knows how to make my body vibrate with arousal. This is the man who can make me writhe with pleasure. This man can make me abandon all sense of shame and crave things I've never even known I wanted before. And yet, I worry that he doesn't know me at all.

"I hoped that you'd learn to love me," Jonathan says.

"I do."

It's as close as I can come to saying the words, and it startles him.

Then doubt spreads over his features. "If that's true, why wouldn't you ever say it? I told you that I loved you . . . before we were even married. But you never said it back."

My tongue trips over the words. "B-because I never believed you."

He accepts this answer with equanimity, seeming to weigh it in his mind. Sprawled on the bed, he closes his eyes. I know that he's thinking, because I can see his fists clench and release. Eventually he sits up, both feet on the floor, head bent over clasped hands, elbows on his knees. "I don't suppose I could make you believe it now . . ."

"I want to believe you . . . but how can I, if we keep living like this? Alienated. Apart. If we—if we love each other—there's no reason for it."

"You want things, Nora. You need things . . . that I can't give you."

"Like what?"

"Like respectability. After last night, I doubt we'll receive many invitations into society again."

His naiveté is endearing. "Oh, but we will. We gave everyone something to talk about. The ladies will clutch at their pearls and call me names behind my back. The men will feign disapproval, all while secretly admiring your nerve or wondering if they can seduce me. And they'll invite us everywhere, so that they can point at us and shake their heads with distaste when they think we aren't looking."

"You shouldn't have to endure that kind of censure," Jonathan says.

"It will sting, I admit. The next time I walk into a room and see any of those men from last night, I'll die a little in shame. But the heat of that shame will burn between my thighs, and it'll only make me want you more." I've never spoken so brazenly to him before when his hands weren't on me. He looks up in surprise. "I want your approval, Jonathan. I don't care about anyone else's. I don't care about society."

"Spoken like someone who was born into it. Like someone who

has never been on the outside of it. You say you don't care, but you just don't know any better."

"I tell you, I don't care." Then I stop and stare at the man who has had to claw his way to the top. Who has worked tirelessly, under constant scrutiny. "Oh, but *you* care, don't you? You care, Jonathan."

"You're damned right I do," he breathes.

I want to rail at him for his materialism, for his shallow desire for acceptance. But he's the son of a field hand. He's a man who has come from nothing. And I want him to have everything. "I can behave myself in public, you know. If you care so much about society—"

"Not more than I care about you," he says. "Let's be clear on that. If society was the only problem between us, Nora, I'd let them all go hang."

"Then what keeps us apart? Is there something else you don't think you can give me?"

"A child," he says. "After the miscarriage, I swore to myself that I'd become a better man. That I wouldn't touch you again until I was worthy of you. Well, I'm not. And after last night, I don't know that I ever will be. I *hit* you, Nora. And I *enjoyed* it. So we can't simply return to the way things were, pretending that I'm not going to crack one day and do it all again. Because I will. I don't know how to love you gently."

How is it that he won't hear me? That he won't understand. "I never asked you to treat me gently!"

"Listen to me. If we stay together as other men and women do, I'll look for excuses to yank at your clothes, to bite at the back of your neck and turn you over my knee. What I want is wrong and it's sinful. I am a depraved monster inside, Nora."

If there were anything near enough, I would throw it at him. "Stop saying that!"

"Oh, for the love of God, I don't need your pity. I'm not one of the poor orphans at your charity house."

"It isn't *pity*, you horse's ass. I'm insulted. When I went with you that first time, when I let you put your hands up my skirt, let you bed me, I thought that I wasn't a virgin. But I was. Because you were the first man to ever touch me. Truly touch me. Or at least, the first man to touch what was really inside of me. Everything about myself that I'd been afraid of came awake in a moment, and it wasn't ugly. I'm not twisted and ugly inside, Jonathan."

He stands up, rounding the bedpost to face me. "I never said you were."

"You say it every time you call yourself a monster. Because if you're a sick and sinful and depraved man for what you want to do to me . . . what does that make me for wanting you to do it?"

His eyes narrow. He exhales sharply from his nose. He looks away.

"*Oh*," I whisper, both hands to my face in despair. "Oh. You *do* think there's something wrong with me."

He takes my hands, pulls them gently from my horrified face, and clasps them in his. "It's just . . . I used to see men beat on their women on the farm. Drunken sots, big fists, lots of tears. I'd see those same women go back to those men. Make excuses for them. Just like you're doing for me."

"We're not like that," I say, wishing there were words for it. "If I'd asked you to stop last night, would you have?"

"Of course."

"Then it's play. It's a game."

"Games have rules," Jonathan says.

"Then we'll make some."

He hesitates, as if tempted. "People don't . . . *do* this, Nora."

"How do you know? Maybe they do. Just not, perhaps, in the middle of a party. And maybe they don't. Maybe no one in the world plays these games. Maybe that's why we were drawn together out of anybody else in the whole world. We're perfect for each other."

"We can't just do anything that feels right to us."

"Why not?" I stare at him, hard, waiting for an answer that doesn't come. "Why not, Jonathan?"

The more we argue, the more sure of myself I become. The certainty spreads through me, limb by limb, transcendent. I know myself as I've never known myself before. And I can say all the things that have been caged inside my head. "Our whole marriage, I've done nothing but try to hold on to you, Jonathan. I've done so very many things I'm not proud of, not the least of which was withholding from you the truth of my own feelings. *I love you.*"

His expression lightens and I see that he believes me. He reaches for my face and I let him kiss me. It feels so right that I cannot bear to deny it anymore. My palms skid down his bare chest, stopping to lace my fingers through his. And then I say the most difficult thing I've ever said in my life. "These hands have never hurt me. But *you* hurt me. You've hurt my heart and you've hurt . . . something deeper. Something uniquely me. And if you're going to keep doing it, keep denying what we both want, then I want you to leave. Right now. This afternoon."

He draws back, obviously shaken, trying to gather his composure. Silhouetted against the fireplace with its carved rosettes, he rubs his face in thought. He's withdrawing into himself, which only makes me feel more raw and exposed. Desperate now, I go to my knees in the pile of clothes that I've knocked to the floor, digging into the back of the suitcase. I don't stop until the touch of a metal buckle bites at my fingertips and I pull out a brown leather belt.

Stumbling over the suitcase, I get back to my feet and hold it out to him. "Use it on me."

He recoils. "For Christ's sake, Nora!"

I plead with him. "Hit me with it. Just like you did that night. I'll make you see that you didn't hurt our baby."

A wordless shake of his head.

"What's the matter, Jonathan? Can't you do it unless I provoke you? Do I need to kiss someone else? Do I need to go to bed with another man this time? What is it that you need me to do to make it alright?"

He swallows as if there is something caught in his throat that keeps him from speaking.

"I'm strong, Jonathan," I say, hoarsely, finding my own courage. "And you can't break me. I thought you could. I thought you *did*. But you can't."

"Perhaps you're right," he says, dropping his gaze. "But what you don't seem to realize, Nora, is that *you* can break *me*."

His words reverberate through me. The lump that rises in my throat threatens to strangle me. It hurts, a painful throb at my center. Tears roll down my cheeks. So here it is, then. All this time, he thought he needed to protect me from his own worst instincts. Now he realizes that he needs to be protected from me.

I am the monster.

"Then it's up to you, isn't it?" I ask quietly. "My father used to say I was a spoiled and willful child. I was. Because I always knew that I didn't belong to my father. I knew I didn't belong to Robert Aster. I don't belong to you, either—not unless I want to. I'm mine to give, Jonathan. And no one can decide, but you, whether or not to give yourself to me in return."

I twist the gold wedding band from my finger. It's a perilous journey to the carved marble mantelpiece, where I gently set the ring down. I'm too near to him, overwhelmed by his scent and his warmth. He hasn't changed posture. Hasn't moved a muscle. Rigid in tormented thought.

"But you're going to choose me, Jonathan. You're going to choose us. I have faith in you."

When I lean close to kiss him, he flinches.

"I'm going down to breakfast," I say, my voice as flat and emotionless as I can make it.

"Of course," he says, almost absently. "You must be wanting breakfast . . . why it's almost afternoon . . ."

"Will you join me?" It's the only fissure I allow in my newfound self-possession.

"I don't know." A mask has descended over that impossibly handsome face and I cannot read him.

"Shall I have a tray sent up to you, then?"

His eyes are blank. "Whatever is most convenient."

CHAPTER
Six

In the dining room, Dolly is stiff-lipped as she pours my tea. It is lukewarm. The biscuits on the sideboard are cold now, but I take three of them and smother them with butter and strawberry preserves. As I pile my plate with food, I notice that since I went upstairs to confront Jonathan, someone has set the table with the best china, as if we were expecting guests.

Then Dolly reminds me. "Your father, ma'am. He's expected this afternoon, remember?"

Most of me dreads the idea of seeing him. Especially now. But some tiny, infuriated part of me eagerly readies for a fight. I've faced almost all my demons today—what is one more? That my father should have lied to Jonathan and made him suffer for so long . . . I can't begin to guess how my father might have known the exact words to crush my husband's spirit, but I want to make him sorry.

I'm hungry. Hungrier than I think I've ever been. And while this morning, the pear tasted quite nearly like ash, now it bursts in my mouth, juicy and fresh. My taste buds are as oversensitive as the rest

56 · Stephanie Draven

of me. The flake of the biscuit against my tongue melts swiftly in a pool of butter and I want more.

More of everything.

It's only after I open the soft-boiled egg in its cup, scooping out the tender insides and washing them down with tea, that I begin to feel better. Jonathan won't leave. He can't leave. Not after everything we've said to each other today. If he's the man I've come to love, he'll find the strength within him to stay. To make something with me that's new . . . and unbreakable.

The pendulum sways in the grandfather clock on the far wall. I eat slower, my bites getting tinier until finally, I hear Jonathan's footsteps on the stairs. The servants wisely scatter; Dolly disappears behind the pocket door that separates the dining room from the kitchen, and draws it shut.

Please, God, let him choose to be himself, I pray. *Let him choose me.*

So sure am I that my wish will be granted that I look up at him with a beatific smile. I want him to see me like this, sitting at his table, confident and happy. Open, body and soul, to every kind of pleasure.

But then I see the brown leather suitcase in his hand.

He might have had a servant carry it down for him, but the square luggage looks to weigh nothing from the way the handle settles in his calloused palm. He's dressed now. Cuffed trousers, shirt and tie. Slim-fitting jacket, cut high at the waist. A gray fedora hat, perched upon his head at an angle that shadows his eyes.

I set down the butter knife at the edge of my plate, letting my hands fall to my lap, where I clasp them so hard that the nails dig into my palms.

"Is there anything else you want to say to me?" Jonathan asks.

Lifting my chin, I fight back the tears, shaking my head in disbelief.

"Then stand up," he says, setting the suitcase down by his ankle.

What can he want from me? A hug good-bye? A tender kiss? I won't begrudge him. Even if he isn't the man that I hoped he was,

I loved him. I love him still. Folding my napkin on the table, I rise to my feet.

I wait for him to come closer, but he doesn't.

Instead, he removes his hat, crushing it with his fist. "Turn around and put your hands on the table, Nora."

I understand each of the words but can't decipher what they mean all run together. I stand there, stupefied, until he grabs hold of one of my wrists and spins me towards the table. His grip is like iron, merciless in its intention. He dips his head, his hot breath sweeping down the back of my neck. "Put your hands on the table, palms down."

Before I can think to do anything else, my fingers splay on the table, next to the silver salt and pepper shakers. Warm dappled sunlight filters through the window, making the hair on my arms look golden. He runs a warm palm down my shoulders, resting it on the small of my back. A broad arm reaches over me to deposit my wedding ring on the table in front of me, where it winks in mockery.

My mind swirls with confusion, and I start to stand up, but he holds one hand pinned to the table. "Nora, do you have any idea how sexy you are, bent over for me?"

I remain bent like that, paralyzed, letting him touch me. Letting him toy with the garter suspenders that hold up my stockings. Then I hear the jingling of his belt as he moves behind me. "I don't understand, Jonathan. What are you doing?"

"I'm taking off my belt," he says, very calmly. "And I'm going to hit you with it."

A tremor goes through me, leaving my knees soft and spongy. A thousand questions fly through my mind but the only one I ask is, "Here?"

"Right here," he says. "Unless you're not as brave as you claim to be."

He won't find me lacking in resolve, if it's a demonstration that he needs. Though my arms shake, I don't move, not even when I hear the sound of the leather slipping through the loops of his trousers.

He'll fold it, I think, imagining the leather looped over his fist. He must, because his arm swings in only a tight arc, the crack of the belt on the backs of my legs more weighty than sharp. The next blow forces me to hiss with the impact, and everything on the table jiggles. Glasses and plates tinkle together, but it doesn't stop him. He hits me with the belt again, and I glance over my shoulder at him in . . . what? Disbelief? Anger? Pain? Arousal? Admiration? Adoration?

All of those things and more.

"I'm not nearly done," he says. "Unless you tell me to stop. Are you going to tell me to stop?"

"No."

"Then this time tomorrow you won't be able to sit down. Do you know why?"

Truly, this time, I don't. And I'm hypnotized by his lips, utterly captivated by whatever he might say next.

"Because it excites me," he says, pressing the length of his erection against my sore ass cheek. My muscles go limp with desire. He must know it, because he loops his arm around my waist to steady me against the table. "I'm not hitting you because you kissed another man. Not because you've done anything to anger me. I'm doing it because I want to . . . and because you want it, too."

His voice is throaty, strained with emotion, as if he needs to hear it as much as he needs to say it to me. And by god, as much as the pain bites through my skin with each blow, I don't want him to stop. Another blow jolts me forward into the table so hard that breakfast cream sloshes out of the decanter, spilling into the saucer beneath.

Jonathan bends over me, covering his body with mine, and I take several desperate breaths as he smoothly unzips my gown in the back, easing it over my shoulders. "Step out of it," he says, and I let the fabric skim down my arms and over my belly. There's something outrageously erotic about the way it slips down over my legs to puddle around my ankles on the floor. Standing in nothing but my corset and girdle, I feel exposed. It's our dining room—not a dance floor, not a desk in someone else's parlor, not the back of a car. And yet, I bring my hands up over my breasts, suddenly shy.

"Do you want to go upstairs?" Jonathan asks.

"Yes," I whisper.

"We're not going to," he says, staring at me, his eyes burning over the curves of my body as if he's never seen them before. "You are a choice dish, Nora. You're built like you were born for a burlesque house. But there's one thing I don't enjoy about burlesque. I don't like being taunted with fans and peeks of flesh. I don't want to be teased. Are you going to tease me?"

I shake my head, lowering my hands, leaving myself open to his hot gaze.

He rewards me with a kiss on my shoulder, then says. "Hands back on the table."

He waits until my palms are flat on the table to strike me again, and this time, the sugar bowl crashes to the floor. I start to protest, but whatever I'm going to say is cut off by a shriek when the belt lashes me.

"Too much already? I haven't even hit your bare ass."

He yanks at my undergarments, and the cool air is almost a respite against the burning stripes of heat he's laid on me. Then he cracks the belt across my bottom again, so hard that he grunts with the effort. His arm swings down again, and the blow makes me keel forward. A plate crashes to the ground. "Jonathan!"

"Had enough?" he asks, nuzzling the back of my neck.

Though tears blind me and shrieks of pain have become tiny sobs, I shake my head.

"These are going to leave welts," Jonathan says, the flat of his palm pressing down warmly between my shoulder blades until I have no choice but to bend forward, my cheek on the tablecloth. "I've marked you."

I wilt against the table, grateful beyond measure. Too overcome to choose words that might express how wonderful I feel. I let my body do the talking, rubbing back against him like a cat.

"I'm going to put down the belt," he says. "But I'm not done hitting you."

He sets the belt where I can see it, coiled on the table next to my cheek. Then he presses tight up against those stripes of pain and I feel his erection throbbing against the cleft of my ass. I yelp at the drag of rough trouser fabric against my bare, sensitive skin, wanting more.

"You're mine," he says, fingers pushing between my legs where I'm softest and most vulnerable. One dexterous finger swims through the damp curls of my sex and thrusts up inside me, forcing me to cry out. I'm sore from last night, swollen and tight. Still, not too tight for him to push inside.

"Do you feel that, Nora? How wet you are? I love that you get wet so easily. The way you arch your back for me, like you're in heat. I think I could just look at you from across a room and you'd be clenching your thighs and squirming in your chair and ready for me. Are you ever *not* ready to be fucked by me?"

"No," I groan, because everything he says is true, and on the rare occasion he's caught me by surprise, I'm wet enough by the time he's inside me.

"That's proof that you belong to me."

"Jonathan . . . I . . . I don't understand. The suitcase . . ."

"I'm leaving, Nora. But I'm taking you with me."

"I—I . . . but I thought . . ."

"We're going to a summer house once we get a few things straight between us." I want to turn to look at his face. To know that he means it. But the rude thrusts of his finger inside me keep me pinned to the table. Then the pleasure and joy are so intense that I squeeze my eyes shut and concentrate on his voice.

"The first thing we're going to get straight is that I love you," he says. "And I'll tan your hide every day of the week if that's what it takes for you to believe me. And I need to know that you love me, too."

"Oh god, I *do* love you, Jonathan," I say, frantic to twist from his grasp so that I can kiss his mouth.

But he won't let me up. "Hands back on the table." He waits for me to obey, then says, "The second thing we're going to get straight is that you're not going to kiss other men."

"No, I won't, of course I won't."

"You're not going to kiss anyone, fuck anyone, dance with anyone, or even shimmy for them, Nora . . ."

At this moment, Jonathan fills all my senses. I cannot even fathom a world with other men in it. "I won't!"

"Unless I tell you to." It's those last words that force me to glance over my shoulder at him, this time, gape-mouthed. And when I catch sight of his devastatingly handsome face, his eyes are lit with blue mischief and a tiny smile creeps into the corners of his mouth. He looks utterly devilish. "Do you understand?"

I should be saying no, but his finger is banging into me, making me moan my consent.

"I need you to say it, Nora. Do you understand? Unless I tell you to."

"Yes," I whisper, through lips parted in ecstasy. "I won't do any of those things . . . unless you tell me to."

"And when you put that wedding ring back on, you're never going to take it off again."

"Yes, yes, Jonathan, yes," I cry, reaching for the golden wedding band.

He stops me. "Not yet. Because you need to know what you're getting into. Do you remember how I made you touch yourself last night?" I nod in wordless surrender, my whole world seeming to narrow to his hand between my legs and his voice on my ear. "You're going to do it again, Nora. You're going to do it for me. You're going to do it in front of a mirror. You're going to do it anytime I want you to do it. Do you understand?"

"Yes."

"You're also going to spend more time on your knees, because I loved your mouth on my cock."

"Yes." Now that I've started saying it, I can't stop. "Yes, yes . . ."

A second finger pushes inside, and as it sinks into my body, I sigh.

"*Christ*," Jonathan says, his breath catching. "Do that again?"

"Do what?"

"Sigh like you do when I'm touching you. Like you're going to swoon away if I stop."

There is no difficulty, no hesitation, no artifice when I sigh again, and I'm rewarded with a third finger slipping inside me, spreading me to the point of aching. Then, all at once, he pulls those fingers out, one of them drifting between my upturned ass cheeks. The sticky feel of his finger at the puckered entrance makes me stiffen and thrash, which only makes him laugh. "Oho, have we found the one place my wife is still a virgin?"

An incoherent protest bubbles up as he eases his finger in to the first knuckle. "Jonathan!" I gasp, hating every moment of it, but loving the way it turns me to clay to mold in his hands.

"I'll always stop when you say to stop," Jonathan tells me. "But I don't think you will. I think there's nothing you're not going to let me do. Starting with all the ways I plan to take you on this table."

Jonathan's free hand reaches around in front of me and slips over my corset, nails raking the swell of my breasts. I know that I won't have any mastery over what happens to me next. He reaches into my corset, finding the swollen nipple there, torturing it between his fingers until I can't stand it anymore. Then he finds my other breast and tortures it with equal malice. Both nipples ache so much so that I beg him to undo the corset. I can't bear the fabric scraping the stiff peaks, but he's merciless, rolling them like hard pebbles in his hand until some invisible cord of arousal is pulled taught between my breasts and my womb. When I'm so needy that I think I'll scream, he withdraws his finger from between my tight, forbidden passage, and takes the time to remove his jacket and tie.

"Will you wear my ring again?"

"Yes," I say, this time from somewhere deeper than where I've found the answer before.

He takes it and slides the glowing circle of gold back onto my finger, brushing his cheek against mine, the stubble of his beard prickly against my skin. "I love you," he murmurs.

I die a little watching him roll up his shirtsleeves before he picks the belt back up.

"And I love you, Jonathan. I love you, I love you, I love you."

I don't know how many times I say it, even when the belt slams down on my tender flesh. The words dissolve into cries of pain as he swings his arm back and lashes me again and again. I don't know how long he can do it. Each stroke becomes harder than the last. He's testing me. Testing himself.

It isn't until I'm howling, gripping the table in pain, shifting on legs that no longer seem strong enough to hold me, that he stops to wipe sweat from his brow. "I think you've had enough."

Inconceivably, I moan in protest. "No . . . no . . . you're not hitting me with your full strength."

He stills behind me. "I don't need to."

"I want you to. Please . . . please . . . hit me harder." What drives this fit of masochism I cannot say, except that I am desperate now to prove to him that he cannot break me. Frantic. So frantic that if he doesn't do it, I think I'll scream.

The next moment, all my panic is obliterated in a flash of red-hot pain. My husband is stronger than I knew, and the next stroke of his belt hisses through the air. I hear him grunt with the effort, but the impact no longer registers as pain at all. A rush of euphoria runs through my blood, like a splash of cherry syrup. It stings so sweet that I'm in a place now beyond pain.

Finally, Jonathan drops the belt. "My arm is starting to tire."

I scarcely hear him anymore as he strips the clothes from my oversexed body.

I do nothing to stop him or help him. I do nothing but stand there, letting him peel back every layer of clothing until I'm standing naked in my own dining room, palms flat on the table. When he nudges my knees apart to enter me, I close my eyes and lose all sense of time and place.

His hands clamp down on either side of my hips, pumping my body in an exquisite rhythm. Then his thick, muscled arm slips over mine, his fingers twining with mine in a fierce grip. Something warm, something wet is trailing down my back and I realize it's his tongue. Licking me. Tasting me. Kissing my shoulders and the slope of my spine. The hair of his abdomen scratches the tender inflamed skin of my bottom as he grinds into my body.

"I want you," Jonathan murmurs behind my ear.

"You have me."

"Not yet, I don't."

He shoves aside plates and bowls, which clatter to the floor.

"Jonathan!" I cry, shaken from my reverie.

He withdraws, turning me to face him and he's smiling. "You don't care about society, but you care about the place settings?"

I glance down at the broken shards of dishes and crystal, then back up at the sharp blue eyes of a man who loves me, and I say, "No. No, I don't care."

I knock a saucer to the floor, utterly indifferent to its fate.

He grins. Then Jonathan sweeps the rest of the table clean, tablecloth and all.

The noise is cacophonous, an irrevocable crash that shatters everything we've known.

Two hands on my waist, he gingerly lifts me up onto the table. "It seems sturdy enough," Jonathan says, crawling atop me. "And I suspect it's about to become a very treasured family heirloom with a great deal of sentimental value, given that this is where I intend to conceive our child."

Joy forces me to gasp and my eyes frantically search his for any wavering, any sign of doubt. "Do you mean it?"

By way of answer he presses me down to the table with his weight, he kisses my mouth, my nose, my cheeks, my chin. I kiss him back, like a woman dying of thirst, drinking him in. My hand on his cheek, his fingers tangled in my hair, our noses pressed together, not a hairsbreadth between us. I cannot get enough of the way his mouth tastes. We kiss and kiss.

It's some kind of rapturous insanity we're caught in now, and I splutter with laughter every time he lets me take a breath. Then he is laughing, too. We are filled with a mad joy.

I throw my head back, my hair in a wild tangle on the table behind me, my throat quivering and bare, and he buries his head there, nuzzling against me with a gentleness that is completely at odds with the desperate clutch of his hands.

"I love you," I say, gripping his hair. "I need you to know it."

He smiles and takes deep breaths, like he has been delivered from some manner of drowning. I reach for his shirt, yanking it free, deftly opening the buttons and popping them when they won't come free. I use my feet to help him ease his pants down, and then he positions himself over me.

It takes only the nudge of his swollen erection at the entrance to my defenseless sex to start me careening wildly towards the edge. And when he pushes inside me, this time inch by slow inch, I exhale with a long shuddering sound of pent-up desire. "Jonathan . . ." I murmur, a warning.

It doesn't deter him. Pulling my leg up over his hip, he hits bottom and draws out again, the slide of his engorged cock through the velvet of my insides making the edges of the whole world blur. "Jonathan . . . Jonathan," I cry again, pushing against his chest, trying to stop it, even though it is the thing I want most.

There is nothing either of us can do or say to keep me from pleasure. "Do it, Nora."

With his permission, the flutter in my abdomen opens into a soaring expanse of ecstasy. I come. I scream. I lock my knees around his waist, pulling him into me, battering myself against his body as if swept up in a storm. The chandelier overhead blinds me with its brilliance, and I have a pure, white climax in which the world goes silent.

I'm the earth to his plow, unbreakable, depthless, enduring anything. I writhe, my insides tumbling over one another as I squeeze him inside. He finds a rocking pace that I think he cannot possibly maintain. His arms strain, muscles bulging. The cords of his neck are visible as sweat trickles down between us. He's a man possessed, his thighs flexing, his body thrusting into me. Though my whole body vibrates with the impact, I settle into it, a honeyed sweetness making me languid beneath him.

The doorbell rings.

I don't care. It jars Jonathan, but only for a moment, because I kiss him, biting down softly, inhaling his breath, tasting his sweat. There is no one and nothing else in the world. He continues to piston down into me and a smooth answering heat coils inside. I tingle from the tips of my ears, to my curled toes. It doesn't seem possible that I could be so aroused again, so swiftly, but we're both close now.

It's going to happen again. I know it. When I'm under him, when his hands are on my body, I am insatiable. I will never stop coming. Our hands clasp together, fingers straining as Jonathan's excitement makes him swell and throb inside my pussy. I whimper as the pleasure sweeps over me, as I'm utterly at its mercy, whispering, "Jonathan, give me a baby."

That's what he needs. A sound catches at the back of his throat. He convulses, eyes half-closed, and makes a guttural cry as his seed pulses up into me. It's the feel of it, the rush of warm fluid from his body into mine that opens my womb for him and sends me into oblivion.

He pumps his hips more slowly now, a new spurt of seed with each thrust. The cream pools deep inside me, so warm and filling. And I flush with the pleasure of knowing that in a few months, it will make my belly swell.

I'm not sure which of us starts laughing first, but he laughs louder and I love the sound of it. His forehead touches mine, and we are tangled together in a heap. The doorbell rings again, and I wipe the sweat from his face with my fingertips, kissing him. "You know who that is."

"Your father, I expect," Jonathan says, glancing at the empty foyer. The whole house is silent, as if it had been listening. "I think the doorman's too afraid to answer it."

"I can't blame him," I say.

Jonathan strokes my hair, lips at my temple, rolling me over so that I'm cushioned against him. "I didn't realize this table is so very hard on your back," he says, absurdly rubbing my spine, as if *that* were the sorest part of me.

"I don't mind," I say, burrowing beneath his arm. "I have a special fondness for this table now. You're teaching me to appreciate things I've taken for granted."

A clang sounds out. It's the door knocker. Three angry taps.

My father is not a man used to being kept waiting.

"Do you want me to answer it?" Jonathan asks, one eyebrow raised.

"No. I don't want to see him. I don't have anything to say to him."

"Oh, but I have a thing or two to say to your father," Jonathan says, inhaling the scent of my hair. "Maybe it can wait, though. I'll send him a telegram from our summer house."

I imagine my father twisting his mustache in fury, red-faced and enraged. Receiving a telegram from Jonathan might well cause him to spontaneously combust. I am painfully curious. "What would you say?"

Jonathan's hand runs sinuously over the curve of my hip. "Most of what I'd like to say to him isn't suitable for a telegram, but I can think of at least two words: *I quit.*"

When I laugh, he nips at my earlobe, stroking me tenderly, kissing the supple peak of each breast in homage. Then he sits up and fastens his pants, threading the belt around his waist. I know I'll never be able to watch him fasten a belt again without remembering this day.

"Aren't you going to get dressed?" Jonathan asks.

"I don't think I can. I'm sore to the bone."

He looks vexed until he sees me smile, then admits, "I worked hard to make you that way. And I'd like to look at you naked all day. But, I don't think they'll let you on the train unless you're wearing at least a frock. You are looking forward to our summer together, aren't you?"

"But what if I can't move?"

"We'll do it together." His arm slips beneath the small of my back, and he scoops me up. He helps me dress, taking special care fastening my gown, his mouth pressed to the sweat-damp nape of my neck.

"Careful of the glass," he says, stooping to find my shoes.

More knocking comes at the front door. I think I also hear my father's muffled shout.

Slipping his jacket on, and leaving his tie askew at the open collar of his shirt, Jonathan retrieves his hat and suitcase. I put on my shoes, preparing for the confrontation with my father. But Jonathan twirls me to him and says, "We have a back door, you know, as long as Dolly and the servants aren't cowering in it."

Sputtering with something akin to delight, I say, "We can't just slip out the back door and leave this mess behind!"

"Why not?" Jonathan asks, in an echo of my earlier question.

"And just drive off in the Bentley in a cloud of dust like a gangster and his gun moll?"

"Why not?" he asks again, holding his hand out to me. "Will you come with me, Mrs. Richardson?"

"Yes," I say, breathlessly, lacing my fingers through his. "Yes, I will."

when i'm bad i'm better

CHAPTER

One

Clara

"Are you having an affair with him?" asks the stranger as he stoops to light my cigarette.

In the chaos of the party it would be easy to ignore him. After all, there has already been a drunken fistfight and a couple caught having sex on the desktop in the parlor. Now the ragtime piano player is hammering at the keys with feigned gaiety while the guests talk too loudly, clinking their glasses of illegal liquor as if to banish the unpleasantness.

If I want to turn my back on the handsome and impertinent stranger, no one would blame me, but I'm intrigued. "Am I having an affair? That's not the kind of question someone normally asks before a formal introduction."

The stranger smirks and snaps his lighter shut. "You don't need an introduction. Everybody who reads the scandal sheets knows who you are. Clara Cartwright. Box Office Gold."

"Then you have me at a disadvantage. I didn't catch your name, Mr.—"

"Vanderberg," he says. "Leo Vanderberg."

It sounds familiar, but I can't place it. "German?"

"Dutch," he says quickly, exhaling a long ribbon of smoke from the corner of his mouth.

I like his mouth. Firm lips beneath a shadow of stubble he ought to have shaved for this party. Lips that part in a narrow expression of vague amusement at our obvious instant attraction. I feel it, too. The inexplicable tug between us. "Well, Mr. Vanderberg, exactly who do you think I'm having an affair with?"

He grins, leaning against the wood-paneled wall, priceless artwork framing his square shoulders. He holds an icy glass of bourbon at a precarious angle, and yet his hand is steady. Then his eyes motion to the host of the party. "I want to know if you're sleeping with Big Teddy Morgan. He's the fat cat throwing this bash in your honor, isn't he?"

"This party is for the *studio* . . . or didn't you read the invitation?"

His heated gaze slips over my silver sequined gown in apparent appreciation of the way it hugs my hips. "Maybe I don't need an invitation."

He's bold but I've managed bold men since I was fourteen. I let the smoke at the long end of my cigarette holder encircle my head like a wreath, then turn to my best angle to give him a better view. "Do you always go where you're not wanted?"

He smiles with those dark, dangerous eyes. "Oh, I'm wanted wherever I go . . ."

This makes me laugh. "That's a good line. I should steal it for my movies . . ."

"Do they let you write your own lines now?"

"Nobody *lets* me do anything, Mr. Vanderberg. I've scraped and clawed for everything I've got."

He nods, sipping from his crystal glass and I see that he's not wearing a wedding ring. There's a lean hungry look about him from the shine of his neatly barbered Valentino-style hair to his polished wing-tip shoes.

"So are you?" he asks. "Having an affair with Teddy Morgan, I mean?"

I don't see the point in denying it. "What's it to you if I am?"

He leans in, close and predatory. I catch a whiff of the spicy scent of his aftershave. "I like to know the field before I make a battle plan. I like to know who I'm up against."

He's so sure of himself that I have to knock him down a peg or two. "I'm a fight you can't win, I'm afraid."

He glances over at my sugar daddy. "Why? Are you in love with him?"

"I don't fall in love, Mr. Vanderberg. When I take a man to bed, it's got everything to do with the size of his bank account and what he's got between his legs."

I say it to shock him. Possibly to offend him. But he just kicks up a brow in wry amusement, the sparkle of the chandeliers overhead reflected in his eyes. The ritzy glitter and glam of this party is getting to me and if he asks me to dance, I decide that I'll say yes.

But before he can, our host ambles over and throws one meaty arm around my waist. I don't mind terribly; Big Teddy is just one more man in a long string of them who thought they were using me, and he's not the worst of them by far. "Clara, I see you've run into our resident war hero! This is Leo Vanderberg. Flying ace."

I've met plenty of soldiers before but never a genuine flying ace. That explains the boldness. It takes a special kind of man to brave impossible heights in nothing but a little box. And that's to say nothing of the kind of man who can shoot another person out of the sky. I look at Mr. Vanderberg with a trifle more wariness than before, then extend my hand as if we hadn't already been introduced. "How nice to meet you, Mr. Vanderberg."

The aviator takes my hand. He kisses it. His lips linger too long. "Call me Leo."

Big Teddy doesn't seem to notice the spark that crackles between us. "So, how many German aircraft did you shoot down in the Great War, Leo? Seven?"

"Seventeen," Leo murmurs.

I blow a perfect ring of smoke. "Goodness! And what does a flying ace like you do with himself now that the war is over?"

"I'm a test pilot," Leo replies, his gaze steady on me. "I take the finest pieces of equipment available and push them as far as they'll go."

Oh, my. Now I know where I've heard his name before. He's not the *most* famous American aviator . . . but just about.

Big Teddy snorts. "Sometimes you push too far, Leo. You wrecked the last plane my engineers designed. You may have walked away with your life, but you lost your chance to make that first transatlantic flight. You let Lucky Lindy beat you to it and it serves you right."

The mood abruptly changes and Leo sets his jaw. "Lucky Fucking Lindy."

His bitterness amuses me, and I can't resist getting in a dig. "It usually *is* the rich or lucky who get to do the fucking."

Teddy Morgan roars with laughter, yanking me tight against his fleshy side. The big man pawing at me is a collector. He collects priceless items and unusual people. A silent screen starlet. A war hero. It makes his parties interesting. But he also expects us all to be at his beck and call. "I've got a new plane for you, Leo. She's state of the art. A masterpiece."

"I heard you haven't been able to get her off the ground," Leo replies coolly.

"That's where you come in. This plane is an advance . . . we'll make aviation history if you can get her into the air."

Leo's eyes lock with mine. "Can't wait to get my hands on her."

"Can you be ready next week?" Teddy asks, oblivious to our flirtation.

"I'm always ready," Leo replies with a smirk.

Across the room, a well-heeled guest waves to our host. "I'd better mingle," Big Teddy says. "But you'll stay for a nightcap, Clara, won't you?"

I smile. "Of course."

Then the tycoon releases me and wanders off.

Leo finishes his drink in silence. He's all angles and shadows. The camera would love him, and I don't mind the looks of him, either.

"Come home with me," Leo finally says.

My sigh is one of regret. "I'm afraid Big Teddy and I have an understanding. He's bankrolled my last three films . . ."

"Because he makes money off them. When Clara Cartwright stars in a motion picture, odds of a safe return are almost two-to-one. You don't owe him more than your name in lights on the marquee."

I've never let myself think about it that way before and I might be grateful to Mr. Vanderberg for pointing it out were it not for his self-serving motive. "Even so, you're not likely to offer me a better deal, are you?"

Leo laughs. "Why are you so determined to convince me you're *that* kind of girl?"

I feel a spark of mischief heat my blood. "Maybe because I *am* that kind of girl."

"So, you're jaded," he says, stubbing out his cigarette into a crystal ashtray.

"A true cynic."

"You've done it all . . ."

I grin. "At least twice."

"Then level with me," he begins, leaning in close. "How do you fuck him?"

My smile dies away. "I beg your pardon—"

"Did I shock you already? What happened to the jaded girl, the true cynic who has done it all twice? You're not getting a case of the vapors just because of a lurid question, are you?"

My pulse quickens, my blood rising to his bait. "You surprised me, that's all. Ask again."

He circles behind me, coming close enough that I feel his hot breath on the back of my neck. "So, how do you take him? On your back? On your hands and knees?"

"I straddle him," I say, bold and sultry. "It's easier that way. There's a reason they call him Big Teddy, you know."

I wonder what kind of suitor Leo Vanderberg really is that this kind of talk doesn't run him off. Instead, he trails his warm lips over the back of my neck. I shiver and give a little toss of my head, but I can't shake him. "Why, Miss Cartwright, that's a nice picture you paint. I can see it in my mind. You straddling his lap, riding him, sweat dripping down your spine. It excites me."

Flushing with heat, I stare off at the dance floor where flappers dance the Charleston and a few couples pair off into quiet corners. "You're a strange man to get excited by the idea of a woman having sex with someone else."

"Is it strange? I don't have to be the only man to lift a plane off the ground to appreciate its capabilities. Anyone with eyes can see you're a perfectly built vessel. You weren't made to sit idle in the hangar, were you?"

I want to get a little sore at him for comparing me to a cold hunk of machine, but he's got me running so hot I don't care. "You're right about that. I do believe I was made to fly."

"That makes two of us then, doesn't it? Now, about that deal . . ."

"What deal?"

His voice is a purr. "You said I wasn't about to offer you a better deal, but I am. I'm about to give you something for nothing."

"There's no such thing."

He laughs. "This is a gift. No strings attached. I'm going to make you come tonight without laying a hand on you."

My eyes go slanted and sleepy to make it seem as if I'm bored, but we both know I'm wide awake. "Is that so?"

"Tonight, when you're in bed with him, working those hips of yours, close your eyes. Imagine my breath on the back of your neck, like it is now. Imagine my hands cupping your breasts . . ."

I feign a yawn. "Oh, how droll. You want me to pretend that I'm with you instead of him."

"No, I want you to pretend that my cock is buried in you from behind and that I'm grinding you against him. Pretend that I'm making you take him deeper. Trapping you between us so you've got nowhere to go but where I tell you to. Pretend that I'm pushing you to see how much you can take. It's going to drive you right over the edge."

Another woman would probably slap him, but my knees turn to jelly. And when he withdraws, I'm left to grasp the ornately carved wooden back of an upholstered wing chair for balance.

Satisfaction spreads across his face. "And now I'll be going, unless you'd like to give me a kiss good-bye?"

I finally find my voice. "Sorry, Ace, the bank is closed."

"Then have a pleasurable evening, Miss Cartwright."

When the party is finally over and the mansion is quiet, I sit at the abandoned piano in the alcove. My mother used to play organ at church but I never picked up more than a few notes. Still, I can't resist plunking at the keys. The maidservant finishes sweeping up some confetti and broken glass, then quietly withdraws when the master of the house returns.

"Sorry to keep you waiting." Teddy stumbles in, having abandoned his waistcoat somewhere along the way. "I just needed to make sure my wife is asleep."

His wife is barking mad, as everyone well knows. Mrs. Morgan hasn't left her room for more than a decade. Sometimes she awakens the household late at night with incoherent rages, and when she does, he always goes to her. Other men of his social standing would have institutionalized or divorced her, but I think Teddy Morgan would give up all his fortune—and any mistress—just to have his wife back the way she was before.

Which is why I chose him.

You see, these days, every mogul keeps a starlet for a mistress. Joe Kennedy has Gloria Swanson. William Randolph Hearst has Marion Davies. William S. Paley has Louise Brooks. I figured I'd better pick a big shot before one picked me. And as far as fat cats go, Theodore "Big Teddy" Morgan isn't a bad egg. He's lonely but he won't fall in love or demand more from me than I'm willing to give.

Dropping heavily onto the high-backed leather sofa, he pats the seat beside him. "Take a load off, you've been on your feet all night. But you charmed them all, doll. They'll be lining up on the street to see the film."

"At least until the reviews come in," I say, slipping out of my shoes and joining him. "The producer was a fool. I can make a better picture. I know I can."

He's already pulling me into his lap, hands fumbling for the fastenings of my dress. "Clara, you're a fine actress, but I've already told you. I'm not about to finance a film produced by a woman."

I pull away. "Don't be so old-fashioned. Mary Pickford's been producing films for almost ten years."

"But she's America's Sweetheart," he says, moving my hand onto the growing hardness beneath his pants. "Whereas you warm people up somewhere far south of the heart . . ."

My eyes narrow at the challenge. "I bet I can get you excited in more ways than one. Why don't you drop by the little studio I've been renting and take a peek at some of my projects? I think you'll agree that I should have control over the production of my films."

"Behave yourself, Clara."

"I didn't get anywhere in life by behaving."

His voice lowers an octave. "Then, by all means, let's misbehave . . ."

He unfastens his pants and I take a good look. Teddy Morgan drinks too much and he's going a little soft in the middle—but his giant erection is a thing of wonder. He's wide, thick, and dangerous. He could hurt a woman if he isn't careful. I don't mind though, because I've always wanted the best and biggest of everything.

I know what he wants and I find that I want it, too. I shimmy out of my drawers and kick them onto the floor. My body is already pulsing in anticipation when I hike my sparkly gown up around my waist and climb aboard. I like to to feel the width of him between my thighs. My bracelets jingle as I grasp the back of the couch, gasping a little when I feel his bare flesh press against mine.

"You're not the first woman to rub against me tonight, you know. That vamp, Mrs. Richardson, was like a cat in heat on the dance floor before her husband took her on my desk like a common strumpet."

It surprises me that he seems genuinely angry. "Why are you so upset about having caught a woman having sex with her own husband? Who was it that got slugged, anyway?"

"Only the most eligible bachelor in the country," he says, fleshy hands caressing my hips. "The ambassador's son."

Robert Aster, he means. The youngest of the Aster brothers, heir to a fabulous fortune. I caught a glimpse of him earlier in the evening and thought he had boyish good looks. "Well, I hope he wasn't hurt too badly. I'd hate to think of that face being bloodied."

"I'm just sorry the incident nearly ruined your party."

"Oh, I had a grand time. Everyone will be talking about this party for a while to come."

Teddy chuckles. "I suppose you're right. You know, I got an eyeful of Mrs. Richardson spread out under her husband . . . does that make you jealous?"

I can't afford to be jealous. Men can be possessive of their mistresses, but if you turn it around on them you're a shrew. Worse, he might use my jealousy as an excuse to take the relationship more seriously, and I'm not the serious kind. Not about any man. So I smirk and say what we both know is a lie. "Of course I am."

Our entire relationship is built upon such polite lies. Like the lie that he bankrolls my movies because he's a great appreciator of the arts and not simply because the more money he sinks into my career, the more often I let him fuck me. I'm going to let him fuck me tonight. He knows it. I know it.

But we both pretend it isn't a foregone conclusion.

I tease him, pulling back like I'm having second thoughts. "I can't say that I approve of Mrs. Richardson's behavior."

"I'm surprised," he says, sliding the strap of my gown down over one shoulder to nip me there. "After all, I'm told *you've* been caught having sex on *film*."

"No one's ever produced the reel to prove it," I say, but it's not a denial.

"Good thing, too. It would ruin you. So you're hardly in a position to judge Mrs. Richardson."

"Oh, I'm not judging her; I just don't approve of anyone causing more of a scandal at a party than I do."

"You caused plenty. Your dress is cut so far down in the back you can see where the Lord split you. The gents couldn't tear their eyes away. Leo Vanderberg was like a hound on the scent . . ."

So he *did* notice our flirtation. Now that he mentions the dashing pilot, I flush with heat. I said I was jaded, that I'd done it all, twice. And that's true, for the most part. I've been sleeping with men since I was fourteen, when the landlord forced me to do it or be kicked out into the street. I decided then and there if a man thought he was gonna use me, I was gonna use him right back. I learned to like it. I learned to love it. I did whatever I wanted . . . every position. Every taboo. But Leo Vanderberg somehow latched on to the one thing I haven't done. Now his words swirl deliciously in my mind.

Pretend that my cock is buried in you from behind and that I'm grinding you against him.

As I lower myself onto my lover's erection, I hiss. It always hurts a little at first, no matter how wet I am, but soon, the pain will turn to pleasure, so I screw up my courage. Teddy's eyes go heavy-lidded when I've got only an inch of him inside me. He likes to watch me work at it.

Sometimes we do it in front of a mirror so I can watch, too.

Tonight, it's easier.

While Big Teddy squeezes my breasts, I'm imagining another man's hands on my hips. I'm imagining Leo Vanderberg behind me. Yet, how is it possible that there'd be room inside me for two men? There's not even room enough for this one. But the fantasy makes me slick with arousal. I can feel the flutter of my heartbeat as if it's dropped between my legs.

I get another inch into me. Maybe two. I moan at the feeling of fullness.

"Good god, woman, I love the way you move your hips," Teddy says, while I perform for him.

Pretend that I'm making you take him deeper. Trapping you between us so you've got nowhere to go but where I tell you to.

I work myself on his cock, but get only halfway down the shaft. I hold back; I tease. This is usually as far as I can take him, and it's usually enough to bring Teddy off. In fact, I'm near the edge now myself. His thickness presses deliciously in every direction.

Pretend that I'm pushing you to see how much you can take.

I want more. Tonight, I want to take my lover deeper. Letting gravity pull me down, I fill myself. His big throbbing erection stretches me to the limit. "Oh god, you're so big . . . ," I moan, but it isn't a complaint.

Teddy's red in the face with arousal, his hips making awkward little jerks off the sofa. He palms my ass cheeks as he looks down between us. His voice is husky. "Do you think you can take it?"

It's a matter of pride now. "Yes. I want it all."

My words force a shudder of arousal from him, his eyes suddenly burning with lust. I worry that he'll finish too fast. Instead, he flips me onto my back. I grab the arm of the sofa for balance as the big man rouses himself to pump into me. He's not used to this kind of work and the sweat beads on his brow, but he's like a man possessed. I won't deny him. God, I don't *want* to deny him.

He uses his tool to open me and I cry out. Again and again, I'm impaled until the pain melts into pleasure. I'm stretched so wide now that he's gliding in and out of my pussy with ease. I look down between us, quivering with the thought that his belly might touch mine. He's fucking me with a strange jerking rhythm, as if he were afraid I'll ask him to stop at any moment. But he can't stop. Not now. "Please take it all, Clara . . ."

The start of his orgasm robs him of all self-control and he slams home.

I scream fearing that he's torn me in two, but when I feel his thatch of pubic hair wet against mine, when I feel it scratch my thighs, and the press of his sweaty belly against my own, joined together so tightly that we'd have to be pried apart . . . my screams turn into something else. I've done it. I've taken all of him and the filthy satisfaction with myself makes me come.

It's going to drive you right over the edge.

I don't care that I owe it to Leo Vanderberg; I've never been one to turn down a free gift.

I clutch at my lover while waves of orgasm wash over me, my muscles contracting then giving out with fatigue. I'm aware of Teddy grunting over me, driving his seed into me with wild strokes and spasms. We're locked together for several minutes afterward, until he's soft enough to withdraw from my aching body.

He grunts, then pants, rolling to the side to stroke my hair with unexpected tenderness. "If I weren't already married, Clara, I'd be down on one knee."

"Horsefeathers," I pant. "Wouldn't you rather marry a nice girl?"

"You *are* a nice girl, Clara. You just don't want anyone to know it."

"Don't be sweet." I give his shoulders an affectionate squeeze as I'm fonder of him than I'd ever admit.

Which means it might be time for me to start thinking about moving on.

CHAPTER

Two

"*Whore.*" She spits at me.

Taking a deep breath, I root around in my pocketbook for a hand-kerchief, then wipe the spittle from where it landed on my arm. Then, so as not to frighten her, I smile. "Are you feeling any better?"

Her heavy metal chair slides against the cement floor. "Don't sit there and pretend you can't hear me, girl. I know what you are."

I tuck the cloth back into my purse, smooth the long wool skirt over my legs, then squint into the sun streaming in from the high window, watching the dancing specks of dust she thinks are angels. "Are you sleeping? Last time I asked your doctors, you weren't sleeping."

"We have her on a regimen now, Miss Cartwright," the orderly says. "The sedatives help."

She begins rocking, staring at me, scrutinizing my prim appear-ance and old-fashioned straw hat. "Let me see you, Clara. You know I don't like it when I can't see you."

Removing the pins from my hat, I slowly unfasten it, though I leave the gossamer scarf around my neck. When I look up at her, I say, "There. Now maybe I can read to you. Would you like me to read you a story?"

"You washed your face."

I wish I hadn't. Without the ruby lips, the dark-lined eyes, and the rouge, I'm somehow more vulnerable. But I can't leave my house like that without being recognized; people sometimes follow me on the street and I don't want them to follow me here. So I made myself as plain as possible. "Every girl needs to give her skin some time to breathe, don't you think?"

She says, "I can still see your sin even without all your harlot's paint. I know what you do at night with the men who pant after you. Those men who give you all your baubles. I know any man can have you on your knees by giving you something that sparkles, and they know it, too. You should be on your knees begging the Lord's forgiveness."

I tell myself that her words can't cut me. I won't let them. Still, I pull my hat back from the table for fear she might grab at the pins. It would not be the first time she left me bleeding. "I've brought you some crossword puzzles. I know you like them. You can do one every day and when you're done, I'll send you more."

Normally, working at the puzzles steadies her. Today she throws them on the floor. "One day, you'll be sitting here alone, just like me, Clara. Just like me. Except that at least I have a husband, worthless as he is. When your nerves are shot and they lock you up, who will care?"

Unable to bear it even one more moment, I leap up from my chair and flee for the door, murmuring, "Hopefully, I'll drink myself to death long before that happens."

At home, from the safe height of my fancy penthouse apartment with its gilded furniture and velvet drapes, I find my stash in the sideboard and pour myself a shot of hooch. Downing it too quickly, I cough at the burn. Then I wipe my lips and hurriedly hide the evidence of my distress only moments before the doorman brings me the red roses and the note attached.

The man who sent them is waiting downstairs.

"Can't you shoo him away, Charlie?"

"He's not the sort to be given the bum's rush, madam," the doorman replies.

No, I don't suppose he is. Leo Vanderberg has come at the worst time, but I find that I want to see him. Maybe the reckless aviator is just the tonic I need. "Alright, send him up. Wait fifteen minutes, then have the car brought around, won't you?"

The penthouse, the doorman, and the driver are all perks of being a kept woman. I can afford them without Teddy Morgan's generosity, of course. But like I said before, I never turn down a gift. The days when I was clawing for crumbs in a cold one-bedroom apartment are over, but I haven't forgotten them and I'm never going back.

When I hear the aviator's footsteps in the hall, my pulse quickens. I can see his lean body in my mind's eye, and those dark looks, hot and heavy. I still remember what he whispered in my ear, and it makes me a little shaky to think of it. I don't have to guess what he wants.

When he comes in, I don't turn around right away. "Why, Mr. Vanderberg, I didn't expect to see you again so soon, much less bearing gifts," I say, arranging the roses so the blooms are on fine display. I have to admit, their perfume lifts my spirits. "Are you falling in love with me?"

"Of course not. That would ruin the whole arrangement."

I want to turn around and look him in the eye, but I don't. "What arrangement would that be?"

"The one where I'm planning to debauch you and you're planning to let me."

My lips part in amusement. "I'm afraid I was *thoroughly* debauched long ago."

"I'd like to test that—" He catches his breath when I finally turn around. He has both hands in his pockets, a languid slope to his shoulders, a snappy hat shadowing his face, but he can't hide his surprise.

And his wide-eyed astonishment makes me laugh. "What's the matter, Ace? Haven't you ever seen a girl without powder on her nose before?"

"I—I just . . . I just need a second to get used to it, is all."

"Is my skirt too long, my hat too wide, or don't you recognize me without my war paint?"

"You look younger . . ."

"Like a farm-fresh, freckled milkmaid? Like a sweet daisy ready to be plucked from a field?"

He shrugs. "Something like that."

"Well, don't let the baby face fool you. I only go out like this when I don't want anyone to recognize me."

"You're Clara Cartwright. Why the devil wouldn't you want anyone to recognize you?"

There is nothing I can do but lie. "Because, I'm going to a matinee at Grauman's Chinese Theatre. I can't go there looking like myself. My handprints are in the concrete forecourt right next to Charlie Chaplin's. I'd spend the whole afternoon signing autographs."

He smirks. "Must be hard to be you."

"Positively a trial."

He's still smirking—and I see it's his natural expression, as if he has the utmost contempt for the whole world. "If you're going to the matinee, Clara, let me take you. My treat."

My voice is low and husky with regret. "I'm not interested, Mr. Vanderberg."

"Yes you are. And like I said before, you can call me Leo."

"I haven't decided if I want to be on a first-name basis. At the party I got the impression you weren't just another wet blanket . . . you seemed reckless. A little bit dangerous. But flowers and a movie? Rather conventional, wouldn't you say?"

"The courtship's for your benefit, doll, not mine." Then he leans in and everything turns deadly serious. "See, it's like this. When you're in bed with me, squirming in embarrassment for all the filthy things you've let me do to you, it should comfort you to remember that I did court you as a lady . . . even though I intend to treat you as anything but."

There's something about him that's so potent, so alluring, that I can hardly stand up straight. It's not that he's such a brash pursuer; I've been pursued by brash men before. It's that I think he means it. He means every word he says and that sends the blood rushing past my ears. "You don't need to try so hard, Mr. Vanderberg. I assure you, it's more difficult to make me embarrassed by anything I do in a bed than to get me into one."

He leans close enough to kiss me. "Now that sounds like a challenge . . . so, what do you say? Are you gonna see a picture with me or not?"

I tilt my head, look him in the eye and smile. "Not."

This doesn't dissuade him. "Oh, good. I was hoping you'd make things difficult."

"I wish I could say that I was playing hard to get, but the fact is, I'm spoken for."

"I don't see a handcuff on your finger," he says.

"I'm not the marrying kind."

"That makes two of us. See? We're a matched pair. Last night, you said I wasn't likely to make you a better deal than the one you've got with Teddy Morgan but—"

"Oh boy, did you prove me wrong," I say with a saucy tilt of my hips.

That admission earns me a big toothy grin. "How'd you like it?"

In spite of myself, I grin back, remembering the pleasurable fantasy. "It was swell."

"*That* gift didn't come with any strings but the next one will."

"The next one?"

"I've got something that I think belongs to you, but if you want it back, it'll cost you."

"Now I'm intrigued . . ."

His shoulders tense as if he's bracing for something. "It's a stag film. You know the kind."

He's bluffing. He has to be. I call upon all my acting talent and hide behind a facade. "And what makes you think it belongs to me?"

"Well, I could give it back to the fella I got it from, but it seems like the kind of film that should only fall into the hands of the girl who starred in it."

My chest rises and falls and I think I should say something, but I can't think of a good line. I can't think of much of anything except the fact that he might *not* be bluffing. If he really does have the film that could sink my career, what am I going to do about it? "I've made a lot of films, Mr. Vanderberg. I can't remember them all."

"Oh, you'd remember this one, I think. Two flappers walk up to the bartender in a Parisian nightclub—"

"And you have the film?" I ask flatly, all business.

"I do. And I'll give it to you tonight if you want it."

"In exchange for?"

"A private screening," he says. "You arrange the showing and I'll bring the reel at eight sharp. Watch the movie with me and you can keep it."

I can't decide if I'm offended or fascinated by his nerve. "So, you intend to blackmail me."

He makes an indignant sound. "Blackmail requires a threat. I'm not threatening you with anything."

"The threat is implied."

He puts a hand over his heart as if wounded. "Do you always attribute such sinister motives to people?"

"Nearly always. This way I'm seldom disappointed."

My hard-boiled attitude only seems to charm him, and he plucks one of the roses from the vase and taps it against my cheek. "Call it blackmail, then. Or call it smart business. Either way, it's a one-time offer. Take it or leave it."

The decision is already made, but a girl has to keep up appearances. "You just want to watch the movie with me. That's your price?"

"That's right."

I eye him dubiously, taking the rose, careful to avoid the thorns. "You're sure you don't want more than that?"

"Oh, I *want* plenty more. I'm just not willing to bargain for the rest."

CHAPTER

Three

I don't like it when a man thinks he's got something over me. I seduce men; I don't get seduced. So I decide upon the siren red dress just short of my knees. Then I wear a matching feathered headband and paint my lips a poisonous shade of scarlet.

It's armor, the only defense I've ever had. And I *need* a defense against Leo Vanderberg. He's dark and dangerous—perhaps he's even a predator. It was ungentlemanly to let me know that he had the stag film; to insist that I watch it with him bespeaks a certain depravity that I ought to find quite off-putting. So why don't I?

My mother always said I'd run headlong into the devil's arms if he opened them to me.

I fear I'm about to prove it.

Promptly at eight, Leo Vanderberg shows up at the darkened studio with the reel. When he sees me in my skimpy red dress, he stares at me so hard I think I can see the veins in his forehead pulsing. "You look like a goddamned movie star . . ."

I merely curl my lips around the end of my cigarette holder in the way I know drives men wild. It's a battle of nerves, I think. If I make his mouth run dry with desire for me, maybe he won't realize that I'm trembling. "I don't mind the looks of you, either."

He clears his throat. "Nice little studio. Is it yours?"

"Not yet. I just rent the space when I'm working on a project."

He lifts an eyebrow. "What kind of project?"

I want to tell him about my own films. I want to let him know I'm not just the little chippy he thinks I am, but something stops me. I'm vulnerable enough. No need to give him anything more than he's already got. "Are we here for small talk, Ace?"

He shows me a glint of teeth, undressing me with his eyes. "No, I don't suppose we are."

Then, mercifully, he glances away and I turn to see my rival for his attention—one made of lights and lenses. He whistles in appreciation of the machinery. "A motorized projector . . ." He caresses it with one hand, as if he wants to take it all apart and put it back together again. "That had to set you back a few clams."

"You didn't think I was going to hire a projectionist tonight, did you?"

"Why not? Would it embarrass you to watch this film with two men?" He circles closer as if scenting blood. "Do you think it's going to embarrass you to watch it with me?"

I don't answer, fighting off a blush.

My bashfulness makes him laugh. "I thought you said you didn't embarrass easy. You've appeared half-naked on a big screen for audiences for years now. You know men fantasize about you and I think you like it. But this is going to be different, isn't it?"

I tilt my head so that I can look him in the eye. "I've learned that in the end, all movies—and all men—are just the same."

It's a bald lie. If he were to press me, I'd crack. My stomach knots at the thought of seeing myself naked on screen, having sex with a man whose name I can't even remember. In other movies I'm a star, but in this one . . . the only thing worse than watching myself will be letting this man take pleasure from my shame. So why do I sud-

denly want it? Why do I crave it? Maybe I'm mesmerized, like one
of those little mice at the circus who stare too long into the eyes of
a snake they're being fed to. All Leo has to do is kiss me and I won't be
able to keep up the pretense of bravado for even one more moment.

Instead, he gives my hand a squeeze. "You can have the film,
Clara. You don't have to watch it with me. You can have it."

Hiding my relief, I ask, "Are you going soft on me, Ace?"

"I can be a hard man when I have to be," he says, gripping my
fingers tighter, just short of the point of pain. "But I lured you here
for pleasure tonight. Now here we are, so you can set the film on fire
if you want."

"Why would I?"

"Because I'm starting to think that maybe you didn't star in this
film voluntarily. Maybe someone made you do it."

What a laugh. "Nobody makes me do anything."

"I made you come here tonight, didn't I? It simply never occurred
to me that coercing you into watching this movie might actually
upset you."

"I'm not upset," I protest, because whatever is happening in me
goes much deeper than upset. "But I'd like to know how this film
came to be in your possession."

"You're not going to like the answer."

I lift my chin. "Try me."

"Teddy Morgan asked me to track it down for him."

"Why would he do that? Are you moonlighting as a detec-
tive now?"

"It's the kind of film that is bound to show up on an Air Force
base in a private showing at the officer's club," Leo says. "Besides,
I'm a man of various talents."

"What did Teddy Morgan want with a stag film?" I ask, my nerves
on edge.

"He didn't say. I suspect he wants an insurance policy to keep
anyone from taking you away from him."

At this, I shake my head. "You're wrong. If he asked you to find this film it's because he . . . collects interesting things. He might have even wanted to get his hands on it so he could protect me."

"If that's true, then he won't mind that I gave it to you."

I can't argue with his logic. "Maybe not, but he won't like it when I tell him that we watched it together."

He lifts a brow and the knot in my belly starts to melt away into something hot and molten. I want this strange, mysterious man with a fierce lust I haven't felt in years. Maybe not ever. A lust that defies all good common sense. I peek at him from beneath long lazy lashes. "I've never seen it before . . ."

He's all in shadow, but I hear him breathe deeper. "Would you like to?"

My whole body screams its eagerness, from the tingling tips of my fingers to the upturned curve of my hips. "Why not? Unless you're bluffing and there's nothing on this reel at all . . ."

"I never bluff."

He's got me now, with or without the film. I'm going to let him have his way with me and he knows it.

"Turn it on," he says.

My fingers tremble as I adjust the machine. Then, when the film flickers over the title to a grainy black-and-white scene of a bartender in a white jacket, Leo Vanderberg settles into a seat and pats the one next to him.

The bemused set of his sensual lips draws me in. He straightens the crease of his pants, then pulls a silver flask from his jacket, uncaps it, and holds it out to me. "Here. You look like you need a little Dutch courage."

I take the flask and drink in deep, wondering if it's his mouth I taste on the rim. My cheeks burn as I watch myself on-screen flirting with another flapper who orders two cocktails, then presses her pretty lips on mine.

I'd almost forgotten the girl.

I watch, fascinated, as the actress's hand drops between my legs. Then I'm too embarrassed.

"Don't turn away," Leo says. "It's just getting started. Besides, this is one of the best parts."

"I did it on a lark you know," I say, wondering how many times he's seen the film and if it excited him. I want to know if it excites him now. "I was only eighteen. I was sleeping with the actor playing the bartender. When he suggested we make a movie of it, it sounded exciting."

"Whose idea was it to involve the other girl?"

"His," I reply, deciding I need to be drunk. I gulp down the rest of the contents of the flask, then hand it back to him, waiting for my head to swim.

When he takes it, our fingers touch and another arc of electricity passes between us. "I like how you writhe against her hand as she strips you. It looks as though you're moaning at her touch."

"I'm an actress."

This makes him laugh. "So you're saying you didn't like it; you were just putting on a show."

"I didn't say that. Girls are soft and pretty but don't thrill me like men do. If I was excited kissing her, it's only because it was so forbidden."

"So you have a taste for the taboo. I just wonder if there's more to it than that."

"Maybe," I admit, finding myself more and more aroused by his interest, by his casual acceptance of the lurid sex act depicted on-screen—one that would earn me the scorn of the society I'm accustomed to keeping, if not get me arrested in some places. He gives off the air of a man who can't be shocked by anything, and that makes me feel safe enough to tell him the truth. "I liked being naked for the camera. Being naked when everyone else was still dressed. She wanted me; he wanted me. I like to be wanted, so I let them have me. It made me feel like a glorious object of pleasure . . ."

"That makes sense. You're a performer. You like to make people laugh and cry . . . why wouldn't you want to excite them?"

He puts into words what I've never been able to and now I *do* feel drunk. "I think I was born to do it . . ."

Leo nods. "But I've seen you seduce a hundred men on camera, you're all vamp, taking charge. Not here. Look at the way your eyes drop so shyly when the bartender comes around the bar to pick you up. You wilt like a virgin in his arms."

I laugh. "I assure you, I wasn't one."

"I think you want to be. You want to feel shivery and nervous like you did making this film, doing something you've never done before. You want to feel like your innocence is being taken from you all over again."

My mouth runs dry and I squirm in my seat, not sure what's exciting me more: the things he's saying, or watching myself be seduced on the screen. "And you think you can make me feel that way?"

Leo dips closer, his voice low by my ear. "I think I'm making you feel that way right now."

My breath catches. "I think you are."

Leo makes his move, tracing the tip of his finger down my bare arm. "I'd like you to undress for me."

This unapologetic statement of his desire quells any resistance. I turn away from him, looking back over my shoulder to ask, "Will you help me with the hooks in the back?"

The corner of his mouth curls with approval. He runs a palm between my shoulder blades before setting to work on the clasps. He doesn't fumble; he isn't at all clumsy. His warm breath sweeps down my spine as he opens the hooks one by one. When he's finished, he slides my gown down over my arms until it reveals the silk of my skin-tight chemise and bloomers. I stand, letting the gown fall to my feet.

Leo's hot gaze sweeps over my body. The high rounded breasts. The long, lanky, stocking-clad legs. He takes his time, drinking me in from head to toe.

"Aren't you going to take anything off?" I ask, low and sultry in the dim light.

"No. You just told me you liked being naked while everybody else is dressed."

"That was when I was eighteen," I protest, giving him my trademark pout. "I'm not a girl anymore."

"But you *are* an actress," he says, snagging my wrist. "So let's pretend you're just a girl again." He draws me into his lap and I let him do it, settling with satisfaction against the hard ridge of his erection.

It's easier for us to watch the film this way and on the screen, the bartender lays me naked on the floor behind the bar. Watching my younger self shiver with anticipation creates an echo of that emotion in me now, and I lean back against Leo and sigh. He cups my breasts, weighing them in his hands, squeezing them with satisfaction. On the screen the bartender strokes his hands down my naked sides, trying to coax me to relax. In the here and now, in Leo's arms, I don't need any coaxing. Whatever this is between us is something dark and dirty and desperate. He runs his hands down my body as bold as you please. And when he uses his fingers to tug at my garters, I spread my knees for him.

"Tell me what you want, Clara," he says, the deep resonance of his voice making me quiver.

"I want you to touch me," I breathe.

The warmth of his palm travels higher to the heated valley between my legs. When the evidence of my arousal kisses his fingertips, he growls like a hungry animal. "You're so wet, Clara. I hoped you would be."

In the movie, rendered in grainy black and white, I see the pale expanse of my hips undulating as the other woman strokes the bartender's cock, then guides it into me. It's close-up and I can see everything vividly. If I was mesmerized before, now I'm paralyzed with the pleasure of watching myself getting fucked by a man who hasn't even taken off his underwear. The woman keeps hers on, too, even as she playfully licks at my young breasts, drawing my nipples up tight and hard.

"You like watching this movie," Leo murmurs, his mouth behind my ear, his other hand up under my chemise, rubbing my nipples until I'm caught in some world between reality and film. On the screen, my mouth falls open in silent pleasure at her touch. In Leo's lap, my mouth falls open with gasps of pleasure that supply the missing sound.

"Tell me you like it, Clara."

I do. I can't help but think that I would have filmed it differently, but I'm caught up in the magic of the movie. I had no idea it would be so raw. But I don't want to admit it to Leo. Not even when he draws my own hand down, using my fingers to rub the damp curls between my legs. I'm eager to touch the place that throbs with need. I want to touch it while he pushes his fingers inside me, but he doesn't allow me to disentangle my fingers from his. He sets the rhythm. He strokes me over and over, until I'm squirming in his lap, the friction of his tweed slacks warming my bottom.

"Keep your eyes on the screen," Leo says. "This is my favorite part."

I look up to see the lean bartender roll onto his side, pulling me with him so that one leg is up over his thigh, and the camera has a better view of his swollen member disappearing into me. With one hand on my ass for leverage, the bartender strokes in and out and in and out. I love watching the tension in his muscles, the tightening as he gets closer to orgasm. I loved it then, and I love watching it now.

"Did he make you come?" Leo asks.

We can't see my face on the screen, of course, because the picture is so tightly focused on my widespread legs. We're just a tangle of aroused bodies and the memory of it is flooding back. "I came when he did . . ."

Leo's clever fingers force me to stroke myself in just the right way. "Let's see if you can do it again. I'm guessing a lotta guys jerked off watching you in this film. Seems only fair you should enjoy it, too."

The thought of men watching me like this is too much. The fires of arousal lick up my insides until all my skin prickles with heat. "And what about you, Ace? Did you jerk off watching this film?"

He chuckles. "Till my hand blistered."

The idea of him masturbating to these flickering images of me is such an overwhelming rush that I clamp my thighs. It doesn't stop him. Leo Vanderberg pushes on, pushes past the cries of protest that die in my mouth. He's still a veritable stranger; it can't be possible that he should know my body so well, but he's such a quick study that I'm already on the edge.

"You like that, do you, Clara? Knowing that I saw you naked before we met and that I've already fucked you a hundred times in my mind."

It makes me so excited that I can only whimper in helpless reply.

"Let me taste you," he says, encouraging me to lift my sticky fingers to his mouth.

I do it only because I'm utterly under his spell. He catches my fingers with his lips, then sucks them between his teeth, groaning as he continues to stroke me, giving me no room for reprieve.

On the screen the bartender stiffens in orgasm, and Leo rubs me, faster and faster, biting down softly on my fingertips. I'm coming. I'm coming on the screen. I'm coming with the bartender. With the flapper. With Leo Vanderberg. I cry out, immersed in pleasure, my body arcing back against him, thighs shaking, eyes tightly squeezed shut. The waves of ecstasy wash over me again and again until I collapse against him. I would fall to the floor were it not for the tight hold he keeps on me. He cradles me until the sweat cools and makes me shiver. Then he takes off his jacket and wraps it around my shoulders, saying, "Easy, Clara. That was just a test run."

On the screen, the bartender wipes me clean with a napkin, as if he were a gentleman, then kisses me with a great deal of affection. For some reason, I hadn't expected to see that in a dirty stag film. This film has always been something shameful in my past, something I feared. Somehow, I didn't expect the affectionate kissing and stroking and holding of hands afterwards. There's an adorable mischief to it all as the bartender, the girl, and I peek our heads up over the bar with naughty twinkles in our eyes.

At this cheeky end to the film, I find myself smothering a giggle.

Leo laughs, too. "That's what charmed me. You enjoyed every minute of that, Clara. And when it was over you wanted to do it again. You brought a joy to it that made it almost wholesome."

"I feel anything but *wholesome*," I say with a come-hither look.

My climax hasn't satisfied me and I want him, badly. When he lifts me out of his lap, I expect him to unbuckle his belt and bend me over. Instead, he deposits me back into the chair and goes to turn off the projector. I see him in silhouette, standing there next to the expensive machine.

"Aren't you coming back? I have more buttons you can push," I purr.

He folds his arms over his chest. "Why don't you come to me . . . on your knees?"

Surely, I've misheard. "You want me to crawl to you?"

"I wanna learn you, Clara. I *do* wanna push your buttons. I want to push them in ways they've never been pushed before. I wanna test your limits. So do it. Get down on your knees and crawl."

Annoyance flashes through me. "I don't crawl for any man."

"Don't do it for me, then. Do it for the jaded girl, the cynic who thinks she's done it all twice and that life's got no more surprises left for her."

This argument is strangely compelling, so I shrug out of his jacket and drop down to my knees, inching my way towards him, the carpet rough on my bare hands. I feel his hungry eyes on me, his breath heavier with each move I make. "You want to throw me down and fuck me, don't you, Ace?"

"More than words can say, but I'm slow to pull the trigger, Clara. I know how to wait for my moment . . ."

"Your moment may have passed, because I'm feeling awfully sore at you."

"What else are you feeling?"

I keep crawling and once I settle into it, I feel the seductive sway in my own hips. "I feel like a cat in heat."

He beckons me closer with one finger. I nuzzle my forehead against his knees, then slide my cheek up his leg until it's resting on his throbbing erection. His hand goes into my hair, taking a fistful of it, and then he bends my neck back.

That's when he makes the mistake of looking into my eyes. I know how to make my big brown eyes smolder, how to pull a man into their dark depths and make him weak in the knees. Leo's not immune. His breath catches, and I take advantage of the moment, skimming my hands up his long, lean thighs. Mesmerized by the flash of my red painted nails as I unfasten his belt, Leo says, "Oh, you really are a dangerous woman . . ."

That makes me grin with lascivious intent, a grin that only widens when I open his trousers and his steely erection springs free. I love the look of him. He's ramrod straight and thick, though not so much that I shouldn't be able to take him all the way. And that's just what I do, sliding the red circle of my lips down his shaft in one smooth stroke that makes him unsteady.

Pulling back with a profound sense of satisfaction, I say, "You might want to take a seat . . ." Before he can argue, I trail my tongue over the swollen knob of his cock and little drops of salty fluid coat my tongue. Given the way his hand flexes in my hair, I know he wants to stop me, but when I bat my eyelashes at him as I work his member, the fight goes out of him.

He sinks down into the chair like a man without free will.

Every man likes it a little different, and I quickly learn that a swirl of my tongue over his shaft drives him wild. A lustful growl rumbles up from his chest as his legs tense. Using my hand as a guide, I thrust him between my lips, taking him hot and hard as he mutters a dark oath. He likes it. And I like it, too. Especially the way he's already throbbing against my tongue, ready to explode.

He fights for control, saying, "That's a pretty lipstick stain you're leaving on the base of my cock."

I don't let him rally. I rub my whole body against him, drawing his leg between my thighs, letting my swollen sex rub against him for relief even as I suck him like I do when I want a man to lose himself in me.

Leo curses again and twitches in my mouth. He's going to come. All I have to do is close my eyes and let it happen. That's just what I do.

His grip in my hair tightens and he holds me still as his body tenses, then releases into my mouth. "Good god!" he cries, as if his orgasm takes him by surprise. The sounds of pleasure he makes seems to set my skin on fire. He tastes clean, masculine, salty.

I let him watch me swallow, then lick at the corners of my mouth like a cat who has discovered a bowl of milk. "And here I thought you said you were slow to pull the trigger, Ace."

He gulps at the air, as if he's run a marathon. "Well, that wasn't supposed to happen."

I'm too smug to let him get away with it. "Says who?"

He taps me on the nose. "You just taught me an important lesson about underestimating my opponent. Now I know what kind of woman I'm up against. Next time, I'll know better than to let you have your way with me."

"I hope next time comes soon, because I need you inside me."

"Oh, looking at you on your knees like that, I could go again right now," he says, fastening his pants with a rueful sigh. "But we've both had enough for tonight."

I'm so worked up that I grab at his belt. "I haven't had enough!"

With a look of delight, Leo jerks me up into his lap, bringing his face so close to mine that our noses nearly touch. He speaks softly, with devastating confidence. "Listen, Clara, the day I fuck you—and trust me, I *am* going to fuck you—it's not going to feel like this. It's going to feel like the first time. You're going to be scared. Embarrassed. Needy. And you're not going to be in control."

I've got no snappy comeback. I can't even find the words to reply. Everything inside me goes soft and I'm *afraid* to speak. I don't know why I want that so badly—or how he could know something about me that I don't even know about myself. And it makes me so angry that I break free of his grasp. "Don't say it like it's a promise."

His voice lowers dangerously. "But it is."

I thump his arm. "What if it's a promise you can't keep? What if it's something you can't make come true? You can't say a thing like that to a girl and then let her down." I barely know what I'm saying. It's all half-drunken gibberish to me. Maybe I had a little too much of that Dutch courage.

Still, he doesn't dismiss what I've said. "You and me, I think we're a lot alike, Clara. We live by our own code, but we *do* have a code, don't we? I'm not gonna let you down." He disentangles from me, takes the reel off the projector and puts it back into its canister. "Here you go. Here's your film. See? I keep my word."

I shake my head. "I don't want it."

"Yes, you do. I love this film and I'll be sad to see it go, but it can hurt you. Destroy it before someone uses it against you."

"I wouldn't be here tonight if you didn't have that film," I argue. "You may think otherwise, but you're wrong. I wouldn't have come if you didn't have something to hold over me. It was the excuse I needed to see you. And it's the excuse I'll need to keep seeing you."

His eyes narrow. "What a very bad first impression I've made if you think I'd ever use this film to do you any real harm."

I give a shake of my head. "I don't think you would."

"Then what the devil do you expect me to do with it?"

"It'll be enough to know that you have it. That you could do something dastardly with it. That you could show it to someone else, anyone else you like, whenever you like."

Leo tilts his head, eying me as if for the first time. "Well, aren't you just full of surprises . . . Would you like me to show it to someone else, Clara?"

"No, but the fantasy arouses me so much I don't think I can stand."

He tucks the reel under one arm and steadies me with the other. "Well, then. By all means, let's find you someplace comfortable to sit."

CHAPTER

Four

Miraculously, he finds a diner car open at this hour. It's all shiny stainless steel, too bright and glib, but glitter has always cheered me. A few people in the car recognize me and the waitress has to shoo them away so we can have our coffee and dessert. Still, they're staring at us, so I cross my legs under the table to affect a pose of elegance. "Tell me, Mr. Vanderberg—"

"Back to Mr. Vanderberg again?" Leo asks, taking a healthy bite of blueberry pie. "I'd rather hoped we were on a first-name basis now . . ."

Given that I can still taste him on my lips, I concede the point. "Tell me, Leo. What is it that you really want?"

He swallows, wipes the corner of his mouth with a napkin, then leans close. "I thought I'd made that abundantly clear, but in case I've been too subtle . . . I want to fuck you."

"You could have done that half an hour ago in the studio," I say, trying to ignore the way his words reignite the fire in my loins. "Which tells me there's something else to it. You're a good-looking man. You could have it from a hundred girls. You could have that waitress taking orders at the counter. She practically swooned when she saw you."

He grins. "So did you."

I don't deny it. "Maybe it's ego. Maybe a flying ace like you needs a movie star on his arm to feel the rush he's used to. You don't want to settle for an average girl—"

"I've never settled for anything in my life."

"Or maybe you've got a score to settle against Big Teddy Morgan, so you decided to take me from him."

Triumph gleams in his eyes. "So you admit that I've taken you from him."

I shouldn't admit it, so I sip my coffee.

Leo tilts his head, staring. "Well? Are you going to break it off with him?"

"Why would I?" Even though I'd been thinking about moving on, it just isn't sensible to break things off with Teddy Morgan. This is nothing more than a torrid affair that will burn itself out in a day or two. There's no good reason not to cling to the security that comes with being the mistress of a very rich man. No reason except that I just wouldn't feel right about it. "Alright, I will. I may be a hard-drinking gold digger with loose morals, but I do have some small sense of decency."

"As do I," Leo replies, stabbing another bite of pie. "Which is why you ought to know better than to think this is some scheme to get back at your Daddy Warbucks. I've got nothing against Teddy Morgan, unless you count the business about the war memorial."

Now here's a new wrinkle. "A war memorial?"

He looks abashed. "I shouldn't have mentioned it. I don't wanna spoil the mood."

"A little late for that. Tell me."

Leo shrugs in the way people do when they don't want you to know just how important something really is to them. "I mean to build a war memorial for aviators in Elysian Park."

"And what's Big Teddy got to do with it? Won't he lend you the money?"

Leo bristles like I've questioned his manhood. "I've got a nickel or two of my own to rub together, you know."

"And you want to spend it on a memorial?"

"That's right. But the city council won't approve it—and Teddy Morgan isn't keen to persuade them in my favor."

Without a fat cat to back you, you can't do anything in this town, so I say, "That's the end of it then."

"The devil it is," Leo says with a look of fierce determination. It relieves me to see that he's as passionate about his other ambitions as he is about seducing me. "I'll get it done if it takes me the rest of my life . . . which admittedly, might not be that long, given what I do."

"You say that so lightly. Aren't you scared? To die, I mean?"

"When Germans aren't shooting at me, I feel a lot better about my chances."

I find that I can't eat even a bite of my dessert. I just stare at it. "Terrible thing . . . the war . . . you must have stories."

Seeing that I haven't touched my plate, Leo snags a bite off it. "None of my stories are easy to tell."

"I'd like to hear one anyway."

"Ask me just before I'm about to go up into the air. I'll brag about all the Germans I shot down, ready to tell anyone who will listen that I'm the best goddamned pilot in the country. And I'll mean it. I'll believe it. It's the only way I'll be able to take to the skies. But tonight? I'm prouder of the fact I got your clothes off than I am of anything I did at war."

I've lived my whole life doing and saying outrageous things to distract anybody from ever asking me anything serious about my life; I recognize evasion when I see it. Leo Vanderberg may have come home from the war without any visible scars, but I'm willing to bet he's got them on the inside. As if to confirm it, Leo keeps talking. "Besides, my stories aren't all that important. It's the story of American aviation that's worth telling. The story of all the other pilots who weren't lucky enough to come home. Who gave their lives not just for the war, but for progress. Airplanes are going to change the whole world, Clara. I'm a part of that."

"I salute you on behalf of a grateful world," I say, like a smart-mouthed kid. "It's awfully dangerous."

He shrugs. "I've had a few crashes. Only planes, though. I've been fixing cars, building cars, designing cars, and driving cars all my life. The faster the better. Never crashed a car. But I've gone down in a plane more than once and had the broken bones to prove it."

"Good god. All I've gotta do for money is vamp around on a set. Your parents must be nervous as cats."

"They both died when I was still a kid."

My hand goes to my cheek. "Oh . . . oh, I'm so sorry . . ."

"It's alright. It was a long time ago. My mother died of a fever before I was old enough to remember her, and my father dropped dead plowing the field on our family farm. It taught me not to worry about dying. You never know when your time's up. You can go just like that." He snaps to emphasize his point. "Never had any family needing me to come back home, so if there's a man alive who ought to risk his life for his country, you're looking at him."

It's a curious thing to hear from an even more curious man. "So how does the orphaned son of a Dutch farmer become a pilot?"

He shrugs. "Even as a kid, I was always taking things apart and putting them back together again just to see how they worked. Loved machines. Wires. Electricity. Had my own set of tools even before my father died. When he passed, I sold the family farm so I could become an engineer. Self-taught. Took a correspondence course then went to work for a motor company before the war. When I was called up for service, I knew how to fix the planes so I got to fly."

He says it all matter-of-factly, but there are layers of emotion in his story that his flat delivery can't hide. I'm not like him; I've never had a hankering to figure out how something worked—at least not until now. I find that I want to know all the hidden gears that are turning in his head. All the things he isn't saying. But before I can think of the right question, he leads the conversation in another direction. "What about you, Clara? Who waits for you to come back home at night?"

I stir more sugar into my coffee, because it's never sweet enough for me until it makes my teeth hurt. "Just my Pops. He ran out when I was growing up. Hadn't seen him until about three years ago when he heard I had money and showed up on my doorstep. I had a speech all prepared; I was ready to blister his ears but good. Yet, somehow, when I saw him again, we fell into each other's arms and cried like a couple of fool kids."

Leo looks astonished.

"I bet you think I'm a sap, don't you?" I ask.

"Actually, I think you're the cat's meow . . ."

"You think I'm a pushover."

He grins as if I'm just too adorable for words.

I know that look and decide to warn him. "Don't get attached, Ace. Remember, I have a roving eye."

"I'm not afraid of competition." He reaches for a silver cigarette box in his pocket, flips it open, and offers one to me. When I decline, he takes one for himself.

"You're awfully sure of yourself."

He lights up, then leans back and stretches his arm along the top of the booth. "Clara, I want to see you again tomorrow night."

"Why wait? There's still a few hours left before daylight. You can take me home to bed and finish what you started, Ace."

He looks as if he's considering the idea. "I'd love to, but first I need to know how to get your engine going."

"Oh, you've already got me hitting on all six cylinders."

Smiling, he taps the barest hint of ash off the end of his cigarette.

"Let me take you to dinner somewhere swanky. This is a courtship after all."

"It's a little late to pretend your intentions are honorable."

"What makes you so sure they aren't? You're a grown woman. I'm a grown man. We've both got each other straight—there's no pretense to it. You don't get more honorable than that."

CHAPTER
Five

When I miss my cue the third time, the director of the sword-and-sandal epic calls the shoot for the day. As the handlers begin pulling the makeshift chariots off-set, I escape to my dressing room and my costar Brooke Gordon follows me. "What's gotten into you, Clara?"

Not Leo Vanderberg, I think. Not yet. And it's driving me to such distraction I can't concentrate on a thing. I shrug, yanking off the Roman sandals and rubbing my ankle where the strap dug in. "Just tired, I guess."

Brooke is playing the wife of an emperor, her blond hair piled on top of her head into an impossible shape. She collapses into a seat to wipe the perspiration from her face. "God, I hate Hollywood. It's so unbearably hot. I'm still too young for hot flashes, aren't I? It was always cooler making films in New York."

"Sure," I murmur. I'm also weary from the heat. The camera lights. And whatever fever it is that Leo Vanderberg has put into my blood.

"So who is he?" Brooke asks, fanning herself. "I've heard a dozen different rumors."

Remembering the hard-bodied aviator whose hands seem to have left burning traces all over my skin, I bite my lower lip. I may be a movie star but Leo's famous enough in his own right that it'll be all over town the moment I admit it. "I'd rather not say."

"Given the look on your face, he must be worth it."

"Oh, I certainly *hope* so," I whisper.

"Clara! Are you saying that you haven't had him yet?"

Brooke has made more movies than any actress I know, and taken almost as many lovers, so I tell myself that it's safe to confide in her. A slow smile spreads across my face and I'm unable to keep the desire out of my voice. "Not yet, but there's something about him. Something so . . ."

"Rich?" Brooke asks, jiggling her wrist to show off the shiny jeweled bracelet that I'd mistaken as part of her costume. "You can't possibly let yourself sigh like that over a man who can't shower you in jewels."

As always, my attention is caught by everything that glitters. "He says he's got a nickel or two to rub together, but I doubt it's serious money."

"And yet, you're going to throw over Big Teddy Morgan for him? Be careful, Clara, or you'll turn into a sentimental little fool."

No one has ever accused me of *that* before . . . "So where did you get the bracelet?"

She slips the bracelet off her wrist so that I can try it on. "Isn't it pretty? I don't want to tell you what I had to do for it, but I probably ought to get used to swallowing my pride . . . among other things."

I slide the gold over my forearm, adoring the way it warms to my skin. "That bad?"

She gives a sigh. "This is my last film. My voice won't work in the talkies. It's too low. And I'm too old to play the waifs and damsels in distress now."

"I think your voice is smooth as velvet."

Brooke turns to the mirror and starts taking the pins out of her hair. "Which is better for the bedroom than the talkies. What else are girls like us to do when our looks start fading? If you were smart, you'd be sweet to Big Teddy Morgan and consider it an investment in your retirement. When rich men make offers to girls like us, we have to take them or else we'll end up staring at padded walls in our old age."

I'm silent as the grave.

Brooke's hands drop from her hair and she shakes her head. "I'm sorry, Clara. I shouldn't have said that."

I give her a pretty smile without meeting her eyes. "Don't be silly, Brooke. Everything's jake."

"No it's not. I'm sorry. I don't know *why* I said it. I just forget that you're not like me. I don't know the first thing about cameras or making movies. I'm not talented like you."

"Sure you are."

Brooke chuckles. "You're a good little liar, kiddo. And listen, if you don't want Big Teddy Morgan anymore, I wouldn't mind taking him off your hands."

"It's a free country," I reply.

"You're a sweet kid, Clara. Don't ever let anyone tell you different."

I don't feel sweet or like a kid that night at the supper club. Not even when Leo presents me with another bouquet of fragrant flowers and tells me that I look lovely. I feel wild and reckless and I keep wondering if I'm making some horrible mistake, like those girls in the movies who always end up tied to train tracks.

Like an oncoming engine car, Leo is interrogating me before we're even in our seats. "How'd Teddy Morgan take it?"

"He was surprisingly decent about it," I say, both relieved and a little saddened.

"Did you tell him about me?"

I wait for the coat-check girl to take my fur wrap, then say, "No. I didn't want to provoke him."

Leo pulls out my seat for me. When I slide into it, I shiver at the feel of his knuckles as they graze my spine. "He's bound to find out. Someone's likely to see us together in the next few weeks."

"The next few weeks? My goodness, you're optimistic, Leo. Do you really think our affair will last that long?"

Leo smirks. "I think I can keep you stimulated and entertained at least that long."

"Truly? Because I'm beginning to think you're all talk and no cider."

He laughs and orders a fine meal for us both, something French that I can't pronounce, but it sounds rich and decadent rolling off his tongue. I think he's forgotten my taunt, but when the white-coated waiter leaves, Leo says, "So you think I'm all talk . . ."

The dangerous way he curls his lips around those words sends a flush down my neck. Nevertheless, I opt for bravado. "I haven't seen much evidence to the contrary."

"Oh, haven't you?" he asks, taking a sip of water. "If I've left you with the impression that it's safe to challenge me, then we're starting the evening off on the wrong note . . . something that can be remedied easily enough. I'd like you to remove your knickers. Unless of course, you're not wearing any."

I jerk my head up. "*What*?"

"You heard me. Go on . . . this is a quiet corner of the restaurant. You have a white table linen to hide behind. Nobody's going to know about it but you. So wriggle out of your drawers and hand them to me."

A thrill goes through me at the thought of doing something so wanton. "Why would I?"

"Because if you don't, I'm going to come round to your side of the table and yank them off for you."

My breath catches. "You wouldn't."

"Do I look like the kind of man who would lie about such a thing?"

Leo's fiery gaze is filled with daring. When I don't answer, he begins to rise to his feet and I'm half-convinced he's going to reach across the table and pull my dress off if I don't do as he says. Why that should make me burn hotter with arousal, I can't say.

"Alright, I'll do it." I say, wriggling, adjusting my dress until the cool air hits my bare hips and thighs.

"Atta girl," Leo says, sitting back down again.

I pull my drawers down over my knees. As I settle back down in the chair, feeling vulnerable and exposed, I have to make myself look at him. It's not that I don't want to. I do. I want to see myself, all wanton and lustful, reflected in his eyes. But his attention is so intense that it's a little bit like staring into the sun.

He turns his palm up on the table, expectantly.

Glancing about to be sure no one is looking, I slide the undergarment over the table to him. Leo rubs the silky fabric between his thumb and forefinger before tucking it neatly into his jacket. "Thank you, Clara."

"What are you going to do with them?"

He leans back in his chair. "I'm going to add them to my collection of things that once were yours and now belong to me. After all, it's not the only thing I'm going to take from you tonight."

"Oh . . ." It's my eagerness that makes me blush.

"But first, we're going to enjoy a meal together."

He's half right. He enjoys his dinner, cutting into squab with a hearty appetite, but I can't seem to eat more than a few morsels. I'm burning with a different kind of hunger. One that consumes all my other appetites and leaves me picking at my plate like a dainty damsel.

"Try this," Leo insists, holding a forkful of something in a rich buttery sauce. He feeds it to me. My lips part for him, then our eyes meet and I can think of nothing but teasing his shaft with my tongue. The same memory seems to occur to him because he groans. "Good god, Clara . . . that heart-shaped mouth, those big brown eyes. How does *anyone* resist you?"

"They don't," I say, then swallow the bite whole.

"Do you have the key to your rented studio with you?"

"Of course, but I can think of more intimate places for us to go . . ."

"Tempting, but if sex was all I wanted, I'd take you to the cloakroom and put you up against a wall."

Oh, I wish he would. Instead, he pushes his plate back, then draws his chair closer to mine so he can whisper into my ear. "Take the key from your pocketbook and set it on the table."

I've no idea what new game he's devised, but I've enjoyed all the other ones, so I do as he says.

Then the metal key rests heavily on the table between us, like scintillating possibility.

He strokes my arm in approval. "However do you get your skin to be so soft, Clara?"

"I soak in baths of donkey's milk. Or didn't you see that movie?"

Leo's very close to me now and he doesn't withdraw when the waiter comes to take our plates. He's so brazen that he takes a cube of ice from his water glass, and runs it slowly over the overheated curve of my shoulder. I shiver at the chill and the waiter averts his eyes, quickly finishing his work at the table until we are left alone. Me and Leo and the trail of kisses he now lays on top of my chilled shoulder. "Mmmm," he murmurs at the taste of my skin, and the whisper of his stubble against my bare arm is nearly my undoing. "I'd like to bathe you."

"I'd rather you did something else to me," I say, trying not to slide off my chair.

"All in good time. You see, I like to talk, but I'm not *all* talk. It's just that you've got me in a bind."

"Oh?" I ask casually, as if I weren't thoroughly rattled. I'm grateful that our table is in the corner and that we might appear, to the casual observer, to have turned our attention to the man playing at the piano.

The bill cannot come quickly enough.

Leo's hand drifts under the table, sliding beneath the beaded fringe of my dress in an attempt to coax my thighs apart. "You see, I'm wondering who I should invite to watch your stag film. I've a few candidates in mind. Maybe you'd like to help me choose."

I gasp, nearly leaping from my chair. "No!"

Leo traps me between the table, the wall, and his arm. He's cut off my retreat as if he planned this assault in advance. "No, you don't want to help me choose?"

"No, I don't want you to show it to anyone!"

"Sure you do," he whispers into my hair. "That's why you wanted me to keep it."

I didn't know what I was saying. I was too dizzy on drink and desire. "I didn't mean any of it!"

He doesn't waver. "You meant it, Clara."

My stomach clenches. "Well, I've changed my mind. I want the film. I paid the price you asked—"

"That was a one-time offer. I told you that you could take it or leave it. You left it. And with good reason. Just the idea I might show that film to someone else made your knees buckle. Now that you know I'm actually going to do it, I bet you couldn't even get up and walk out on me if you tried."

I go weak all over—too weak to stop him from pushing his hand under my dress, and my traitorous body coils tighter in arousal at his touch. "So wet," he whispers, sliding one finger back and forth. I grip the table's edge, straining not to show my anxiety to onlookers. His voice lowers so that he can't be overheard. "So who should I show it to, Clara? Who is it that you want to see you like that, writhing around on the floor at the center of a threesome, getting licked by another girl, letting a man fuck you for the camera . . ."

I'm shaken. I'm so shaken by the question that I can't even slap him, like I should. Like any woman would. But I did this to myself. I walked right into the devil's open arms. Why should I be surprised that he wants to take me straight to hell?

Leo's still waiting, but I can't make my throat work. My mouth is dry. My tongue seems swollen in my mouth. It won't move. I hear myself swallow, but that's the only sound I make as he rubs in a slow circle. "Here's how it's going to happen. You're going to give me the key to your studio. Tomorrow night, I'm going to invite a friend to meet me there to watch the film. When he leaves, I'll drop by your place and you can thank me properly."

My nostrils flare. "You expect me to thank you?"

"I expect you to give me permission to take the key."

"That's not going to happen."

"Clara, look at me."

"No," I say, twisting my head away, even as my hips press forward against his hand.

"You're scared of two things right now, Clara. The first thing you're scared of is that I'm going to let someone else watch your stag film. The second thing you're afraid of is that I won't. But you don't have to be afraid of either of these things because it's out of your hands."

"You don't seem to understand how blackmail works," I manage to choke out, even as the ache between my legs feels heavier and more insistent by the moment. I dig my fingers into his arm to make him stop stroking me, but his touch only intensifies. Dear god, does he mean to make me come right here?

"You don't seem to understand how *I* work, Clara. Look at me."

"No," I murmur. I should make him stop. I should make him stop right now. But his touch is the only relief against the burning heat searing through my body.

I'm undone by him.

Lifting my eyes, I'm met by a gaze that burns dark as coal. "Clara, I'm going to do it whether or not you give me that key. I'll build my own projector if I have to. It's going to happen . . . and what I want to know is, would you rather that I show it to a man or to a woman?"

The idea of Leo in a darkened room with another woman sends a stab of jealousy through me so sharp that I gasp, "A man."

My admission forces a moan past my defenses and I snap my eyes shut. Too late, though. His finger slips into me and his thumb takes up the task of tormenting me. Twin spirals of pleasure coil up into my belly and now all I want is to satisfy my hunger.

"You're close, aren't you, Clara?"

I nod, wordlessly.

"Give me permission to take the key."

Rocking against his hand, biting my lower lip so hard I think I taste blood, I whisper, "Take it!"

At his triumph, he smiles against my bare shoulder and fetches the key into his hand. Then he trails his fingers wetly down my thigh, leaving me shaking and unfinished. I writhe in misery at being left empty. Then I'm furious. I'd batter him with both fists if it wouldn't attract an audience. "You bastard."

"I'm going to show your stag film to someone else, Clara. Then I'm going to tell you all about it. When I do, I'm going to make you come harder than you've ever come before. I'm going to turn you into a quivering mess. And the only thing that's going to turn you on more than knowing that I did it is knowing that you gave me this key."

CHAPTER
Six

The critics hate the studio's latest Clara Cartwright movie. Nevertheless, it's a box office smash. Good thing, too, since I've snubbed my financier to take up with a sadistic aviator who seems intent upon ruining me. Maybe I want to be ruined, I decide. It's what I deserve. Mama always said that everything I had was the wages of sin; maybe I'm trying to pay it all back with interest.

The night Leo calls, I give Pops enough cash to go on a bender at the speakeasy. I ought to feel guilty giving that much money to a drunk but I can't bear to have anyone here while I wait, pacing back and forth in a satiny robe with feather trim. Leo promised me he'd make me shiver. Make me tremble. Make me afraid.

He's certainly giving it a go.

I try to work, making notes. I've been making movies in my head all my life. But I can't concentrate tonight. All I can think about is two men ogling me in my stag film. Not that being ogled has ever bothered me, mind you, but there's something more perverse about this. Something more objectifying. As much as I said I enjoyed being a glorious object of pleasure, I can't shake the baseness of it.

Maybe they're sitting in silence. Maybe they're talking about me. Maybe Leo is saying something about the way my breasts felt in his hands; maybe the stranger is talking about the curve of my ass . . .

The stranger.

I'm dying to know who he is. I ought to drive over to the lot right now to see who leaves my studio, but that'd be too risky. I remind myself that rumors about this stag film have been circulating for years. Leo Vanderberg isn't the first man to get his hands on the reel. The idea that there are countless men out there who may have seen it makes me shiver—and not with revulsion. So what's one more?

The phone doesn't ring until ten o'clock and by then, I'm jumping out of my satin slippers. "Send him up, Charlie."

My doorman sounds rueful. "Miss Cartwright, I don't think I could stop him if I tried."

Leo walks into my penthouse like he owns it then takes off his overcoat and hat. He hangs them on the hooks by the door, just as casual as you please. But I'm a trained actress; I know when someone is faking. He's strung tight, shoulders squared, sexual need rolling off him like some kind of nectar I want to catch on my tongue.

His skin is so hot I can feel it even before he catches me by the waist and pulls me against him. "Do you want me to tell you about it, Clara?"

"You didn't do it," I say, breathless. "Tell me you didn't do it."

He backs me against the wall. "I told you before that I don't bluff. I did it and you know I did it. Which is why you're shaking like a leaf."

I'm so grateful to be trapped between the solidity of the wall and his body, because I feel as if I'm going to shake apart. Leo's erection is hard as steel, painful where he grinds it against my hip. And I can't seem to get enough air. Winding my fingers through his hair, I keep gasping. I think I'll drown if I don't get him inside me.

"Where's the bedroom?" he asks.

"It doesn't matter." I'm the kind of girl he can lay down on the floor. The couch. Anywhere.

But he hoists me into his arms, carrying me into the hall, trying each door until he finds the room with my four-poster canopy bed. He drops me down on the glamorous blue and gold damask bedspread, knocking tasseled pillows to the floor as he crawls over me. I love the weight of him as we sink into the softness of the mattress, the long arms that pin me down as he kisses the base of my throat.

My heartbeat leaps under his lips.

"My friend and I started the night with drinks," he murmurs between kisses. "He had too many. He's in love with a woman who doesn't love him back, so I offered him a little distraction. I invited him to your studio for a smoke and a movie."

"Oh god," I say, arching my neck as his teeth graze my collarbone.

"My friend didn't recognize you on the screen at first, Clara. You were just some bright young thing with a talent for living, eager to get naked for anyone who wanted to watch. Then he realized it was you."

I whimper. "No. No, he didn't."

"Of course he did. You're the most famous woman in the country. He said your name. He asked me."

I moan, stricken with equal parts humiliation and lust. "Did he touch himself?"

"You'd like that, wouldn't you?"

I close my eyes, imagining it. Leo strokes my thigh and catches my nipple between his teeth, biting it through the fabric of my robe. The sensation is electric. "I can't think when you do that, Leo."

"Good," he says, with immense satisfaction. "And to answer your question, no. My friend didn't touch himself during the film but he's probably stroking himself now, thinking about you. I'd wager that any time he sees you on any movie screen, he's going to be thinking about your naked body."

Between panting breaths, I whisper, "That doesn't make you jealous?"

"It makes me hard, Clara." He presses his erection against my hand to prove it. "It makes me feel like a goddamned god. Because I gave him that sexy image of you like a gift. I gave *you* to him. And you don't even know who he is."

I moan again. I clutch at him. I'm dying for him. "Tell me . . . tell me his name."

"Not yet. I wanna keep you like this for a while. Nervous. Unsteady. A little thrill in your belly every time you meet a man on the street, wondering if it's him. Wondering if the twinkle in a stranger's eye is because he knows how you like to get fucked and he's seen you do it. I like having that power over you."

"Bastard."

"You like it, too."

It's true. It's so true I don't dare deny it. I never liked anybody using me or trying to tell me what to do, but with Leo everything has changed. He's making me feel things I didn't know I could feel and I wonder if there's anything, *anything*, I won't do to have him inside me. I reach for his shirt, popping the buttons in my hurry to get it open. "I can't keep my hands off you, Leo."

He levels me with a heated gaze. "You're going to have to, because you turned me into a thirteen-year-old boy the last time you touched me. You're a force of nature I'm not ready to unleash, so keep your hands over your head."

I don't pay him the slightest heed, reaching to unclasp his belt. He lets me do it, but when I pull the leather free, he takes it from me and uses it to bind my hands to the headboard. I cry out, kicking at him in sudden frustrated rage. When he's got my wrists fastened good and tight, he asks, "Do I need to tie your legs down, too?"

"Leo!"

"I like to drive, Clara. Just enjoy the ride."

Now that sounds more like it. "Fuck me, Leo. Just do it before it kills me."

"It's not gonna kill you," he says with a wry smile. "I know a survivor when I see one."

He opens my robe, blowing the feathery fringe away from my skin. I spread my legs so wide, so eagerly, that they ache at the stretch. I catch the scent of my own arousal as he dips his head to trace a hot wet trail down my belly with his tongue. When I realize where he's going, I try to twist my hips away from him. "No, Leo. I don't like *that*."

His breath caresses the soft thatch between my legs. "You liked it in the movie. When the girl did it to you."

"That's different."

"How so?" he asks, petting the vulnerable spot.

If my hands were free, I'd shove him away. I'd break out of his grasp. But now I pull against the belt that restrains me until my arms tire from the effort. "I don't know. It just was. I don't like men doing it."

"Good thing you don't have much choice in the matter." Defiantly, he dips his head for a long lick. "Mmmm. Do I taste something floral?"

"It's the gardenia from the soap in my bath," I say, nearly spitting the words.

If he notices that I'm furious, he doesn't seem to care. "I have a new favorite flower."

"Stop teasing me!" I cry. I know that he's aroused. I can see the flush of it on him. His skin is burning with it. So why won't he take off his pants and thrust inside me?

"You're right to scold me," Leo says, strong fingers with short, clean nails, scraping lightly over my skin, leaving gooseflesh in their wake. "It wasn't right of me to leave you unsatisfied last night in the restaurant, was it? Well, let's see if I can make up for it."

With that, he pulls my knees up over his shoulders, and then I'm there again in that stag film. Lying on that floor behind the bar.

Naked and splayed and exposed and vulnerable. He strokes me softly, my cunt, my belly, my thighs. Then he drops little kisses between my legs as if to soothe me. "How curious . . ."

I groan, no longer wanting him to stop. "*What?*"

He pauses, drawing the moment out interminably. The amusement in his voice makes me feel even more exposed. "It's just that all the women I've been with are darker here than on their heads, but these very wet curls of yours are fair."

"I'm strawberry blonde by nature," I snap. "I dye my hair to make it a richer red."

"Why?"

Trembling with unfulfilled need, I whimper. "Do we have to talk about this now?"

Mercifully, he presses his hot tongue right where it aches. He wriggles it a little bit until I sink deeper into pleasure. Then he stops again. "Actually, now seems like as good a time as any to talk about it."

"Damn you!"

He laughs. "Why do you dye your hair?"

"I never liked the way fair hair looks on film." Maybe if I say it all quickly, he'll touch me where I need to be touched. "You can't see much variation in color on the screen so those blondes always look all angelic like Garbo. That's not me. So I put henna in my hair. I never thought to do it down there as well."

"Well, your pussy is hot enough without the fiery red hair," he says, mischievously. Then he presses his tongue even harder. I try to pull my hips back to escape the unexpected assault of his mouth, but there's no resisting him. Every time I shift away, his tongue finds me again, flicking in ways that arouse me as much as surprise me.

He's not sloppy or overeager. He has a dry, dexterous tongue that teases and tortures the swollen little button at my center. He pokes. He prods. He's learning me, just like he said he would. And when he finds just the right way to circle his tongue, he drives me to a place of utter, helpless surrender.

Then he stops again. "Have you ever heard of an Immelmann turn?"

"Oh, I hate you, Leo. I hate you!"

He grins, his fingers doing the work his mouth leaves undone. "In a dogfight, after an attack, the pilot takes the plane straight up to the sky, climbing higher . . ."

He's very slow with his fingers, circling around the swollen pearl until I moan.

"You take the plane higher and higher . . . until the whole craft is shaking around you."

It's coiling inside me, the pleasure, tightening until I do start to shake. I think I'm going to fly apart.

"Do you know what happens then?" he asks. "To the plane I mean? It stalls out. It hangs there, nearly motionless, as if the whole world has frozen."

I feel that way. Suspended. Lost. The rest of the world no longer any concern at all when he lowers his mouth to lick me once again in earnest. It takes only a few moments before a scream of pleasure tears itself from my throat, and then I'm bucking underneath him. He stays with it, he stays with me, laving me until it's so intense I can't stand it, then easing off into little kisses that trail all the way to the edge of my stockings.

I go limp in my release, my head lolling to the side, luxuriating in the little spasms that slowly fade away.

But Leo keeps going.

"No, Leo, I—I can't. Not so fast . . . I need . . ." Every bit of me is oversensitive to the touch. What was so deliriously pleasurable before is now too much. I can't stand for him to keep rubbing, but he doesn't listen. He doesn't stop. He refuses to let me come down from the high. Not even when I'm thrashing. "Oh god, Leo stop . . . I can't . . ."

"You're close, Clara. Try riding it out and maybe I can get you there again. See, when the plane suspends in the air, that's the point of maximum vulnerability. After the stall, the plane starts falling. Plummeting really. But a good pilot has already applied full rudder to yaw the plane in a new and unexpected direction."

His palm comes crashing down between my legs, and the sting of it shocks me. It stills me. And before I can even yelp out a protest, his kisses soothe my stinging flesh, the pain alleviated by the pleasure of his soft tongue.

"*What* are you doing, Leo Vanderberg?"

He lifts his head again, one finger pumping very slowly inside me. "It's a difficult trick to do properly. It involves precise control of the aircraft at low speed. But with practice and proper use of all of the fighter's controls, the plane can be positioned for a second attack."

Then he does it again.

Again.

Again.

Spanking the damp thatch between my legs, then licking it until some sort of floodgate inside me crashes open. He's going to make me come again. And I'm going to let him. Even if it's like this. The sound I make isn't one I recognize. It's pure animal need as Leo uses his mouth to exert new pressure, eliciting unusual sensations that make the heat rise. I'm climbing again to climax, higher and higher, until my back arches. My arms go rigid, and I undulate under him. My hips feel like a wide expanse of need and my skin is burning up. He keeps doing it until an explosion of ecstasy makes me blind to the world.

My sweat-damp hair flies wild and I call out his name. I scream it, really, almost a keening wail.

When I'm done, he looks up at me from the cradle of my quaking thighs with immense satisfaction. "That was two."

"No more," I pant, so spent I just want to die. "Stop."

"Stopping now would defeat the purpose of the experiment."

Breathless, I plead for mercy. "No more. I'm begging you. I'm *begging* you!"

"Oh, you're *begging* me? Well, then." He reaches up and unstraps my hands. They sag onto the bed where I lay like a corpse. He turns me gently onto my side and when I curl into a ball, he wraps himself around me. "That's a good girl."

I muster up *just* enough energy to elbow him in the ribs.

He grunts in agony, rolling onto his back. "Christ, woman! A sneak attack . . ."

"You deserved it."

He's still grimacing when he says, "That was my bad rib."

"I hope I broke it!" After all, I've heard of people having bad ankles or a trick knee, but never a bad rib.

"It wouldn't be the first time," he pants, laughing and groaning in pain at the same time. "Maybe I did deserve it. But it was worth it. Level with me, when was the last time you came that hard?"

"Never."

"Glad to hear it. I like to know the score."

I'm pouting. Brooding. But the blood is pounding through my body with such delicious satisfaction that I can't remember what I'm so sore about. "You broke a rib before?"

"Two ribs, one collarbone, and various smaller fractures," he says nonchalantly. "I've survived a lot of crashes."

I don't even know what to say to that. It *almost* makes me sorry for having elbowed him.

He takes my wrists, which are both red where his belt cut off the circulation, and gently massages them. "Good god, Clara. You're a fantasy come alive."

"You're not half bad yourself. That's was a good opening act, Mr. Vanderberg, but I'm still waiting for the feature film."

He grumbles. "Believe me, if I had my way I'd be plowing you into this bed right now, but I made you a promise to make it feel like the first time, didn't I?"

"I release you from that silly obligation—"

"It doesn't work that way."

I could cry. "How long are you going to keep doing this to me?"

His lip curls with amusement. "How long am I going to keep driving you wild?"

I lower my eyelashes in a way that even he can't resist. "When are you going to fuck me properly?"

He swallows and his eyes trail down my body. "Propriety's got nothing to do with it."

He can still taste me, I know. I see temptation written all over his face. But before I can get his pants off, his self-control rallies. "Not tonight, Clara."

"You have no idea how good I can make you feel, Leo . . ."

"Oh, I've got a *damn* good idea."

"Let me show you." I run my hands down his body, aiming for the erection straining against his pants.

He rolls out of my grasp. "I told you, Clara, I can't let you put your pretty little hands on me. I know myself. Once I give in, there's no going back. I'm an all-or-nothing fella and resisting you is more difficult than I thought it would be. Which is why I've been staring at all the photos on your walls in a desperate attempt to keep the blood flowing in my brain. They're brilliant, by the way. Who took them?"

"I did," I say, taking his thumb between my lips and sucking on the tip.

He growls in appreciation. "Don't worry. I won't be able to hold out much longer. I've just got a few more things about you I need to figure out."

"Like what?" I ask, propping myself up on one elbow.

"Like how many lovers you've had."

It's a question I know better than to answer, so I adopt a flippant tone. "I lost count."

"No you didn't."

"Sure I did. I can't even remember their names. What about you?"

"Five," he says with distressingly little hesitation. "And I can still remember *all* their names."

"I don't believe you."

He begins to count on his fingers. "Sally, the bordello girl who relieved me of my virginity. Marguerite, the French farm girl. Helen, the army nurse. Pauline, the English socialite. And Susan, the suffragette."

"I meant I didn't believe there were only five! I didn't want you to list them."

He laughs. "Well, what do you think of my list?"

Looking away in a state of anxiety, I murmur, "I think that my list is much longer."

"Good. I'm glad."

This shocks me. "*Glad*?"

"I hope your list numbers in the hundreds . . . this way, when you admit I'm the best you've ever had, it'll really mean something."

I shriek with laughter. "Leo!"

Leaning into me, he nips at my earlobe. "Surely you've surmised that your sordid past arouses me."

"That's why you want to know about it? Because it makes you hard?"

"Among other reasons . . . Tell me, Clara. How many stag films have you starred in? How many threesomes?"

I oughtta make some smart remark. I oughtta give some sassy, sexy line like the ones Mae West gives whenever anyone challenges her virtue, but the question actually makes me flush. "Just the one."

He touches me now like he has the right, running his hands over my backside. "Have you taken a man in your ass?"

"Once, but I didn't like it."

"You didn't much like being licked before, either, but I think I just changed your mind."

He thinks that if he's the one doing it to me, I'll like it.

I think he's right.

"You know what I've never done, Ace? I've never had sex with a man who was blackmailing me . . ."

His eyes twinkle. "If only I'd known that before. Now it's too late."

"Why? You still have my stag film."

"Yes, but it's mine now. You said you liked the idea that I could show it to anyone, anytime, whenever I wished. Well, I have to tell you, I enjoy it even more than you do. I wouldn't give it up now for any price."

"I've created a monster," I say, then whimper. "*Are* you going to show someone else?"

He looks like he's pondering the matter. "Do you know what I like about how you asked that question, Clara? There's no doubt in your mind that I'll do exactly as I please. And that's why you let me keep your reel."

"That's not the only reason. After all, if I took it when you offered it to me, I'd have cut it to ribbons."

"Which is exactly what you should have done. That would have been the safest thing."

I creep into the hollow he makes with his arms, resting my head upon his chest. "Safe for Clara Cartwright, maybe. Not safe for me."

"What do you mean by that?"

I'm too tired to lie, so the words come out soft and sincere. "If I cut up that film, it'd be like slashing myself to pieces. Like killing my own past and all the things I've done. Making it like it never happened is worse than saying it's a sin. It'd be like admitting that what I did was *so wrong*, that what I did was just *so bad* that the part of me who loved doing it can't even exist."

His self-satisfaction melts away. His brow furrows. He struggles for words, and when he finally speaks, he says, "Well, I think this just stopped being a game."

"It wasn't ever a game to me."

He shifts to get a better look at me. "Clara, I never want to make you feel like you did anything *wrong*. Shocking. Sordid. Scandalous, sure. But not wrong."

"My mother used to pray for me. 'God, please don't let the movies turn my daughter into a whore.' She never turned away the food I put on the table but she's so ashamed of me . . . and she doesn't even know I made that stag film. It wouldn't surprise her, though; it's just exactly what she expects from me."

Leo's jaw tightens. "If you take me home to meet your parents, I'm going to find it difficult to be civil to your mother."

"I don't take men home to meet my parents and even if I did you couldn't see her. She's in an asylum."

He tries, but fails, to hide his shock. "What's wrong with her?"

I don't want to tell him this story. I don't want to tell anyone this story. And yet, I start telling him.

"It happened after the fifth movie I made, the one with the camels and all the veils . . ."

"I remember that one," he says, coaxing me to go on.

"The critics loved it. One of them said that I was a revelation. That I lit up the screen. I was just starting to make money—real money—so my mother and I were still living in a little apartment together. One bedroom. We shared the bed, like we always did. And I came in late one night after work. Rehearsals always sap my pep, so I was so tired I was wobbling on my heels. I'd had a little hooch, not too much. Forgot to wash the makeup off my face. I just climbed under the covers and closed my eyes . . ."

He doesn't rush to fill the silence. Even when I can't seem to continue with the story, he just waits. I've gotten to the hard part now. "When I woke up the next morning, my mother was kneeling over me with her dark hair wild. Calling me names that frothed off her lips. I couldn't answer back—I couldn't defend myself because she had a knife against my throat."

Leo sits up, all his concentration on me now. If he says anything, I don't think I'll be able to go on. But the only words he speaks are with his eyes, which radiate concern.

"She was going to kill me, Leo. She was asking God for the strength. She told me that if I just kept still and let her slash my throat like a lamb to the sacrifice, that I'd be forgiven my sins and allowed into heaven."

Leo twitches, both hands clenching at his sides. "But you didn't keep still . . ."

I shake my head. "I fought her with everything I had. I kicked and punched and elbowed until I knocked the knife out of her hand."

"Atta girl," he says, with soft approval.

"Then I ran out into the hall, screaming. The neighbors came rushing to help when they saw the blood dripping from where she'd cut me. Not deep, but it bled a lot. There's a little scar. That's why I wear so many scarves. It isn't for fashion; I just like to keep the scar covered."

The concern in his eyes becomes stone cold anger. "Let me see."

I hesitate, then tilt my head back, exposing the line where my chin becomes my neck.

Leo gently brushes the scar with his thumb. "Does it hurt?"

"Not exactly," I whisper, closing my eyes.

Then Leo startles me by pressing his lips to the scar.

It's not a fevered kiss, not lustful in any way. It's intimate. Reverent. Almost . . . worshipful. And I can't stand it, so I shy away. "See? I'm marked by my sins."

"You didn't do anything to deserve that," he whispers against my throat.

"I drove my mother mad."

"She was already mad. No sane mother can be driven to slit the throat of her own child."

"Well, I had my revenge, didn't I? I locked her away. If I were half the person that Teddy Morgan is, I'd have kept her at home and hired a nurse. Sadly, I'm too scared to fall asleep in the same house as her . . ."

"You've got every right to be scared. Anyone would be."

"Maybe I'm just too filled with guilt for my sins to stand listening to her point them out."

"You're not a sinner, Clara."

I give a delicate snort. "What do you know about sin, Leo? What's the worst thing *you've* ever done?"

He withdraws from the intimate embrace to look me in the eye. "I killed seventeen men."

"Oh . . . oh, Leo, no. You were at war . . ."

"Yes and I'm not sure I'd do anything differently if I could. But I took men's lives then let them be counted up as kills to be celebrated. And I've witnessed what men can do to each other. It's made me give a lot of thought to right and wrong. I know what it's like to hurt people and bear the guilt for that. But all *you've* ever done is use what God gave you to give other people pleasure."

I want to believe him so badly. Emotion is so thick in my throat I can barely swallow. Our eyes meet and for just a moment, I think he glimpses past all the veils and costumes I hide behind.

I'm afraid I'll cry if I speak, so I don't.

This time, Leo *does* fill the silence. "Be embarrassed that you're an oversexed vixen. Maybe you oughtta be a little ashamed at the way you always need to be the center of attention. But you're not a sinner, Clara. You might even be a saint."

That breaks through my melancholy.

"St. Clara Cartwright of Hollywood," I hoot. "I'd rather be dead!"

Leo's tone is gentle, encouraging. "Think about it. Most people can only do good deeds for their friends and neighbors. Through movie screens across the country, you've touched *millions* of people."

"Now that sounds filthy," I tease, because I hate to be maudlin.

He just keeps stroking my hair. "I like every wicked, lurid, wanton thing about you, Clara. I'll push you, rattle you, and make you do things you never thought you'd do. Maybe even things that you shouldn't do. But I won't let you turn against yourself."

"I know."

"Do you?"

"I figured that much when you accused me of being *wholesome*."

That makes him crack a smile.

"Leo, you made me think I could put myself—my film in your hands for safekeeping. If you give it back to me, I'll cut it up like my mother tried to cut me."

He looks more serious now than I've ever seen a man look. "Well, don't worry about that, because I told you. I'm never giving it back."

Something flails inside me. "You say that now, but what about when the affair is over and we go our separate ways? You're not going to want to do the decent thing?"

Leo kisses my nose. "I'm not that decent, Clara. I can be ruthless when I want to leave my mark. And I want to leave my mark on you. So, I'll level with you. You can leave me. You can hate me. But you'll never forget my name in your long list of lovers because from this moment until the day you die, you'll know that I own a little piece of you."

My instinct is to lash out. To set him straight that nobody has ever owned me and nobody ever will. But his certainty quiets me inside. "What if you die first?"

Given his profession, it seems only fair to ask.

He hesitates only a moment. "I'll make a provision for it in my last will. I'll leave your stag film to someone who will make sure you never get your hands on it. You'll always know it's out there. My guess is that it'll be worth a lot of money, so if I were you, I'd say a few prayers that I live to a ripe old age."

I hear myself swallow.

Then he moves in for the kill. "That scares you, doesn't it?"

"Yes," I say, unable to catch my breath.

"But it excites you, too," he says, moving his hand down my belly. "What is it? The uncertainty? The idea that another stranger might see you naked? Is it the mystery that gets you running hot or the fact that it's out of your hands? That I'm going to make all the choices. Just like I made a choice for you tonight . . . I decided to let someone else know your secret . . ."

"All of it," I whisper, writhing in helpless desire. He said that one day I'd be next to him in bed, squirming with shame for all the filthy things I'd let him do to me. Today's the day. "I've never wanted anyone to choose anything for me. I've always done just what I wanted and resented anybody who got in my way. So I can't figure out why I like it so much when you decide things for me."

"Maybe because you've never had anybody who took the time to figure out how you work. Nobody else has ever known what to do with you, Clara. I do. And I'll prove it to you."

"How?"

"I'm going to choose your next lover."

CHAPTER
Seven

It's like he's dropped me into a bath of ice. I go from hot to cold to chills. And as my wits slowly come back to me, I must be the picture of outrage, because as I start to scramble up, Leo catches me by the arm. "Let me finish speaking before you slug me."

My heartbeat gallops in my ears like a stampede of furious horses. "I don't need you to find me another lover. I *had* another lover and I gave him the high-hat for your sake. I'm not looking for anybody new."

Leo's strong hands hold me still. "First of all, you ended things with Teddy Morgan for his sake, not mine. And maybe you shouldn't have, because I suspect the old bastard would have enjoyed sharing you with me."

I'm not sure if I'm going to swoon or run away before I can even consider being *shared*. But the thought is already there, burning like a coal through my paper-thin defenses. And now I can't think of anything else. Remembering the way my fantasies ran wild at the thought of being trapped between Teddy Morgan and Leo Vanderberg, I try to wrench myself out of Leo's grip before I make a complete fool of myself.

"Don't be a hypocrite, Clara. I know you like the idea."

Oh, how I hate to be called that. "Well, it's not possible now, is it?"

"Sure it is. Just not with Teddy Morgan. I know you've never been with two men before."

"Who says I haven't?"

He gives me a little shake. "*You* did. I asked you how many stag films you'd been in. How many threesomes. You told me it was just the one. Did you leave one out? Forget an orgy or two along the way?"

"Maybe I did."

"If you did, you wouldn't be crimson from your ears to the tips of your toes. Half of you wants to haul off and punch me right in the kisser, and the other half can't sit still just thinking about the idea of being the star attraction in another threesome. I want to be the one who does it to you."

The strength of him, the scent and power of him—it overwhelms me. I've already surrendered so much this night that it's become a habit. And I find that I don't want to fight him. He is every temptation I've ever had rolled into one. I want to fold into him and let him do anything he pleases. I can't help myself. I just can't.

"You're the devil, Leo Vanderberg. The *devil*!"

"And you're the sexiest woman alive," he says, trailing his mouth down my jaw. "That's what happens next, Clara, and you want it so bad you can't even admit it to yourself."

He's wrong. I can admit it to myself.

I just can't admit it to him.

"I'm not going to do it, Leo. I may not be very selective in the men I take to bed, but at least *I* select them."

"Not anymore you don't," he says with conviction. "But I'll give you a day or two to adjust to the idea. Tomorrow, I'll take you on a picnic. We'll play a little backseat bingo but I'll have you back home at a respectable hour and kiss your hand at the end of the night as if you were a well-bred lady."

At this, my nostrils flare. "And that's all?"

"So suspicious . . ." he says, as if taking umbrage. "I like spending time with you."

"That's what men say when they want to convince a girl to let them ruin her."

"True. I definitely want to ruin you."

I cross my arms over myself. "Then do it. Right now."

"Not until you agree to all my terms." When I don't say anything, he laughs. "You're actually sore at me."

"Maybe I am. And I haven't agreed to anything. In fact, I'm starting to wonder if you're worth the wait."

He taps my nose like I'm a naughty child. "Don't give me that adorable pout, Clara. I promise you, I'm worth the wait."

※

Leo drives my car with perfect confidence, and watching him work the steering wheel puts me under some kind of spell. He won't put the top up, even though the wind has my hair dancing like a dervish under the blue sky. Leo puts one arm around my shoulders when we hit the open road, and gives me a sidelong glance. "They say a picnic is a splendid tonic for frayed nerves."

My nerves aren't just frayed. They're snipped in a thousand places and my temper is foul. "Says who?"

"Those etiquette books. You know the ones. They spell out correct behavior for every situation."

I scowl. "I've never had any use for those books, and you don't follow any rules but your own."

He glances over at me, reading my irritation. "Clara, can we call a truce? It's a beautiful day and I'm with a beautiful girl. I'd like to enjoy them both."

"I don't believe in truces," I sniff.

"Even the Germans believe in truces. Be reasonable. I'm waving the white flag here."

Somehow I doubt he's ever surrendered in his whole life, but I can't resist his charm. Thermos bottles and lunch baskets in the backseat rattle louder the faster that he drives. And he drives like a demon, leaving a cloud of dust in our wake. I wait until he looks over at me to see if I'm scared, and give him a sly smirk. "Can't you go any faster than that, Ace?"

He grins, putting both hands on the wheel. "You'd better hold on for the ride."

We speed up the country roads, racing any car we pass by. I hold on to his waist, squeezing close at every tight turn. My kerchief goes flying and I'm too giddy to care. He makes the tires squeal and I tingle with the thrill of it. We're daredevils, him and me, and I'm suddenly glad to remember it. I think I never want him to stop driving, that I could spend forever right here next to him, shrieking with laughter until my sides hurt.

When he finds the ocean overlook, he slams the brakes, sending a spray of gravel into the air. We clamor out of the car and race up the hill. I'm faster than he is. "What's the matter, Leo? Not so easy when you don't have a motor to do the work for you?"

Hampered by the baskets, blankets, and Thermos, he shouts, "You left me holding the bag!"

With those long legs of his, he's on my heels, but I'm fleet-footed and sure. I'm going to beat him to the summit and he knows it. I look back just in time to see him drop everything and lunge for me. He catches my ankle and we both go tumbling down into the grass.

I wrap my arms around his shoulders, laughing. "Aren't we going to eat lunch, Leo?"

"Just a little bite first," he says, nuzzling under my chin and opening the ties of my sundress. My pale breasts come spilling out, nipples glowing pink in the sun, and he nips at them until they're taut and rigid, stopping only to admire his handiwork. "Your breasts are a work of art, Clara. They could make a grown man cry."

"That's not anywhere near the top of my list of things I like to make grown men do . . ."

He drags his head up from my bosom. "I'd like to know what *is* at the top of that list."

"I'm not inclined to tell you. I've already revealed too much and I haven't even seen you with your shirt off. It isn't fair."

"Well, let it not be said that I tolerate injustice." He reaches to unfasten his shirt at the starched collar. Just watching him undo the buttons mesmerizes me. Then he pulls his shirt over his head, revealing a lean, muscular torso and I'm devastated.

My hands go to my mouth. "Oh, no . . ."

Leo squints. "That wasn't the reaction I was hoping for."

I cover my eyes. But then I can't resist peeking between my fingers at the lines of his strong shoulders gleaming in the sun. "Oh, noooooo."

Looking down at himself, Leo rubs the dusting of dark hair on his well-hewn chest. "It can't be that bad."

"It's horrible," I say, reaching out to thrust his shirt at him. "Put this back on!"

Leo practically stammers. "Uh . . . well . . . you really want me to put my shirt back on?"

"I've never been more certain of anything in my life."

It's gratifying to see him off balance for a change, but I'm not cruel enough to keep up the ruse. "I need you to put your shirt back on because if you don't, I'm going to throw you down, claw the rest of the clothes off your body, and eat you alive!"

He barks with sudden laughter. "I can handle you, Clara . . ."

"Don't be too sure of yourself, Ace."

Grinning, he pulls his shirt back on. "You had me worried that you preferred chubby, balding tycoons."

"You leave Teddy Morgan alone."

"You know, Clara, I can't decide if I'm charmed or offended by your loyalty to him."

"You're charmed. Anything else wouldn't be worthy of you."

"Well, I'm glad to see that your opinion of me is starting to improve. Unfortunately, I'm about to irritate you by insisting that you fasten your dress so that we can eat lunch like civilized picnickers."

The only thing that gratifies me is how much he seems to regret the sight of my breasts disappearing back into my dress. "You just want to drive me into a fever of frustration, don't you?"

"That's not anywhere near the top of *my* list of things I want to do to *you*. Believe me, Clara, the self-denial is wearing thin on me, too. But tomorrow I'm going to give you everything you want and more."

To acknowledge it would be to consent to all his terms. So I don't reply until he hands me a cream cheese and olive sandwich. I survey the hillside and say, "This would be the perfect location to shoot a film."

He leers. "What kind of film did you have in mind?"

"Not that kind."

I tell him about my projects—the ones I've been producing myself with younger actresses and actors who are looking for a break. He rolls onto his side, eating while he listens, stopping to ask a question now and again. "And these will all be talkies?"

I hug my knees against my chest, wiggling my bare toes in the grass. "I hate talkies. They're so stiff and limiting. But you can't buck progress. You saw *The Jazz Singer*, didn't you? It's going to be the standard. My big eyes and exaggerated peek-a-boo gestures . . . they'll look silly."

"You'll always have that trademark pout."

I give him one of my best.

"Very nice . . . I think that'll translate just fine."

"I dunno, Leo. In talking pictures an actress has to rely on her voice to do the job her whole body used to. I'm not sure my voice is up to the task."

He sits up. "I like your voice. In particular, I like the sounds you make when—"

"Don't start," I warn him.

"I'm teasing, Clara. Truthfully, I'm awfully impressed at the way you're thinking ahead."

"Nobody else is gonna do it for me," I say, though this treads too close to matters that fall under our truce. "It isn't just planning, though. I've always wanted to make movies. You saw the photos in my room. I've got a good eye. I think I could be brilliant if someone gave me the chance."

He crumples the paper wrapper of his sandwich, then reaches for another one. "What kind of film would you make?"

"Something no one would ever expect from me. Something serious and innovative and a little bit dangerous. Something that has meaning to somebody beyond the day they bought the ticket."

He stares at me for a long time. "You're quite a package, Clara Cartwright."

"That's just a stage name, you know." I'm not sure why I tell him, but once I do, it seems easier to tell him the rest. "It's Clara Flannagan, actually. My people are from Brooklyn."

"Never been there," he says, chewing. "What's it like?"

"Noisy. Crowded. Cold in the winter . . ." I don't want to tell him about the nights I spent huddled under a wool blanket with my mother, shivering so hard that I couldn't sleep. "Hotter than hell in the summertime."

"What did you do for fun?" he wonders.

"What's with all the questions, Ace? Is this an interview and nobody told me?"

He gives me a long and lazy smile. "I like to inspect my equipment thoroughly . . ."

"The way you compare me to machines is starting to rub me the wrong way."

"Don't worry. I plan to rub you the right way." He props himself up on one elbow to stare at me. At the sight of his easy masculinity, hair tousled by the wind, something inside my chest squeezes. He's a beautiful man and I mean to have him, but I know I can't keep him. And I can't seem to shut him up, either. "Come on, Clara. Tell me what you did for fun in Brooklyn."

"I sucked off men under the boardwalk for a nickel apiece."

He snorts. "Did you?"

Hugging my knees tighter, I look straight at him. "What if I did? What would you say?"

He doesn't look away. "I'd say you didn't charge enough."

"Be serious."

"I am. Having sampled your talents, I know that no man could ever pay you what you're worth."

Turning from him, I glare into the bright sun. "So, you're saying you wouldn't care."

He sobers, then sits up so that our knees are touching. "What do you want me to say, Clara? Do you want me to be angry or aroused? Because the former would damn me in my own eyes and I worry that the latter would damn me in yours."

That catches me by surprise. The idea that Leo would worry about anything, much less how I judged him. He's always exuded a strong confidence in his sexual desires. I've been embarrassed by the things I want to do for him; is it possible he feels vulnerable because he wants me to do them? The idea of hurting him is so awful that I tell the truth. "I'm sorry. I never did that under the boardwalk. I did plenty of other things but not that."

"Why did you want me to think that you did?"

"I don't know," I say, but that isn't true.

He's getting into me too deep. He's seeing more of me than I ever let anyone see.

"Is it a fantasy?"

"No."

"Then you're looking for the escape hatch," he says, his stare unblinking. "But you can't shake me, Clara. I have you in my sights. Go on. Try to shock me. Tell me the *worst* thing you've ever done—

something that doesn't involve another person walking away supremely satisfied."

He makes me feel so foolish all of a sudden, that I can't do anything but bite my lower lip.

"Did you cheat on your tests at school?"

"No."

"Did you lie to anyone?"

A blush creeps onto my cheeks. "Whenever the truth seemed too dull."

He chuckles. "Did you steal anything?"

My cheeks get hotter and he seems to know that he's hit upon something that genuinely shames me.

"What did you steal, Clara?"

"Other women's husbands . . . well, I've just borrowed them, really." I try to make light of it because it pains me. I've always steered clear of married men. The few I *have* taken to bed were special cases like Teddy Morgan, whose wife isn't lucid enough to care what he does. But the thought that I might have hurt some poor woman haunts me.

Leo knows it's not something to joke about. "Do you think you'll do it again?"

"No," I reply, suddenly sure of it. "No, I won't ever."

"What else have you stolen, other than hearts?"

I squirm in discomfort at the memory. "When I was ten years old, I pinched a sparkly silver hatpin from a shop. I thought I could pawn it for bread money, but then I couldn't part with it. It was too pretty and shiny."

"What a little magpie you are," he says, dragging me over his knees and giving me a slap on the rump. He has me half turned in his lap so that he can see my face, but my bottom is still in easy reach of his warm palm, which he slowly rubs in a circle. And now I'm squirming with more than just discomfort. "What else did you steal, Clara?"

"Cotton candy. My mother called it 'fairy floss.' We couldn't afford it, of course. When she took me to Coney Island she only had enough for hot dogs. But when I saw that sweet spun sugar displayed in a rainbow of colors, it seemed like magic. Then the devil got into me. I grabbed a pink one as big as my head and ran!"

Leo throws his head back and roars with laughter. "Did you get away?"

"I did. I ran like the wind, stopping only to shove little sticky bits into my mouth. It was so sweet it made my teeth hurt, and I loved it. I still love it. I could eat it until it makes me sick."

"Bad girl," he says, giving me a harder spank. As the sting of it spreads across my bottom, we both stop laughing. I look up at him, and he looks down at me, and something magnetic passes between us. I wonder if he's going to bend his head and press his mouth to mine. Instead, he says, "I'd have liked to see you then . . ."

"No you wouldn't. I was skinny as a rail. Built like a boy. Nobody wanted to kiss me."

"I don't believe that for one second."

"Well, when they tried, I had a mean right hook and I licked 'em good every chance I got. When they came after me, they couldn't catch me. I ran track in school and even won a shiny trophy or two."

"Then I shouldn't feel too badly that you almost beat me racing up this hill."

"I *did* beat you, Ace. Least, I woulda beat you if you didn't cheat and tackle me."

He flashes me a pearly white smile. "Was that against the rules? You need to remember what you said before. I don't follow anybody's rules but my own . . . which makes me the perfect partner for you."

Though the grass feels wonderful on my feet, I sit up to look for my shoes because he sounds like he's working up to a conversation I don't want to have. "Who says I need a partner?"

"You need one for the movies you want to produce, don't you? Unless you plan to finance them yourself."

Now he has my full attention. "That's bad business. No smart filmmaker takes on all the financial risk."

"What if I give you the money to produce a picture about American aviation? In honor of all the pilots who didn't get to come home to a hero's welcome. A film about the friends I lost."

I throw my hair over my shoulder and look at his face to see if he's on the level. To be able to produce a film like that . . . why, that'd be a dream. And even though he's dangling it before me like a sparkling trinket, I'm smart enough to be wary. "I dunno, Leo. You'd have to tell me those stories. The ones you don't like to talk about. You'd have to tell me all the details so we could shape a film out of it. What makes you so sure you could even do it?"

"I'm not sure I *can* do it, but if you were the one listening, I'd try. I want to make a fitting memorial . . . I just never thought about putting it on film before today. Hearing you talk about the kind of movies you want to make got me thinking . . . so what do you say?"

The weight of his proposition settles over me and my confidence wavers. "I've only made small films before. Nothing for the public. Why would you trust something like that to me?"

He takes my hand, lacing my fingers with his. "You gave me *your* movie. Seems right that I should trust you with mine."

I don't think we're talking about films anymore and I'm struck with a pain in my heart so sharp I can't bear it. I want him. More than that, I want to take his face in my hands and kiss his mouth, his cheeks, his eyelids. I want to kiss him so hard that I forget who I am.

And the urge scares me worse than waking up to a blade against my throat.

"Looks like rain," I say, lifting my eyes to the sky.

He reaches for my cheek, brushing it with his hand, but when he can't make me look at him, he says, "Alright, Clara. We'll go back."

He puts the top up on the way home because it does rain. It's a long drive and I drowse in the seat next to him, lulled by the pitter-patter.

He insists on walking me in, holding his coat over me to shield me from the rain. When we get inside, he goes up with me to the front door. I lean back, pushing wet tendrils of hair out of my eyes. "Why don't you come in?"

"You know I want to, but I can't," he says, lifting my hand to his lips and kissing it.

Just then, the door opens from the inside.

Leo has to catch me before I stumble back. We both turn to see Pops standing there, gray hair all askew, an umbrella in one hand. My father clears his throat, darting a quick glance at me, then at Leo. "I was just on my way out. Don't let me interrupt . . ."

Leo should step aside, but instead, he leaps into the breach, extending a hand to my father. "Mr. Flannagan, I presume? I'm Leo Vanderberg. Your daughter and I had a splendid picnic this afternoon and I was just seeing her home for the night."

I've never let my parents catch me with a man before and Pops has no idea what to do. I have to jerk my head to the side to prompt him.

Then the two men clasp hands, and Leo gives my father's a firm shake. "With your permission, sir, I'd like to call on Clara tomorrow afternoon."

My jaw drops open at this farce. I positively gape. "I'm a big girl, Leo."

But my father huffs. "Let a man be a gentleman if he wants to. God knows none of the rest of them ever bothered."

"Oh, dry up, Pops!"

My father, the drunk who never did a thing with his life, looks the war hero up and down. "What did you say your name was again? Leo Vanderberg? I've heard of you. Famous pilot. Like Lucky Lindy, right?"

Leo nods, managing not to grind his teeth. "You should know, I think quite highly of your daughter. Quite highly indeed."

At hearing this, my father's chest puffs up and his eyes shine. "Clara is a smart girl. Everybody knows she's pretty, but she's smart, too. Always was a little scamp, too clever by half. But she's the best thing her mother and I ever did."

The lump that rises in my throat keeps me from hushing them both.

"I'll take good care of her, Mr. Flannagan," Leo says.

"See that you do." My father clears his throat. Then Pops ambles down the stairs, leaving us quite alone.

My eyes sting with tears and I give Leo a shove. "That was quite a performance!"

"I didn't say anything I didn't mean, Clara."

"Don't, Leo. Don't act like this is something different than it is. I don't want any more games."

He moves in, one palm flat to the wall behind my head. "No? What about the game I have planned for you tomorrow? You want that badly, don't you? I'm going to pick you up and take you to the movie palace. We're going to meet another man there, and then I'm going bury myself inside you like I've wanted to do from the first moment I laid eyes on you."

I stare at him, breathless. Leo has always told me exactly what to expect. I should know better than to think I can make him deviate from his plan. But I try. "I don't think I can go through with it . . ."

"Why not?"

I have a thousand reasons, starting with the fact that he's already got too much over me. More important, he's starting to make me see myself a different way. I've had a few dangerous glimpses at a different reflection that's going to shatter the moment I give him everything he wants.

"Are you scared?" he taunts. "Remember that I told you that you would be."

"I want to be with you more than I've ever wanted to be with any man, but I don't think I can do it."

He presses his forehead to mine and I feel his breath on my cheeks. "I told you that I wouldn't let you down, Clara. I'm a man of my word.

I'll be here to pick you up tomorrow afternoon, but you're the one who has to decide whether or not to answer the door."

I hold him against me, hoping to say with my body what I can't with my words, and we cling together. Then Leo kisses my forehead, slowly pulls away, and turns to go. He gets only two steps before he stops. "Clara . . . there is something else you need to know. I told you before that I was Dutch. That's not true. My mother was, but not my father. He came over from Germany before the war."

I tilt my head and stare at his back. "You're the strangest man I've ever met."

When he turns to face me he's shamefaced and his head is bowed. "What with the way people are . . . you know they'd hold it against me. As it is, I always feel like I have to prove my loyalty. Maybe I wouldn't have killed so many men in the war if I wasn't afraid that someone might think I was a collaborator. So, I lie about it."

He's grim, his expression touched with an emotion that other people might confuse with aloofness. But I recognize it as fear. He's squeezing his damp hat in his hands, waiting for me to say something. "Oh, Leo. Were you worried that I'd think you were a Mad German Brute, like the giant ape carrying off the girl in those war propaganda posters?"

He winces and I realize that it's no joke to him. One more wrong word can wound him. An answering sharp pain in the middle of my chest tells me that I'm in trouble. Big trouble. I wanna wrap my arms around this man and never let him go. And I know now why they call it a crush. Because it *hurts* so very much. "I don't care where your people are from, Ace. I'd want you whether you were German or Dutch or a green man from Mars."

He lets out a long breath. "I just don't want to lie to you, Clara. Not about this or anything else."

"Don't try so hard to be an angel, Leo, when we both know you're the devil himself."

He smiles a little, shoving his hands into his pockets. "I'll be back with the pitchfork and brimstone tomorrow."

"I might not open the door when you come knocking," I say.

"If you do, make sure you're not wearing much, because it's only going to get in the way."

CHAPTER

Eight

In spite of all my bold talk, there isn't any possibility that I won't open the door for him.

I've never been one to turn down an adventure, sexual or otherwise. My body is anxious and eager. It doesn't matter that I don't know who the other man is. The truth is, I'd go to bed with a turnip, just as long as Leo was there with me. It doesn't matter that it's the foolish thing to do—the one thing I can do that will tarnish the last bit of shiny goodness he may see in me. In the end it all boils down to the fact that I want him so badly I'd sleep with Leo Vanderberg and *anybody*.

Something's happening to me. Something awful. And I'm afraid it's only getting worse. This man has somehow gotten inside of me, without even taking me to bed. I feel him, just beneath my breastbone, where I breathe in and out. How empty and hollow is that place going to be when we finally part?

I've never been so afraid to lose a man before; certainly not before I've even had him.

I wear the siren red dress again, with the feather headdress. I've no illusion it will serve as any defense against Leo's charms, but I'm sentimental. When Leo shows up at the door, I paint my lipstick on thick then go to meet him.

He's wearing an overcoat and a hat that shadows his eyes. His nearness burns a hole through me, but neither of us says a thing. We stand there by the mirrored bureau near the front door, locked in each other's gaze. He takes a fur from the coatrack and holds it open for me. I step closer and he wraps it around my shoulders, pulling me against him until I inhale his scent and close my eyes.

He hears my sigh and knows it's surrender. "Are you scared, Clara?"

"Yes."

"Are you needy?"

"So much that I'm shaking."

"Does that embarrass you?"

My cheeks must be scarlet. "More every time I admit it."

"Then I think it's finally time you get what you want, isn't it?" he says, stroking me softly, his warm hands carrying the promise of deeper intimacy. "And today, you don't have to worry about anything . . . except pleasing me."

"I'd like that. I'd like to please you," I admit.

"You will," he says, pressing a kiss to the top of my head.

On our way out past the doorman, Charlie gives a tip of his hat, as if this were any normal day and I weren't filled with a craving for wickedness. I'm silent during the car ride. Leo takes me to the Moroccan Theatre and escorts me past the velvet ropes into a side door before the crowds catch a glimpse of me.

Then we push through the beaded curtains into the plush anteroom. They used to serve champagne here, before Prohibition, but now the room is reserved for big shots and performers. I don't know what I'm doing here. The truth is, I love not knowing. I love the idea that any man here might be Leo's friend who saw my stag film, might be the one he wants to share me with. I love it so much I think I might be the most wicked woman ever born, and it twists inside me with every step I take.

Amidst the opulent Eastern decor of the movie palace, we make small talk with a few people who know me. They seem surprised to see me with Leo, especially when he touches me in ways that leave no doubt that he's taken me as a mistress. Maybe he wants to show me off. If so, I don't mind, because I feel a thousand stabs of envy from all the women in the room.

They all lust for the dashing aviator, but he's mine, at least for one more night.

After a few minutes, Leo spies a young usher with a mop of blond hair. The two men exchange a knowing glance and I think my heart is going to beat its way out of my chest. Leo squeezes my arm in reassurance while he presses an envelope into the usher's white-gloved hand. The young man tucks the envelope into his jacket, beneath the shiny metal buttons, then bows smartly. "If you'll follow me . . ."

I begin to sweat at the back of my knees.

The band's already playing and the lights are low, so the usher uses his flashlight to guide us up the stairs and through the aisles to the balcony box, shrouded with crimson silk draperies embroidered with gold. The empty chairs are carved, polished wood. Only when the usher leaves with our coats do I dare to show my astonishment. "You rented the whole box?"

"I think we'll want the privacy," Leo says, crossing his legs and smoothing the crease in his pants.

Apprehension dawns slowly. "Oh, no. Leo, you can't mean . . . you can't mean to make love to me *here*. A movie palace is about as close to a church as it gets for a girl like me."

"Oh, come now, the whole place is a petting pantry. With all that chatter going on down there, they probably wouldn't even hear you if you screamed."

He might be right. Over the balcony, I can't see individual faces but I hear a sea of voices. People laughing, clapping, engaging with the band. The projectionist has his part to play, too, speeding the movie up and slowing it down for artistic effect. I wonder how it will be when people have to be quiet to understand a movie because they can't read words on the screen.

As always, I go with hubris. "So what's the main feature, Ace? I didn't even ask the name of the movie."

Leo shifts against me and goose bumps race up my arms. His proximity is something that I'm always aware of, but now he seems to loom over me. "It doesn't matter," he says, taking a feather from my headdress. "You're not going to be able to pay much attention."

In the darkness, the feather tickles its way down my neck, over my bare shoulder, and down my arm. I react as if he's singed me with a lit candle, hissing at the trail of heat.

"You're so responsive. You say a thousand words with every move you make," Leo says with admiration, as if it weren't exactly my talent. "Remember how you said that you'd like to please me?"

I nod.

"Then pull up your dress, spread your knees, and touch yourself."

It doesn't even occur to me not to comply, so I slide my hand over my trembling belly, burying my fingers into the heat of my own sex. I'm wet enough to ease the friction, so it doesn't take but a moment before the sound of the musicians below fades away and I'm slowly pumping my hips in reverie.

"That's my girl," Leo says. "Close your eyes and keep doing that. Don't stop unless I tell you."

With my eyes closed, the sensation of the feather over my skin intensifies. The tickle of it drives me to distraction as I rub myself. I'm vaguely aware of the curtains rustling near the back of the booth and I gasp, but Leo grips me hard by the knee. "Don't stop and don't open your eyes until I say."

There's someone else here. Maybe it's the usher with his flashlight cutting through the darkness. I don't know. But my desire to please

Leo, to do as he wants me to do, is so strong that it overcomes my terror. I tremble from head to toe, but continue to gently stroke myself.

"Good afternoon, Miss Cartwright," someone says.

The breath goes out of me at the sound of a stranger who knows who I am. Of course he does. The shame of my position, with my dress up around my hips and my fingers sticky with my own arousal, turns my blood to liquid fire. I think I'm going to melt into a puddle, just melt away into nothing.

"You can open your eyes, Clara," Leo says.

I do but it's too dark to see more than shadows as the stranger takes the seat next to me.

The stranger's voice is rich, like he hails from some wealthy New England town. "Don't let me interrupt. You've got the body of a goddess. I can't blame you for wanting to touch it . . . I know I do."

Leo laughs indulgently. "Don't tease her. She's had about all the teasing she can handle . . ."

"I just want to lend her a hand," the stranger says, laying his palm on my knee.

My breathing stutters the way delicate ladies breathe just before they faint dead away.

"Let him touch you, Clara," Leo says. "This is what you wanted. And it's what I want, too."

And nothing else matters. Not now. There's no fight in me. I drift away to a place of such frightful submission, that I don't even think I remember my own name. This is by design. This is happening exactly the way Leo engineered it to happen and that's all that I care about. He said he wanted to choose my next lover, and he has. I embrace the idea with an open heart . . . and widespread legs.

"Yes," I whisper. "Please touch me."

The stranger shifts closer, bringing with him the scent of expensive forbidden liquor, and kisses my neck. In a moment, both men are kissing my neck in perfect symmetry. Leo cups my breast with his right hand, squeezing it, kneading it until I sigh with delight. The stranger reaches between my legs and after a few moments of soft petting, he increases the tempo until he's rubbing my pussy the way one scrubs a pot.

I've never been touched that way. I shouldn't like it. The stranger is touching me the way men masturbate themselves. I've passed through fear and shame into eagerly embracing the depravity. I moan low in my throat. I've allowed my lover give my body over to a man I don't even know and I've never felt so excited by anything.

It also makes me frantic. I've lost my moorings. I need something to anchor me. "I want to touch you, Leo. I *need* to touch you."

"That makes me a very happy man," he says, alleviating my panic by drawing my hand between his legs where he's hard as iron. I know how to stroke a man through his trousers, and Leo growls his approval of my technique. "Clara, do you want to stroke him, too? You can if you want. Go on."

With only this slight encouragement, I fumble with my other hand, running it up the stranger's leg. When I find his rigid erection, the stranger groans. I stroke both men, one in each hand, surprised that it comes so naturally. As if I were born knowing how to do it. The harder they get, the harder I fall. I've forgotten the music. The audience. The wispy curtains. The whole movie palace could burn down around me and I wouldn't care because I'm already consumed with the flames of desire.

Leo's mouth clamps over my nipple, sucking it through the thin fabric of my dress, and the heat of it shoots straight through my body. The stranger dips his head and catches the other nipple, and then they're both doing it. Both of them leaving wet spots over each nipple, and I don't care. I don't care about anything but pleasure.

I squeeze my eyes closed as the explosion flashes white behind my eyelids. I swallow back a silent scream as the orgasm washes over me, thrashing my head from side to side. I think both men know they've brought me off, but how? It must be that I stop breathing. That I go perfectly still everywhere but my sex, which pulses steadily against the stranger's palm.

Only when I'm done do I take big gasping drags of air, like I've just been born.

Leo whispers, "That makes one."

"Well, isn't she splendid?" the stranger asks.

"That's not all she can do," Leo says. "Let her put those pouty lips of hers on you and you'll be a goner . . ."

"Not a bad way to go," the stranger replies.

Leo pushes gently on the back of my neck, and I know what he wants. It's the same thing I want, so I slide to the floor. I'm all vamp now, looking up with seductive eyes, ready to perform. I'm kneeling there on the floor of a public theatre, ready to suck off two men. There's a moment—just a moment—that I hate myself.

Then I see through the haze of low light and smoke that both men are staring at me like I'm a sex goddess. And I remember that I'm Clara Cartwright. I can make a grown man shake in his shoes. Now I've got *two* grown men. I'm kneeling in front of them, but they're both mesmerized by what I might do.

And I'm going to do *everything*.

I start with Leo, wrapping my lips around just the swollen head of his cock until it jumps on my tongue. He growls at me and I'm not sure if it's with pleasure or frustration. Frankly, I don't care. I wriggle my tongue up the underside while I stroke the stranger with my other hand, and now I have both men squirming.

Glancing up at the shadowed face of the stranger, I pause to lick my lips and he lets out a quick, sharp gasp of arousal. Unlike Leo's, the stranger's erection isn't a ramrod-straight bar of steel. His manhood curves upward, and I want to taste him so badly that I inch towards him like a jungle cat. I slowly slide my lips over the stranger's shaft a little bit at a time, taking him so deep that he bumps the back of my throat. I pull up, then do it again, which causes the stranger to grip the arms of his chair.

Leo slides into my seat so I can take turns licking each cock, savoring the differences in taste and texture and sound. Leo mutters a dark oath that makes me feel like he wants to devour me. And the stranger jolts every time I suck him, like my lips are electric. I could go on like this forever, back and forth, sucking these men, but Leo is just not the kind of man who can let me have my way with him. "I can wait, Clara. Give him your best."

He shifts me so that my face angles into the stranger's lap. Running my hands back to the warm recesses behind the stranger's hips, I start sucking so hard he mutters a string of whispered curses that would shock a sailor. I'm going to make him come. I'm going to make a stranger come and it turns me on so much that I won't—I can't—deny myself.

I start touching myself with my free hand, and am startled when Leo stops me. "You can wait, too, Clara. Perform just for him."

The challenge and the frustration mix inside me. He wants me to show another man how good a cocksucker I can really be? He wants me to do it, like a whore, without any pleasure for myself? Fine. I'll show him.

Covering my teeth with my lips, I bob my head up and down in the stranger's lap with utter determination. I'm good at this. And I know the stranger is perilously close to orgasm. "Good god!" the stranger grinds out through clenched teeth.

Then I feel the splash of semen on my tongue in more quantity than I expect. I start to pull back, but Leo forces my head back down. "Swallow, Clara . . . be polite."

There's more than just one swallow involved. Four, five, maybe six thick gushes of salty fluid rush to the back of my throat in quick succession. I lose count because I'm suddenly so thirsty for the stranger it that I don't want it to stop. I milk him, swallowing it all down like precious cream.

Then, haughty as a queen, I wilt in a wicked posture of repose.

Leo says, "Oh, Clara, you can be such a good girl when you want to be."

Licking my lips with satisfaction, I say, "But when I'm bad, I'm better."

Both men chuckle, but the stranger's voice is shaky and breathless. "Thank you, Miss Cartwright. That was most enjoyable."

His good manners, at a moment like this, make me laugh with just a touch of hysteria. You see, I'm wrong about there being no pleasure in it for myself. My own body gets the better of me. I'm so needy that every brush of my gown against my skin pains me. I'll go right over the edge with just a little stimulation. I'll explode. Which makes it all the more frustrating when Leo gently pulls me up into his arms, giving the stranger a moment to fasten his pants.

Clearing his throat, the stranger says, "Once I can walk again, I'll go up and order ahead for us."

"Thank you," Leo says, his voice utterly calm, even though I can hear his racing pulse.

After a few moments, the stranger stumbles out of our box, disappearing behind the curtains beyond.

Then we're alone.

"Are you alright, Clara?"

"No," I whisper, dizzy with sexual need. "If you don't fuck me, I'm going to cry."

"I'm going to," Leo promises. "But first, I need to know . . . do you need that man to stay a stranger?"

What a question! As if there were some set of social niceties for this kind of thing. "I don't know. I can't think. You're the one who chose him, so what do you suppose I need?"

Leo falls silent a moment, clasping me tight against him. "I suspect you need to know that when you put yourself into my hands, that I took the responsibility to heart. You gave me a very special gift, Clara. It might be nice for us both to know whether or not I chose wisely."

"That all sounds very sweet, but I can't make sense of any of it in my condition."

"That was Robert Aster," Leo tells me. "He's a good friend of mine."

That sobers me. "The son of the ambassador?"

Even in the dark, I can see that Leo is watching me closely. "Yes."

"You're telling me the man I just *serviced* is one of the Aster brothers. Heir to the Aster fortune. *That* Robert Aster?"

"You know of him."

"Of course I do. He got into a fistfight with some poor woman's husband at my party!"

"Oh yes. I'd forgotten. I was distracted that night by the most beautiful woman I've ever seen."

For once, his flattery doesn't pierce the tension. I've no idea what to think. How to feel. But I think I'm angry. No, I'm *sure* I'm angry and I start to yank my dress back down. "Goddamn it, Leo! You could have chosen anyone. You could have chosen the damned usher. Someone without any power or influence. Someone nobody would ever believe if he decided to spill the beans. But you decided on one of the richest men in the country. Where did you even meet him? At some billionaire bad boy's club?"

Leo grimaces. "I met him at war."

"Oh." I put my face in my hands. "I should have realized."

"I trust Robert Aster with my life . . . I thought . . . well, maybe I was wrong. Since you're considerably more valuable to me than my life, I may have made a mistake."

That place where I feel him inside me when I breathe seems to swell. "No, you didn't make a mistake, Leo. Of course you didn't. And don't say a thing like that to me unless you really do want to make me cry."

"Are you alright, Clara? That's what I need to know."

I know what he's really asking. He wants to know if I can live with the idea of what I just did with Robert Aster. I'm the one who was just stripped down to my rawest sensuality, but somehow, while he waits for me to answer, Leo's the vulnerable one. I build him up a little. "You must be the most self-assured man alive, Leo Vanderberg. You know I'm a gold digger, yet you just introduced me to the most eligible bachelor in the country. Aren't you worried I'll want to see him again?"

In the dark, I see a hint of that reassuring smirk return to his face. "I'm rather counting on it, since I told him we'd meet him in the billiard room during intermission."

"Is that such a good idea? I'm a very alluring woman. What if he falls in love with me?"

Leo lights up a cigarette, casual as you please. "I'd feel very sorry for him, because you'd break his heart. You belong to me and I'm about to prove it."

CHAPTER

Nine

The billiard room is normally crowded during intermission. The harem-style decor, complete with silk pillows and plush couches, makes it a popular gathering place. But when the usher leads us through the giant carved-wood doors into the sandalwood-scented hall, it's eerily quiet.

"I'll see to it that you're not disturbed," the usher says, just before pulling the doors closed behind us.

"You rented out the billiard room, too?" I ask Leo.

"*He* didn't." Robert Aster answers from the far end of the room. "I did. I ordered us a meal, as well."

I look over to see the man who is no longer a stranger, sitting at a table set with fine china and crisp white linen. In the light, he cuts a dashing figure. The scion of a big, wealthy family has fair hair slicked back, and a boyish, dimpled smile. He's almost as attractive as Leo, but only almost, and his good looks are marred by a fading bruise. When he sees my eyes fall on it, he says, "Courtesy of a jealous husband."

"Ah. The fistfight," I murmur. "Yes, I remember."

Leo remarks, "He has a taste for women who belong to other men, so I knew he'd enjoy you."

Leo's becoming entirely too possessive; normally, this would be the time in a relationship that I'd say or do something to discourage it. But I can't and I won't. If anything, Leo's sense of mastery over me seems to be the only thing keeping me from coming unhinged.

"You can't get anything stronger than lemonade here," Robert says apologetically, snapping his napkin with an aristocratic air. "But may I offer you a cup of tea, Miss Cartwright?"

He's offering me tea. I've swallowed his seed and he's offering me tea! I giggle before I can help it, slightly hysterical at the sexual need still coursing through my body. I don't even know how my legs carried me here because all I can think about is touching these men and being touched.

At my odd behavior, the ambassador's son raises a brow in concern.

Leo guides me into a red velvet chair. "She's just a little drunk on sex, I think."

"I must confess, I'm a bit light-headed myself," Robert says, sliding a cup of hot tea over to me. "Miss Cartwright . . . I am *definitely* a fan."

Leo keeps his hand on the back of my chair, staking his claim. "I warned you about her."

I probably shouldn't enjoy the way they're talking about me, but I do. It brings out my sass. "Such flattery, Mr. Aster. Next you'll be telling me that you've seen all my movies."

Robert exchanges a quick glance with Leo. When Leo nods, his friend says, "Now that you mention it, I saw a most compelling film of yours just the other night, but I confess, the camera doesn't do you justice."

I swallow with the certainty that he's seen the stag film and find that it only makes me hotter. There's food on the table. Beneath silver domes arranged over the plates, steam rises. But both men stare at me as if I were the main course, and I'm hungrier for sex than anything else. Glancing around the empty hall, every flat surface looks like someplace I want to sprawl naked. The linen-covered tables. The gilded couches. Even the plush red-carpeted floor. And the realization of what I'd be willing to do, right here, right now, staggers me.

I've let Leo drive me completely mad. Something has to give and it can't be my sanity.

Gulping down the tea in a few swallows, I set the cup back down on the saucer and stand up.

Robert stands, too, as if it were only the polite thing to do.

"Listen, fellas," I say. "This has been swell. Knowing Leo, I'm sure you've made some elaborate plan for the rest of the night. But I'm afraid I've had enough."

Leo's brow furrows. "Clara—"

"I like you, Ace," I say, my voice filled with regret as I back away from the table. "But if this is the way you're going to treat me, I don't think we can see each other anymore."

Stricken, Leo rises to his feet. "Clara, wait."

"I'm done waiting," I say, sliding the strap of my dress over one shoulder, then shimmying out of the other one until the bodice falls down to my waist. At the sight of my rounded breasts gleaming under the sparkles of the chandelier, both men go slack-jawed. "You've made me wait, and wait, and wait, Leo Vanderberg, and I'm not going to wait anymore."

He should be chagrined, but that infernal smirk creeps onto Leo's face again.

So I get naked. The caress of my dress as it slips over my hips and pools at my feet makes me shiver. Both of them stare at me where I stand in nothing but my shoes, stockings and garters. Their heated reactions thrill me to the tips of my toes. Robert Aster grips the back of the chair while Leo crosses his arms and gives a low, appreciative whistle.

"Flattery isn't going to work this time, Leo. Do you know what I'm starting to think about you? That you're an amateur. You're like

one of those men who want to pose in front of a genuine airplane but
don't have the courage to climb into the cockpit."

Leo is entirely indignant. "*Amateur?*"

Leaning against the billiard table, I hoist myself up so that I can
sit on the edge. Then I cross my long legs to show off my garters.
"Mr. Aster, do you know how many times this man has promised to
fuck me?"

Robert actually blushes. "I—I can't say as I . . ."

"Clara, lay off him," Leo says. "He's already had more excitement
than he can handle."

"I dispute *that*," Robert hastens to protest.

"Mr. Aster, what would you call it if someone promised you something over and over again, and never came through? Wouldn't that
be a double-crosser? I think Leo is a dirty double-crosser."

Robert shrugs. "She makes a valid point, Leo."

Leo glares at us both. "Clara, be reasonable. I've planned it all
out. We'll have dinner—"

"No more dinners. No more picnics. No more flowers and gallantry in the rain . . ." Both men watch my hand's journey as I run it
over the pale flesh of my breast, then down my tight belly to the cleft
between my thighs. "There are a hundred men in this building who
would be happy to give me what I want, Leo. They'd line up—"

"You'd probably like that," Leo says.

"I probably would. So, if you don't go all the way with me, *this
minute*, I'm going to walk out those doors, naked as the day God made
me, and find a man who will."

"Trust me, Miss Cartwright," Robert says, dimpling a boyish
smile. "You won't have to walk out the doors to find such a man."

At that, Leo stubs out his cigarette. Then he snaps off his jacket
and thrusts it against Robert's chest with a thump. "Hold this, will
you? I have something to attend to that apparently can't wait."

Then Leo starts towards me, working at his silver cuff links,
yanking at his tie.

I'm the one who waved my red cape at the bull, but as he advances on me my bravado falters. Perhaps taunting him wasn't such a bright idea. He's got his shirt open by the time he reaches the billiard table, and I shrink back in fear. Leo ignores my squeak of apprehension as he unfastens his belt. Under any other circumstances, I'd be eager to help him with the task, but the menace in his eyes pins me in place. Then he produces, from his pocket, a sheath to prevent pregnancy.

At my obvious surprise, he lifts a smug eyebrow. "*Amateur*?"

I inhale sharply, overwhelmed by the nearness of him as he opens his trousers and pulls out his cock. Oh god, it's more beautiful in the light, and already hard as a rock, pulsing and sticky with dew. He's as ready for me as I am for him, and I want him inside me so badly that I whimper like a puppy.

That's when Robert Aster clears his throat. "Would you two like some privacy?"

"No need," Leo says, grabbing my legs, throwing them open and stepping between them. "Clara loves an audience."

I'm so eager for him that I fall back against the table in utter invitation. It's not good enough for Leo; he grabs my hips and yanks me into position. I love how that feels. The lewd angle that exposes my throbbing sex to him. The smooth felt of the billiard table under my shoulder blades as he puts me where he wants me. The look of fierce lust in Leo's eyes as he rolls the sheath onto himself.

Yanking me by the hips, he buries himself to the hilt. The sudden intrusion makes me cry out. He doesn't move for a moment, staring into my eyes. He forces my body to make room for him. I spasm around him. And I *adore* the feel of him. The weight of him. The scent of him. The strength of him. There's something intensely pleasurable about the way we fit together. The sense of relief I feel at being filled, that empty ache finally soothed has me arching my back, trying to get more.

"You're always so wet for me," he says, shuddering with pleasure. He lowers his face to my neck and his chest hair rubs deliciously against my hardened nipples. The tension in my body eases as he slides deeper. Then Leo narrows his eyes and asks, "All warmed up?"

"I'm on fire, Ace," I breathe.

"Then you'd better brace yourself."

I start to laugh, but when he slams back into me, my laughter dies away. That's the opening salvo—to show me just how much force he can bring to bear. He does it again. His hips move faster, his pelvis banging against mine, his testicles thudding with each thrust. I cry out, first with shock, then with fear.

Then with dark, libidinous satisfaction.

He doesn't show the slightest mercy. I'm forced to grip the wooden lip of the billiard table in white-knuckled desperation because it's the only way to keep him from driving me right off the edge. He fucks me so hard that I don't dare let go—not even to hold my breasts, which bounce as he pumps harder, faster.

Leo's body becomes an unrelenting fucking machine that I can't escape.

Oh god. He's every bit as good as I hoped he'd be. Better, even. He's better at this than I imagined any man could be. He has me panting, both with pain and pleasure. Each thrust makes me moan like an animal. The heels of my shoes dig into the table as my body goes rigid. I knew I was wound tight, but I didn't know how close I was.

Leo tosses a lock of sweaty hair out of his face and asks, "Did you think I didn't know how to fuck you, baby? Did you think I wouldn't be able to figure out how you like it? You're already coming on my cock aren't you?"

I don't answer. I can't answer. I'm coming too hard. It hits me like an avalanche, tumbling over me until I'm buried beneath a wall of pleasure. I'm gasping and clawing for air and can't help but be swept away. And when it's over, I can only cling to him as little tremors and aftershocks rock my oversexed body.

I've never come so fast in my life, and given the way Leo is staring down at me, I'm afraid that he knows it. Worse, he's managed to ride out the storm without reaching satisfaction himself.

So this is what it's like to be taken by a man who has studied you, learned you, conquered you . . .

"Well, that was splendid," Robert says from the chair where he's watching us.

In my heated state, I'd almost forgotten the other man was in the room, and I cover my face with my hands in sharp embarrassment. It's not the first time Robert Aster has seen me have sex, of course, but the unmistakable leer in his eyes makes me feel small and fragile, like a butterfly pinned to a felt mat by the force of Leo's still-hard erection.

Drawing my attention back to him with a bite on the shoulder, Leo says, "That makes two, Clara."

"Oh, no." I put my palms flat to his chest to fend him off.

But there's no fending off Leo Vanderberg.

"I've been waiting for this a long time, Clara, and I'm going to have things my way." Leo calls to his friend. "Do you have a watch?"

I turn my head to see Robert pull out a golden pocket watch and flip it open. "Of course."

"I like to know what record I have to beat," Leo says, still buried deep inside my body.

"My guess is no more than two minutes," Robert replies. "She was quick out of the gate."

"No, no, no." I pant, squirming under Leo to get away. "I can't take it . . ."

"No?" Leo asks, cruelly pressing all his weight down on me. "Don't you want me to break you, Clara?"

I catch the meaning of his words and moan with helpless desire. All my life I've been a wild creature but now I want someone to tame me . . . at least for one night. And Leo means to do it. He means to break me like a mount, and the idea of it makes me thrash my head with denial even as my body reacts to him.

"Don't you want to please me?" he asks.

"Yes," I breathe in utter surrender. My god, yes. I want that desperately.

"Good." Bending my knees up and back, he rests my legs over his shoulders. "Because every machine in existence has a purpose, and yours is to *perform.*"

Leo Vanderberg then sets about the business of giving me the hardest ride of my life. He batters his body against me with the stamina of a soldier. Whatever fitness regimen Leo subscribes to lends him a superhuman strength that nearly destroys me and the billiard table beneath us, which creaks as if the legs might give way.

Each stroke makes me gasp until I'm hyperventilating. And when I turn my head to the side, I see that our voyeur is excited, too. Robert holds a watch in one hand and his cock in the other, slowly stroking. His eyes trail hotly over my body, his gaze filled with lustful admiration.

Seeing the effect I'm having on the other man is so electric that I throw my arms tight around Leo's neck, cries rising in pitch. I clutch at Leo as if he were the only sure thing in the world. Leo called *me* a force of nature, but I'm caught up in the storm of his making and I can't stop it. I don't want to stop it. I'm going to come again. I want it. I need it. I want to be under him, just like this, forever. Even if it leaves me raw and weeping.

He angles his strokes to drive me over the edge and I hear myself shrieking. It feels so good that I revel in pure bliss.

Red-faced and perspiring, Leo speaks with utter glee. "That makes three . . ."

He doesn't need to count anymore. It'll happen again if he wants it to. My body knows no limits now. I must be sore and swollen, but I don't feel anything except pure exhilaration.

"Sorry, old boy," Robert says, snapping the watch shut. "Didn't beat the record."

Leo doesn't seem disappointed or in a hurry. He rolls onto his back, carrying me with him. I spread over his body, melting like butter, too weak to lift my head from the pillow of his chest. He can do whatever he likes to me. He can make me come until it kills me. I don't care. I'll let him do anything.

"I could use a bit of assistance," Leo says.

Robert rises from his chair. "I thought you'd never ask."

Where Leo threw his clothes on the floor, Robert folds his and tucks his shoes neatly under the table where dinner has no doubt gone cold. But it's the only thing that has. Watching Leo's friend undress is like a spark to kindling. I thought I was spent, but now desire roars awake again. The sound that comes out of me is a low, throaty moan of eagerness. All I've wanted of Leo is more, more, more. Now his friend seems to be a deliciously sexy extension of him. It's not in me to even *pretend* that I don't want Robert Aster.

The other man hops onto the table with us and takes it upon himself to undress me completely—removing my shoes, rolling down my stockings and removing my garters. When he's done, I find myself between both men, a pampered pet, being kissed and stroked.

I do my own bit of exploring.

Where Leo's skin is tan and weathered, Robert's is freckled and fair. Where Leo's hands are calloused, Robert's are soft and well manicured. Where Leo's body is sinew and steel, Robert is fleshier but strong. He has the hands of a patrician but the body of a farm boy, and when I scratch over his nipples, he hisses with pleasure. He seems almost giddy to be touched by me, easier prey than Leo has ever been.

Watching me toy with Robert seems to amuse Leo, who rolls me onto his body again, palming me, flesh to flesh. Leo is still hard and needy—he hasn't found his own satisfaction yet and I want to give it to him. It doesn't take much urging for me to mount him. There's something incredibly arousing about the way Robert Aster helps me into position. Enticing both men with every roll of my hips, I ride Leo's cock with shameless abandon.

Well, that's not quite true. There's plenty of shame; it's just that my sense of shame never stands a chance against my fevered lust. I keep waiting for Leo to rein me in. But it's Robert whose hand goes into my hair, gently pulling me up so that I need to rest my palms on Leo's chest for balance. "If you don't mind terribly, Miss Cartwright, I'd like to see your breasts while you fuck."

Oh, hearing that from him shocks me. And that hard look in his eyes under the civility makes me start to wonder if I've misjudged the rich boy completely. He caresses my breasts, catching the nipples between his fingers and giving them a squeeze. Being touched by both men sends a jolt of electric heat through my body. Leo likes it, too. I know because his cock swells even bigger inside me. Right now, pleasure is the only thing I know. Maybe my mother was right and I was a born whore, because I begin to make frantic motions with my hips, trying to prove to them both that I can take anything. Leo lets me thrash against his body, until I'm filled with frustration, and pleading with him to fuck me even harder.

"I *really* like when you beg . . ." Leo says, using his legs and back for leverage as he gives me just what I want. He strokes up into me like a jackhammer until my teeth rattle. Meanwhile, Robert squeezes my nipples, twisting them between his fingers to the point of pain, and I wail with pleasure.

Pink and breathless, I'm vaguely aware of Robert sheathing himself just as Leo pulls out of me, his shaft resting like a broom handle between my belly and his. Even so, my whole body stiffens in shock when Leo asks, "Are you going to let him fuck you, Clara?"

I'm shamed by how eagerly I say yes. Then Robert Aster, a man whose acquaintance I've known less than the length of a feature film, slowly sinks his cock into the emptiness that Leo has left behind.

I can't see my new lover, but his breath is warm on my back. The feel of his groin pressed tight against my upturned bottom is warm and arousing. No two men fuck in the same way, and these two are no exception. Robert is gentler, sliding smoothly against the flesh that Leo has left sore and swollen. Meanwhile, Leo cushions my body for the other man. He holds my hair back so that he can see my reddened face, my parted lips, the wanton desire in my eyes when he says, "Make him feel good, Clara . . ."

The expression on Leo's face is one of complete mastery. He's entitled to it. I've never felt like I belonged to anyone before, but there isn't a doubt in my mind that I belong to him.

How strange that I should realize it while another man is thrusting up inside me.

They trade me back and forth between them. First Robert is stroking into me, then Leo, then Robert again, until we've all melded into one humping, panting, undulating creature. It makes me shameless. It makes me wild. It makes me want to scream. It makes me want to come.

Leo knows it and he increases the tempo of his fucking. I bite down on his shoulder till I think it'll draw blood. It doesn't stop him. And while Leo has me so distracted, Robert produces a tiny bottle of oil and dribbles it over the puckered entrance I'd rather no one ever touched. He's lubricating me, and I know just what for. I try to evade his slippery fingers as they press into the tight hole, but I can't escape them and I squeal at the indignity.

It isn't only that I don't like being penetrated there; it's also that Leo hasn't done it to me first. I don't want Robert—whose winsome manner would have led me to believe him incapable of this particular obscenity—to be the one to take me there first.

Ignoring my objections, Leo spreads the cheeks of my bottom with both hands. "Let him do it, baby. I think you're going to like this an awful lot."

I've never liked doing it; it always hurts. I'm already so full that I can't possibly take more. But I do. Robert prepares me with his fingers, until the pain dissipates into raw pleasure. Then he works his prick into my ass. Leo hisses as if the tightness hurts him, but he grinds his teeth against it. Then they're both inside me.

My god, they're *both* inside me, and I'm a glorious object of pleasure once again.

Robert strokes himself into me slowly, alternating strokes with Leo until I think I'm going to shatter into a million pieces. The sounds I make this time are low growls of pure primal instinct. "Oh my god, oh my god, oh my god!"

Nothing in my life has ever prepared me for sex with two men at the same time. It's all new. All of it. Everything I've ever done has been child's play. I must have been a virgin because I've never felt like this before. Not my body. Not my mind. Not my heart.

Suddenly, my eyes are watering.

Leo takes hold of my face. "You don't like it?"

"I love it, you bastard!"

Leo looks like he might burst with pride. "You wonderful little slut . . ."

The word doesn't sting, but I sob, "I *love* it . . ."

Robert curses, as if this statement of mine was designed to make him spill his seed with embarrassing haste. I'm too greedy to give him even a moment to steady himself. "Please don't stop!"

With my encouragement Robert grips me by the hips and drives into me. The searing, shocking pain of it makes me scream. But I'm not sorry. I find myself moaning, crying out filthy words, thanking them, begging them. I'm sandwiched between them. My breasts glued to Leo's chest. My back sucked tight against Robert's body. Bodies slick and tangled, hands on me everywhere, and their mouths . . . oh, the feel of their mouths pressing kisses to my fevered skin.

Two men are working inside me and I'll do anything—*anything*—to please them.

I throw my head back, and Leo's mouth finds the scar on my neck. Kissing it, running his tongue over it like an animal licks at a wound to heal it. Maybe that's what he's doing. Trying to heal me. Or maybe he's broken me completely. I'm raw and vulnerable in a way I've never been before. He's taken me apart to see how I work, but what if he can't ever put me back together again?

Leo's eyes flash, the look of a man about to find his own pleasure. "Baby, do you want to make us come?"

That's all the encouragement I need. All I want is to make them come, to feel both men stiffening, to hear the erotic symphony of their grunts and groans. Robert thrusts home, pushing into me with more urgency.

I think he'll be the one to find release first, but I'm wrong.

I do.

The sensation of coming on both men's cocks is more than I can bear. My insides clench tight on the men inside me, and I start sobbing.

"Jesus Christ!" Leo cries, tapping his head back against the table a few times before he lets go completely. A moment later, Robert groans as he thrusts home, twitching with orgasm.

We are, all three, doing it together, and my senses give out.

The world becomes a blur of panting breaths and slippery skin and stuttering sighs.

And when I finally open my eyes again, Leo kisses me.

He kisses me full on the mouth. Our first real kiss. I taste the salty sweat of his upper lip. I feel the caress of his breath on my cheeks. His lips are soft and masculine. Sweet enough to make my teeth hurt. The tenderness turns me inside out.

He kisses me like he cherishes me.

He kisses me like I'm something precious.

He kisses me like he loves me.

And it breaks my heart.

CHAPTER

Ten

The regrets come later when I'm soaking in a hot bath, listening to jazz phonographs playing in the bedroom nearby. In Leo's claw-foot tub, I loll shyly in the steaming water while he washes my back with lavender soap and a soft scrubbing brush. All my life, I've chewed up men and spit them out and never cared a damn what anyone thought about it. But all that's changed now; I'm terrified that he'll see it.

"How badly do you hurt?" Leo asks.

More than he'll ever know, but not the way he means. "I'm just sore, is all."

"So what do you say? Did I keep my promise?"

"You'll wish you didn't," I say, trying to put some distance between us. "Now I'll just want to do it again."

He grins, sliding his hand under the water. "Can't I keep you sated for even a few hours? If you need more . . ."

I hiss like a cat. "Don't you dare. I'm *quite* sated."

"Good." Leo kisses my wet shoulder. "I wanted to wreck you just a little bit."

"You certainly did that."

He's holding me, caressing me, kissing me, practically humming a little tune against my skin. I'm all broken inside and yet, he seems so . . . *happy*. "That was even more fun than I thought it would be, Clara. I think you'd better tell me everything else you've never done before."

"I've done everything."

Doesn't he, even now, know what kind of girl I am?

"Well, I don't object to revisiting old favorites. But I'm sure there's something else you've never done before."

"Nothing," I snap.

"I don't believe you."

"Well, I've never been in love before." It just slips out, and when it does, my eyes fill with tears. It's not like me to be so careless with words. Not like me at all to tell the truth when artifice would suffice. And now that they're out, the words just float there in the bath between us.

Leo clears his throat. "Are you saying that you're in love with me, Clara?"

I try and fail to swallow back my tears. "Don't be silly, Ace. If anything, I've fallen quite helplessly under Mr. Aster's spell."

His expression falls. "You'd better be joking . . ."

"Of course I am," I say, wiping my tear-streaked cheeks with the backs of my hands. "I don't fall in love. It would ruin our arrangement and I'm enjoying our sordid affair too much to spoil it."

He isn't fooled for one moment and rushes forward in gallantry. "Well, I'm in love with *you*, Clara. I have been from the start."

"Leo, *stop*," I say, trying to get out of the tub before he feels the need to save me from further humiliation.

He folds me into a towel. "I'd have said it before now if I thought you'd wanted to hear it."

"Well, I don't want to hear it."

"Too bad. You're gonna hear it. I'm busting to say it. I loved you the moment you said, 'When I take a man to bed, it's got everything to do with the size of his bank account and what he's got between his legs.'"

I'm appalled at myself for having said it and at him for remembering it, but now he has me laughing through my tears. "You really are the strangest man."

"Clara, I loved you the first time I met you. Maybe even before I met you."

My heart swells inside my chest until the ache is unbearable. "You don't know what you're saying, Leo. Every man in the country thinks he's in love with me if you believe the papers, but that doesn't make it true."

"Every man in the country probably *is* in love with you, Clara. But they don't know what to do with you. I know exactly what to do with you, or do you still have any lingering doubts?"

His words recall to mind the wicked way we spent the afternoon, and I can't look at him.

"I love you, Clara Flannagan."

At the sound of my real name, I flinch.

"I *do*, Clara. I love the way you taste. I love the way you smell of gardenias. I love the way you sound when you come. I love the way you respond to my touch, to my words, to my every perverse desire . . ."

"That's lust, not love, Leo."

"I'm not finished. I love that you're loyal as a hound. I love that spunky kid inside who stole a giant pink ball of fairy floss. I love the hard-boiled act you use to hide your big sappy heart. I never thought I'd meet a girl like you—never thought a girl like you existed. You're bright and talented. You've got something about you, Clara. You *sparkle*. So I want you to know, right here, right now, that I love you."

"Oh, Leo . . ." I stroke his beloved cheek with my wet hand, terrified to believe a word. "You'll feel differently in the morning."

"Why the devil would I feel differently in the morning?"

I'm silent. My insides writhe like snakes. I think I'm on the verge of a breakdown.

"Clara, is there something you need to tell me?"

I shake my head, unable to speak.

Bitterness seeps into his voice. "Am I going to find out you never broke things off with Teddy Morgan?"

This finally loosens my tongue. "Of course I did. I wouldn't lie about a thing like that."

Leo grunts. "Good."

"But I don't see what difference it makes to you. Whether it's Teddy Morgan . . . or Robert Aster."

"Ah," he says, as if a lightbulb has blinked on. "At least twenty years difference in age, for starters. But the important difference is that Teddy Morgan wants you for himself whereas Bobby knows you're just on loan."

"Why, Leo, you sweet talker."

He's unapologetic. "We Germans can be very territorial . . ."

"Well if you're so territorial, I don't see why you're not angry about the way I behaved today."

"Now that you mention it . . . I *am* a little sore at you. I was looking forward to the expensive meal at the Moroccan you caused to go to waste. I'm willing to forgive you because you turned out to be far tastier than anything the chefs could have prepared."

"You know what I meant, Leo."

"Haven't you figured me out yet, Clara? What thrills me is getting in your head. I'll exploit every fantasy you've got as long as I can make you look at me the way you did this afternoon. Fuck Lucky Lindy. What I did with you today was better than flying a solo flight across the Atlantic. Every single thing we did proved that you're mine. Today, you let me give you away. And a man can't give away what doesn't belong to him. So I'm glad to hear you say you wanted to do it again. Because we *are* going to do it again."

I slant him a glance. "Oh, are we?"

"Yes. We are." Leo's tone brooks no argument. "We definitely are."

The thought of it makes me shiver before I can put on a false mask of modesty. "With Mr. Aster?"

"Why? Do you have another man in mind? And before you

answer, realize that if you say Big Teddy Morgan, I'm going to turn you over my knee."

"Now you're just tempting me . . ."

Leo laughs. "And *that* is why I'm in love with you. And why I'm still going to love you in the morning."

"Don't worry, Ace," I whisper to myself. "I won't hold you to it."

He takes me to bed. And by that, I mean he towels me dry, carries me into his bedroom, then tucks me under the covers. I sigh at the feel of the cool, crisp linens against my skin and delight of the scent of him on the scratchy wool coverlet. There's nothing glamorous about his bedroom. It's spare and well-ordered, with framed drawings of engines and flying machines displayed like artwork on the wood-paneled walls.

"So, what do you think?" Leo asks, climbing in bed with me and nuzzling my damp hair. "I know it's not a penthouse apartment or an oceanside mansion, but I'm rather proud of this place. I bought it with the first prize money I ever won on the racing circuit. Six bedrooms. A pool around back and a gated garden . . ."

A girl could get comfortable here if she let herself, but I say, "It's not bad."

His medals of valor hang over the headboard. The oak-leaf cluster. The Distinguished Service Cross. The French Legion of Honor. The Belgian Order of Leopold II. He tells me their names when I press him, but he won't tell me what he did to get them.

He'd rather talk about his next mission, the upcoming test flight for Morgan Industries. He talks about his plan to circumnavigate the globe. He talks airships and flying machines and filmmaking.

It isn't until the wee hours of the morning that he's willing to tell me about the war.

His voice is flat when he describes the bombing raids. The dogfights. The artillery fire that killed so many of his friends. Sometimes a young Lieutenant Robert Aster gets mentioned in these stories as an officer who found creative ways to reequip their unit with the machine guns they so badly needed, but most of the stories are about men I've never heard of. Men who were shot down and taken prisoner. Brave, gallant, fierce warriors who never lost an aerial battle but died inglorious deaths by way of dysentery.

When he speaks of them, his eyes are red-rimmed. "Sometimes it fell to me to write a letter to their kin, or maybe a sweetheart back home, and . . ." I catch a glint of guilt in his eyes and wonder just what it is that he feels so awfully sorry about. Until now, I didn't know it was possible for someone to feel guilty just for surviving, but I think he does. These men were his family. Now they're dead, just like the mother he never knew and the father who died in a cornfield. And he thinks it should have been *him*. "There's no justice in the world, Clara. I had nobody waiting on me back home, but no matter what risks I took, whether I shot down another plane or crashed my own in a fog, I just kept coming back."

I listen to everything he says, touching his stubbly cheek to soothe him during the hardest parts. When he finally closes his eyes, I think he's fallen into a deep sleep, but then I realize he's just putting everything away again inside his head. He's told me stories that would make a riveting, gut-wrenching film, but that can wait. It'll have to wait.

"Why do you keep flying, Leo? In war, men risk their lives for a good cause. But the war's over. It's been over for years."

He leans back on his headboard. "When I go up now, it's not about killing anybody else. The only life at stake is mine. Aviation is opening the skies for the future. Because of what we do, you can see more of the world. You can take an airship to Paris. When pilots try to cross the ocean, it's to prove that it can be done. That it *should* be done. Someone has to go first and change everything we think we know and it might as well be me."

"That all sounds rather high-minded but you make me wonder if you have a death wish."

He knows I'm serious but shrugs it off. "Planes are better designed and safer than they used to be. When I started flying, wings were practically made of paper and wire. And we didn't use parachutes during the war. The German pilots had them, but Allied aircrew flew without. I was glad we didn't have parachutes because when we were going down that left only three choices. Ride it out and risk a fiery crash. Jump to your death. Or use a revolver to end it quickly."

This chills me to the bone. My mouth falls open in abject horror.

He chucks me under the chin. "Clara, I always rode it out. And the plane I'm taking up next week for Morgan Industries has a metal frame. I've studied the design. The fuel tank's in front, which reduces the possibility it might crush me to death in a crash."

How am I stuck on a man who views falling from the sky and crashing his plane as less dangerous than being crushed by a fuel tank? And how can he speak of it with such resignation? Maybe he's just tired. He *looks* tired, his eyes hooded, his strong shoulders slumped. If he's as exhausted as I am, he's a man in desperate need of sleep, so I say, "I should go, Leo. It's late."

Leo narrows his eyes. "Where the devil are you going?"

"You don't expect me to stay the night, do you?"

"That's exactly what I expect. I want you right here until the sun rises . . ."

"Haven't you ever kept a mistress before, Leo? That's not how it works."

Leo reaches into the drawer by the side of the bed and takes out a pack of smokes. He doesn't offer me one. He just lights up. "Tell me, how is it supposed to work?"

"You keep a mistress tucked away in some apartment that you can visit when it pleases you. On special occasions, you might have her come to your bed, but you always send her away when you're done."

"Well, I'm not done," Leo says, taking a deep drag of his cigarette.

The way he looks at me makes me very afraid. "Leo, I'm in no condition—"

"I want to sleep next to you. Or do I have to marry you to get you to spend the night in my bed?"

I snort. "Neither of us are the marrying kind, but I'll get into bed with you whenever you want me."

"Now there's the little vamp I love," he says, pulling me against his chest.

Then he turns out the light and falls into deep slumber. I watch him. The way his chest rises and falls, rumbling with contentment. The rhythm of his breath. The way his eyes move beneath his lids as if he were dreaming of a future with me. It's a dream I want to share, but I know it's *only* a dream.

And by morning, I'm gone.

CHAPTER

Eleven

Rehearsal goes badly. Dressed in a grass skirt and Hawaiian lei, I'm supposed to be dancing the hula for the camera and all I can think about is Leo. Later, sprawling in the grass on set, I'm supposed to entice the hero of the movie to kiss me. Instead, I turn my head away.

Twice, the director scolds me until it becomes clear that I'm not paying any attention at all.

"What's the crisis this time, sweetheart?" the director asks.

I don't answer him. I just leave the set.

At home, Charlie says, "Miss Cartwright, there is a gentleman caller waiting for you. It's Mr. Vanderberg. Your father said it would be alright if I let him upstairs."

I wish he hadn't. "I don't think I can face Mr. Vanderberg today . . ."

My father is coming out just as I'm going in, and he overhears. "Throwing him over already, Clara? He seems like a nice fella."

From the man who abandoned my mother and me, that may not seem like much of an endorsement, but there's something so sweet and hopeful in my father's eyes that I don't want to disappoint him. "Who says I'm throwing him over? I'm just tired, that's all."

Pops nods, takes a few steps, then stops. "Clara, I hope you know . . . not every man is like me."

I just stand there, my hand on the doorknob, pretending I haven't heard him. But he knows. We both know. It just seems kinder this way. And after a few moments, I hear his steps fade away. They echo in my mind with the words he's said, and I wish I could believe him.

Forcing myself to hang up my coat and pour myself a drink from the sideboard takes all the strength I've got left. Leo is sitting on the divan, head down, elbows on his knees, holding his hat. When he looks up, everything inside me comes awake and I have to fight my urge to rush to him and throw my arms around his neck.

"You skipped out before breakfast," Leo says crossly. "And what are you wearing . . . is that a grass skirt?"

Glancing down at myself, I see that I was in such a stupor I didn't remember to change out of my costume. Trying not to show that I'm flustered, I flash him a leg. "Do you like it?"

Leo makes a sound of approval in his throat. "You were right, you know. About this morning. When I woke up, I did feel differently."

An arrow of agony rips through me but I force a bright smile. "Wonderful!" It's an award-winning performance. "Now that we're done with that silliness, maybe you can help me out of this outfit and into something a little more comfortable."

Leo frowns. "I wasn't happy to wake up alone, Clara. More specifically, I wasn't happy to wake up without you. And I realized how I poured my heart out to you like a sap last night and you didn't say anything at all. It occurred to me that you may not share my feelings . . ."

"If that's what occurred to you then you're a fool, Leo Vanderberg."

"Don't toy with me Clara. I'll *make* you love me if I have to. But I need to know how you feel about me."

I've been pretending all my life that everything was fine, so why shouldn't I go on pretending? But the way Leo is looking at me now, so earnestly . . . I don't have the heart to pretend for one more moment. "How do I feel about you? I love you, Leo."

He starts to smile, but falters when he sees my expression. "Well, you couldn't look less thrilled about it."

I promptly burst into tears.

"Because it's awful! I can't imagine why anyone would ever want to be in love. I look at you and my belly flutters. I haven't been able to eat more than a few bites since the day I met you. I can't sleep because whenever I close my eyes I remember how it feels to be touched by you. I daydream about you when I should be working. Sometimes, I even start shivering just at the sound of your name. It's like I've fallen ill with something that could be fatal!"

The tension goes out of Leo's shoulders and he laughs. Then he rises to his feet and enfolds me in an embrace, patting my back. "There, there. It can't be all that bad . . ."

"It is," I sob. "I don't want to be in love. Don't you know what I do for a living? Tomorrow afternoon, I have to pretend to drown in a lily pond so some handsome actor can rescue me and kiss me passionately. I have to be Clara Cartwright. Fiery, fearless, and independent as a cat. I've never loved any man and never needed one. But I need you so badly that I think it's going to kill me."

He's grinning now. "You do have a flair for the dramatic, don't you, darling?"

The tears won't stop and Leo has to offer me the handkerchief from his pocket. I'm sniffling and my make-up is smearing. I dab at my eyes, which feel puffy. My nose is probably red. Even my lower lip is quivering so badly I doubt I could force it into a seductive pout. How hideous I must look. "You shouldn't see me like this."

"Marry me, Clara."

My heart stops. It stops right in my chest. "*What?*"

"You heard me."

"That's not funny, Leo. It's not funny at all."

"It's not a joke."

"Then you've lost your wits."

"That's true," he says. "I'm crazy about you."

My hands go to my cheeks. "What are you thinking? I'm not the marrying kind, Ace. Neither are you."

Leo clears his throat. "I know I said that. I believed it, too. But that was before. Everything is different now. I got to thinking about all these rules for mistresses. Did you read all that in one of those etiquette books you've got no use for, or is it something I did or said? I don't know how I made you feel like I don't want you near me always. Or how I made you feel like I only want you until I'm done with you. But let me clear it up now. I'm *never* going to be done with you, Clara. So why don't you marry me?"

My broken heart cracks into several new pieces. "Because I'm not the girl men marry, Leo. I'm the girl men share on a billiard table."

He reacts as if I've flung frigid water in his face; he goes white to the tip of his nose. And he responds with a cold fury that frightens me a little. "Why, Clara, I do believe we're about to have our first serious quarrel . . ."

"It's only the plain truth."

Grabbing my arm, he tugs me towards the bedroom. "Come here, I want to show you something." For a moment—just for a moment—I think he means to carry our quarrel onto the bed. Instead, he pulls me to my dressing table, where my matching brushes and gilded perfume bottles mock me from their tray. Easing me onto the vanity seat, Leo says, "Tilt your head back."

"What?"

"Just do as I say, will you? Tilt your head back."

"No, Leo. Stop it."

Giving my hair a good yank, he exposes my throat. I stare up at him, wondering if he's going to strike me. Instead, he says, "You're the only one who can see it, Clara. Do you know that? In your mind, that scar is so red and vivid that it marks you. You think that part of you is unlovable. You're wrong."

This raises the ire in me. "Let me go, you mad German brute, or I'll elbow your bad rib into next week."

"Look in the mirror, Clara. Look at yourself."

"I don't have to look! I'm a vain, shallow, woman, and all I *ever* do is look at myself. I see myself on every movie poster. In every theatre."

"That's a persona, Clara. It's not you."

"It is. At least, it's a part of me."

"Yes and so is the scar. But it's not the whole of you. So look at it."

My eyes well hot with tears as I dare to glance in the mirror. To see the scar, I have to squint. But when I see it, all I can hear is my mother's voice, and I want to clamp my hands over my ears to make it stop.

"I know what this scar means to you, Clara. What you think it says about you. But do you know what it means to me? It means that you're a fighter. You don't need my money. You don't need my name. You don't need a damned thing from me except to embrace your dark secrets and protect them, even from you."

Tears slide down my cheeks, hot and salty. "But you don't have to marry me to give me any of that. I'll be your mistress for as long as you'll have me and a mistress is more fun than a wife."

His grip loosens, and he strokes me softly. "Oh, Clara. Are you afraid marriage is going to put an end to our games? I know you're a scarlet woman and I plan to be a nefarious husband. Especially once I get you to promise to love, honor, and *obey*." When I wilt a little, it only encourages him. "See, you like that idea. You're thinking of all the wicked ways I could abuse that power, aren't you? Maybe you'd like a little preview . . . maybe that will help convince you."

In spite of everything, my body buzzes with renewed interest. "You're the devil himself."

"And you look surprisingly sexy in a coconut brassiere," he says, cupping my breasts. "Still sore?"

"Yes," I whisper.

"Do you think it's going to stop a 'mad German brute' like me?"

"I hope not."

With that, he grabs me up into his arms and slings me over his shoulder.

"Leo!"

He drops me onto the bed, then crawls over me. "It's time for a change in strategy. I assume you want to be ravished by me over and over again."

I moan, unable to deny it. "Yes, oh yes."

Leo grins. "See how easy it is to say yes to me?"

"Shut up and make love to me," I say, clamping my arms around his neck.

He yanks the Polynesian flowers off me and reaches under my grass skirt. His hands caress me and he starts nibbling his way down my body, then looks chagrined. "Unfortunately, I really am an *amateur* today. I didn't think to bring precautions."

"I don't care," I whisper, lost in the reverie. "I want you inside me, bare."

Leo's self-control unravels. "You know exactly what a man likes to hear, don't you?"

He fumbles with his belt buckle, kicking his pants off in his haste. But when he enters me, he's gentle. He's gentle in a way I didn't know he *could* be gentle, kissing my throat over and over again, kissing my scar until it feeds me with sensation. Until it becomes a new place of pleasure all to itself. We make love, my legs wrapped around him tight as I stroke his back, his arms, his chest. It feels different this time. Tender, loving, languorous as we strain together. But every time I near the summit, Leo shifts subtly or slows down to keep me on the edge.

"Leo, please," I murmur.

"Do you want to come, Clara?"

"Yes."

"Say it again."

"Yes, Leo. Yes."

"Very nice. Say it again. I want to get you used to the idea of saying yes . . ."

"Yes, please, please, yes!"

"Then marry me."

"No!" I sputter my indignation. "That's not fair."

Leo gives a small push with his pelvis, anchoring me to the bed, destroying my resolve with the promise of pleasure. "Fair? You know better than to think I'm going to follow the rules, don't you?" he asks, lifting up so that I can see where we're joined together in such beautiful, carnal intimacy. "Say you'll marry me and I'll make you see stars."

I groan with frustration, squeezing my eyes shut. "No."

"I can do this to you all day, every day, Clara. If I get tired, I'll call Robert Aster to help. Eventually, you're going to give in, so why not now?"

"Because you're not the only one who can do this all day, every day," I say, sliding my hand between us to touch where I so need to be touched. My brazen sensuality delights him and he watches the trail of my fingers like a man enchanted. I stroke myself, using my body and his for satisfaction.

"I knew I should have tied your hands to the headboard again," he says, but he doesn't stop me. I use every trick I know, nipping at his nipples on the upstroke, caressing the small of his back, which flexes with each thrust. It excites me to see how his desire for me shatters his resolve. And when I hear him moaning my name, again and again, we send each other into a spiral of pleasure.

The moment he begins to pulse and throb, I lock my legs around his waist so he can't pull free. He struggles against me, but I won't let him go. "Come inside me, Leo . . ."

His face contorts with an ecstasy that matches my own, and we cry out together as he floods me with warmth and my body grasps hold of him, with its own designs. After, we lay panting together, our sweat-slick limbs wrapped in intimate embrace, and Leo gives a rueful chuckle. "Well, *that* wasn't supposed to happen."

I stretch, content as a cat. "I wanted it to. I want it to happen again and again."

"If it does, you'll get knocked up and *have* to marry me . . ." He turns to look at me with a gleam in his eye. "Which, on second thought, is a rather good argument for the idea."

In spite of my bliss, this talk of marriage has to stop, so I confess, "I can't have children, Leo. I've been sleeping with men since I was fourteen and I never got knocked up. Not even once."

"Which proves exactly, nothing, but it's neither here nor there. When did you hear me say that I wanted to raise a bunch of little ankle biters?"

"That's why people get married, Leo. To start a family. And I can't be anyone's mother. Even if I could, how do you think kids would fare growing up the children of Clara Cartwright?"

"Like spoiled little brats, probably. You're a movie star, Clara. Any kid would be proud. If you want to worry, you should worry about how they'd fare as the children of a German American."

"Oh, you and that sauerkraut on your shoulder . . ."

"I have no interest in children unless you do, Clara, in which case I'm happy to give them to you."

I've never even thought it a possibility, and the strangeness of a man offering to give me children, a home, a family, fills me with happiness, even if it's a dream that can never be mine. "Why do you want to get married then?"

"Because you're *it* for me, Clara. I want you. And I get what I want."

"You *have* me, Leo. But if you're trying to show the world that I belong to you, marrying me isn't the way to do it. People know that you're sleeping with me. They admire you for parading me around like the fallen woman I am. But if you marry me, that'll change."

"How the devil do you think things will change?"

All my life, I've clawed to get what I wanted. Now all I want is him so why am I so determined to let go of him? I suppose it's because I love him too much not to tell him the truth. "For starters, if we get married, the scandal sheets will call you Mr. Cartwright, and that's just when they're being nice."

"Clara, the first time a scandal sheet calls me Mr. Cartwright, I'll fuck you so hard that you consider changing your stage name. But it isn't going to change the way I feel. I want to marry you. Only you. I don't want to marry you to convince the world that you belong to me. I want to marry you so that the world knows that I *love* you."

Temptation. It's like the spun candy at the carnival I couldn't ever afford as a kid. The only way I could get it was to steal it from someone else. And the harder I fall for him, the more determined I am not to steal anything from Leo, especially not his future. Every reason I give him, he's only going to argue down, and there are some arguments I can't bear to have. So I say, "I love you, too, Leo. I really do *love* you. Which is why I have to do the decent thing and say no."

Standing behind the boxy camera on the tripod, I film Leo as he works on the plane. I have my crew adjust the lighting while Leo patiently explains the controls. We don't know how we're going to use the footage yet, but we both think it'll be valuable to have. I'd like to film him for hours, until he forgot anyone was there, and maybe I'd catch a glimpse of what makes him the man he is.

I *love* to film him. The way he moves, with such sureness. The way he uses his tools to adjust and inspect and master the machine. More important, it gives me a chance to stare at him from behind the camera, where I keep myself safe from my fears and his resentments.

It's a monstrous thing, this plane with its Morgan Industries emblem on the side. I don't want him to go up in it. It doesn't look as if it could possibly protect him. In the shadow of the engine, Leo is meticulous, wiping the grease from his hands on a rag that he tucks in his front pocket. Wrapping up for the day, he waves off my crew and then we're alone.

I sneak up behind him and wrap my arms around his waist.

"You're going to get dirty," Leo says, rattling around as he puts his tools back into their box.

"I don't mind if you don't," I say, letting my hands drift over his hips. "Unless, of course, you're still angry with me."

"You'd know if I was angry," he says, though his tone is clipped.

Maybe he's not angry. Maybe he's hurt. Or maybe he's focusing all his thoughts on how he's going to get this plane in the air and keep it there. And maybe I should let him do just that. Instead, I press myself against his back.

Growling low in his throat, he says, "Clara, if you keep doing that, I'm going to take you to the other end of the hangar, spread you over the hood of my car, and rip that pretty summer dress off you."

"Oh, no. Please. *Anything* but that," I say, backing away in mock horror.

"And here I thought you were such a good actress . . ."

We laugh but the laughter between us is strained since I turned down his proposal. He's slipping away from me. I knew it would happen eventually, I just don't want it to happen so soon. "C'mon, Ace, let me take your mind off any jitters you may have about tomorrow."

"You're the only thing that's giving me the jitters, Clara."

I sigh. "I just don't know what you want."

"*Baloney.* You know exactly what I want. I want you to marry me."

Something darkly antagonistic in me forces me to shout. "You don't even know me!"

Turning to face me, Leo says, "I'm the only one in the world who *does* know you."

"You think marriage is going to be so perfect, Leo? You lost your parents when you were too young to know better, but mine are both still alive and I can tell you, marriage isn't perfect. Not perfect at all."

"I never said it would be perfect."

"Then how do you think it'll be? Me in an apron, cooking meals in your kitchen, tending a garden out back?"

In spite of my belligerence, Leo's tone is patient. "Clara, if I want a cook or a gardener, I'll hire one. Not that I object to the sight of you in an apron, but I know you'll spend your time in a studio or behind a camera. I *do* know you. I know exactly who and what you are."

"Well, maybe I don't. Maybe I don't know myself at all. Maybe I'm still figuring it all out. I'm still trying to figure out how to be in love with someone. How can you be so sure when I'm not?"

"I'm used to making snap decisions."

I believe him. "It's so fast. It's too soon. Why can't you just settle for what we have?"

"I told you before—I've never settled for anything in my life."

"Then don't settle for me."

Leo peers at me. "What do you mean by that?"

My throat is raw with the words as they scrape their way out. "I'm not good enough for you."

Leo throws a wrench down. "*Goddamn it*, Clara. How can you love yourself so little when I love you so much?"

His question sends a tremor through me and my voice comes from somewhere very far away—somewhere gray and quiet where the light comes in only from a window high above. "Every morning, I wake up with a knife against my throat, Leo. And I fight it. Every day of my life, I kick and punch and elbow my way past it. But sometimes I get tired. Some days, I don't think I'm going to be strong enough. Someday I'm going to *lose*."

I spit the last words out like a poison and they leave me nearly retching in their wake.

I expect to see that white-nosed fury again, that near-violent anger. Instead, Leo comes towards me, pulls me into his arms, and strokes my hair. When he speaks, it's a whisper. "On those days when you think you're not strong enough, I'll fight for you."

"You shouldn't have to. It's not fair."

"I gave up on thinking life was fair a long time ago. I don't want you to wake up every morning with a knife to your throat, Clara. I want you to wake up in my arms. Safe. Loved. Cherished. I'm not going to leave you."

Everything inside me rebels against the idea of letting myself be duped. "You don't know that. You can't know that."

He lifts my chin so that I can't look away. "Listen to me, Clara. As long as you have me, you don't have to fight anything alone ever again. I'm never going to leave you. Not by choice. Do you hear me?"

Blinking back tears, I nod. Then Leo kisses me. Soft and reassuring. Our lips meet in a soft sacred seal. The hunger, the poverty, the loneliness of trying to handle my mother's madness when my drunken father was nowhere to be found . . . all these memories rush at me like conspirators ready to snuff out this precious moment Leo and I share.

It takes everything in me to beat them back.

To my astonishment, he has me considering his proposal. Really considering it. "I'm not easy to live with, Leo. There's not a director I've ever worked with who didn't leave with a few gray hairs. I like things the way I like things. I'm used to getting my way. I'm a diva. We'd argue all the time."

"We already argue all the time, Clara. Sometimes it's even fun."

"It won't always be fun."

"Then it won't always be fun. And when it's not, you can console yourself with the shiny ring I bought you."

My breath screeches to a halt. "Y-you bought a ring?"

He gives me his devil-may-care look. "It's a real sparkler, too . . ."

"You're not teasing?"

"You like when I decide things for you. Well, I've decided that we're getting married." With that, he reaches into the pocket of his jacket and produces an engagement ring.

I cover my eyes too late. I've seen the glitter. The sparkles are still dancing behind my eyelids. The greedy girl inside me sighs with avarice. "Oh! Dear god, Leo, is that a diamond? It must be two carats!"

"More than that," he huffs. "But you can't have the ring until you agree to marry me."

The ring is as potent as any aphrodisiac. I want it. I'm tormented. "You know how to sweeten a deal . . ."

"There's my little gold digger. Maybe I should have started out with the diamond rather than making pretty speeches about love." His tone is slightly bitter, but when he sees me struggle with my greed, it makes him laugh deep in his belly. "Are you going to marry me?"

"I'll think about it," I say, tasting a sweet syrup on my tongue.

"Good enough for today, Clara. You can say no all the way to the altar, but eventually you're going to give in. On the other hand, if you say yes now, you can show the ring off at the airfield tomorrow."

My stomach knots at the realization that tomorrow is the day he's going to climb into that plane. Morgan Industries has arranged for a celebration for investors complete with canapés and champagne. "I wouldn't want to take away from your glory, Leo. After all, everyone will be there to watch you make history."

"One way or another," he says.

A chill goes down my spine. "See, that's the kind of talk that makes me know I shouldn't be there."

"I want you there, Clara. At least come give me a kiss. Every newspaper in the country will have a camera. Think of the scandal you can cause."

I feign outrage. "Do you think I need a war hero to get my picture taken?"

He chuckles. "If you do show up tomorrow, I'm going to kiss you right on the mouth. Hell, I might grope you in front of the reporters with Teddy Morgan standing right there, and I hope he chokes on it."

"You've won me, Ace. Can't you be gracious in victory?"

"I've only won a dogfight or two, Clara. Until you marry me, I'm still fighting the war."

Three outfits land at my feet before I decide on the right one to wear to the airfield. You'd think I'd be running late, but instead, I'm so nervous about Leo's flight, I'm dressed and ready hours too early. I tell the driver to circle the city while I try to calm myself. I don't want Leo to see me so nervous.

The driver is used to chauffeuring me around town. He knows all my usual haunts. Maybe that's why he pulls onto the street I've spent so many miserable hours. But today as Leo bravely faces death, the least I can do is face *her*.

"Stop the car," I say, thumping once on the back of the seat.

Today the dust dancing in the sunlight from the high windows of the sanitarium *does* look like a choir of tiny angels. "How are you feeling, Mama? Are you sleeping better?"

She reaches for me, her fingernails like talons in my arm. "Look at your red painted lips. Wipe that off. Don't you know that you're ruining yourself? No good man will ever have you."

Perhaps it is folly that drives me to argue with a madwoman. Or perhaps it is something infinitely more fragile than folly . . . it's hope. "Actually, a good man *has* asked me to marry him . . ."

My mother jolts with surprise, the hard lines of a difficult life softening on her face. "Oh, Clara. That's wonderful."

She can't know what I've said, can she?

"Who is your beau, Clara? Who is he?" I dare not be too optimistic, but she seems *happy*, and the talon grip on my arm turns into a motherly stroke. It's been such a long time since she's touched me that way, as if I weren't an abomination . . .

I can't remember the last time we've shared a moment of genuine connection, and that lures me to reveal more. "He's an . . . an engineer. He's smart and brave and kind."

"And he wants to *marry* you?" she asks, latching on to the present.

My lips wobble into a smile, unexpected joy spreading through my whole body. "He rather insists upon it."

"Well, we won't tell him," she says, conspiratorially. "We won't tell him about your past. He doesn't have to know what you've done, Clara."

With the joy inside me threatening to turn to vinegar, I lift my chin in defiance. "He knows, Mama."

She doesn't hear me and her voice becomes more urgent. "I won't tell him. He doesn't have to know what you are. And as long as he doesn't know, he can love you."

"He *knows*, Mama. And he *does* love me."

He really does, doesn't he? And that ought to be enough.

She looks through me to some other place. "Well, that's wonderful. Clara, that's just marvelous. And don't you worry. We'll change the color of your hair. We'll go somewhere people don't remember, so he doesn't have to be ashamed."

My scarred throat closes with regret.

I have nothing left to say.

CHAPTER

Twelve

It's a bright blue-skied day, but so windy I have to tie my hat on with a kerchief to keep it from blowing away.

Leo exaggerated when he said every newspaper in the country would have a photographer on hand, but it is a bit of an event. A few journalists cloister together by the hangar, and important investors and wealthy men sit on chairs under big white pavilions set up for just this occasion.

"Clara!" one of the reporters calls out. "Miss Cartwright, will you give us a pose?"

But today I'm one of them. My crew sets up and I take refuge behind a camera of my own.

Maybe this footage will end up in the movie Leo and I make together. Maybe it will just be my homage to the man I love. Either way, my eyes are all for him.

In a short double-breasted leather flying coat, a cap, and goggles strapped tight to his head, Leo is the very picture of an aviator. He exudes confidence beyond anything I've seen from him before. He's worked himself up for this, I realize. He's telling himself about all the Germans he shot down, convincing himself that he's the best.

That he's invincible.

I wish I believed it.

It takes him a moment to realize that I'm there. When he sees me, he grins. He strides from where the plane sits on the tarmac, pushing past my equipment to catch me up in his arms.

"You came," he says with a smile. "And you look like a goddamned movie star."

Then he kisses me. He kisses me, dipping me back so far that the wind catches my dress and exposes my legs. And I want him just as fiercely as the day I met him . . . if only I weren't so terrified. In my business, we say, break a leg, but I can picture that happening all too clearly, so I say, "Good luck up there."

"I don't need luck," Leo says with a wide grin, helping me find my footing again. "I just need you."

It's never been so hard to let him go. But I give such a brilliant smile that it ought to blind anyone to the dread that coils within me. Leo retreats to the plane and I retreat behind my camera.

As it turns out, the camera isn't defense enough. Brooke Gordon is on Teddy Morgan's arm and when she sees me, she seeks me out. "Oh, Clara," she whispers. "Please tell me you don't mind."

"I'm happy for you both," I say, with genuine affection. Teddy Morgan is a lonely man and Brooke will give him the attention he deserves. He'll treat her kindly. I have no cause to complain.

If anything, I'm enormously relieved.

Seeing us together, Big Teddy meanders over. I worry that it's going to be awkward, but he gives a booming laugh. "I take comfort in the fact that if I had to lose you to another man, at least I lost you to the man you're going to marry."

Good god, how many people did Leo tell about his proposal? "I think you have the wrong idea, Teddy."

"My daughter was in the jewelry shop the other morning when Leo Vanderberg went ring shopping."

With all the talent I've ever mustered for any film, I force myself to shrug. "You know I'm not the marrying kind . . . actually, I'm not much for exhibitions, either. The wind is awfully strong and I'm not feeling well. I don't think I can stay."

I have the crew pack up my camera. Leo will expect me to be here when he lands. He'll be furious if I'm not, and maybe that's what needs to happen.

"Miss Cartwright!"

Someone is calling my name, but I don't look back to see who it is. I keep walking from the airfield.

"Miss Cartwright, wait!"

I walk faster. I shouldn't have come. Reporters are here. Ex-lovers are here. All the people who know my shame. And the wind is howling like it was the morning my mother tried to slit my throat.

Someone grabs me and I whirl around, shocked to come face-to-face with Robert Aster. One look into his boyish face, and I think I'm going to cry. He is a reminder of everything in the world I should be ashamed of. A photographer snaps our picture and the flashbulb makes me see spots. No doubt the scandal sheets will spill a load of ink speculating on how many lovers I have and whether Robert Aster is one of them.

For the first time in my life, I actually mind.

"Miss Cartwright, it's good to see you," Robert says, his touch entirely too familiar.

Ignoring the absurdity of being called Miss Cartwright by a man who has taken every pleasure available from my body, I hold my hat against the wind and say, "You're being rather unchivalrous."

This seems to take him aback. "I haven't said anything out of line."

"You're thinking plenty!"

"I'm only thinking that I've acquired a passion for billiards . . ." When I don't smile at his joke, his grin fades away. "Whatever is the matter?"

"I can't stay. Please give Leo my regrets."

"You can't go. He's about to get into that plane . . ." The thought of it only makes it worse. To think of how many checklists Leo is going through now in preparation of climbing into that cockpit. "Is this about the proposal, Miss Cartwright?"

Apparently, Leo's told *everyone*. "It's a mistake. Better off forgotten."

I've wondered all along what kind of friend Robert Aster really was to Leo. Now I'm about to find out. "Why won't you marry him?"

"I have my reasons."

"Is it the money? He's got more squirreled away than you think."

"It isn't the money. Truth is, I have plenty of money. It's just that when you're a poor kid, you think you can never have enough." It's time I grew up. Glancing back over my shoulder at the gaggle of reporters watching us, I say, "Mr. Aster, it doesn't trouble me when newspapers write about my affairs. I'm a vamp. It's my reputation. I fostered it. And it doesn't hurt Leo as long as everyone thinks that he's just the man I'm bedding. It only adds to his mystique. He's the sexy war hero who seduced the silent screen siren. But if we get married, he'll be the sucker. The dupe. The cuckold."

The ambassador's son—a young man trained to political realities—understands this in a way that Leo probably never will. "I see . . . but you must know that Leo doesn't care about that kind of thing."

"Then it's up to the people who love him to care about it for him."

Robert folds his arms over his neatly tailored suit. "I'm not sure I understand."

"I'm not much of a hero, Mr. Aster. I've never fought in a war. I'm not like other women; I'm selfish and vain and greedy. But I can protect the man I love by saying no. And I'm not very good at saying no, so you can imagine what it costs me. Will you help me convince him to let go of this idea to marry me?"

"I'll do my best," Robert says.

So it's done then. I should be relieved, but I'm suddenly so tired. Sapped of all my pep.

"There's just one thing you ought to know," Robert says. "He won't give up on the idea no matter what I have to say about it." When I start to protest, Robert shushes me with an affable shake of his head. "I've known him a long time. You can tell him that a car won't go as fast as he thinks it will. You can tell him that a plane won't get off the ground. You can tell him he's not going to make it out of a dogfight when he's outgunned. The only thing he's going to believe is that *he* can make the car go that fast. He'll believe *he* can get that plane off the ground. He'll believe *he* can win that dogfight. He'll believe whatever he needs to believe to accomplish something no one else can."

"So you're saying if you tell him not to marry me, it will only make him want to do it more."

"I'm saying it doesn't *matter* what anyone tells him. You say you're not like other women. Well, he's not like other men. He doesn't get up in the morning and worry about catching the morning train or what his boss is going to think about his new suit. He wakes up and thinks about how to strap himself onto an engine and change everything we think we know about the world."

Robert Aster is a persuasive man, and I feel myself getting turned inside out. I glance over my shoulder at the plane on the airstrip. That hunk of junk doesn't look as if it will ever get off the ground, and the reality of it hits me.

I've been fretting about playing pretend, gossip, and scandal. The concerns of Hollywood. I've been worrying about all the things my mother, the madwoman, thinks I should be worried about. Maybe I just haven't wanted to face the truth about how scared I am. There's a thousand *real* ways I can lose Leo. He's going up in a real plane—not some Hollywood invention. He's climbing into an untried machine with a fuel tank that can kill him. With wings that can fall off. With bolts that can come loose.

He *knows* how dangerous it is. He just does it anyway.

Robert catches my eye. "In the war, he never flew with a parachute, you know. He thought he was better off without."

"He told me."

"Well, he was wrong. He needs a parachute, Clara. He *needs* you."

The words flatten me and my heart begins to pound. "Oh . . . oh, my."

"He used to volunteer for the hazardous duties. He said he should go, because nobody was waiting back home for him. Don't you see, Clara? When he asked you to marry him, he was asking you to be the one he comes back for."

I go to stone. Then I fracture. For a moment, I even miss my step and Robert has to catch me by the elbow. My hand goes over my mouth and I shake my head. "Oh, have I been a fool?"

"I'm afraid so," Robert says. "But I admire it a little."

"Leo!" I cry. He's already got one foot in the cockpit, but he hears me even over the roar of the wind and turns his head. He sees me and gives a little wave. "Leo wait!"

I run to him. My hat slows me down, so I let the wind take it and it floats up and away. The crowd turns to watch me race down the runway toward the plane and a few of the mechanics even try to stop me, but I'm too fast for them. "Leo!"

He climbs out and jumps down from the plane, taking a few purposeful strides towards me. I'm running so fast that I crash into his chest and he grabs me by both arms. "Clara, what the devil are you doing?"

"Marry me!" I shout over the wind.

"What?"

"Leo Vanderberg, will you marry me?"

He pulls the goggles back over his head, looking vexed. "Clara, I've already proposed to you. All you have to do is say yes."

"I'm sorry. I don't know how to do this. I never expected to be anyone's wife. It's no excuse but I love you so much that I was too afraid to say yes."

He gives me a cocky grin. "Are you still afraid?"

"Of course I am." But if Leo has taught me anything it's that you have to take the risk to accomplish something wonderful. I want something wonderful. I want him forever. And that certainty stiffens my spine. "I'm terrified, but I'm going to do it anyway. I think it might just be glorious."

Leo grins. "It's already done, Clara, whether you know it or not. The moment I told you that I was keeping your film—that I'd keep it the rest of my life and yours—we made a lifelong commitment. The rest is just a formality."

I blink and some of the terror *does* fade away. It seemed different with him than with anyone else from that moment. Maybe we've been married all along, which makes me feel like even more of a fool for saying no. "You told me that you'd always own a little piece of me, Leo. I just didn't know it was going to be my heart."

"Say yes, Clara."

The sun on my face feels like God's blessing, and I find myself beaming up at him. "Yes, Leo. Yes, I'll marry you. Yes, to anything. Yes, to everything."

With a smug smile, he takes off one of his leather gloves, reaching into his jacket for the ring that flashes so brilliant it nearly blinds me.

I gasp. "You just *happened* to have an engagement ring in your jacket?"

Leo laughs. "I knew you were going to say yes eventually, so I wasn't taking any chances."

He slips the golden band over my finger. A perfect fit. It's a dazzling rock, round and brilliant. Showy as a star. A squeal escapes my lips before I can stop it, and I find myself hopping on my toes with joy. "Is that it? Are we engaged? I've never done this before . . ."

"I've never done it, either."

I clasp him against me. "Then how do we know we're doing it right?"

"Oh, I think we're probably doing it right."

He dips his head and kisses me hard.

Leo climbs into the plane, situating himself in the cockpit. He gives a wave to the crowd, then starts the engine. When the plane rolls forward, everyone applauds. The plane rattles when it takes off. It stutters in the air, then glides up and up and away. I hold my breath as Leo takes that plane and pushes it as hard as it will go. He climbs with it, straight up. An impossible angle and as the machine gets tinier in the air, I know what he's doing. He's attempting an Immelmann turn and I have to stuff my fist in my mouth to keep from screaming when we all hear the engine cut out.

The whole world freezes. Then the plane literally falls from the sky.

I don't know how he does it; I don't know how he gets control of it again. But the engine fires again, and we see him hurtle off in a new and unexpected direction. We cheer for him. Grown men jump up and down, while the women throw their hats. I clutch my hand against my heart as Leo changes aviation history.

And then he comes back to me.

CHAPTER

Thirteen

It isn't always perfect.

We argue on set because Leo is always fiddling with the machinery when we're losing valuable light. Sometimes we argue about foolish things like whether or not engineering plans are suitable artwork for the bedroom. But every morning I wake up next to my husband loving him more than the day before and wondering how that is even possible.

Every morning, the warmth of his smile lifts my spirits the whole day long. At breakfast, I like the lazy lurid slide of his eyes over my body as I serve his eggs and pour his coffee. Some Sunday afternoons we spend the whole afternoon in bed with the paper. On Sunday evenings, we have dinner with Pops—who has been surprisingly sober since the day he gave me away in marriage at the chapel.

And though Leo refuses to speak my mother's name, he saves the crossword puzzles so I can take them on my visits.

The first time the scandal sheets call him Mr. Cartwright, Leo *does* fuck me so hard that I *do* consider changing my stage name. But it feels so good I secretly hope it will happen again.

He never lets me near the stag film. He never even tells me where he keeps it. We watch it sometimes, together. Sometimes with Robert Aster. Somehow, it always disappears before I can think to destroy it.

In this, and in everything, Leo keeps his promises to me.

We fuck, we make love, we play bedroom games the rules of which are known only to us. We're a couple of fools in love. And we're happy. We're madly, *deliriously* happy.

My husband, after all, is a man who can change everything we think we know about the world.

let's misbehave

PROLOGUE

Robert

My lover coaxes the last shudders of orgasm from me, then rolls off my body into the waiting arms of her husband. Mewling with pleasure, she buries her face in the dark hair of his naked chest while his fingers lovingly trail down the pretty line of her spine. She kisses him with aching tenderness and he strokes her with lusty approval. Meanwhile, I pant from our exertions, my pleasure ebbing, my arms empty.

It's always like this afterwards.

I'm usually aroused by the sight of them together. The rough way he grabs her hips and shoves her back to the mattress as if to reclaim her when I'm finished. It's as reassuring as it is erotic to watch. His steely arms locked tight around the curves of her voluptuous body. The sheen of perspiration that glistens on the pale insides of her thighs when she spreads them for him in eager welcome.

These heated visuals often awaken me, stiffening me for an extended performance, but this evening I'm strangely dispirited by the fact that she's crawled to him and left me covered in cooling sweat.

The jazz playing on the phonograph has begun to skip. I can just reach the cabinet from my side of the bed, so I fix the needle while wondering what accounts for my lack of satisfaction. Perhaps it's that despite the many times and the many depraved ways in which I've enjoyed the famous movie-star body of Clara Cartwright, we rarely touch.

By this, I don't mean to say that I haven't explored every inch of her velvety skin. I don't even mean to say that she hasn't caressed me or scraped her nails up my back, nor dragged her lips down my body to engulf my cock between her lips. We've done all those things and she's given me thrilling pleasure. What I *do* mean to say is that when Clara touches me, I suspect that she's really touching her husband.

I'm an extra arm, leg, or other limb she caresses to heighten the experience.

For that matter, Leo and I touch only incidentally when sharing her body. I've felt him moving inside her when we've trapped Clara between us. Sometimes our legs brush or our hands tangle in her hair at the same instant. This is as much contact as either of us would desire. The male form holds no allure for me, but the Great War brought Leo and me together in ways that go beyond flesh. And sharing Clara has only deepened that bond.

There's a camaraderie in what we do to her—how we taunt her, tease her, force whimpers from her that are at once desperate and seductive. Given how we are made, sharing his wife is the only way in which Leo and I can enjoy an intimate sexual act together.

She is the conduit between us and yet, she remains slightly beyond my reach.

It has never bothered me before, but it does tonight.

Maybe it's the way they kiss. Full-mouthed, passionate kisses, laden with secret meanings to which I am not privy. They are staring into each other's eyes, breathing each other in, and instead of sinking back down into the tangle of sheets to join them in their marital bed, I reach for a deck of cigarettes thrown casually upon the night-stand.

Normally, I prefer the Gitane brand, with its bite of dark tobacco, but tonight I content myself with Clara's Lucky Strikes. When Leo sees me light up, he taps Clara's nose in admonishment. "You've tired him out already."

She turns to face me, the flush on her neck drawing the eye down to the swell of her magnificent breasts. They seem *especially* magnificent tonight, and I'm aroused by the way her nipples darken and peak under my gaze. I want her . . . but then, every man does. She's a Hollywood legend. It's half the thrill of bedding her. Unfortunately, my mysterious malaise triumphs over my ardor. "It's only that I rather feel as if I'm intruding."

Clara bats her eyelashes at me. "But I enjoy when you intrude, Mr. Aster."

She and I play at formality with each other; it intensifies the arousal to pretend we're strangers, but the game has quite suddenly lost its charm. I suck in a deep lungful of smoke and try not to scowl at the unfamiliar taste. An entire wall of their modest bedroom is dedicated to framed photographs of Leo's planes—those we flew together in the war and those he's flown since. I'm present in many of those photographs, but as Clara adds her feminine touches to this room, I assume there will be less and less space for me.

Clara draws herself up. "Is something wrong?"

"No, of course not," I say.

Unfortunately, Clara is rather an expert at reading emotions. "Liar. Poor Robert. Have I left you feeling debauched and ill used?"

Leo barks with laughter, and in spite of myself, I laugh, too. Pressing a relatively chaste kiss to the corner of her mouth, I say, "I'm afraid I feel positively defiled."

She strokes my cheek. "Come on then, out with it. What's the matter?"

"Is it your father again?" Leo asks.

The thought of my father makes my mood even darker. "No. The ambassador is still harping on me to come home and either campaign for political office or run the family hotel, so there's nothing new in that regard."

"Tell him to go straight to hell," Leo says, nuzzling his wife's hair. "If you go back East, you'll end up drinking yourself into an early grave."

"I'm sure my father would prefer that to the alternative of my living a long and colorful life as a dissolute playboy."

"If the trouble isn't your father then it must be a woman," Clara announces with a note of triumph.

"It's nothing," I insist, unwilling to put a damper on the occasion. It's clear from the way Leo fondles his wife that his sexual interest hasn't cooled, and I shouldn't like to spoil it for them. But Leo is patient. I've always been prouder of the athleticism I bring to the bedroom than any careful seductive calculation, but given Leo's example, I've begun to reconsider. As it happens, Leo is older than either of us, and I like to think it's his age and experience that renders him capable of amazing feats of patience both in the bedroom and out of it.

It gives me hope that in a few more years, I might be able to modestly impress someone with something more than my physical talents. Maybe even myself.

Leo watches the thin trail of smoke escape my lips. "You might as well tell us; Clara won't be of any use to me until you've satisfied her curiosity. What's happened?"

I yank the bedsheet, covering myself from waist down as heat prickles my face. I find the matter painfully embarrassing. "It's only that I saw Nora Richardson today."

"That damned woman," Leo grumbles. He's a good friend; he's never met my former fiancée, but that doesn't stop him from having the utmost antipathy for her on my behalf.

Clara is more circumspect. She steals the cigarette from between my fingers and inhales. "I thought the Richardsons moved away."

"They only went on holiday." I don't take the cigarette back from Clara; I'm rather certain that I need something quite a bit stronger for this conversation. "Are you dry? I'm feeling a bit parched."

"You're a boozehound, as bad as Pops," Clara accuses. "We've got a stash. Will cognac do?"

"I'll get it," Leo says, heaving himself up, but Clara lays her hand on his shoulder, as if to display her half-moon manicured fingernails, all lacquered in black and white.

"Let me be a good little wife for a change, Ace. I'll get you both a glass. With ice."

As she rises from the bed, both of us watch her go. There's a reason she's a movie star; when she's in a room, you can't pull your eyes away—especially when she's as gloriously flushed and fleshy as she is now, swaying those ample hips of hers with every step.

Upon her departure, I raise an eyebrow at Clara's uncharacteristic burst of domesticity.

Leo grins. "She'll make any excuse to parade around naked."

I've no doubt of that, but in this case, I suspect Clara intended to leave us alone. Leo must suspect the same, because he eventually asks, "Where the devil did you run into Nora Richardson?"

"On the street, if you can believe it," I say, clenching my teeth against the memory and violently shoving Clara's lacy pillow under my arm. Given my former fiancée's gaiety, I may not have recognized her beneath that elegant hat today. The woman I intended to marry might have passed by me on the street without my having recognized her at all, but she was walking some horrible little dog on the end of a leash that got tangled round my leg. That's when I had the shock of looking up to see her swollen belly. "Nora is pregnant, you know."

"Pregnant?" Leo stares at me for a moment. Then he reaches for his drawers and pulls them on as if this revelation has ruined all his plans for the evening. The expression on his face is disapproving. "I see."

I don't know whether to laugh or punch him in the mouth. "It's not mine, if that's what you're thinking."

"You're sure?"

"I'm as certain as a man can be about that fact," I reply, more irritated by the moment.

"Her husband's baby, then?"

"Yes." I hate to admit it, but I sense that every time I acknowledge reality it will help me put my past firmly behind me. "She tells me that she's very happy with him. That she's happier than she's ever been in her life. And if she was lying, she's a better actress than Clara."

"No one is a better actress than Clara," Leo replies, a touch defensively.

As if summoned by her name, Clara returns with two crystal tumblers full of ice and liquor. She hands me my drink, then sashays to Leo's side so they can sip from the same glass. He pulls her into his lap and though they're a comfortable tangle of limbs, they both turn to me, attentive.

In this moment, it strikes me that they're both offering the kind of intimacy I craved, so why am I so reluctant to share my woes? "It's really of no consequence. Or at least it *should* be of no consequence to me. I'm not even in love with Nora anymore . . ."

"Robert, I had no idea you were so sentimental," Clara says, reaching to smooth my hair. "Whatever did this woman do to you?"

"She broke our engagement," I say, hoping to prevent Leo from offering his less diplomatic assessment.

In that endeavor, I fail utterly.

"She skated around," Leo seethes. "She got knocked up by one of her father's drivers and married the chap."

Clara is instantly and powerfully infuriated on my behalf, those expressive eyes of hers narrowing to dangerous little slits. "She did that to you, Robert? Why, the next time I see her, I'll blister her ears good."

"Just let me be there to see it," Leo says, kissing the top of her head with an audible smooch.

I cringe at the idea of my favorite brassy starlet accosting my pregnant ex-fiancée on the street. "I'd really rather you didn't cause a fuss, Clara. Not on my account."

"I'll do it for my own reasons. She caused all that trouble the night I met Leo. The next morning all anyone could talk about was the brawl and sex show on the desk—nobody was talking about my movie."

"The brawl was my fault." It's easier to admit in the presence of friends who are willing to defend my behavior, no matter how abominable. "I should've known better; the bastard took it out on her. I think he struck her that night. In fact, I'm sure of it. It kills me to think I gave him an excuse—"

"There's no excuse for that," Leo insists.

"What a *beastly* man," Clara adds, hugging closer to her husband.

"Do you know she claims she wanted him to do it?" I blurt out, because I'm still bedeviled by the remark.

When Leo grinds his teeth and Clara's eyes bug out a little bit, I've never been sorrier to have broached a subject in my life. Usually, one or the other of them fills a silence with laughter or witty banter. This time, neither of them rescue me from myself. I take a swallow of the cognac. It isn't top-shelf, but it does the job. "We argued today. I think her husband is a brute—I think that he knocks her around. But she says he never lays a hand on her without her say-so. That it's some kind of bedroom game between the two of them."

Leo looks dubious. He's likely to dismiss anything Nora—Mrs. Richardson, I remind myself—has to say about anything. It's Clara who knits her brow in careful consideration, and perhaps a bit of sympathy for Nora's point of view. "And what sort of bedroom games did you two used to play?"

"None. She was a virgin—at least, I thought she was—and as I intended to marry her . . ." Clara blinks in surprise, which rather offends me. "All appearances to the contrary, Mrs. Vanderberg, I *am* a gentleman."

Fortunately, Clara never worries about offending me. "Well, there's your problem. It doesn't sound as if she wanted a gentleman."

"No, I don't suppose she did." I swirl the liquor around in my glass, watching the ice melt. Clara hasn't said anything that I haven't said to myself before. I wonder if I've had the wrong idea about women all along.

"Her loss is our gain, isn't it?" she asks, turning to glance at Leo.

Clara and Leo stare at each other, some manner of wordless discussion transpiring between them, and when she turns back to me, she drags both their hands atop mine. It's a tender gesture and when I look into her eyes, then at Leo's face, I see an opportunity present that has not been there before.

A tentative invitation.

A subtle shift between them as if to make room for me.

It is a humbling thing. A thing that a better, braver man would seize. But I have no idea how to cross the space that separates us and find a way to fit into their lives. I'm not like Clara or Leo, both of whom do whatever they like with complete disregard for public opinion. They're splendid immortals who break and bend rules to suit them at their whim.

But as it happens, I am altogether too mortal.

CHAPTER
One

Sophie

"Now, Miss Sophie, you don't wanna be starting trouble 'round here, do ya?" Hamilton asks me, removing his bellboy cap to scratch the wooly curls at his aged brow.

"Oh, horsefeathers!" I thread the posy I grabbed from the garden outside into his buttonhole so he'll look dapper.

I can see that I make him nervous, but then again, I make most people nervous.

Anybody who wants to change things usually does.

"I'm not trying to cause any trouble, Hamilton; I'm just trying to improve things around here."

Hamilton looks over his shoulder, a little bit relieved that the hotel's elegant breezeway is empty and no one is waiting for the elevators who might overhear us. "I dunno, Miss Sophie. Maybe things'll git better with the new management."

By *new management* I suppose he means young Mr. Aster, the prodigal son, returned to the city to take over for his father, the cranky old Robber Baron who somehow bribed a few corrupt officials to make him an ambassador to China. Young Mr. Aster is rumored to be a shiftless wastrel who will assuredly run the Aster Hotel into the ground and as far as I'm concerned, it's already halfway there. "He's not *new* management. He's been here *six months* and things haven't changed a bit."

Well, that isn't entirely true. They just haven't changed for the better. Whereas the ambassador arrived each morning at precisely eight o'clock, doffing his top hat to important guests and scowling at everyone else, his son usually stumbles into the lobby after carousing all evening, then sleeps in late as a lollygagger.

Of course, every girl in the hotel strains her neck trying to get a glimpse of the new boss, whether he's sober or stumbling drunk and unshaven. This is because the younger Mr. Aster has a bedazzling smile. Even *I* find his dimples disarming. One morning, he made a wrong turn into the boutique and grinned with such wattage that I nearly stumbled blind into the counter.

But I've got my senses about me now, so I show Hamilton where to sign.

"You heard what happened to Gertrude, didn't you?" I mimic the harsh nasal tone of Mrs. Mortimer. "'We won't tolerate immoral women who flaunt their depraved and wicked behavior.' That's what she said before giving Gertie the sack. And we both know Gertie didn't make a baby all by herself."

Hamilton ignores my petition to stoop down to haul luggage onto the shiny brass cart. He's done this job half his life, but at his age, it's getting harder for him to manage the parcels. He won't accept help if I offer, though, so I wait until his back is turned to drag the heaviest trunk closer. Suppressing an unladylike grunt, I use my free hand to give the iron-banded chest a good yank trying not to slip and slide on the marble floor in my heels. I keep arguing all the while. "It isn't right to fire Gertie for something that isn't anybody's business."

"I'm awful sorry about Miss Gertie," Hamilton admits, "Still, it ain't right for folks like us to be running 'round with petitions and starting a fuss. You're a smarty, you are. Always got your nose in a book or writing in one. But can't you ever behave like other girls your age, Miss Sophie?"

"I do!" I protest. "Other girls . . . like books."

Of course, I have to fight a blush, because the book I intend to spend the evening with is my own private diary, in which I write wild, untamed thoughts that have nothing to do with being a smarty . . .

"You should let a fella take you to see the latest Clara Cartwright film."

Oh, cruel *temptation*! Miss Cartwright is my favorite movie star. Something about her confidence just makes me want to sing. But I can't let Hamilton distract me from the task at hand. "I'll go when I can afford it, and *not* with a fella, thank you very much, because I can pay my own way. Of course, I could pay my own way a good deal more often if there were fair wages around here. What about you, Hamilton? You make three dollars a week less than every white bellhop and now they're shaving off another because of your age."

Hamilton frowns. "I don't load the luggage as fast as I used to, Miss Sophie."

"But you've still got to load them, don't you? And I've never seen you take a day off work, not in all the time I've been here."

Hamilton gives a rueful smile. "You're gonna git yourself fired if you keep on, but you sure is a girl with gumption."

"What a very nice compliment," I say, pressing the pen into his gloved hand. "If you promise to keep it quiet, I'll leave this petition with you to think over. We've got somebody from every department except for the bellboys. If we all speak with one voice, the big shot will have to listen."

The next morning, Mrs. Mortimer tells me to report to the boss, and my heart sinks. So this is it. I'm getting the sack. And even the supercilious elevator operator knows it. "You couldn't leave well enough alone, could you, Miss O'Brien?" he asks, shutting the elegant doors carved with the Aster family crest, then pulling the grate closed behind me like a prison door.

I clench my pocketbook in my hands. "At least I'm trying to keep food on the table for your child, Mr. Underwood. You oughtta thank me."

He stiffens at my frankness. "There's no way to know the baby is mine."

I can't imagine how Gertie could have lost her head over such a man because I hate him all the way from the tilt of his cap to the rows of shiny buttons on his uniform. "You know bloody well whose baby it is and if you'd only used precautions, like I told you both to do—"

"Well, it's all spilt milk now, isn't it, young lady?" he asks, cheeks ruddier than usual as he works the manual controls that take us to the top of Aster Tower. "Gertrude's out of a job, you're about to be out of a job, and given the mischief you're making around here for Mr. Aster, you'll likely take a few of the staff with you."

Mr. Aster. The reminder of the playboy millionaire who holds my fate in his hands makes my knees shake. I should take a seat on the posh velvet bench or steady myself against the brass handrails, because if I lose my balance and crack my head open on the marble tiles, the pretty bastard is likely to charge me a fee to clean up my blood from the floor.

At the thought, I hold my chin up high, because I'm going to give the man an earful before I go.

In fact, I walk into his office spoiling for a fight.

Gallingly, Mr. Aster welcomes me with a bright smile, as if summoning me like a naughty schoolgirl is the highlight of his day.

He's a big man; you don't realize it at first, because everything about the Aster Hotel is big, too, and this office is no exception. He's dwarfed by the giant Art Deco sunburst on the wall, wrought in polished brass. And sitting behind the massive walnut desk with its curved, geometric legs, his broad shoulders are effectively masked. If I don't think about it too much—his size, his wealth, and the fact that he has all the power here—I might be able to stop my knees from knocking. I remind myself that he's nothing to admire or fear; just a callow capitalist who stiffs bellboys of their hard-earned wages and puts pregnant shopgirls out onto the street.

"Good morning, Miss O'Brien," he says. "Please have a seat."

I sink down onto the oversized chair in front of his desk, straightening my dress over my knees and removing my cloche hat as Mrs. Mortimer didn't even give me the chance to take it off this morning before sending me upstairs.

With blond hair slicked straight back, an aristocratic nose covered with freckles, and long lashes that frame hazel eyes, Robert Aster is something to look at. I'll give him that. Then again, it's always the people who are blessed with an abundance of everything who never seem to worry about taking what little the rest of us have got.

"Miss O'Brien," he begins. "How long have you been working here?"

"Two years, sir."

We both know what's coming and I wish he'd just get on with it.

"Has Mrs. Mortimer been your supervisor all that time?"

"No, she was promoted just a few months before you came to work here . . . and the pinch-mouthed harpy has been lording it over the rest of us ever since."

There. That ought to move things along.

To my surprise, he laughs. "You're very young, aren't you?"

He must be almost thirty years old, but I won't have him thinking he can treat me like a child. I sit straighter, so that my spine doesn't touch the chair. "I'm twenty-one."

"And not a day over, I'd guess. As it happens, there's been some discontent amongst the employees of the hotel. Some whispers of an organized protest. It was brought to Mrs. Mortimer's attention that you might be one of the *agitators*."

The way he says it, with such an air of amusement, gets my dander up—as if a fair Irish lass could never have thoughts in her head beyond the frilly things in the boutique. But before I can make a sharp retort, he sets a number of items on the desk where I can see them. Pamphlets from the Civics League, the Humanist Society, and the Birth Control Federation. A few flyers for talks that I wanted to attend in the coming weeks. My books. And, most incriminating of all, the leather-bound journal of my secret thoughts.

"You ransacked my locker?" How naive I was to think ordinary courtesy might shield me from the ruthless types like him, men who own half the city.

"*I* didn't, no," he says, quickly. "Mrs. Mortimer took it upon herself to go through your belongings looking for evidence of suspicious activity."

A flash of temper overtakes me, and I cross my arms over myself. "She had no right. I keep a change of clothes in my locker, too, and ladies' undergarments and a few nickels for fare. I've a right to some privacy and security, don't I?"

Mimicking my posture, Mr. Aster pretends to consider the merits of my argument. "I don't suppose you hold with the notion that the locker room is in my hotel and only afforded to you by courtesy, therefore you ought not use it to store anything you'd be distressed for someone else to find?"

"No, I don't hold with that notion at all."

He picks up one of my books and glances at the spine. "Upton Sinclair. I keep meaning to read this . . ." Then his eyes drift back to me and he pushes the birth control pamphlets my way. "Do you know that two nurses and a doctor were recently arrested for distributing similar information?"

I tilt my chin defiantly. "I do and it's unjust, if you ask me."

"So, I take it that you feel married persons are perfectly free to take their pleasure from one another without fear of consequence."

I'm surprised, and a little delighted at the freedom of knowing I'm going to get the ax. I won't know where my next meal is coming from, but at least I'll know I spoke my mind. "I *do* think married persons ought to be free to take their pleasure from one another without fear of consequence . . . and unmarried persons, too, if it comes to it."

He flashes me a smile as shiny as new silver coins from the mint. "You're a rather liberated young lady, aren't you? One of the *new women* we keep hearing so much about?"

His implication makes me swallow hard. He thinks he knows what kind of girl I am, but he's got the wrong idea. On the other hand, the way he's looking at me makes my toes curl, so maybe his idea isn't so far off the mark. "I just don't think anyone should be ignorant of such matters."

"So you have the pamphlets for the sake of intellectual curiosity, of course . . ."

The pamphlets were for Gertrude—not that she took them. She'd believed that preparing herself, making a decision about what might happen with her lover, would turn her into a fallen woman. But it wasn't the pamphlets that got her into trouble.

It was the elevator operator.

And in spite of the trouble she's in, I admit, I envy her a little. Taking a lover is sophisticated and modern, but I don't have Gertie's looks and I've always been too practical to get that carried away . . .

Mr. Aster tilts his head, apparently amused at my silence. "The notion of men and women in sexual congress for the sake of recreation doesn't offend you?"

Why won't he just get on with it and fire me?

"I don't see why it should offend anyone, what two people do behind closed doors. Certainly, it ought not be the cause of a dismissal—"

"What about more than two people?"

"Pardon me?"

His gaze intensifies. "What about sexual recreation between more than two people?"

The thought intrigues me as much as it scandalizes me. Does he *mean* to shock me or is that genuine curiosity? No, he must be trying to knock me off balance. I'm being toyed about like a mouse in the paws of a cat, but I don't intend to squeak.

He sighs at my silence, as if it disappoints him. "Miss O'Brien, I've concluded that you're some sort of *radical* stirring up trouble in my hotel."

"And I suppose you expect me to deny it, do you?"

There's a bit of a twinkle in his eye as he leans towards me. "Oh, no. I'd never encourage anyone to lie. Besides, I admire unconventional women."

I can't imagine that's true; if it were, he'd be a much different sort of man, wouldn't he? Even so, I have to shake away my potent desire to believe that the look I see in his eyes *is* admiration. "Then what is it that you want me to say? That your workers are all merry and without complaint? Because we aren't. We have a right to bargain for better treatment and we've written up a list of complaints—"

He holds up a hand to silence me. "That's a discussion for another day. The truth is, Miss O'Brien, I called you here to discuss your journal."

He reaches for the leather-bound book that belongs to me, then absently thumbs through the pages. It's too much. My Irish temper can sustain me through a great deal, but not this. The scribblings and fantasies are so deeply private that I lose my nerve completely. "What makes you think that's my journal?"

Mr. Aster raises a perfectly groomed brow. "It isn't yours?"

It's more mine than anything else in this world; it's filled with dreams and forbidden thoughts. It's the only place I give voice to my secret self. And it ought to have remained a secret. That's why I have to lie. "No. It's not mine."

His expression tells me that he doesn't believe me. "What an *enormous* disappointment . . . May I ask to whom it belongs?"

The problem with telling lies is that once you start, you have to keep on telling them. "It belongs to a friend, but don't ask her name because I won't say."

"Then how can I return it to her?"

"I'll return it," I say, eagerly extending my hand.

But he shows no sign of being willing to relinquish the journal. "I'm afraid I can't let you have it. You see, I assumed it might contain the names of other dissatisfied employees but I found matters of a much more personal nature inside."

My stomach falls away. So, he's read it. There's no question of that now. The idea that a man—any man, but especially this man—has read thoughts and feelings that I scarcely admit to myself makes me feel as if I've been stripped naked. He has a window into my soul and there's nowhere to hide.

Mr. Aster stares straight at me. "The author of this journal is a lively writer with a certain creative genius; her stories are so intriguing that I want very much to meet the woman behind these words, so please tell your friend that I have her journal and she may retrieve it at her earliest convenience."

He's going to keep the journal, the bloody bastard. He knows it's mine but he's keeping it!

As if unaware of my distress, he says, "That will be all, Miss O'Brien. I'll reprimand your supervisor for her zealotry in this matter and have your things returned."

I blink so hard my lashes tangle. "You're not giving me the sack?"

A sardonic expression touches his features. "I should, shouldn't I? But I'm told that you keep the company of scientists and socialists and intellectuals. It would infuriate my father to know we employ such free-thinking girls. And infuriating my father is a sport at which I greatly excel, so as far as I'm concerned, you still have a job here at the Aster Hotel."

My relief at having slipped the noose is palpable. I want to shoot up out of my chair and bolt for the door. However, to do so would be to abandon my journal entirely . . .

I can't seem to go. He watches me and I can't look away.

We stare and stare until he breaks into a bright dimpled smile.

He's got no right to go around smiling at girls like that. It's the kind of smile that could blind a woman to all good sense. I can't imagine that Mr. Underwood ever smiled at Gertie that way but if he did, I begin to see how she stumbled.

In fact, Mr. Aster's smile is so keen that I have to fight one of my own and when one of the corners of my mouth quirks up without my permission, he seems encouraged. "One more thing, Miss O'Brien, if you'd be so kind . . . I need a bit of advice. I'm afraid that the journal inspired me to a reckless act. My father says that I'm always most reckless when it's likely to do me the least advantage. In this case, I'm inclined to agree, but I really couldn't help myself."

Now that sounds ominous. "What did you do?"

"I was inspired to buy a gift for the woman who wrote this journal. Now I realize you're not that woman . . . I'm quite embarrassed, really." He doesn't look *at all* embarrassed, but I'm feeling noticeably warm and I've the sneaking suspicion that he's mocking me. "I wondered if you might take a look at the gift and tell me if your friend would appreciate it."

I feel a pang of jealousy for my imaginary friend when he produces a white box topped with a bow. I know better, but curiosity gets the better of me. I pull the end of the ribbon off, lift the lid, and carefully open the tissue paper to reveal a silk crepe chemise step-in with lace insets and a red rose boutonniere sewn into the bodice. The peach-colored lingerie is more beautiful than anything we have in the boutique, and I can't help but marvel at the ribbons sewn into the garment and the intricate beauty of the lace. But it's also such an inappropriate gift that a blush crawls up my neck and burns all the way to my ears. "You're a very presumptuous man."

He chuckles. "So I've been told. It's a rather close reproduction of a garment described in this journal, don't you think?"

My temper runs hot. "Just because a woman writes a fantasy in a journal doesn't mean she wants it to come true."

"Naturally," he says, leaning back in a posture of thoughtfulness, fingers laced and thumbs tapping together. "Especially in this case, as many of the imagined couplings in the diary aren't even possible."

This time I'm *sure* he's mocking me. "And just what do you mean by that?"

He lowers his voice to a seductive tone to boast, "In my experience—and in these matters, my experience is considerable—the laws of physics and human anatomy would seem to preclude some of the more adventurous positioning described."

A new blush burns right over the first one. His experience in these matters might be considerable, but mine is limited. And I'm more than a bit mortified. If only the carpet would swallow me up like the sea, I might welcome it. I try to disguise my little panicked breaths, but the rapid rise and fall of my chest must give my panic away.

"Miss O'Brien, I apologize for making you uncomfortable. Sometimes there's a fine line between seducing a woman and frightening her. It's a line I never want to cross . . ."

The casual admission of his intentions—and his regrets—astonishes me. Why, he's *insufferable*. That's what he is. "You're trying to seduce me, sir?"

His eyes twinkle. "I'm trying to seduce the author of this journal; she isn't as timid as you are."

"I'm not *timid*," I protest, with a toss of my head. "I'm just stunned at your nerve. I believe a person might find pleasure in thinking about things she might never actually want to talk about . . . or do."

"Quite right. But do you think it's likely that a woman might not want to do *any* of the things she imagines?"

We appear to be having a philosophical argument and every word we say is like a thread weaving us closer together. As much as I want to escape his dangerous web, I feel myself drawn closer. "This lacy garment isn't the kind of gift an unmarried gentleman gives to an unmarried lady."

"Right you are. It's the kind of gift that a married gentleman gives to his mistress. But as I'm both unmarried and endeavoring to be less of a gentleman, I hope this gift might signal my willingness to help you experience some of your fantasies."

I hear myself gulp. How many times in a girl's life does she hear an offer like that one? Not many, I think. And in spite of my sweating palms, my nervous little breaths, and my general sense of outrage, temptation tugs at me. I'd best put a stop to it before I end up just like Gertrude. "Mr. Aster, I told you, the journal isn't mine. And even if I—even if *my friend* wants to experience those fantasies, it doesn't mean that she wants to experience them with *you*."

He takes a moment, scratching his chin in feigned humility. "Why not? Am I too repulsive for her? Too rich? If she's a friend of yours, I assume she's attracted to Bolsheviks and penniless professors, but I'm told I have a certain appeal."

He does at that.

There's something about those gleaming teeth in that brilliant smile that make it hard to stay sore at him. In fact, I'm starting to feel something altogether different. Something that's making me sweat behind the knees. It's terribly warm in here and the decorative tie at the front of my dress is suddenly rather constricting.

Mr. Aster, on the other hand, is wondrously pale, cool, and collected. "If *your friend* doesn't like lingerie, I have other tricks up my sleeve."

"That's the problem with men. They all want to trick a woman into bed."

His head bobs up, as if I've finally offended him. "It was merely a turn of phrase, Miss O'Brien. I assure you, I've never tricked any woman into my bed. And in your case, I've been remarkably frank about my intentions."

With that, he pulls a stack of cream-colored envelopes from the drawer, then piles them in the middle of the desk until the edges line up.

I stare, shocked to the marrow of my bones.

In one of the stories I wrote, a girl receives anonymous letters in the mail, each of them daring her to take some provocative new risk. I'd described the notes as being written on cream-colored paper with a silver trim. The envelopes on his desk look just the same—as if conjured from my own imagination.

I know what they are, and he knows I do. He doesn't have to say it. It's all in his gaze. And a little thrill goes through me that any man should go to such lengths to impress me. His meticulous attention to detail is flattering, overwhelming, alluring. I'd be lying if I said otherwise. But what kind of man does this? Is he mischievous, obsessive, dangerously eccentric, or depraved?

"You wrote on all these cards?" I ask, my mouth dry.

"I did." Maybe he finally feels the heat, too, because he removes his closely tailored linen jacket to reveal a pale gray vest underneath. Then he rolls up his shirt sleeves and comes round to the front of the desk. ". . . and it was rather time-consuming."

My eyes widen at his sudden proximity, large and looming. I motion to the wide shiny expanse of his bare desk. "Don't you have a hotel to run, sir?"

He chuckles, leaning towards me. "Yes, which is why I'm so *bored*."

"What a luxury. Most of us are too busy trying to earn a living to have time for boredom."

His grin widens. "Sorry, *Comrade*. Most of my business is finished by noon and I'm ossified by dinnertime. So, I've plenty of time for recreation . . ."

Emboldened by his teasing, I put a hand on my hip like Clara Cartwright always does in the movies when she needs to knock a man down by a peg or two. "If you've so much time on your hands, perhaps you ought to make time to hear the complaints of your workers. I've a list of grievances, starting with a friend of mine who—"

"*Another* friend, Miss O'Brien?" he says, his eyes sweeping up and down my body. "My, you're a popular girl . . . but I'd rather not talk about business, if you don't mind."

I do mind. Or at least, I should mind. It's just that I never knew how very difficult it is to champion a cause—even a very good cause—when a man smells so wonderful. Soapy, spicy, and clean. My nostrils twitch in delight, which I fear must make me look like a timid little rabbit after all. Bloody hell!

"Aren't you curious about what's in the envelopes?" Mr. Aster asks.

"Painfully." My fingers itch to open them. But when I reach for one, he stops me.

His eyes crinkle at the corners. "Those aren't for you, unless you want to admit that you wrote the journal."

Such an admission is going to cost me. It's going to cost me dear. It better be worth the price. "Will you give my diary back to me if I admit the journal is mine?"

He nods, his eyes shining with challenge.

I'm sure I'll regret it, but that look in his eyes goads me to make the confession. "Very well. I wrote it."

"That wasn't so hard, was it?" he asks, his voice low, seductive, and approving.

It was harder than I imagined because now he knows all sorts of things about me and I don't know anything about him. "It's extremely embarrassing."

"I wish you wouldn't be embarrassed. I think most women are ashamed of thoughts like these, so men don't know that you have them. We assume you're all angels we taint with our own base desires rather than earthly creatures with desires of your own. That's a tragic mistake I've made at least once before."

With that last bit, he takes it a touch too far. He's been seen on the arm of pretty husband hunters and socialites. Why, before he returned to the city he was even linked in the scandal sheets with movie stars. It ought to serve as a warning to me what kind of man I'm dealing with. "I'll wager that's more than a bit of blarney, Mr. Aster. You've quite a reputation with the ladies."

"My reputation notwithstanding, I won't force unwanted attentions on a young woman in my employ. If you want to take your journal and go, this can be the end of it . . . but if you *would* like to make any of the stories you've written come true, I'd be happy to be of assistance."

"Would you now?" I grin, in spite of myself.

He levels his gaze on me. "I doubt you'll find many men better suited . . . especially for the more outlandish and expensive fantasies."

His self-assurance must come from knowing he can buy whatever he wants, and whoever he can't buy, he can probably charm into submission. I wonder what it must feel like to be him—able to live his life with no limitations but the ones he puts on himself. I call myself a modern thinker, but feel like an unsure girl inside. And here's a man offering me a chance to become a woman in all the ways I've only imagined. Would I be a fool to refuse? "Just how far are you prepared to take this, Mr. Aster?"

"As far as you'll let me," he replies, tapping the pile of envelopes. "What do you think?"

I think that I'm two breaths away from forgetting all good sense. "I need to return to work, sir."

Standing up, I dare to pluck my beloved journal from his hand. He follows me to the door and when I start to turn the handle, he angles his shoulder to block my exit. "Aren't you forgetting your lingerie?"

Something flutters in my belly. "It seems like a dangerous gift to accept."

"Oh, it is," he says, leaning lazily against the door frame. "But I want you to have it. I want to imagine you wearing it. I can't quite get the picture of you naked right in my mind, though. I can't decide if your breasts are round or pointy, with low nipples or high nipples, and the curiosity is driving me mad."

"*Mr. Aster.*" I laugh, shocked, amused, offended, aroused, and uncertain which is the strongest emotion. I've imagined men of all sorts in my fantasies: strong and shameless men, controlling and crude. But I'm not sure I ever imagined a man quite so playfully debauched.

"Take the lingerie," he insists.

I don't own anything like the garment in that box. It's pretty and feminine and utterly impractical. It would be a gift I couldn't tell anyone about, a gift just for me, secret and sinful and forbidden, just like him. "I don't think I should."

"Then don't take it. Just stay. Because this is the most interesting morning I've had since returning to the city and I'm not ready for it to end."

"So I'm a source of amusement to you." It ought to offend me, but it doesn't. Everything is crowded out by the coiling desire in my body.

"I mean to be a source of amusement for you, too, Miss O'Brien. Haven't I already amused you? You came into this office such a serious girl, but you're on the verge of laughing now . . ."

I have to bite my lip to hold back the merriment he senses. "What happens if I stay?"

"Then I'll let you open an envelope . . . but there are rules. If you find that you don't want to obey the command written there, the game stops and you don't get to open any of the other ones."

Obey? So there are *commands* in those envelopes. The thought of it makes me bite my lower lip even harder. The secret notes were my own idea, drawn from little dreams that gave me pleasure in the dark. Will I still like them in the light of day?

He returns to his desk, taking the topmost envelope from the stack, then holds it out to me like forbidden fruit. I shake my head. Better that I take my journal and go. Better to pretend that we never had this conversation. For all that's said about him, Mr. Aster seems like the kind of man who would keep his word about letting the matter drop. All my best judgment tells me that I should go back downstairs as swiftly as possible and return to my job while I still have it.

That's exactly what I decide to do.

Somehow, I find myself reaching for the envelope anyway.

CHAPTER

Two

I can't say why I take it. Maybe it's because he said my writing was lively and that it showed creative genius. Maybe it's because I'm flattered by his attention. Or maybe it's because my fantasies are even more seductive to me than the man who claims he's willing to bring them to life . . .

I slide the cool linen paper through my fingers. I open the envelope carefully, skimming my nail under the seal so as not to tear it. Then I draw forth the little card and swallow at the two words written there: _Touch me._

I study him. No boyish grin graces his features now; his eyes are fastened on me like there is nothing and no one more interesting in the whole wide world. A tremor goes through me as I contemplate all the possibilities. "Touch you?"

"If you like."

Touch me.

Those two little words seem so harmless, but carry such gravity that all my limbs go heavy. I glance at him, suddenly struck by the idea that, like some dresses in the hotel boutique, he's too expensive to risk touching. In his monogrammed shirt, Brooks Brothers vest, and perfectly pressed oxford trousers, there isn't much exposed skin. Just his face, well-formed and patrician, and his hands and forearms—the backs of which are dusted with pale golden hair.

I find that I want to touch him. I want to touch him very much. I come closer to him and hear his intake of breath. But my boldness falters, and there's an awkward moment as I reach forward with a trembling hand, not sure where to put it. "Like this?" I brush my fingers against the back of his knuckles. It's an innocent gesture, the kind of contact strangers make on the train without ever knowing. It binds neither of us to anything.

It also risks nothing.

That's what his eyes say. He's taken a gamble. Will I play it safe?

Letting my hand drift up his arm, I rest it on his chest where I can feel his skin burning through the fabric. He's hot as a furnace and both of his hands grip the edge of the desk as if he were struggling not to make any sudden moves that might frighten me. So close to him now, I'm overwhelmed by the urge to kiss him. But that's not what the card said to do.

Touch me.

Sliding my hand down, I rest both my palms on his thighs. The firm muscle there takes me a little by surprise. The tailoring of his clothes understates the power of his physicality. Beneath the slightly scratchy wool fabric, I feel the evidence for myself and it makes me tremble. A bulge of arousal has risen beneath his trousers and if I move my hands only a little bit, I can stroke him. But do I dare? What if his mask of civility is hiding darker impulses he's barely managing to restrain? Our eyes meet, our gazes lock, and then I wonder which one of us truly has the darkest impulses.

Maybe it's me.

Spreading my fingers wide, I slide my hand over the hardness of his erection and am delighted by the answering pulse beneath my palm. His low growl of approval warms me all over. It makes me feel

238 · *Stephanie Draven*

sexy and powerful. Womanly. When I press harder he groans and his eyelids lower, heavy with desire. It makes me giddy to get this kind of response from him with nothing but my touch . . . I rub him, enjoying the size and firmness of him against my hand.

"More?"

He doesn't answer right away. Perhaps he hasn't heard me. Then he swallows. "What do you want, Sophie?"

The use of my given name pulls me closer to him in intimacy. I want to keep touching him. I want to make him growl again, that pleasurable sound deep in his chest. I want to undress him and see what he looks like under his clothes. I want him to undress me and see what I look like under mine.

But all of these things are new fantasies; the old one still has more power over me.

"I want to open another card."

His hands flex on the desk, like little invisible bands were holding him still. Nothing is holding him but his own self-control. "Same rules as before," he reminds me. "Whatever is on that card, either you do it, or the game is over."

I'm afraid of the eagerness with which I tear the next note open. Glancing down at the card, I see four words this time.

Let me touch you.

I look up to see the question in his eyes. It's both a plea and a promise.

"You want to touch me, sir?"

"*Very* much."

His enthusiasm makes me stammer. "W-where? I mean, where do you want to touch me?"

"Everywhere."

My throat convulses in a little gasp.

"Oh." I feel as if I must understand *all* the rules. "And what if I ask you to stop, Mr. Aster?"

"Then I'll stop. But the game will be over."

"And what if *you* stop before I want you to?"

His dimples deepen with his smile. "If I do it right, you won't ever want me to stop."

Let me touch you.

The question is still in his eyes and I answer it with a single nod.

Knowing he has my assent, he breaks those invisible ties on his wrists and reaches for me. Drawing me to stand between his legs, he surprises me by first stroking my hair. Then his thumb brushes my lips. The sensation is so intimate that the hair raises on my nape.

While I'm still reeling, he puts both of his warm hands on my shoulders and I realize how big they are. Big, warm, meaty hands that inch themselves down to my breasts, cupping them. Most women wrap their breasts to fit the popular flapper style, but mine aren't big enough to need flattening. I find myself suddenly quite grateful for that, because I don't want anything else to come between my skin and his.

Following his example, I keep my hands still, letting them dangle uselessly to give him the best access to my body. My head tilts back in pleasure. My nipples tingle and I wish he'd take them out and suck them into his mouth, but he's in no hurry. He kneads my flesh, squeezing my breasts, rubbing them in a circle, first this way, then that. It feels so good, I don't think of stopping him.

I worry that he's right and I might *never* want him to stop. And isn't that just how girls get into trouble?

His hands slip lower. He strokes my belly, my hips, my thighs. It's only when arousal makes me unsteady and I lean against his leg for balance, that his hands slide round my back, then down, down, down to cup my bottom in his hands and draw me tight against him.

The hardness of his erection meets the heat between my legs, sending a jolt through me. Face to face. Hip to hip. It's a perfect preview of what it might be like to be joined with him. To have sex with him . . .

He murmurs, "I'd like to kiss you . . . you're actually quite lovely, Sophie, do you know that?"

I'm no bug-eyed Betty but my face is big and round as the moon, so I've never thought of myself as a beauty, either. "I'm going to let you kiss me whether you sweet-talk me or not, Mr. Aster."

He chuckles. "I hadn't any idea what you looked like when I read your diary and I don't think it would have mattered. I wanted you and was willing to go to great lengths to get you. But when you came into my office, I couldn't stop smiling because you were prettier than I had any right to hope."

He knows how to talk to women, I remind myself. He's had practice charming all manner of beauties, foreign and domestic. It's probably a skill he's cultivated, so I shouldn't take it to heart . . . but I do. And when his mouth closes over mine, I'm lost. He kisses me slowly, teasing at my lips until I kiss him back. Until my arms go up around his neck and I dare to brush my fingers over his golden hair, releasing the scent of Brilliantine. I imagine being cradled against him like this, naked. The big bulk of his body around me. A desire made only more intense when he begins unfastening the belt around my drop-waist knit jersey dress. When he's done with the belt, he pulls the garment up over my body, and I find myself lifting my arms even higher so that he can remove it.

Standing before him in nothing but my white chemise and pantaloons, I'm again beset by rapid-fire breathing and a stuttering tongue. "T-the n-note only said that I should let you touch me, not that—"

"You get to say stop at any time," he reminds me.

And I will, I promise myself. I *will* stop him. But not now. Not when his hands slide so deliciously beneath my undergarments, fingers sweeping over the wide areolae of my nipples. And not when the flat of his palm skims into my drawers and cups the pulsing mound of my sex.

His hand lingers there, fingers slipping up inside. My squeak of surprise gives me away, and he murmurs, "Why, Miss O'Brien, you're not a virgin, are you?"

"Of course not," I say, afraid to reveal the truth. Afraid that if he knows, all these sophisticated womanly feelings might disappear. And anyway, it isn't much of a lie. There was the Irish revolutionary who cornered me after a lecture and very nearly seduced me with his tales of woe. I didn't stop him until we were both half-dressed and panting against a tree in the park, his fumbling hands urging me to recklessness. And that doesn't even count the boy back home . . . but no, I can't think of *him* now.

Not with Mr. Aster's clever fingers finding the secret swollen place between my folds that makes me cry out. He strokes between my legs until my head swims with pleasure and my whole being seems cradled in the palm of his hand.

In a husky voice, he asks, "Will you let me see you naked?"

Unlike the stark commands written on the cards, this is a request. There's no challenge or threat. Just his own admission of what he'd like. I've already let him touch me and undress me. I'm ready to let him do even more than that. By way of answer, I slip out of my undergarments and let them fall to the floor.

He smiles, stooping to kiss the tips of my nipples. "Splendid. Upturned and rose pink. Just like your lips."

"What about yours?" I ask. "Time for you to show a peek, don't you think?"

"All in good time."

He spins me around, away from him, confusing me. Then, the warmth and weight of his hand presses down on my back, forcing me to lean over. With the iron of his erection pressed tight between my buttocks, I feel trapped. Somehow taken prisoner by his masculinity alone. I can't make a sound of protest.

I need to say something to make him stop. Because I know what he's going to do! But I'm wrong. His fingertips skate through the slickness between my legs, then draw the wetness back to an even more forbidden place that makes me arch up in surprise. "What are you doing?"

"I'm touching you *everywhere*," he murmurs, pressing the wet tip of his finger at the tight opening. I don't expect the rush of heightened sensation and yelp with distress. "Relax, Miss O'Brien, I won't hurt you."

And he doesn't. The pressure is insistent, but gentle. His thumb slides in only to the first knuckle and my body squeezes and tenses around it. It isn't the pain, but the idea of what he's doing that makes me spiral down into myself, into a place that feels entirely sinful. For these aren't the fumblings of a nervous boy or a drunk revolutionary. Only a man with perfect confidence in what he's doing would dare to touch a woman's body this way.

Facedown on his desk, my nipples hard to the point of pain against the unyielding lacquered top, I ask, "Is this what you do to other women, sir?"

"I've never played this game with the note cards before, no. Or do you mean to ask whether or not I've fucked a woman in the ass?" The discourteous words shock me and set the mood. "I've done that several times."

I speak in a breathy little whimper. "Oh."

"Do you want me to fuck your ass? I don't remember seeing that in your journal."

His erection presses hot and hard against the backs of my thighs, and though the desk takes most of my weight, my legs strain under me. I press the burning blush of my cheek against the cool wood of the desk and I say, "I—I don't know. I never thought about it before."

My eyes are on the stack of envelopes while his finger slips shallowly in and out of that nether passage. I'm struck by an overwhelming sense of gratitude. That he's so shameless gives me a freedom I've never felt before and likely never will again. I'm so eager to claim this freedom that I reach out and snatch the next envelope from the top of the pile.

"Wait!" he barks. "Don't open that yet."

"Why not?"

He pauses just long enough in his answer that I'm afraid he'll have a good reason and I'll never find the courage. So I tear it with my teeth, yanking the card out, and everything inside me catches fire at what I see.

Let me fuck you.

"That's why," he says, easing his finger from me and turning me around to face him. "I was going to switch it with the next one."

Gooseflesh rises on my skin. It feels so strange to be exposed to a man, here in the middle of the morning, with sunlight streaming through the tall windows that overlook the rest of the city and no shadows to hide behind. And since I can't hide, there's no choice but boldness. "Why did you want to switch out the card? Don't you want me?"

"Oh, I want you. I've wanted you from the moment you walked in the door. My cock is *aching* from wanting you."

"Then why didn't you want me to open this card?"

"I didn't think you were ready. But now it's too late for second thoughts . . ." He bends to nip at the hollow of my throat and when he speaks, his voice is steel. "You opened the envelope, Sophie. You know the rules. If we start breaking them now, it will set entirely the wrong tone for this affair."

Are we having an affair? I'm already writhing against him. My body is already dancing to this tune. The part of me that isn't all desire is having to fight for every word. "Right . . . here?"

His eyes are half-lidded and lazy with lust. "Remember, your story about the man who takes the woman on the floor. Fast and hard and abrupt . . ."

I hear myself swallow. What would it feel like to do it? To lose my virginity right here and now to a man I barely know? I can think of a thousand reasons not to—not least of which is my own promise to myself that I'd stop this before it went too far. But we O'Briens have always had more courage than good sense. If I say no, it'll all

244 · Stephanie Draven

stop and I may never again feel the way I do right now. I may never know this sexual creature inside me that I've only ever let out to write on a page. "Do you have . . . would you take . . . precautionary—"

He takes a French letter from his pocket and it stuns me that he has it at the ready. "You know what this is, don't you?"

Only from the pictures in the pamphlets do I recognize it, but I affect nonchalance. "Of course I do."

He uses two fingers to lift my chin so that I'm forced to look into his eyes, which burn with fierce desire. "Then you know how I'm going to use it. I'm going to slide it on my prick and then I'm going to push inside you and thrust hard, with very little regard for your pleasure. I'll work myself in your pussy, all to spill into this sheath. So you won't have my seed in you; you'll know it isn't about love or children or anything but *fucking*. The second time . . . that will be for you. I'll make sure you enjoy every moment of it and beg for more. But not the first time."

His words are casually crude and they steal the breath from me, not only because they are so unexpected, but because they're so familiar. They're my own words, rearranged and rephrased, but somehow more wicked and sinful coming from his lips than from the tip of my pen. Only now does he show the slightest doubt. "That's what you want, isn't it?"

Jesus, Mary, and Joseph, I'm going to do it. I'm going to do it because with other boys, it was always about how much they wanted me. How much they wanted to satisfy *their* hunger. But this time, this man, is torturing me with *my* blueprint for seduction . . .

I'm not as foolish as Gertrude. I've no expectations of this moment beyond my own hungers. And all of it is my idea, my choice, my needs, my desire. "Yes," I gasp. "It's what I want."

He doesn't hesitate for a heartbeat. He drags me down to the floor where a sheepskin rug cushions our fall. He's on me like a madman, biting at my shoulder while my hands tear at the buttons of his waistcoat. When I have them undone, I yank the vest down his arms and run my hands up under his shirt. Meanwhile, he works at the fastenings of his trousers, pulling them just far enough down his hips to free his erection.

I get only a glimpse of it, thick and pale and slightly curved towards his belly. It's far more impressive than anything I've seen in a pamphlet, and it's difficult to believe it's meant to fit inside a woman. He slides the sheath on. Then he works his legs between mine so swiftly, there's no going back. He pillows my head on his forearm and, with deep ragged breaths, encourages me to lift my hips for him.

He guides himself, then, all at once, thrusts and breaks my maidenhead. Amidst a wash of pleasure comes a wave of pure agony, and I bite the inside of my cheek to keep from crying out. I'd known it would hurt a little, but not quite so much, and I have to fight the tears that threaten to spill over.

Oh, it's *very* bad. Much worse than the little pinch I'd been told to expect. I tell myself that it can't hurt for much longer. But my bravery does no good; he notices. He blinks, long eyelashes sweeping against my cheek. "Sophie . . ."

"Please don't stop," I cry, because pleasure is my only bulwark against the pain. I batter at his shoulders. "Don't you dare stop now!"

Maybe he knows the way a woman looks at the edge. Maybe he knows just how to push her all the way. Because he strokes into me, deep into me, the hairs of his groin tangling with mine. The wickedness of being taken on the floor this way, the buttons of his shirt scraping against my breast and belly, it all builds inside me. This is how dirty girls get taken, I think. Sluts and harlots and whores do it on their backs, on the floor under any rich man who can pay for it, under rich men just like him. That's all I can think about as he fills me in long smooth strokes; the sharp pain fades to an insistent throb of pleasure that grows more intense until I'm clinging to him.

"Are you going to come for me, Sophie?" he asks, low and husky.

And then I don't care what kind of girl I am.

The shuddering orgasm forces throaty cries from me as all my insides collapse around his cock. My body milks him and the feeling of fullness makes the pleasure stronger. I'm in the grips of it, overwhelmed. I dig my nails into his hips, which thrust faster and faster as he finds his own release. He grunts, his face slightly reddened with his exertion, collapsing down onto me with three or four more thrusts before he stills.

Then there we are, a sweating, panting heap of limbs and half-removed clothing sprawled on the floor. In spite of the pain, the experience was vastly more exciting than I imagined. How was I to know that something so sudden could leave me filled with tiny quakes of delight? The lingering joy of it makes me laugh when I can breathe again. "If that's how it feels when you show very little regard for my pleasure, I'm looking forward to the second time."

But Mr. Aster isn't at all amused. Rolling onto his side, his eyes are stormy. "You lied to me."

He's got no right to be sore. No right at all. "And you read my journal without permission, so that makes us even."

"But why? Why would you lie about this being your first time?"

For so many reasons, not least of which is that I didn't want him to think he was so much better and more experienced than I am. And just as important, "Because I was afraid you'd stop."

"Of course I'd have stopped. Gentlemen don't despoil virgins!"

"I thought you said you were trying to be less of a gentleman."

Under the force of his anger, I reach for my discarded undergarments, but they prove too little to shield me from his anger. "See here, Miss O'Brien. When the newspapers call you the most eligible bachelor in the country, you learn to avoid husband chasers; I don't intend to be forced into marriage."

The fact that he says it with such a note of accusation, makes me want to laugh in his face. Curling one lip with contempt, I say, "I can see how that'd be a hazard. I bet women force you to steal their diaries and ravish them all the time . . ."

His frosty expression melts under his chagrin.

"Touché, mademoiselle."

"I didn't do it to trap you. I did it just to enjoy the look on your face right now."

His embarrassment seems to deepen, and he strokes me, almost apologetically. "You're a very odd girl."

"I'll take that as a compliment. You needn't worry, Mr. Aster. I don't want to get married. Marriage isn't fair to women. It isn't to our advantage. We've had the vote for less than ten years and we're still making medieval contracts where all the terms disfavor the wife. I let you take my virginity because I wanted to know what all the fuss was about."

"Now you think you know?" he asks with a smirk. "You don't. I promise you, that wasn't *remotely* the best I have to offer."

This makes my body roar awake again. He tempts me. Is it possible that this gets better? Because I can't imagine how, once anyone discovers this, they want to do anything else. "I never knew it would feel so different from when I touch myself."

He groans. "Do you touch yourself often?"

"Only in the bath," I admit, too exposed to be embarrassed anymore. "But it was so lovely and different today when I found my climax . . . and you were inside me . . ."

He groans again, turning to me, so that I can feel him stiffening against my side. "I like knowing that I'm the first man to have you. That my cock is the first to ever make you come. That when your insides gripped me and you cried out, that was the first time you'd ever felt that . . ."

"Why?" I ask, my breath catching.

"Because it makes me feel extraordinarily possessive."

"I'm not a possession," I say, though I'm far too pleased with myself to put true fury behind my rebuke.

"Then why do I feel so proprietary? In fact, at the moment, I feel rather free to do with you as I like."

I give him a seductive grin. "And what are you going to do with me?"

"I'm going to send you back to work," he says, shocking me into silence.

As I sputter, he removes the used sheath from his member, then begins to fasten his clothes.

"You're *finished* with me?" I ask, appalled.

"The very opposite of that, Miss O'Brien," he says, tucking himself back into his pants. "When you first came into this office, I was hoping you'd prove to be a diversion, but now I feel a responsibility to take this game quite a bit more seriously."

That I can see he's still aroused only confuses me more. "What does that mean?"

"It means I'm going to take you as a mistress and see to it that you understand *what all the fuss is about.*"

A *mistress.* I can't quite fathom the word. And while it clangs about between my ears, in all its bewildering implications, he gets up then offers me a hand. I take it and rise shakily to my feet.

"I also intend to keep my word to you that the second time will be for your pleasure," he says. "You *will* beg for it, but given what I know now, that will take time to arrange properly."

He takes another envelope but instead of giving it to me to open, he pulls the card out himself.

I see what's written on it: *Come back tomorrow afternoon.*

Now he takes a fountain pen and adds more words. *Come back tomorrow afternoon . . . for a spanking.*

The sexual heat in my body kindles into anger. My temper must show because he says, "Don't you think you need a spanking, Sophie? Haven't you been a very bad girl today?"

I'm not sure if I'm more upset by the fantasy that he's chosen to play out next, or by the fact that he's dismissing me. He takes the lingerie from its package and holds it for me to step into. "I wouldn't want you to have to explain the box."

It's a courteous gesture, but it makes me feel patronized. I decide to let him dress me in it anyway, because I want a token of remembrance. Then I yank my own dress back on, glaring at him all the while.

So, he has it figured out, does he?

He seems sure I'll return, but maybe I won't. Would he care? He probably is the kind of man who has stolen encounters like this one every day. For all I know, there's another woman ready to climb into his bed tonight. The idea of it makes me wonder if it isn't better if we pretend that none of this ever happened. "What if I don't come back tomorrow?"

"You'll come back," he says, brushing a tiny kiss over my lips.

It's strangely sweet, gentle, and not at all in keeping with what's just happened here.

"What makes you so sure?"

"Because, if you do, I'll listen to some of the grievances you've so helpfully gathered from my staff."

My mouth falls all the way open at the casual way he mixes business with pleasure.

"Also, I'm keeping your journal."

Now my hands ball into fists at my side. "You told me you'd give the journal back."

His features light with amusement. "And you told me that you weren't a virgin."

CHAPTER

Three

There's not a lick of privacy to be had in the room I share with Ethel and Irene—which is why I kept my diary in my locker at work to begin with. It's a nice boardinghouse and our flat has a view of the city from the fire escape where Irene grows a flowerpot garden every spring. It's also across the street from the Civics League where we're sometimes invited to listen to talks from progressive leaders in science, economics, and politics—real visionaries who want to modernize the country.

Given the wages we make, none of us could afford to live in the neighborhood on our own, but with three beds crowded in, we make do.

It's just that when anything happens to one of us, the rest of us know about it. So it seems odd that they don't notice anything different about me. I've finally *done it*; or at least let a man do it to me. I still catch the scent of him on my skin from this afternoon. But the girls haven't suspected a thing.

"Mrs. Mortimer turned you in? That old bluenosed prune," Ethel says with disgust, throwing her purse onto the bed. "Well, we'll all just know better than to keep anything at the boutique, won't we?"

"And how!" Irene cries, taking off her earbobs and hopping out of her heels. "It's a good thing you left your petition with Hamilton. When they called you upstairs to see the Big Cheese, we thought you were finished, Sophie."

"But he knows we're organizing and he didn't fire you," Ethel muses. "That's something . . . what's he like, anyway?"

I hesitate. "He isn't . . . what you'd expect . . ."

Given all the time in the world, I don't know that I could find the words to describe Robert Aster, and I'm afraid to try, lest I slip up and spill something I don't want either of them to know. I can't very well tell them about the diary, can I? I can't tell them about the lingerie, either, which even now slides sinuously beneath my clothes. And if I tell them what I let him to do to me, they'll be scandalized.

Well, Irene will be scandalized.

Ethel's a wild flapper. She isn't scandalized by anything. She'll want to know every salacious detail. In fact, she's already changing into an evening gown, slinky and short. "Come on girls, let's get a wiggle on. My guy is going to take us to the new juice joint on Forty-ninth Street and he's bringing friends."

Irene rubs her toes. "They'd better be buying dinner *and* cocktails, because I've been on my feet all day and my dogs are barking."

Ethel finishes changing, then purses her lips in front of the mirror, dabbing on lipstick to make a perfect cupid's bow. "If we play our cards right, they'll even take us to the Clara Cartwright movie afterwards. When are you gonna learn, Irene? Give 'em a few kisses and they'll buy you whatever you want."

Irene swats at Ethel in mock outrage, but even she can't resist a Clara Cartwright film. In the movies, Miss Cartwright always plays girls like us, shopgirls and secretaries and factory workers, and *boy* does she do it with panache. We all love her. Ethel even stole a movie poster from the nickelodeon to hang on the back of the door.

"Should we check on Gertrude before we go?" Irene asks.

"Poor Gertie," Ethel says with a sentimental sigh. "I guess there's no use boohooing about it again. We'll get her job back for her, won't we, Sophie?"

"Mr. Aster seems willing to hear our grievances," I admit, reluctant to tell them the price he put on that willingness. Even more reluctant to tell them I'm eager to pay. "And if he won't, then we strike."

Ethel puts the finishing touches on her lips, then glances at me. "Sophie, you're not wearing that out, are you? You haven't even powdered your nose!"

"You two go on without me. My nerves are shot and all I want is a hot bath." It's all true. Of course, there's also the fact that if I undress in front of them, I won't be able to hide—or explain—the lingerie.

"Oh, don't be a flat tire!" Ethel cries. "There'll be too many fellas without you."

But Irene tugs on Ethel's arm. "You know this one. If she wants to spend all night with a book instead of a boy, let her. One of us has to be smart enough to negotiate with fat cats and tycoons."

When they're gone, I cross the hall, slip into the lavatory and lock the door behind me. Removing my dress, I look at myself in the full-length mirror and bite my lip at the vision. I've never seen myself like this—not even in my own imagination. I like the sight of me in this suggestive lingerie. I really do. The fabric is so sheer I can see the dark pubic mound between my legs and the wide nipples of small, upturned breasts . . . and yet, I present a far more scandalous picture than if I were entirely naked.

I doubt reformers like Mrs. Sanger and Mrs. Garvey and other women I admire would be caught wearing such a thing. But wearing this makes my blood fizz in my veins like soda at the fountain . . .

A little stain of blood on the fabric reminds me of why.

Of what I am now.

A bad girl, that's what.

I let a man undress me, pull me down to the floor, and make love to me—no, that's not what he did. He *fucked* me with such little fanfare it might as well have been a handshake. He just did it. Hard and fast and seemingly without regard for my pleasure . . . even though it gave me quite a bit of pleasure after all.

And now he wants to spank me.

That's all I can think about as I fill the tub with hot water and give myself a good soak, hoping none of the other boardinghouse tenants knocks to interrupt my bath.

He'll want to spank me and then he'll want to fuck me again. He'll expect that he can do it any time he likes now. And what if he's right?

The parish priest back home would call me a fallen woman. Mrs. Mortimer would say I'm ruined for marriage, not that I care about *that*. But she'd also say I'm one step away from working in the brothel. And that's to say nothing of how I've disgraced the memory of the boy back home.

That does sting.

It's perfectly humiliating to think about what I've done and even more humiliating to admit how much I want to do it again. So much so, that I can't stop clenching my thighs together and touching myself in the bath.

I *am* ashamed, but I don't think it's going to stop me . . .

The next morning, Mrs. Mortimer's pinched face is decidedly pale.

"Sophie, I'd like to apologize," she says.

Never in all the time we've worked in the boutique has Mrs. Mortimer apologized for anything. But if this is a prank, she's not in on it, for there's not a tickle of mischief in that woman's bones. I peek past her out the glass doors of the boutique into the luxurious lobby where white-gloved bellhops rush past with parcels and luggage. Even in the summer, the Aster Hotel is buzzing with ritzy guests, men dressed in straw Panama hats and three-piece linen suits, women in long strands of pearls and sleeveless pastel dresses designed by Coco Chanel. With ostrich feather fans in hand, they mingle on the red carpet beneath the murals and potted palms and none of them pays even a wee bit of attention to the dragon lady of the boutique humbling herself before me.

At Mrs. Mortimer's apology, however, Ethel coughs from behind the perfume counter and Irene nearly stumbles off the ladder she's climbed to retrieve a hatbox. I find myself quite speechless and when I don't make a reply, Mrs. Mortimer clenches her teeth to say, "Mr. Aster has informed me that I had no business going through your belongings. It won't happen again."

So he's bawled her out, then. I ought to find it gratifying, but it reminds me just how much power he has over everyone who works in this hotel, including me. "Thank you, Mrs. Mortimer. I appreciate the sentiment."

Her spine rigid, she begins to walk away then stops. "I wouldn't be too smug, Sophie. Mr. Aster assures me he'll be taking private disciplinary action against you; it won't help matters when he finds out that you have a suitor."

Private disciplinary action. I swallow at this. And I worry, too, that maybe she's peeked into my journal. Then I hear the rest of what she's said. "A suitor?"

I see there's a long-stemmed red rose clutched in her talons. She lays it on my counter. "So it seems. Someone sent this for you by messenger without a name or a card. Inform your uncouth suitor— whoever he is—that you're not to receive gifts in the workplace; it's gauche. It's unacceptable. This isn't a bordello, my girl. No matter how standards may have fallen lately, this is *still* the Aster Hotel."

Irene nearly leaps to my defense, curiosity shining in her eyes. "A rose? Well, I think it's sweet!"

"Diamonds are sweeter," Ethel chirps.

"I'll have no lip from you girls," Mrs. Mortimer says in a tone of disapproval one normally reserves for criminals, bums, or lawyers. "Men in this city prey on young ladies and if you let your head be turned with gifts, you'll be ruined like Gertrude."

This is entirely too much for Ethel, who says, "We coulda

clammed up about Gertie. Let her wear a ring on her finger and none would be the wiser."

Mrs. Mortimer stares down her nose. "It is against the policy of the Aster Hotel to employ girls of ill-repute. And even if the father of Gertrude's child decided to make an honest woman of her, customers shopping for elegant evening gowns don't like to see bloated broodmares behind the counter. Remember this: Young ladies who spend more time thinking about beaus than work end up in a bad way."

She's right, because by lunchtime, I'm in a bad way indeed.

When I take the elevator up to Mr. Aster's office, I don't expect to find him sitting facing the door, leaning forward with both hands on his knees in a keen posture. I stand in the doorway, fiddling with the stem of the rose, and he launches to his feet.

I drink him in, convinced that a pale blue linen suit never looked better on any other man. Being near him again makes me wobbly on my heels and I'm grateful when he ushers me inside, a steadying hand at the small of my back.

"How are you feeling, Miss O'Brien?"

Yesterday he was all smiles; today his serious countenance makes me even more nervous, but I manage to hide it. "Just swell, thanks. I'm looking forward to talking to you about the grievances you promised to hear."

"Pleasure before business. I trust you received an apology from Mrs. Mortimer?"

"And a warning, too . . . about men who give gifts to women and ruin them for marriage."

"Yet, here you are."

"Well, I'm already ruined, aren't I?"

He pales. "I'm not a rake. You tricked me yesterday, you know that . . ."

I'm charmed by his use of such an old-fashioned word. "I tricked *you* and you romanced me this morning with a rose. So maybe that makes *me* the rake, sir."

I hope he'll be amused, but his expression gets more serious still. "My father was an ambassador, Miss O'Brien. He's learned a thousand clever ways to lie. He'd like for me to follow him into politics, but I don't have much stomach for deception. In fact, the only good relationship I've ever seen between a man and a woman is one based on a scandalous abundance of honesty and openness. So if we're going to play games, they're going to be honest ones from now on." ·

Why, he's giving me a stern lecture! It should move me to anger or remorse. Instead, all I can think about is what his voice does to me when he takes that tone. All that bossy talk makes me throb in the naughtiest places. Emboldened by my own arousal, I ask, "You're still sore at me then, Mr. Aster? Maybe you should give me the punishment I deserve."

There's a shake of his head and *finally* the hint of a smile. "I've been imagining all morning how you'll look draped over my knees."

He still wants to spank me. The confirmation of it makes me weak— all my joints rubbery. And as I watch him pull the chair from behind his desk to make room for me, the throbbing of my body drowns out all other thoughts. "You're not really going to do it, are you?"

"Miss O'Brien, once I commit to a course of action, I do so with uncompromising certainty. And I am *thoroughly* committed to this enterprise. So, yes, I really am going to spank you."

My mouth goes dry. "You're awfully wordy."

He sits down on the chair, feet flat on the floor. He pats his lap by way of invitation. "I'll say it simply, then: Bend over my knee."

There's no mischief in his eyes now. His gaze is frank, direct, and filled with an expectation I don't want to disappoint. It's bending over his knee that proves to be the chief difficulty because I don't know where to put my hands. To my immense relief, when I tilt over his legs, one of his strong arms comes down over the small of my back and shoves me into position. The warm weight of his hand settles over the curve of my backside and I realize again, with a sense of dread, just how big his hands are. "I'm going to pull your drawers down, Miss O'Brien, because I believe you deserve a bare-bottomed spanking."

I didn't think I could be more embarrassed, but that does it. That and the cool rush of air on my most private parts when he lifts my skirts up and bunches them around my waist. When he yanks my underpants halfway down my thighs, only the weight of his arm in the middle of my back keeps me from bolting up in fear. Then he slaps his palm against my bottom for the first time, and I jolt. It's no playful swat. Nothing tentative about it. And I'm in no way prepared. My back arches right up and I look over my shoulder at him in surprise. I stare at him, agape.

"You want a real spanking, don't you, Miss O'Brien?"

My lower lip wobbles. "I'm starting to think better of it."

"Do you want me to stop, then?"

Dear god, no. I don't want him to stop. So I shake my head.

"Count, if you wouldn't mind," he says, shifting his legs slightly underneath me. When he does, I feel his hard erection press against my side. The urgency of his sexual arousal coaxes an answering rush of heat between my legs. Or maybe it's the outrageous excitement I feel. "You can start at two . . ."

His big hand smacks my flesh again and the sound echoes through the empty office.

"Two!" My voice cracks. It isn't so much that the spanks are excruciatingly painful. It's that I have no way of knowing when or where they'll fall. In addition to the shame of being spanked is the wildly exciting realization that I have no control over it. The next spank makes me cry out. And each one keeps getting harder and harder until the count of ten. Then I can't even gauge it anymore. The sting he's leaving on my bottom spreads lower until my whole body is enveloped in it. My heartbeat is racing, pounding at my wrists, my throat, and between my legs. Surely he can feel the wetness of my sex. I'm so wet and needy now, the pain seems far away, replaced by a sweet ache for satisfaction.

Shamelessly, I angle myself so that my hips can grind against his body with each spank.

When I cry out fifteen, my voice is ragged with need. I clench my thighs together, rocking in a way that urges me towards climax. My voice rises on the sixteenth stroke and I know that I'm going to bring myself off. I squeal on the seventeenth, so close. Then moan low on the eighteenth, nineteenth, and twentieth as orgasm overtakes me. I'm coming, and my climax is like all those effervescent soda bubbles burst at once.

Squeezing my eyes shut and biting the inside of my cheek, I force myself to stillness to hide it. But it feels so good that I could scream. It's sweet relief, but it leaves me damp and trembling in his arms.

All at once, he takes me by the arms and drags me up, seating me in his lap. He wants me to look at him. But I can't. I look away until he catches me by the chin and forces me to meet his eyes. "Miss O'Brien, did you just take your pleasure from me?"

With my bottom burning brighter than my face, there's no denying it. "Yes."

His eyes twinkle with instant delight. "You might have warned me that spankings have that effect on you."

"How was I to know?"

"I'd forgotten what an innocent you are."

"Besides, *you* enjoyed it, too," I say, defensively, eying the rigid evidence in his trousers.

"Of course I did. The way you squirmed against me would excite a statue. Now here I am, hard as marble and without your enviable talent for easy satisfaction."

He says all this with perfect amiability, as if he didn't know it would awaken in me a profound curiosity and desire. "May I touch you?"

Those warm hazel eyes of his crinkle at the corners. "You're quite welcome to touch me whenever you like; you don't need to ask permission, Miss O'Brien."

"I think it excites me to ask."

"Oh?" This clearly surprises him. For a few awkward and silent moments, he's like a man struggling to get his bearings. Eventually, he clears his throat and says, "In that case, I'd like you to ask me again . . . and this time, with greater specificity."

"Greater . . . specificity, sir?"

"I want to know exactly what you're asking permission to do."

"May I please, touch you . . . your . . ." Several words for it echo in my mind. Some clinical. Some vulgar and pornographic.

"You want to touch my cock?"

His having said it first makes it easier. "Yes. May I please touch your cock?"

Part of me regrets having asked at all but the other part of me squirms while he weighs the matter in his mind. "As it happens, I don't think I could bear another day of teasing, Miss O'Brien. Today, I'd like you to stroke it. I want you to use your hand to *make me come*, and I'm afraid that unless you're willing to commit yourself to my pleasure, the answer must be no."

"But I *am* willing," I protest, almost offended.

He dimples me a smile, then unfastens his trousers with an air of magnanimity. "Show me."

I find him hot and hard. His manhood is silkier than expected and my fingertips slide easily down the shaft. When I stroke him, he leans his head back so that it touches the chair, then he closes his eyes.

I like that. It's easier to experiment when he's not watching me. I squeeze tight, marveling at the size of him in my grip. He groans when I do that and groans again when the flat of my palm smears some of the dew on the tip of his shaft. He gets excited. Very excited. Then his big hand closes around mine, and he teaches me to do it just as he likes.

I'm mesmerized by the way he trains me to his desires.

I like it. I like it so very much. And it makes me feel strangely . . . powerful. He's the one who cries out when his cock throbs and spurts warm and sticky semen into my palm. But I'm the one who wants to shout with victory because in this one moment, he is *mine*.

CHAPTER

Four

He takes the pocket square from his jacket and uses it to gently wipe my fingers, but the cloth isn't nearly absorbent enough to clean up all the mess. There seem to be rather copious amounts of the milky remnants of his ecstasy and he murmurs something about having to change his pants.

I glance at the enormous grandfather clock in the corner, almost dizzied by what I see. "I have to go!"

His golden head snaps up. "What? Why?"

"My lunch break is over. Mrs. Mortimer will skin me alive if I'm late."

"What kind of ogre do you think I am, Miss O'Brien? Surely you didn't think I was going to let you return to work without having lunch."

"But Mrs. Mortimer—"

"Works for me," he interrupts. "Mrs. Mortimer works for me and for that matter, so do you. So, if I should require your services on the rooftop instead of at the boutique, neither of you are in any position to complain."

I feel my eyes widen. "You're abusing your power, Mr. Aster."

He chuckles. "Perhaps you ought to bring it up at your next organized labor meeting."

He's teasing; I know he is. But it doesn't stop me from feeling guilty. This is exactly the kind of thing we talk about. Predatory employers who take advantage of their workers in every possible way. Except . . . except, I'm here of my own free will, aren't I? "Speaking of organized labor—"

"Let's save that conversation for dessert, shall we?"

He produces a new pair of trousers from his cabinet, leaving me to wonder how often he finds the need for new clothes in the middle of the day. He swiftly changes into them without any self-consciousness, as if he were quite accustomed to women seeing him in various stages of undress. I watch him do it, my eyes drinking in the powerful muscles of his bare legs underneath his sock garters. As soon as he's made himself presentable, he leads me from his office into the corridor, at the end of which are two beautiful French doors that open into the rooftop garden.

The giant dome of glass and steel overhead affords a perfect view of the city. It's a popular spot for tourists and for the wealthy; it's usually filled with the noise of hundreds of guests clinking their glasses together, forks and knives clashing over elegant meals, waiters hurriedly bustling in and out of the kitchen. But this afternoon, the rooftop dining area is silent but for the bubbling water in the fountain.

I come to a halt beside a lattice all covered in vines. "What—what is this?"

"It's lunch. Won't you please join me?" He takes several purposeful strides to a lone table in the middle of the dining room, covered in white linen and gilded china plate. Then he pulls out one of the chairs for me.

"Where is everyone?" I ask, bewildered.

"I closed the rooftop for us this afternoon. I thought we might like some privacy. I hope you're hungry. The menu is a Waldorf salad to be followed by medallions of spring lamb served with asparagus au gratin and Venetian ice cream for dessert."

My hands go to my cheeks. "Oh . . . I couldn't."

"Why not? Are you too sore to sit?"

The reminder of my spanking makes me flush. "No, it isn't that. It's just that I should be working the counter in the boutique. Ethel and Irene will have to work twice as hard to make up for my absence."

"For a Marxist-Leninist, you have a remarkable work ethic. If it troubles you, I'll give them a bonus. Now, please sit down."

"They aren't the same," I say, annoyed.

"I beg your pardon?"

"Marx and Lenin. They aren't the same. Dr. Marx was a philosopher and an economist who theorized about how to advance justice and prosperity. Lenin was a murderous, power-hungry thug." When Mr. Aster tilts his head as if I were a great curiosity, I quickly add in defense of myself, "I like to read books."

"Admirable. But what does any of this have to do with why you won't join me for lunch?"

It's only the rooftop garden, but at the moment it feels like a foreign world. "This must have cost you *quite a bit* of money . . ."

"As I have rather *a great deal* of money, that isn't a concern for me."

My insides are topsy-turvy. "I can't afford a meal like this."

"Miss O'Brien, I intend to treat you to lunch."

"I like to pay my own way."

"Don't be ridiculous. I said I was trying to be less of a gentleman, not that I intended to forsake all notion of civilized behavior."

Somehow, it seems wrong. I don't know how it can seem so much *more* wrong than bending over his knee in his office, but it does. "Here you are, spending all this money on me when you could use it to pay better wages to your staff. How am I to enjoy an extravagant lunch when thinking about that?"

Mr. Aster crosses his arms. "Has it occurred to you that none of the people in this hotel would have any jobs at all if it weren't for people willing to spend money on extravagant lunches? Moreover, if today were just like any other day, the wait staff would be working themselves into a lather to serve the crowd. Instead, everyone in the kitchen is having a bit of a lazy afternoon because they only have to prepare a meal for the two of us. Besides, when we come to dessert, you can tell me one of your grievances and consider it your good deed to your fellow workers and oppressed peoples of the world."

When he puts it like that, it makes me feel rather foolish. "I wish you wouldn't ridicule me."

"I only meant to poke fun—nothing whatsoever so disrespectful as *ridicule*. You have my apologies. The whole purpose in my arranging this lunch was to make sure that you didn't feel mistreated. I shouldn't spoil it with jokes."

He means it. He's so earnest that I take the seat that he's offered and resolve to be grateful. Still, I worry that I'm too disheveled for a place like this. Trying to smooth my hair back and straighten my clothes, I become aware of every loose thread and wrinkle in my dress. The women he's brought to dine here before have, no doubt, been of a different class altogether, so I try to use my best manners, remember to keep my elbows off the table, and watch him for a clue as to which fork to use.

When the first course is served, he tells me, "I was terribly anxious that you wouldn't come back to my office today."

To be the cause of anxiety for an otherwise carefree playboy is unexpectedly flattering. "Were you?" I ask, as unsure of the man as I am of the apple, grape, and celery salad served with a mayonnaise dressing. "What would you have done? If I didn't come back, I mean?"

He gives a wry grin. "I'd have gulped down enough liquor to put myself into a stumbling oblivion. Which is how I spend most of my evenings, come to think about it, but in this case, I wouldn't have waited for the evening to do it."

"Oh," I murmur, thoughtful. "Why do you drink so much?"

He stops, salad fork poised midbite. "Oh, for pity's sake, don't tell me that you're one of the dries, too. Miss O'Brien, is there *any* cause of social reform to which you do not subscribe?"

His exaggerated look of horror at the idea I might be in favor of Prohibition is so terribly funny that I laugh into my napkin. "So you don't mind Communists but the temperance movement is beyond the pale?"

He smirks at me. "And yet, you told me not to tease you . . ."

"I told you that I wished you wouldn't *ridicule* me. But I can stand being teased a little bit. And you're very good at it."

His gaze narrows provocatively. "It's not the only thing I'm very good at . . ."

As I'm not brave enough to ask about the rest of his talents, I work on eating my salad, the unusual combination of flavors and textures more pleasing than I would have guessed. "To answer your question, when it comes to alcohol, I'm in favor of *temperance*, not abstinence."

"How very dull."

"I can think of more exciting things to do than get drunk."

"Your journal certainly attests to that." The mention of the journal is a sharp reminder that this isn't just a pleasant lunch with a pleasant fellow, but a meal that comes on the heels of utter debauchery with my boss. And at the memory of his big hand crashing down on my bottom, I squirm in my chair. "Have you ever been drunk before, Miss O'Brien?"

"Well, no . . ."

"Have you ever even tasted liquor?"

I press my lips together. "Does the sacrament count or is that the blood of Christ?"

That earns me a belly laugh. "So you've never gone into a speakeasy and asked for a cocktail?"

"I've been to a speakeasy, but . . . no, I haven't had a cocktail."

He narrows his eyes. "What an earnest little do-gooder . . . you're quite charming, really."

"Only accidentally, whereas you seem practiced at it. So much so that you avoided my question completely."

He takes a swallow of lemonade and makes a face. "Which question?"

"Why do you drink so much liquor?"

"I don't have a good answer. Didn't take a drop during the war, but when I came back, I acquired a taste for it."

This takes me unawares. "You served in the war? But you look too young . . ."

A white-gloved waiter takes our salad plates and replaces them with a steaming entree of lamb and asparagus. It seems rich fare for lunch, but my mouth waters at the scent of rosemary, garlic, and roasted meat. Mr. Aster waits for me to begin eating. "I joined up the day I turned eighteen. It was near the end of the fighting, though most people didn't know that at the time. The ambassador had a pretty good idea that the action was nearly over and he didn't want his youngest to miss out on an opportunity to bring glory to the family name. He saw to it that I was made an officer and military aviator."

"You can fly planes?" I ask, decidedly impressed.

"Fly them? Yes. It's shooting them down that proved the difficulty. I'm fairly certain I was the worst aerial gunner in the U.S. Army Signal Corps."

It's strange to imagine him as a soldier and even stranger to hear the tone of self-deprecation in his usually confident voice. "What is the U.S. Army Signal Corps?"

"They call it the U.S. Army Air Corps now."

"So you were a fighter pilot, like the Red Baron."

"*No one* was like the Red Baron. I wasn't entirely useless, though.

I was always good in a brawl and had a talent at getting the supplies our pilots needed that the Army couldn't provide. Guns, mounts, mechanical parts, gas masks, and food . . ."

It's the sort of organizing one expects from a workingman, not from an officer. "How did you manage that?"

"I knew whom to ask. Whom to bribe, to trade with, and to steal from. It became a fun challenge, really. But they don't give out medals for that sort of thing, do they?"

"Maybe they should."

He takes a moment to cut his lamb into neat pieces. "In any case, I came home from the war with shell shock but none of the glory my father hoped for. Those first few months I spent stateside, liquor was the only thing that helped with the insomnia and occasional bout of shaking hands."

He seems so cool, pale, and aloof. A remote Nordic god. It's difficult for me to imagine such a flaw . . . "Your hands shake?"

"Not for years now," he says, holding one out steady. "I've got liquor to thank for that."

"And the insomnia?"

He looks down at his plate. "You shouldn't let your lunch get cold, Miss O'Brien. It's splendid."

I take a bite of the lamb and the way it nearly melts in my mouth is so distracting that I almost let him get away with the evasion. "Do you still have trouble sleeping, Mr. Aster?"

"You can call me Robert when we're alone," he says.

"Do you still have trouble sleeping, Robert?"

"Has anyone ever told you that you're a girl of remarkable persistence?"

"Not usually in such a flattering or approving way."

He laughs. "Yes, I still have trouble sleeping. Especially last night. I've never spanked a woman before and I was fretting about it into the wee hours. I couldn't decide if I should worry more that you'd go through with it or that you wouldn't."

I'm glad he waited to confess these doubts. If he'd let his anxiety show when he had me over his knee, I'd have fled. However, his confession now is so unexpected and endearing that I can't stop staring at him. "You said your experience in such matters is considerable, so out of all the fantasies in my journal, why didn't you choose something you'd done before?"

"I wanted to learn something about women . . . this was the fantasy that I wanted most to understand."

His thirst for knowledge is admirable but I don't know whether or not to believe him. "And here you made it seem as if you already knew everything there was to know about women."

"You've certainly caused me to reevaluate." This cheers me quite a bit—to think that I've surprised a man like him, or confounded him in any way. "Besides, I never said I was an expert on women. Merely that I have considerable experience bedding them."

I let that idea settle for a while. "Only bedding them? Haven't you ever been in love?"

The question seems to amuse him. "I've been in love precisely one and a half times."

And his answer definitely amuses me. "One and a half? You can't be half in love with someone."

"Trust me, you can. And sometimes it's a lot more pleasant than being all the way in love, as I was with Nora, my former fiancée. Though, I must admit, you're helping me to feel quite a bit more charitable towards her."

"Am I?" I ask, not entirely pleased. I chase my asparagus round my plate with my fork until I see him lift a spear with his fingers. "So is there a reunion with Nora on the horizon?"

He coughs. "No. Certainly not. I said you've helped me feel more charitable towards her, not that I've turned into a sap."

It makes me want to taunt him. "So you're a cynic, through with love for good?"

"Oh, no. I'm a romantic at heart."

"And what does the happy future look like for a romantic like you?"

"I imagine I'll eventually fool a woman into thinking I'm worth a damn. She'll reform me of my playboy ways and I'll become a respectable businessman in my father's mold. Then I'll move back into the family mansion and make some little Asters to inherit the family fortune."

"How bourgeois," I say, taking another bite of lamb. "How will you know she's the one?"

"I'll know when I can say I've been in love *two* and a half times in my life."

"You and your half!"

"I've always been good with numbers," he grins. "How many times have *you* been in love?"

My smile fades, never having expected he'd turn the question back at me. "Just once. I was very young."

"You're *still* very young. Tell me about this lad who stole your heart."

I won't say his name, I promise myself that much. "He was a coal miner, like my father and most of my brothers. He didn't have anything to offer as a groom, but he was sweet and proposed marriage to me on my seventeenth birthday."

Robert leans forward, his interest piqued. "I didn't know you came from a mining town. So didn't you marry him, then?"

"He died before I could."

Robert frowns. "I'm so sorry. Was it an accident in the mine?"

"You'd think so, wouldn't you? Rough conditions, long hours, dangerous work. But that's not how it happened at all. He went on strike with the other miners and was murdered by a Pinkerton goon squad."

He winces, setting his fork down.

This is a genteel dining room and I'm having lunch with a genteel man. But even if he isn't the sort to hire goons to bust a union, he comes from the kind of people who do. So I won't spare him. I can't spare him or myself now. "It was a hot summer, like this one. They came in with rifles and herded the strikers into cattle cars. Locked 'em in and rolled 'em into the heat to bake. Our union boys went more than sixteen hours without water before they broke their way out, but it was too late for the one I meant to marry."

Robert silently digests what I've told him, then asks, "You've had a hard life, haven't you?"

"I'm not the one who died in a cattle car."

I don't look at him when I say this because I feel myself hardening. He's a beautiful man and this is a beautiful lunch in a beautiful hotel with a beautiful view. But I know what's behind the veneer, all the ugly parts of this hotel that visitors never see. The way supervisors cheat workers out of their pay, the backbreaking workload of the maids and the poor treatment of the Negro workers . . . I must assume there's an ugly underside to the man who oversees it all, too. Taking my list from my pocketbook, I say, "I'd rather not wait for dessert to discuss the grievances."

"And here I meant for us to have such a relaxing afternoon . . ." He smoothes his napkin over his legs. "But I am a man of my word, so I'm willing to listen to a complaint."

"I've an entire list of them," I protest.

"Traditionally, I have a very short attention span, so why don't we start with one complaint."

"Very well. We'd like you to change hotel policy so that pregnant women aren't summarily fired. So long as a woman can continue doing her job—"

"Any good husband should provide—"

"Not all of them have husbands," I insist.

I tell him about Gertrude's plight without exposing Mr. Underwood, much as I'd like to blacken *his* name. Robert listens patiently as the waiter clears our plates, then takes up his spoon when the Venetian ice cream arrives in delicate crystal cups. He finally asks, "And who is the villain in this story?"

"Robert Aster," I insist.

He snorts. "I meant the name of the man who took advantage of the girl."

"I can't tell you that. You might take action against him."

"Wouldn't he deserve it?"

I straighten my spine. "He deserves whatever the good Lord has to dole out to him, but what he does with women is his own business and I'd be a hypocrite to say otherwise."

Robert sighs. "If you don't tell me his name, I might doubt the veracity of your story."

"Give your word that there won't be retaliation."

"Done."

I tell him. He listens. When I'm finished, he says, "Please tell the hapless girl to report to the front desk tomorrow morning. I'll have a bank note waiting for her."

I think I've misheard him. "A bank note?"

Nodding as he shovels a bit of ice cream onto his spoon, he makes a gesture of dismissal. "I'm prepared to be quite generous. It was a man in my employ who gave her false hopes of marriage and that doesn't sit well with me. I'm happy to pay her rent for the next year or two."

His Victorian attitude and casual assumption of such a large debt staggers me, but also misses the point entirely. "She wants her job back so she can earn her own living."

"Sophie, I can't very well go around rehiring people that my supervisors let go, can I?"

"But you can afford to leave obscenely large bank notes for every girl who gets in trouble in your hotel?"

"This is just one girl."

"I didn't tell you the story so that you'd help Gertie—well, not only her. This is only one story in twenty. I can tell you about a bellboy—"

"One grievance at a time." He looks at me pointedly. "Your ice cream is melting."

Prompted by him, I take a bite. It melts on my tongue, thick and silky—the way I imagine he might taste. And when I think thoughts like that one, it's more difficult to argue with him. "So you'd rather give Gertrude money than deal with the systemic problem."

"*Systemic problem*," he says, mimicking me, his eyes dancing with merriment. "That doesn't sound like anything a mere mortal can remedy. But a girl with a baby I can manage."

"You don't even *know* Gertrude."

"No, but you obviously care about her. There are certain advantages to being my mistress and I'm certain that you'll find a way of repaying me for my generosity."

"I haven't agreed to be your kept woman," I reply, offended.

"You agreed the moment you let me take your clothes off."

This rattles me. And I can't help but think this is not how labor negotiations are conducted; I'm used to men dismissing me because I'm a young woman, but I fear he knows I'm so drawn to him that the idea of exchanging sex for favors seems like I'm getting the better part of the deal. "How many mistresses do you have, anyway?"

He smirks. "You said before that the idea of sexual recreation doesn't offend you . . . and yet, I detect a note of disapproval, Sophie."

"It's a bit intimidating, that's all. The way the tabloids talk about you and all those beauties."

"Yet, I've never spanked any of them. But I *have* spanked you. What's more, I'd like to do it again."

The chill of the ice cream is no help against the heat of my cheeks. "You would?"

"Yes, I would. Tomorrow evening, after the end of your workday, come up to my office. You can tell Mrs. Mortimer that as part of that private disciplinary action, you must stay late and help my secretary file papers."

CHAPTER
Five

At the front desk the next day, there's a bank note with more zeroes than I expected, all strung together like pearls. "Oh, Sophie!" Gertie cries, throwing her arms around my neck, her belly bulging against mine. "Well, ain't this the berries? Ethel told me you were the one to go to for help, but how did you do it?"

"Never mind that," I say. "But you don't have to take it. Wouldn't you rather have your job back?"

Gertie bites her lower lip. "How can I turn down this kind of dough? I can't very well bring the baby to work with me can I?"

She makes a good point, but she wouldn't have the money if Robert Aster weren't trying to impress me, and that vexes me. "We're still organizing, Gertie. And if Mr. Aster won't take our complaints seriously, we'll take steps to see that he does."

"Go easy on him, Sophie," she says, clutching the bank note. "The ambassador wouldn't have given me a red cent, but his son seems like a swell fella."

"He just might be," I say, unable to deny the little glow of warmth

I feel when I think about Robert Aster. "But that doesn't mean we shouldn't deal with him on an even footing."

Seeing how he's made Gertie's life easier softens me, even though I suspect half the good things he does are nothing more than spite against his father. Robert Aster is not a saint and I'm not a sucker, but given how eager I am to be stretched over his knees, I worry I'm going jingle-brained for the man.

Gertie hugs me again, this time so hard my hatpin comes loose. "You know best, Sophie. You always do. And I know you can't stand here bumping gums all day, so I'd better scram."

As I watch her disappear into the crowd near the hotel florist shop, Hamilton looks up from the bellhop stand to give me a little wave. He's wearing a posy, just like the one I tucked into his lapel the other day. That's when I notice all the bellboys are wearing them—a sign of solidarity.

I get a spanking every night for the rest of the week. Each night, Robert is bolder. Sometimes yanking me over his knee before I'm ready. Sometimes spanking me harder, longer, faster. Sometimes he makes me thank him for each one.

I reach climax every time.

The first time took us by surprise, but now he expects it. And when it doesn't happen on its own, he makes it happen, grinding himself against me or rubbing between my legs.

He also teaches me to take him in my mouth, to slip my tongue over the thick, turgid flesh, satisfying him as he's satisfied me.

When he's done, I rush out to catch the trolley home, then run up the stairs to the lavatory, lift my dress, and look at the redness before it fades away. Sometimes I can see the outlines of his hand on my cheeks, and the sight of it is so exciting that I lean back against the door and touch myself.

It's shameful and I wish I hated it, but it feels like freedom.

I don't know what's happening to me. Every day in the boutique, all I want is to step into the elevator and take it upstairs. All I can think about is the depthless sexual hunger that this man has brought out in me. It's a craving. A madness. An addiction.

I'm shaking with it by Friday evening, when I slip into his office.

One look at me and his smile fades to concern. "What's the matter? What's wrong?"

Everything is wrong. I can't imagine that a person ought to feel like this. Like she's under some kind of spell. I think I should tell him that this has to stop. That I'm not sure I know myself anymore. These are all the things I ought to say so I'm stunned by what comes out instead. "Why haven't you given me another card?"

His eyebrows raise. "Because I didn't know that you were a virgin when I wrote them."

"Don't you still want me?" I ask plaintively.

He gives an incredulous snort. "Don't I *want* you? Can't you tell?"

"I can't tell anything about you. I don't *know* anything about you. You know *everything* I want because you read it in my journal, but how am I to guess—"

My words are cut off abruptly by the warmth of his mouth, closing over mine. I moan, first in protest, then in surrender as he sucks my bottom lip between his teeth and teases it with his tongue. A puff of breath stirs between us, warm and sensual. His hands lace into my hair, drawing me deeper into the kiss and my hand cups his smoothly shaved cheek. Though his lips are soft and velvety, there's a firmness beneath them. He uses them to tease, to tempt, and to plunder. Nudging my lips apart, his tongue touches mine and tangles with it. It feels as if we're alone, at the top of the city, locked together far apart from the rest of the world. This kiss is the only thing that matters. And it does matter. It really does.

When we finally break apart, he traces the residual moistness on my lips with his thumb. "Does that tell you anything you need to know, Sophie?"

Dazed, I blink up at him. "I'm afraid it raises a host of new questions."

He puts my hand over his heart where I can feel it beating hard beneath his shirt. "Do you feel that? That's how much I want you. And if you put your hand lower, you'd find even better proof."

"You said you'd go as far as I'd let you. Well, I want to let you . . ."

"I'm not sure you're ready, Sophie. And I don't want this to end."

"I am ready. I'm more than ready."

Robert slowly withdraws to the desk, takes out a card, and hands it to me. "There's no hiding this one."

I open it.

Stay the night with me.

If I say yes, I'll have to tell Ethel and Irene, who are driving me to madness with their curiosity about my mysterious beau. And if there were any question about whether or not I was to be Robert's mistress, staying the night with him would erase all doubt. If Ethel or Irene let any gossip slip, it'll ruin my reputation, but as a champion of several causes that garner social censure, I've no business caring about ruined reputations.

When I was a teenaged girl bringing lunch to miners on the picket line, company men shouted lewd things at me, but it never stopped me. After attending one of Mrs. Sanger's talks on birth control, a policeman on the street corner outside the lecture hall called me a prostitute. That didn't deter me, either. If anything, it made me believe even more firmly in equality for the sexes and the right of women to live as freely as men. I've been called a Communist, an agitator, and a radical. I don't care a bit for societal convention, so why should I care what anyone thinks about my choice to take a lover? "Yes, I'll stay the night with you."

Robert lets out a breath. Only then do I realize how anxious he was for my answer. He was prepared to end it, here and now, should I refuse him. I'm not sure why this comforts me, but it does. He's a man who means what he says and in spite of my fears that I'm slipping into an abyss, he seems like a firm thing to hold on to. Now, knowing that we're both on solid ground, his shoulders relax and he beams with boyish glee. "You'll spend the *whole* night with me?"

My lips draw together playfully. "Will you *need* all night, Mr. Aster?"

"You'll wish I didn't," he says, his eyes burning into mine.

We have dinner in his suite. He calls for it and the wait staff delivers our meal served on silver trays. Striped bass with a cucumber salad, cheese soufflé, and lemon custard pie. I'm dazzled by the sparkle of the chandelier overhead with its blue crystal teardrops, the gilt-edged furniture, and the two giant windows, each framed with blue damask curtains that cascade regally to the floor.

But even the opulence of my surroundings doesn't let me forget that I want him. I want him now. I'm *hot* for him. The glass in my hand feels so deliciously cool that I want to press it to my cheek in the hopes it will offer some relief.

I glance at the open door to the bedroom, and Robert grins. "Finish your dinner, Sophie. You're going to need your strength."

Defiantly, I shove the last bit of pie into my mouth, and it makes him laugh. He grabs me up into his arms and I yelp with surprise at my sudden weightlessness. He carries me into the bedroom, then sets me down on a slate blue velvet coverlet atop a carved oak bed so large it dominates the room.

My whole body tingles from the traces of his touch. I want him to crawl on top of me so that I can pillow his bulk as I did the first time, but I realize now how out of character it was for him to descend upon me in a frenzy like he did then. He was playing a character from my own imagination; I wonder what new stranger he'll turn into tonight.

The answer comes to me in the form of a black silk tie that he pulls from the nightstand and tugs between his fists. I know this fantasy and our eyes meet in recognition.

"Will you trust me?" he asks, his voice soft and intimate even in such a large and ornate room.

Ethel would tell me there's no reason whatsoever to trust any man, especially not this one. But I'm far beyond reason. "Yes. Do it. Yes, yes, yes."

He fastens the blindfold over my eyes and I'm plunged into darkness. But every other sense comes vividly to life. My breath seems louder. The dark scent of tobacco wafts up from the coverlet. I feel the dampness in the air—or perhaps that is only my own perspiration, because the more excited I become, the more I sweat.

He undresses me, peeling away my clothes, kissing my dewy skin wherever it is exposed. My dress comes off. My shoes. My stockings. My chemise. My drawers. Everything is stripped from me until I'm naked and quivering. I feel his lips in the palm of my hand and I tremble, because I know exactly what comes next and it excites me as much as it frightens me.

Perhaps my fear rouses him, because I feel the brush of his erection against my body as he uses his silken ties to secure me to the bed. First a wrist, then an ankle, then another wrist . . .

I can't say why I must test the bonds, but I must. I pull to the point of pain, to the point of reassurance. It's what I wanted. To feel that I can't get away. And the rush of knowing that I'm open to him, helpless to stop him, is worth the bite of the silk into my wrists.

"You can't slip those knots, Sophie. If you want to be freed, you'll have to rely upon me to untie you."

I wish I could see his expression. Wetting my lips, I ask, "Will you? Untie me, if I ask you to?"

"I'll untie you if you beg me to, but that isn't what I want to make you beg for."

In the darkness beneath the blindfold, I'm surprised when his weight shifts and his warm mouth envelopes my nipple. He sucks at one, then the other, making me arch up to meet him, both breasts aching for his attention. The tug of his suckling pulls deep in my womb. His kisses drift lower, tickling my belly, his hands caressing my sides. "Do you feel helpless?"

My answer is a moan, because I can see nothing and feel nothing but what he allows. My whole world has become the sensation of his skin to mine. The intimacy of his fingertips skimming down my body. Of the wetness between my legs, a fathomless hunger for him that I can't hide. "Yes, I do feel helpless."

"And yet, you have me utterly enraptured. I wish you could see yourself now, tied to my bed, at my mercy. I don't think I could stop now even if the Kaiser was at the door."

There is a swish of fabric, a clatter of a belt buckle, and a sound of unfastening. He must be undressing. And I'm distressed by the blindfold that prevents me from feasting my eyes on him. "I don't think I like this fantasy anymore!"

This doesn't stop him. He uses a finger to splay my nether lips, then murmurs, "I bet you taste just as good here as you do everywhere else."

A wet tongue draws shapes on my hip, then laps at the downy curls between my thighs. Liquid heat melts inside me, forcing me to gasp with desire. Then it gets hotter. He licks me, his tongue swirling in maddening little circles that drive me to arch my head back, overwhelmed by sensation. "Oh god, stop or I think, I think . . ."

There is no chance to warn him, because my words become incoherent cries.

I come hard. I come straining every muscle against the silk ties, my hips lifting up off the bed only to press harder against his mouth, my arousal flowing onto his tongue. And when it's over, I'm so embarrassed and there's nowhere to hide. I can't cover my face with my hands; I can only turn my head to the side.

I go silent inside myself.

"Sophie?"

I say nothing.

"You know that's exactly what I wanted to happen, don't you?" Moving between my legs, he presses the crown of his erection against my slickness. "Can't you feel how hard I am for you?"

The desire to reach for him, to touch him is so strong that I writhe against my bonds, and the frustration only grows when he whispers, "Do you remember this fantasy, Sophie? How the man kneels over her, stroking himself until he sprays all over her body. Is that what you want me to do?"

"Yes," I whisper, then change my mind. "No! I just—I want you inside me."

"But I promised to reenact your fantasies in every detail."

"Change it. Please!"

"Do you want me to fuck you instead?"

"Oh, please, please, yes, please!" Shamelessly I spread my knees and I'm near delirious with anticipation when I hear a tearing sound and know he must be rolling a sheath onto himself. If he didn't want to wear one, I wouldn't be able to stop him. And that thought terrifies me as much as it thrills me.

My heartbeat thumps when he slides himself between my legs, teasing at the opening. "Is this what you want, Sophie?"

"No!" I cry with frustration. "I want . . . *more.*"

His swollen erection dips shallowly inside me, then withdraws. It doesn't hurt. Not with the sharp pain of the first time. Instead, it makes me ache. And I don't think I can stand it. "Tell me what you want, Sophie."

"Robert, please, please."

He stretches me a little more, then leaves me empty.

"I want you to fuck me!" I cry, then sob with desire. I am desperate for him. Desperate to have him inside me. "Please, please, fuck me."

I hear the hiss of his desire through his teeth, but he holds back.

"Only if you promise me one thing . . . that when you come—and you will—that you'll call out my name."

I promise, though my words are an incomprehensible jumble. When he fills me, I give out a strangled cry of relief. *Yes*. This is what I need.

"Christ, you're still so tight," he murmurs, seating himself until we're pressed close, his front to mine, and the weight of him on me is delicious. I feel every puff of air against my cheek when he breathes, and my own shallow breaths quicken as he strokes in and out.

He kisses me. And in my fevered state, I bite him. Not hard, but just enough that he notices and growls, making that sound I love so much. I want to throw my arms around him. I want to run my hands up and down his back. I want to wrap my legs around his waist, but I can't do any of those things. Tied still, I can only kiss and bite and breathe him in.

I can only accept all this pleasure . . . and I think I'm going to die of it.

I'm coming. I say his name, moaning it at first, then louder, until the sound drives me to completion. He moves faster inside me, making wet slapping noises that are drowned out completely when I scream his name. My body tightens, grabs at him, and binds us together through my climax.

His jagged breath tells me he's close and I want that, too. But when the last of my tremors pulses through my sex, he withdraws, kneels up, and suddenly I feel the whole mattress shaking beneath us.

"Do you want me to come all over you?" he asks in a hoarse whisper.

The indecent question breaks open a dam in me, and I'm flooded with memories of the fantasy I wrote in the journal. "Oh god, I do."

When the first spurts of his seed splash against my skin, we cry out together. In the darkness of my blindfold, the sensation surprises me. The wetness on my belly. The strand that catches on my lips and clings. It tastes wonderfully salty as I draw it into my mouth, consumed with the depravity of it.

Robert collapses atop me, angling most of his weight into the mattress, but resting heavy limbs over my trussed-up body. Then he kisses me, and the salt of his sweat mingles with the salt of his seed and the salt of my own taste on his lips.

It's an ocean of newness and discovery, and I swim in it.

The fantasy I wrote ends here, the man departing without a word. Thankfully, Robert doesn't go. Instead, he dips a fingertip into his sticky leavings and paints my body with it. "I'm writing my name on you."

"Why?"

"Because you're mine."

He's claiming me. Claiming me more now than when he took my virginity, and though I shouldn't want to be claimed by any man, it touches me somewhere I didn't expect. He's rubbing the sharp, virile scent of himself into my skin, staining me with his essence, and I feel a pull between us, a connection both fragile and irresistible. Can it be possible that there's something sacred in these indecent acts I've imagined?

Or is the magic in the man?

He shifts again and my breath hitches. "Now what are you going to do?"

"I'm going to untie you. I don't like the marks the ties are leaving on your arms, and your hands are bright red."

He reaches to release me and I hiss with pain as my arms fall, one at a time, to the velvet coverlet. Only now do I feel the ache in them, the suffering that couldn't make itself heard over the roar of pleasure. He knew I was in pain, worried about me, sensed this about my body before I did. And his care for me elicits a pang of tenderness that threatens to be my undoing.

How can I feel the way I do about this man, who is nothing like he seems?

He removes my blindfold and I blink at the intrusion of unwelcome light. It's the first time I've seen him in a state of complete undress and it takes my breath away. He's big boned and barrel-chested, with powerful muscles hidden beneath the flesh. I marvel at the constellation of freckles on his skin. We're *both* fair-skinned but his body dwarfs mine and makes me feel like a doll in his arms. And it soothes me.

It also brings out my inner imp. "Is *that* all there is to it, then?"

His hand goes to the nape of my neck. "Oh, Sophie, we're just getting started."

CHAPTER
Six

Late into the night when I'm aching and sore, I ask, "Why do you always get to be the one in command of the situation? Why don't I ever get to yank your clothes off or force you down or make you obey me?"

Robert props himself up on one elbow, idly tracing my collarbone. "Because, my dear lady, none of that was in your book."

Nose to nose with him, I say, "Well, it should have been. What was I thinking, writing all these stories about girls who get seduced and spanked and surrender to a man like he's the lord of the manor? Stories like that probably make people think women shouldn't have gotten the vote."

"I assure you, suffrage was the last thing on my mind when reading your diary."

"I'm being serious," I say, unwilling to let him divert me.

He laughs. "I can see that. Sophie, your stories left me with an impression of a woman who understood her own desires and was unapologetic about them."

A little doubt creeps in. "Maybe there's something wrong with a woman who desires this."

He cups my cheek, adoringly. "There is nothing whatsoever wrong with you, Sophie."

"I'm just thinking . . . wondering . . . I believe people are all equal and that power should be shared. I believe that women are as smart as men and employers ought to respect their employees, but when I'm with you, all I want is to do things that insult those ideas."

Robert scowls. "Oh, for the love of God, if it will put an end to this dreary introspection, have your way with me."

It takes me a moment to recover from the shock. "You'll do anything I say?"

He doesn't look at all thrilled by the prospect, but throws his arms open. "I'm yours to command . . ."

In spite of his words, there is absolutely nothing humble or submissive in his posture. I'm even a little nervous to touch him for fear it's a trick and he'll spank me if I try.

"Well? No idea what to do with me, Sophie?"

"I think I'd better tie you to the bed."

One eyebrow goes up. He doesn't think I'll do it, I realize. He doesn't think I'd dare. But he's changed his mind by the time I've used one of his silk ties to knot his right hand to the headboard.

"Sophie, is this really necessary?"

"Your other arm, please," I say, reaching for his hand.

"This is an experiment," he says with a sigh, allowing me to secure him. "An exercise in trust."

"Mmmhmmm." I lean back and survey my handiwork. I'm overcome by the sight of him, naked, those spectacularly big arms of his spread out and straining like a dangerous beast that I've captured. I'm not sure I *do* know what to do with him.

I start by straddling his legs, kissing him, letting my hair fall into his face. At least I know he likes the kiss, because he murmurs my name. I shiver when my sex touches his and it stiffens with arousal. I grind against him. And I feel an urgent need to have him inside.

"Careful, Sophie." He shifts beneath me, his eyelids lowering in warning. "You're dangerously close to destroying my self-control."

That's when I see that he's loosened the tie holding his right arm. I don't bother to fix it because he could break it if he wanted to. This is, as he said, an exercise in trust. Shamelessly, I slide my body down, taking his cock between my thighs, but not inside me. The sudden motion makes him groan. The head of his shaft nestles against my clitoris and stimulates me in a most delicious and unexpected way.

Resting my palms on his pale, freckled chest, I rub against him slowly. I mean to use his body for my pleasure—to be as wicked and controlling with him as he's always been with me.

And maybe that's how it starts, for the first few moments.

But then we kiss again, the sweat of his upper lip in my mouth, and it's as if I'm the one bound. The undulation of my hips is a dance I do to please him even more than to please myself. And the way he's looking at me makes me feel as if I'd better not stop. The idea that I'm his private dancer sends spirals of arousal up into my belly, but before I can let myself get lost in it, I lift up, leaving him hard, wet, pulsing, and unfinished.

He snarls with frustration. "Where do you think you're going?"

"Remember, you're mine to command."

I arrange my knees on his pillow on either side of his head.

Then he goes quiet and so do I.

I can scent my own arousal, so it must be in his nostrils, too. I was all boldness when I started this, but now my confidence fails. What I meant to do is so brazen that I tremble at my own temerity. I'm frozen above him, paralyzed.

"If you're going to do it," he says, with a growl, "by god, *do* it, Sophie. There's no room for shyness if you mean to fuck my mouth."

That's all I need. Arching my back, I thrust against his mouth. I ride his tongue. I moan as his teeth graze my most sensitive spot, and then it becomes a battle. His is no passive kiss between my legs. He strains, the cords of his neck tight as he sucks my pussy lips into his mouth and takes possession of them.

I try not to melt into him. I try not to surrender. But the way he uses his mouth on me has me panting, moaning, straining. I throw my head, tendrils of sweat-soaked hair whipping at my bare back as I realize that he's going to make me come. "Oh god, oh please."

I shouldn't beg him, but I can't help it. As my thighs clench around his ears, I reach down and grab a fistful of his hair. I'm coming again, crying out, and I think I must be hurting him.

But I can't be gentle.

Rip.

It's the sound of his right arm tearing free of his bonds and it's as raw and primal as my orgasmic screams. In spite of everything, I'm grateful when his freed arm comes round my hips and locks me in place. He's still sucking and licking and thrusting his tongue into me when we begin to roll.

His body is like some enormous boulder, the momentum of which I cannot stop. He's supposed to be submitting to me, but he has me caught in the grip of one arm as he rises from the bed the other arm is still tethered to. He pins me to the wall. The cool grain of the wood paneling scratches my back as I slide between it and his body.

My eyes must be filled with reproach because he says, "I'm sorry. I don't think I'm made that way . . . and neither are you."

Hours later, we're glued together, sticky with sweat and sex. Having taken personal instruction as to exactly which positions *are* possible—quite a few, it turns out—I'm so overstimulated that even the bed-sheets against my skin leave me raw. "I begin to see what all the fuss is about, Mr. Aster . . ."

With great satisfaction, Robert peels himself off me, collapses onto his back, and basks in the morning rays of sunshine that leak in around the curtains. "And *that's* how your first time should have been. Now we can sleep in."

I groan. "I've never been so tired in all my life . . . but I don't think I could sleep a wink."

"I'll read you a bedtime story," he says, reaching to the end table for my journal.

"I'm too tired to even *think* about sex," I confess.

"Nonsense. Tell me, my little bearcat, which of these fantasies is your favorite?"

When this started, it was exciting to have a man cater to me with no expectations in return. Now I find myself wanting to know his fantasies, too. "Which one is *your* favorite?"

"This one." He flips to the right page, holding the journal so that I can see it.

One glance at the page and I feel myself turning scarlet. I curl in on myself, drawing my knees up under the covers as if I can hide what he's exposed. "It was just a whimsy . . ."

"Why are you cowering, Sophie? Trust me, I'm gratified to know that we both fantasize about famous movie stars."

I peek at him. "You are?"

He gives me a lurid smile. "I knew about these fantasies before we met. Nothing in this journal shocks or offends me. I don't know if everything you fantasize about will excite me, but everything I've read in this journal *definitely* does."

There's an easing of the tension in my back and shoulders as I accept his words for the gift that they are. "I think it's just *her.* I love her sass, her hair, and the way she dresses. We all try to imitate her. I think if there was any movie star girls would think about kissing, it'd be Clara Cartwright."

"And trust me, she's the movie star most likely to appreciate that sentiment."

I have to ask. "You've met her?"

"I know her very well."

Remembering the spate of scandal sheet rumors from more than a year ago, my stomach suddenly sours. "You may say that I haven't any business asking, but—"

"Sophie, you've every right to ask," he says, reaching to stroke a lock of hair out of my eyes. "But a gentleman does not tell."

"I thought you were trying to be less of a gentleman."

"Nevertheless, I treat people I care about with respect. If you want to know about my relationship with Clara, you can ask her yourself."

I snort indelicately. "I'm just a shopgirl. I'm not likely to meet the likes of the legendary Clara Cartwright."

"To the contrary, you're going to meet her next week. Clara and Leo are coming to stay in the hotel. Their film has been nominated for an award and they'll be my guests while they're in the city. I intend to introduce you."

If someone told me two days ago that I'd see Clara Cartwright in the flesh, I'd have been over the moon. Now, I'm upset. "I don't want to ask her about you like some jealous harpy! It's not her place to tell me. It's yours."

He pulls himself up, resting his back against the headboard and reaching for a flask by his bedside, as if this isn't a conversation that he can have sober. When I see him pause, unable to take a swallow, I know I'm not going to like what he has to say. "Clara and I were lovers, but I deny it in the scandal sheets and always will."

"Because you're such a *right guy* or because you have something to be ashamed of?"

"I'm not ashamed of Clara," he says with a slight note of offense. "I adore her. She's married to my best friend in the world."

I sigh with relief at this perfectly reasonable explanation. He wouldn't want to rub an old affair in the nose of her husband. It makes sense to spare everyone's feelings. So why does something feel so unfinished about it? "You're not *still* sleeping with her, are you?"

"Not for quite some time." He seals the flask, puts it back without taking a sip, then arranges himself stiffly against the pillows. I'm alarmed by the anxiety in his expression, by the naked emotion in his posture that he's trying to hide.

He's a man who takes what he wants; I've always known this about him. What I don't know is if there are lines he won't cross. "Robert, did you betray your friend with his wife?"

"*No*," he says forcefully, more than a shadow of warning in his eyes. "No, I did not. I *would* not." That's when I realize it's not guilt I see on his features, but some other kind of regret. "It's not what you're thinking, Sophie. But it's too complicated and unconventional to explain."

"I'm a complicated and unconventional girl. If you can't tell me, who can you tell? It's hardly fair that you know all my stories and I know none of yours."

He sighs. "Has anyone ever told you that you argue rather persuasively? Do you have formal training?"

"I've been speaking in union halls since I was a teenaged girl at my da's side." I nestle against him, trying to make him comfortable enough to tell me the truth. I see that his handsome features are marred by dark shadows beneath his eyes. I don't know if it's sadness or exhaustion, but he lets me pull him down so that we're on the same level, face-to-face. "The main thing is that I'm persistent, Robert, so you might as well sing."

I school myself not to show shock or alarm; I don't want to wound him if he opens himself to me. But a little part of me worries whatever he has to say might ruin everything between us. And perhaps my keen desire to protect this relationship should be what scares me most.

He touches his forehead to mine. "What would you say if I told you that when I shared a bed with Clara Cartwright, it was at her husband's invitation?"

The stab of jealousy is blunted by my instant fascination. "He wanted you to make love to his wife?" In spite of bracing myself, I'm wide-eyed, my mouth a little circle of surprise. My words are breathy when I speak, betraying my own excitement. "And you did?"

"Many times."

"Oh." I don't know what else to say. That he would do such a thing makes him seem even more worldly than before. "Are you . . . are you *all* lovers?"

He hesitates. "Leo and I don't . . . it's really of no consequence, Sophie. It's been over for months now, ever since I returned to the city."

"Did something happen? Was there an argument?"

"Nothing like that. Quite the opposite, actually."

It pains him, I realize. And that, in turn, pains me. "You said you'd been in love precisely one and a half times, Robert. Was Clara the one or the half?"

The way he rubs at his cheek tells me I've hit a nerve. "The half . . ."

When I realize he has no intention of explaining more, I guess. "You held your heart in reserve because she's a married woman?"

"Something like that," Robert replies softly. "But I say I was only half in love with her because it wasn't her alone. It was the both of them. I got from her what I couldn't get from him, and from him what I couldn't get from her. But how long can that go on, really?"

"I don't understand."

"My strongest bond is with Leo," he says, his lips thinning with the admission. "But that's not a sexual attraction. Meanwhile, I'm very attracted to his wife, but that never became love—at least not the kind of love that binds a man to a woman forever. What would I have done if it had?"

I lace my fingers through his, fighting back my selfish relief so that I can better understand his complicated heart. "They couldn't offer you more?"

"They offered me more. I just didn't take it. I'm the son of an ambassador. I live in society. Hell, my family *is* society," he says, knotting the coverlet in one of his fists. "What sort of explanation could I ever give for such a relationship? No one can make such a thing work. It just isn't done."

"How do you know if you didn't try?"

He closes his eyes, as if the conversation has exhausted him well beyond the exertions of our lovemaking. "My father reminded me that I couldn't be a worthless playboy and a dreamer forever, and the ambassador is always right. I followed his orders and came back East to be a man and make a name for myself."

"So you left them. You left Clara and Leo?"

"Shouldn't I have?"

How can I answer a question like that, for the man who has become my lover? Can I wish he did anything else? No, I can't and I don't. But it troubles me deep in my bones. "I think if you find happiness, you ought to cling to it no matter what anyone says about it."

"You really *are* a radical aren't you?" he murmurs drowsily. Then, when I don't answer, he says, "I couldn't think of a way to make myself fit with them . . . and it's for the better, because if I hadn't left Clara and Leo, I might not have found you."

Why, what a tender thing to say. It takes me utterly by surprise.

His eyelashes are fair like the rest of him, but they're the longest eyelashes of any man I've ever met. With his eyes closed they give him an angelic appearance. I stroke his cheek softly and say, "But you and I hardly fit in each other's worlds either, now, do we?"

"No we don't," he admits. "But I *thank God* for you anyway because I was drowning here before you . . ."

CHAPTER
Seven

"And you let him *go all the way*, Sophie?" Ethel asks, catching me by surprise with her disapproval.

But even her wide-eyed censure can't spoil my mood. Still giddy, I fling open the window sash and smile at the city below. "More times than I could count."

"Sophie!" Ethel cries.

"What?" I settle myself on the window ledge to get a breeze. "Aren't you the flapper who has kissed a thousand men and claims to want to kiss a thousand more?"

Ethel puts her hands on her hips. "On our skimpy wages, I'd never get to go anywhere or do anything fun if I didn't. But nobody looks up to me. You're the one always telling us to stand up and earn our own way."

I make a sound of annoyance, glancing around our shabby room with its broken closet door. In the corner, a basket overflows with laundry to be washed, hung, and ironed. Even the flowerpots on the fire escape are chipped and cracked. "And what is it you think? That Robert Aster's my sugar daddy?"

"You got him to give all that money to Gertie. Don't tell me he's given nothing to you."

I count my gifts. Lingerie. A rose. Three lovely meals. And more pleasure than I could stand. Even now, the traces of his touch linger on my skin and make me sigh a little. And that makes me defiant. I turn on Irene who, up to this point, has appeared to be in shock. Even now, she's holding the iron up and away from the board as if afraid she won't be able to press her clothes without scorching them. "Well, Irene, aren't you going to add your two bits about my pitching woo with the boss?"

She gives a delicate shake of her head. "I'm just worried for you, Sophie."

"I'm not going to end up like Gertrude!"

"No," she says. "But you're falling in love."

"Horsefeathers." It can't last between us. I know that. Robert has already told me his plan. He's going to meet some girl from his own social circle and let her reform him of his playboy ways. Let her reform him of . . . me. He's going to marry her and show her off on his arm and make little Aster heirs. He's told me what to expect, but the sharp pain of the truth stuns me. "I'm not a fool, Irene. I know better."

Still, in the days that follow, I wonder if she's right.

Robert and I play out each fantasy in my journal, one by one. He takes me to Coney Island late one night; we swim nude at the beach in the frothing waves. Another night we play a card game that leaves me naked and ready to do his bidding. Following that, I dress up in a frilly maid's uniform and pretend to steal the silver from his room, a crime for which I'm exquisitely punished. And after a spirited night in which he introduces me to a vibrating gadget popularized by Dr. Freud for the treatment of hysteria, Robert falls asleep in my arms.

Watching the moonlight play on his closed lashes, something happens to me.

I want to know him; truly know him. Wondering over each object by his bed, I make up little stories about each one, saddened that I should have to guess about anything in his life. I want to know how he looked as a little boy. Who taught him to ride a bicycle. Who tended his first skinned knee. I want to know how old he was when he smoked his first cigarette. When he kissed his first girl. When he did something for which he holds regret. I wonder how he got the jagged scar near his elbow and it seems a terrible tragedy that I've missed all these moments of his life.

All I want to do is be with him so that I don't miss another . . .

It's my night to close the boutique, so I turn off most of the lights and draw the curtain that tells customers to come back in the morning. I'm just about to pull white linen sheets over all the counters to keep dust from settling onto the delicate garments, when someone says, "Don't do that yet."

Startled, I look up to see Robert in the doorway wearing a tuxedo. He looks like a swell, neatly coifed, perfectly handsome, his smile as white as his shirt, which is fastened with mother-of-pearl studs. He's an elite man of society. I'm not sure I've ever seen a man look so dapper.

It makes my insides flutter just to look at him.

"What are *you* doing here, Mr. Aster?"

"It *is* my hotel," he reminds me with a grin. "And I'm buying you a dress. Surely there's something in the boutique you've had your eye on? Choose anything and don't look at the price."

I'm more than a little flabbergasted. "Why?"

"Because you've never been drunk and I'm taking you to a juice joint."

As I stand there stammering, he comes up behind me and touches me with a freedom I've never allowed any other man. There isn't a breath of space between the moment he grabs me and the moment my body comes alive for him. I hear myself sigh, wanting his hands everywhere, but I say, "Getting drunk in a speakeasy isn't one of my fantasies."

"Well, it should be."

I sigh again. "I'm afraid I have other plans. There's a lecture at the Civics League tonight on world peace."

"I did my part to secure world peace during the Great War . . ."

"You can't secure peace with war."

"If only someone had told the President," he says with a chuckle. "Well, I hate to be the cause of bloodshed in some obscure nation because I took you away from a meeting, but come out with me tonight and I'll do my best to make it up to the world later."

"You haven't heard the full list of complaints I wrote up yet. I think you're taking advantage . . ."

He laughs. "Oh, *hell*. Give me your list. I promise I'll read it. As long you let me get you all dolled up. What about the golden gown with the sequins and fringe?"

It's the most expensive and glamorous gown in the shop. It comes with long black gloves, a feather boa, and matching headdress. I worry it won't fit, but once he's stripped my clothes off and put me into it, the gown hugs me tight, baring my shoulders, arms, and back.

That's a lot of skin.

It's so short the tops of my stockings are likely to show when I walk, but when I look from the mirror over my shoulder to see him staring, I can't imagine wanting to wear anything else. "You like it, don't you?"

There's banked heat in his eyes. "It makes me want to burn everything else you own."

"That'd leave me nothing to wear to work."

"Nudity has never bothered me," he says, giving me a little spin. "In fact, by the end of the evening, I expect to have you naked and screaming my name."

Well, I can't say no to that, can I?

He takes the list of complaints from me, glancing at it while I get my shoes on and comb my hair under the headdress. Then he gives me a moment to powder my nose before taking me straight out through the lobby where the bellboys, with posies in their lapels, watch with wide eyes. I don't want them to start doubting me, but right now, the only thing I can see is Robert Aster.

On the street, his driver helps us into the back of his Rolls-Royce limousine and we're off to Harlem. But when Robert leans in to kiss me, I say, "I'd like to talk about wages."

He groans, burying his head against the feather boa round my neck. "You've the most peculiar notions about how to arouse a man, Miss O'Brien."

"Given the way you're panting in my ear, I'd say my methods are working."

He chuckles.

He's indulging me and I'm happy to take advantage of it. "Do you know that the women who work for you make half the wages of the men doing the same jobs?"

He pulls me tighter against him. "We pay the going rate for female employees, don't we?"

He's got me there.

"Just because every other hotel in the city abuses the women who work for them doesn't mean you should, too. You can change the policy."

"I'm flattered you think so, but my father—"

"The boutique makes more money for the hotel than the florist shop or the cigar stand. Yet, as a sales*girl*, I make half the salary of any sales*man* at any counter in the Aster Hotel. I'm paid less than the men who work fewer hours or are still in training. Does that seem fair?"

"You've certainly earned a raise," he says with a suggestive wag of his eyebrows. "At the very least, your paycheck should reflect the extra hours of service you're putting in for me . . ." When he sees my shocked expression, he adds, "You didn't think I forgot *that* fantasy, did you?"

I'm stunned, remembering an errant scribbling in the margin of my journal about a girl willing to sell herself to men. The blood drains away from my face as I realize what he must think of me. And how aroused I am in spite of it. I have to shake myself to keep my wits about me. "I was only using myself as an example. I don't want a raise unless you're willing to give one to every woman who works for you."

"Are you aiming to be the most expensive mistress I've ever had?"

I don't want to laugh, but I do. "Don't do it for *me*; do it because it's the right thing."

He arches a brow. "Why should you care why I did it, so long as you got what you wanted in the end?"

"Because I think you're something special, Robert Aster, and I don't want to be proved wrong."

He blinks. His devil-may-care smile falters. His mouth opens as if he's going to say something of import. Then the car pulls up under the neon sign over the club and the moment is gone.

The chauffeur comes round the side and helps us out. There's been a light summer rain and it smells wonderful steaming up from the hot pavement into the night air. A few drivers honk their horns and swerve round Robert's limousine as he escorts me to the club. The entrance to the speakeasy is in the back, where an iron door bars our way. Robert taps a secret knock, a peephole slit opens, and once the bouncer sees we're the sort he wants to admit, the door swings open.

Inside, we're hit with a wall of jazz and glimpse scantily clad showgirls on stage, all tall and lithe. The dancers wear pasties on their nipples and their breasts glisten with perspiration under the hot stage lights. The flimsy feathered skirts on their hips hide nothing from the mirrored floor, and the men hoot and holler, "Get hot, get hot!"

The place is filled with men in tuxedos puffing on cigars and women in sequins, pearls, and feather boas, just like the one I wear. In my glittering golden gown, I must look like I'm one of them, but this isn't my world. It's too shiny and gay.

Robert's hand closes over mine as he guides me to a table, his ease in this atmosphere of revelry helping to calm my nerves. "I've got a surprise for you."

A little thrill goes through me. I know that I wrote about parties, but not this kind, and I can't think that he means to push me onto the top of the grand piano and make love to me here. The truth is, I don't know and it's exciting not knowing. "Am I going to like it?"

He clears his throat as we approach the best table in the house. "It's going to make you weak in the knees . . ."

That's when I see my surprise.

Beyond a sea of white-jacketed waiters, the contours of a beautiful woman in red emerges from the haze of smoke. She puffs out the long end of her cigarette holder, then smiles like the movie star she is.

It's Clara Cartwright.

Glamorous. Glorious. Gorgeous.

Her red dress hugs every curve, black kohl lines her dramatic eyes, a crimped bob frames her face, and ruby earrings dangle from her ears.

I'm dazzled.

She enchants me such that I nearly overlook her bemused companion, a man of rugged good looks and a slightly world-weary air. This must be Clara's husband, because the moment he spots us, he jumps to his feet and embraces Robert like a long-lost brother. They clap each other on the back, shake hands and then clap each other again.

Eventually, Robert stoops to give Clara a peck on the cheek, which she receives as her due. With a champagne coupe dangling from one hand, she studies me curiously. "Who's the smarty?"

"This is Sophie O'Brien," Robert says, holding a chair out for me. "You're going to love her. She's an anarchist."

What an introduction!

But before I can deny it, Clara's eyes light up. "Oh, Robert. You found me an anarchist to interview for my new film on Sacco and Vanzetti? You're the bee's knees."

I slide into my chair, laughing nervously. "I'd be quite interested in a film about that travesty, but I'm afraid I'm just a reformer, not an anarchist."

Clara snaps her fingers. "*Rhatz!*"

Robert grabs a program from a passing usher and pays a nickel for it. "Don't let Sophie fool you with that adorable laugh. She's a dangerous radical."

He's teasing me again and I glare at him, but Clara reaches out with lacquered nails to give my hand a squeeze. "Well, we love danger and radicals, don't we, Leo?"

Her husband lifts his glass in salute. "Especially danger."

Robert makes formal introductions all the way around, then we order dinner. Soon the table is piled high with shrimp cocktail, blue point oysters, lobster, and roast duckling. I'm the stranger here and feel out of place, but Clara puts me at ease by telling a funny story about nearly drowning on set in a fishpond while wearing a hula skirt and a coconut bra.

Knowing she and Robert were lovers, I don't want to like her. But I do. Everyone does. All the moviegoers, all the men, and especially her husband, whose gaze almost never leaves her face.

Strangely, the only man not stealing glances at her is Robert, whose attention is so riveted upon me that I wonder if he's trying to prove something to them. Or to himself. When a waiter asks him for his order he says, "I'll have an old-fashioned. Actually, make it two. Let's see what Sophie thinks of my usual jorum of skee."

I'm dubious at the arrival of a glass of amber liquid with orange slices placed before me. My nose scrunches at the smell and when I take a sip of it, I cough and sputter. *Jesus, Mary, and Joseph.* "It's terrible! It's like drinking a bottle of disinfectant cleaner."

Clara and her husband laugh, but Robert takes the glass from me, tasting it for himself. He rolls the liquid over his tongue experimentally, then relaxes. "You had me worried there, Sophie. But this is the real thing—the most expensive brand in the country. That's so we don't have to worry about poison."

"Stop scaring her, Robert!" Clara cries. "Just knock it back, Sophie. It's eggs in the coffee."

I've never had a hankering to try liquor. Not because of the laws forbidding its sale, but because it never seemed as if any sensible person made good use of it. And now that I know what it tastes like, I know why. But with Robert and his friends, I *want* to drink it. So with their encouragement, I tip my head back and let it slide down.

"*Atta girl*," Mr. Vanderberg says and Robert beams with pride.

The liquor burns my gullet but warms me down to my toes. It makes the piano tinkle louder in my ears and I sway in my seat, eyes on the dusky saxophone player whose notes make the dancers sway. Some drunk man in the crowd makes a toast to fallen soldiers and Mr. Vanderberg raises his glass.

Robert does, too, though he never lifts his eyes.

"They served together," Clara leans over to tell me.

"So Robert says," I reply, waiting for the heat inside me to dissipate. "Though I'm sure he underestimates his part in the war."

"He always does," Mr. Vanderberg breaks in. "Robert can't shoot straight but I wouldn't be alive today if it weren't for those big mitts of his and his skill with a bayonet."

Robert's gaze trails off to the stage, a slight grimace at the mention. Truthfully, Mr. Vanderberg doesn't seem to want say more about the war, either, but Clara prompts him. "This sounds like a story you've never told me."

The two men lapse into silence. Clara reaches for her husband's hand.

He gives her fingers a squeeze and says, "Once we went down behind enemy lines and had to hoof it through some damned Belgian forest. A German patrol caught us and frog-marched us through the woods. My arm was broken and my ankle was twisted from the crash;

I thought we were going to have to dig our graves. But Bobby waited for just the right moment. Cracked his fist into the jaw of one Hun and had him spitting out his own teeth by time he realized he was disarmed."

"And I nearly sliced my elbow off on an enemy bayonet in the process," Robert adds.

It must be how he got the jagged scar I noticed before. I never gave much thought to the life and death struggles he's survived. I've dismissed him as a man whose led an easy life, but realize now how wrong I was to do so.

"You did what had to be done," Mr. Vanderberg said.

Robert shrugs as if it were a matter of indifference to him, but I see the tightening at the corners of his mouth. "Why talk about this when we were having such a good time?"

"You're right," Clara announces. "The night is young. Let's buy a few bottles and go back to the hotel."

I lose count of how many little glasses I drink before we go, but I can't feel the tip of my nose when Robert leans over to kiss me. The music and the laughter and the voices in the club all fade to a distant buzz when he whispers, "I'm going to make you fuck her tonight."

CHAPTER

Eight

It hits me hard by the time we all pile into the back of Robert's car. I'm blinking too much, too rapidly, trying to pretend that liquor hasn't turned the whole world a bit sooty around the edges, like the windows of every house in the mining town where I grew up.

I try to tell myself that I've imagined it. That he never whispered those outrageous words in my ear, and that it's just my mind playing tricks on me. I convince myself of it because the three of them behave as if this night were nothing out of the ordinary. They're easy with one another. Funny and fun. I like being with them; and just for tonight, I pretend I belong in their magical world.

When Robert's driver brings us around front of the hotel, Clara peeks out the window. "Damn it. The vultures are waiting . . ." Pulling a mirror from her pocketbook, she straightens her hair and puts on a new coat of lipstick. Then her posture changes, shoulders squaring, her expression taking on a hard edge.

"Time to go be Clara Cartwright," she says, sliding out of the car into a mob of people who want to take her picture and get her autograph. Leo climbs out after her, elbowing aside some of the more aggressive admirers, and we trail after them into the hotel and up to Robert's suite.

Excusing myself, I duck into the lavatory and splash a little water on my face. By the time I join them Robert and Clara sit on opposite sides of the sofa and her husband sprawls in a wing chair.

They're talking aviation.

Robert pats the cushion next to him, welcoming me into his arms, while he says, "It was nothing more than a stunt. Miss Earhart didn't fly the plane across the Atlantic. She was just a passenger. And I'm not sure women have any business being up there anyway. It's dangerous."

It always startles me when Robert lets his Victorian attitudes show and this shakes me out of my drunken torpor. "I think she's very brave. Besides, didn't you say you admired unconventional women?"

Robert lowers his eyelashes and leers at me. "That I do."

Leo ignores our flirtation. "Amelia's a fine pilot. She'll make the crossing by herself one day." He pauses here and bitterness creeps into his voice. "And then they'll give Amelia Earhart a goddamned Medal of Honor like they gave Charles Lindbergh."

For some reason, this makes Clara laugh. "Oh, give it up, Ace. You've got more medals than you can fit on that big strong chest of yours. You don't need any more."

"Lucky Fucking Lindy," Leo mutters darkly into his drink.

This makes Clara and Robert howl.

I feel vaguely excluded until Robert says, "Speaking of unconventional women . . . did I mention that Sophie has a splendid fantasy about you, Clara?"

Before panic rips through me, Leo quips, "Don't we all?"

Clara preens like a cat who loves to be admired, but I'm so mortified I want to flee.

Robert's hand closes tightly on mine. "She thinks about kissing you, Clara."

I hate him for saying this. And I love him for it, too. The sudden brutal exposure of my forbidden thoughts cuts me open with desire. I'm bleeding embarrassment and arousal in equal measure.

Clara creeps closer to me. "Would you like to do more than just think about it, Sophie?" Her question slithers between us like a dangerous serpent. I'm not sure if it's so forbidden because she's a woman or because she's a *married* woman. My eyes dart to her husband, and that makes her chuckle. "Oh, don't worry. I'd never do anything my husband didn't approve of."

"Fortunately," her husband says, lighting his cigarette and snapping the lighter shut, "I'm a very approving sort of fellow."

Leo and Clara smile at each other and a spark ignites. Their fiery flirtation singes me, too, and a rush of heat flows through my veins. If they have the same effect on Robert, I can't blame him for having been drawn in. Anyone would be.

Clara turns back to me and tilts her head coquettishly. "What if I kiss *you*, Sophie?"

Robert squeezes my hand in reassurance. He wants me to do it, and the intensity of his stare makes me feel like I'm the center of the whole world. He gives my hand another squeeze, almost turning me towards Clara.

The scent of gardenia swirls under my nose as Clara scoots a little closer. She's lovelier than on her movie posters and her skin looks so soft . . . there will never be another moment like this and I'm not even sure this one is real. I quickly wet my lips with nervous assent, my hands clasped in my lap.

Clara's fingernails trace a sensuous line along the curve of my cheek before she touches her lips to mine. They're plump lips, petal soft and wet. She uses them to tease me, tickling at the corners of my mouth until I gasp. And when I do, she deepens the kiss, slipping her tongue against my palate.

Robert groans and it's at that moment I realize it's *really* happening.

I'm kissing a woman and the thrill of it makes me shiver.

Clara smiles like a cat whose gotten into the cream. I gaze up with wonder and her smile goes from amused to downright wicked. "Aren't you a naughty little thing . . ."

I'm not sure how she manages to speak because I'm breathless.

Leo takes a deep, thoroughly satisfied puff from his cigarette. Robert isn't nearly so relaxed. His voice drops at least an octave when he says, "You've no idea the filthy ideas in Sophie's pretty head."

I think it's the notion that any girl might have filthier ideas than she has that gets her blood up. Clara bats her lashes at Robert and says, "Really? And yet, she seems so innocent . . ."

I'm both jealous and excited by the way Robert knows how to incite Clara. She reacts to him by seducing me. She lets her hand drift over my shoulder in a caress, then down, down, tracing my breast, her thumb finding my nipple and giving it a tweak. The bolt of arousal she sends through me is so strong that I moan.

Then Clara bats her eyelashes at me. "Haven't you ever let a girl touch you before?"

When Robert seduces me, I sometimes have the urge to sass him or test his patience. But the way he's staring now makes me utterly pliant. And with Clara toying with me, I am easy prey. Between the two of them, they've got me mesmerized.

Clara palms both my breasts, whispering, "It feels good, doesn't it? You like it. Your nipples are so hard, you can't hide it. The boys can see it, too. They like watching us. My husband looks like he could devour me."

"Because he's going to," Leo promises, blowing a puff of smoke.

Robert moves to the table where he can get a better view, and his gaze burns a hole through me. "Do you want her to keep touching you, Sophie?"

"Yes," I whisper, because anything else would be an obvious lie.

Clara and I kiss again. Her body is pressed tight to me, her breasts straining under her dress, her tightening nipples brushing mine.

Robert caresses my right leg, but now Clara's fingers slide up the other thigh.

"You didn't seem so shy before," she says and I realize that my hands are squeezed tight between my knees. "Don't you want me to touch your pussy, Sophie?"

"Oh god." I give a sharp exhale, tilting my head back for her as she kisses her way down my throat, leaving a tingling trail in her wake.

"They want us to touch each other," Clara purrs. "It's getting them both pretty hot under the collar. Why, even Robert is sweating, and he never sweats."

Robert tugs at his tie. "That's not true. I sweat."

"No, he doesn't," Clara says. "At least not as much as everyone else. It's something freakish about him."

It sets my teeth on edge the way she reminds me just how intimately she knows him, but just when I want to claw at her eyes, she says, "I've never seen Robert look at another girl the way he's staring at you . . . he looks like he's going to melt into a puddle."

"Touch each other," Robert says, the tone in his voice leaving no room for argument.

I let Clara draw my hands onto her body, and she squirms underneath them, letting me caress the outlines of her generous curves. One shrug and the satin strap of her gown slips over her shoulder; it's a practiced move and I realize that she's performing. I don't think it's all for me, but I don't care.

Her body is so voluptuous, her skin so creamy, her hair so fragrant. I realize how much I want her. How much I want her to touch me. How much I want to taste her. My body throbs with its new and outrageous craving just as her slender fingers slip under my gown to caress my sex.

I moan, but I'm not the only one.

Both men make wounded sounds as if the sight of us together is too much to bear. This excites Clara as much as it excites me. I feel the flutter of her heartbeat beneath my palm as I caress and squeeze her round breasts. I hear myself panting as Clara's gentle fingers stroke between my slick folds. Her lashes sweep down as she gives me a look of pure wickedness. She plays with me, teasing my swollen pussy with a flutter of her fingers that sends a sickly rush of arousal through my belly.

Robert surprises us both by reaching around to grab her by the nape of her neck. "Keep kissing each other . . . and mean it."

Clara goes kittenish, a submissive look in her eye that I recognize because I'm feeling it, too. I want to please him. And her. I think I might even want to please Leo, who stays aloof from us, but has let his cigarette burn to ash.

Deep, sensual breaths fill the room and warm the air. It's the music of utter surrender as Clara and I kiss harder, tongues dancing in each other's mouths. Robert yanks down the straps of my gown, exposing my breasts for Clara, who dips her head. With a mischievous wink, she catches my nipple between her teeth and sucks it. Oh, the warmth of her lips closing around the sensitive flesh . . .

All I can think is that I'm touching Clara Cartwright. I'm kissing her and touching her and being fondled by her like we were lovers, while Robert watches me. When she kisses me again, I moan into her mouth and I arch against her hand, letting her give me pleasure that is itself a confession to a hunger I would never speak aloud.

She rubs me, but not the way that Robert does. I clutch at her, giving myself over to it. "Oh god, I'm coming," I whimper with a note of desperation and surprise as the ecstasy of it explodes behind my eyes. The whole time I'm enraptured with the thought that it's a woman doing this to me . . .

When it's over, Clara says, "I bet Robert loves playing with your pussy. It's still quivering against my hand like a little wet bird." Then Clara flutters her eyelashes and trails her fingers up to Robert's mouth so that he can suck them clean of my taste.

I don't know how to feel. I want them both. I'm shameless now, more needy than I've ever been, but I worry that she's about to steal him. What man can resist that sexy little pout and those come-hither eyes?

Apparently Robert can, because he doesn't kiss her, he kisses me. He kisses me hot and hard and with such a fierce sense of possession that I feel myself totally open to him. If he wants to fuck me here and now in front of Clara and Leo, I won't stop him.

In fact, I think I want him to do it.

He must see it. He must know it. But he pushes me down to my knees.

I bury my head in his lap, enjoying the swollen bulge of his arousal against my cheek. I'm ready to take him in my mouth but he lifts my chin and says, "Don't you want to make Clara come, too?"

I glance up, shocked when she threads her fingers through my hair and spreads her legs with a feline invitation. "Is this where you fantasized about kissing me, Sophie?"

There is nothing I can say. I shrink inside myself. I feel like a tiny mouse. Like a teensy toy that can fit in a box. Like something small and fragile. And my resistance crumbles to dust. I can't speak, I can only nod, stunned at my own willingness when I see she isn't wearing any underwear at all. But that isn't the surprising part. It's that she's totally bare. Shaved of all her hair.

Pink and swollen and twitching with her own sexual appetite.

I don't know what to do and I'm afraid I won't like it. I glance up at Robert and his concentration is so deadly earnest that I'm also afraid to meet his eyes. He wants this maybe more than I do, and that excites me enough to try.

I kiss her sex, tentatively, unsure. But her taste is mild and not altogether different from my own.

That's as far as I thought to go, but Clara tugs me against her. "I'm so close, Sophie . . . use your tongue."

I'm scared to do it, but curious, too. My tongue rolls gently over the pearl between her nether lips.

"More," she whispers, not afraid to pull my hair when I resist. And I do resist.

But she fists my hair in both hands, which excites me. I lick her, moving my tongue faster and harder. The taste of her is in my mouth and the scent of her is in my nostrils and I have a desire to please.

Something must give me away, because Clara gives me a wicked smile. "Ohhhhh, you like it, Sophie."

I try to deny it, but she digs her nails into my scalp. "Don't you stop."

She is hurting me. She is crueler to me than any man has ever been. And it makes it so much better. Her cruelty strips me of pride. It frees me to lick, suck, nibble, and lose myself in the forbidden act.

I like it. *Oh god*, I *love* it.

The men urge us on and a dam of resistance breaks open in me. I bury my face between her thighs, intent on her pleasure. It is my fantasy come true and I want it to go on and on. I think she knows. I think she holds back, forcing me to work harder for it. She wants to give the men a good show. She wants to make an impression. She keeps me on my knees, worshipping her pussy, until the carpet burns my shins and my scalp stings like fire.

The longer it goes on, the more I give myself over to it. I want them to see me do it. I want to do it just the way she likes it. It doesn't matter that my mouth is sore and my tongue is tired. It only matters that I want to make her come. I want to make her come because she wants it. And I also want her to come because Robert wants it.

He's done this to me and I love him for it

Clara finally moans, still pulling my hair. "Don't stop. Just like that . . . oh, just like that, just like that!"

Three rhythmic tenses of her belly and she's pulsing against my tongue, crying out in rapture. But that isn't the end of it. She holds my face there afterwards, making me kiss her pussy softly until she's spent.

Flushed and panting, her grip turns gentle and she strokes my cheek. Then she bends down to kiss me, tenderly and with genuine affection. "Good girl."

The moment she releases me, I look up at Robert and watch him *snap*.

Never in all the times we've been together has he grabbed me with such force. He pulls my clothes off like he owns me, like I'm his, like he can share me if he wants to. I can't escape him. And I don't want to. He has me naked in seconds, spread flat on the coffee table, the cool polished surface slippery beneath my shoulder blades.

I don't know what's happening. I don't much care, as long as his hands are on me. He tilts my head back and presses the shining crown of his cock against my lips. I take him in my mouth and realize there are more hands on me than just his. The silky brush of Clara's hair against my belly makes me cry out, but my sounds are muffled by Robert's shaft as it slides smoothly over my tongue.

The sensation is too much. I'm sucking him as Clara sucks on me and I can't stand it. His testicles bump my nose, forcing me to breathe around his tempo. Clara uses her tongue to torture me. It thrusts, it squirms, it taps and taunts. Her tongue rasps mercilessly against my sex until I'm dying of obscene, wicked rapture.

I want to please Robert. I want to please Clara. I want to please them all. I feel like the tiniest person in the room. A toy for them to play with. And the thought makes me come.

I scream around Robert's throbbing cock, awash in ecstasy.

I want to drink him while my own orgasm consumes me, but he pulls me down to my hands and knees by Leo's feet. I look up at the famous aviator and catch a look that passes between him and Robert. They don't need to speak; whatever they say is in a language all their own, but it looks like gratitude, understanding, and maybe . . . grace.

It's a strange thing to see, especially knowing that Robert is going to fuck me now. I shake with the knowing of it. I smell like Clara and need—I've done something utterly wicked and I'm reveling in it. Sex is base. Sex is animalistic. Sex is rooted in the earth. Its smells, its feel, its fluids, and its consequences are grounded in the here and now. But when he thrusts into me, I feel my spirit fly.

It doesn't take Robert long to finish, and when he does, we collapse together to the floor.

I laugh because I'm filled with unexpected joy. Robert chuckles, too, breathless, clutching me.

"Now *that* would have made a good movie," Leo says, with a tip of his glass.

Clara crawls to her husband. "You don't think I forgot about you, do you, Ace?"

"To the contrary, Mrs. Vanderberg, you sure do know how to show a fella a good time."

Clara and Leo make love in the chair.

Right in front of us.

And why not?

Spooning together in wordless emotion, Robert and I watch them. And they're beautiful to watch. I like the way Clara moves. I like the way Leo touches her. They don't care that we're watching; I think they've forgotten we're even here. They are two people so attuned to one another, so perfectly trusting of each other, that nothing else in the world matters. They're so in love that it radiates off them.

I can feel it. And my own emotions rise up in me.

"Thank you for giving this to me," Robert murmurs.

It was my fantasy and he gave it to *me*. But somehow, I understand. I've closed a circuit for him—I've made the same connections with the people he cares about. I've shared with him something he doesn't allow himself to have anymore. He was discontented and I've given him contentment.

There's something sacred in that.

"I'm falling in love with you," Robert whispers.

My heart fills to bursting, but I'm afraid to believe. "No, no, you aren't."

"Yes," he insists, his lips in my hair. "I am. And there's nothing halfway about it."

The declaration steals my breath away all the more for the quiet, sincerity with which he utters it. A lump lodges itself in my throat as I feel the weight of his stare. I don't know what to say or how to say it because what's inside me feels too big for words.

CHAPTER
Nine

A sliver of cruel morning sun tortures me from the only part of the window not covered by the curtains. My tongue rolls thick and furry in my mouth and a thousand tiny protesters roar their fury every time I move my head.

"Here," Robert says, sitting at the edge of the bed with a tonic in his hand. "This'll help."

I take a sip, but my belly threatens rebellion. "I think I'm going to be sick."

"Allow me to introduce you to your very first hangover."

That makes me laugh, which hurts my head. "You've introduced me to rather a lot of firsts."

He beams, boyish in the morning light. "Your first time, your first drink, your first hangover, your first girl . . . oh, Sophie, don't hide under the covers!"

I do it mostly to keep the sun from stabbing at my eyes, but the sharp edge of embarrassment cuts me, too. "Did that really happen? With Clara. Last night?"

"Oh, yes. I don't have photographic evidence, so you'll have to take my word."

I whimper. "I can't even imagine the discussion you must have had to arrange it—"

"I didn't arrange it."

"But, last night, in the club, you said—"

"By then, I knew," Robert says. "I know their moods."

He takes my hand, lifts my fingers to his lips, and kisses them. "Don't say you regret it, Sophie, or you'll break my heart. I needed that so much. We don't ever have to do it again, but I won't be able to bear it if you remember the evening with disgust."

"Disgust is the very last thing I feel," I confess.

I stand shocked at my own behavior. At my reckless loss of self-control. But the memories that flash through my mind only make me sigh with renewed desire. Clara's lips. Her breasts. Her taste. Robert's encouragement. Leo's cool observation. Somehow, the utter licentiousness of it fills me with satisfaction.

"I understand why you wanted to be with them."

His expression softens. "Sophie, last night wasn't about them. I need you to know that watching *you* excited me more than anything or anyone has ever excited me."

"That can't be true," I say, wary of believing him.

"Do you need proof?" he asks, sliding between the decadently silky sheets with prurient intent.

I hold him at bay with both hands. "Only if you can prove it quietly without jostling my pounding head . . ."

"Sophie . . . I've enjoyed the company of many women; I won't lie about that, but none of them ever needed me before and—"

"And you think *I* do?" I take umbrage.

"You *definitely* do. Spending your days philosophizing and making trouble. Hiding all that sex appeal beneath prim dresses and shabby underwear. Walking around with a head full of wild fantasies and no one to make them come true. It's criminal. You need me badly."

"You're awfully full of yourself," I say, my cheeks hot.

But I don't deny it, either.

"And I need you, too, Sophie. Because you make me feel like a man."

I roll my eyes, then realize he isn't teasing. He's trying to tell me something important.

He clears his throat. "I've been an overgrown boy most of my life because nobody ever expected very much from me and I've never disappointed them. Very few people ever needed me. I can count them on one hand and most of them died in the war. But *you* need me, you trust me, and because of that, I'm starting to trust myself. You challenge me to be smarter, stronger, and more disciplined. You make me want to be better."

"And that excites you?" I ask, thoroughly confused.

"Everything about you excites me. When I tell you to do something and you obey me, it's such a thrill that my cock jumps to attention. And last night, good *Christ*, you made me lose my mind."

"Perhaps you were just aroused because Clara was in the room."

He snorts. "Maybe that's why *you* were so aroused. I adore Clara, but she can't hold a candle to you in my eyes. She's a sweet ball of drama covered in a candy shell, but you're something to chew on. There's nothing jaded or hard about you. You're the genuine article, the real McCoy . . . and I think you were made for me."

Twinkling lights transform the hotel rooftop into an elegant starlit venue. A band plays at the far end and several hundred well-dressed people laugh and dance and swipe hors d'oeuvres from silver trays.

"Is that Douglas Fairbanks and Mary Pickford?" I whisper, in a near panic. It was one thing for Robert to introduce me to his friends in a speakeasy, but now he's squiring me around on his arm in real society. "Are you sure I should be here?"

"I love to introduce you to new things," Robert says with a wink. "Besides, Clara and Leo would be heartbroken if you didn't show up."

Clara and Leo's aviation film won a big industry award and to celebrate, they've rented out the rooftop of the Aster Hotel. Now they're dancing, cheek to cheek, cradling a statuette between them like a love child. They're strange and gay and happy, and their joy is infectious.

I'm happy, too, and why shouldn't I be?

There's a whole night sky of twinkling possibility overhead.

Clara waves us over. I flush and go tongue-tied as I drift into her orbit, but she kisses me on both cheeks, easy as duck soup. "Sophie, say you'll come with us!" Clara turns in her husband's arms, leaning against him. "Leo is taking me to Cape Cod for a few weeks and we're going sailing. You and Robert should join us. Can you imagine the fun we'll have on the beaches?"

It sounds wild and decadent and given Clara's enthusiasm, probably something that Robert has done with them before. But for a man with his reputation, he's strangely reticent. Robert says, "I'm afraid we can't. I have a hotel to run, you see . . ."

Clara laughs, resting her head on her husband's shoulder. "Oh, *bushwa*. You're the boss, Robert. Give yourself a vacation and we'll hit every dive roadhouse on the coast and—"

"Bobby," Leo interrupts. "Eyes at ten o'clock."

Robert glances over his shoulder and stiffens. "Oh *hell*, my father is here."

Following his gaze, I see the portly ambassador in a knot of similarly dressed older men sporting long mustaches that went out of style at least a decade ago.

Leo scowls. "He didn't tell you he was coming?"

Robert gives a shake of his head. "He'd rather make a surprise inspection . . ."

A moment later, the ambassador makes his way over. By way of greeting, he gives a stiff bob of his head. Beside me, Robert steels

318 · Stephanie Draven

himself, tension vibrating through his hand into mine. "Father. It's good to see you. You know Mr. and Mrs. Vanderberg of course."

The ambassador barely acknowledges the duo. "What's this bash costing us? You've got too many waiters working the floor and—"

"May I introduce my date for the evening? This is Miss O'Brien."

The old man nods, indifferently. "A pleasure to meet you, Miss O'Brien. You look lovely tonight." It's a reflexive compliment, dismissive even, as if his son has introduced him to many young ladies. Then something drags his eyes back to me. "You're not Paul Kendrick's cousin from Ireland, are you?"

The old man's scrutiny makes me awfully nervous. "No, sir, I'm afraid not."

"But you look so familiar," he says, puffing on a pipe. "What does your father do?"

Robert starts to say something, but I'm so nervous I talk right over him. "My father was a coal miner."

Old Mr. Aster chuckles until his belly jiggles. "A miner, she says. And I suppose your mother was a kitchen maid. Don't try to pull the wool over my eyes, girl. I've seen you here before."

Robert intercedes. "Sophie works in the hotel boutique."

The ambassador's expression goes sour as spoiled milk. He glares at his son as if he'd arranged my presence just to humiliate him. "Of course she does. Yes, I remember now."

Robert doesn't shrink under his sire's withering glare. "I hope you have a good time tonight, Father. Sophie and I intend to."

With that, he whisks me away to the dance floor.

We dance. We flirt. We sit close together.

But Robert doesn't drink. Not one drop.

And the next morning, he's up and ready for work at eight o'clock sharp.

I know because I see him in the elegant lobby when Clara and Leo sweep out, promising to return in a few weeks on their way back from Cape Cod. Embracing in fond farewell, Clara takes Robert's face in her hands, telling him something I can't hear from so far away. Then Leo shakes Robert's hand and leans in close to whisper something in his ear.

They love him, I realize. They love him. Not in any way that there's a name for. But it *is* love. Deep and abiding. It ought to make me jealous, but I find myself strangely grateful that two people in the world besides me know how special Robert is.

Something has changed.

In the days that follow, Robert actually works at his desk all day. He doesn't laugh as much as he used to and I begin to think that I've done something to ruin his love for me . . .

Maybe that's why I'm so relieved the night he asks me to join him in his suite. When he opens the doors to the balcony, my heart starts to gallop as I remember the fantasy I wrote about the girl who makes love outside, high above the street where anyone might look up and see her. If Robert shares my instant, eager arousal, he controls it and simply lays a card on the balustrade for me.

Oh, good. Our game. Smiling, I tear the card open. Then my smile fades away . . .

Marry Me.

The words seem so stark on the pale paper. I'm suddenly dizzied, hypnotized by the faraway sounds of the car horns from the city below. I turn the card over, as if to see if there is anything more written on the back. I must stare at the card for a very long time, because Robert noisily clears his throat.

I look up to see him grinning at me like a mischievous boy, glee shining in his eyes.

He's very proud of himself and he probably expects a much different reaction than the one he's getting. Knowing how very long he's dodged husband hunters, I'm moved. What woman wouldn't be? But I back away from the railing, suddenly afraid of the height. "I don't understand."

"It's a marriage proposal, Sophie. It isn't very complicated."

"But I don't understand what you mean by it."

"I mean to take you as my wife."

A summer's night breeze catches my hair. "Why?"

He leans dangerously over the rail. "Because it would make everything so much better, don't you think? For one, we could stop using French letters. Wouldn't you like to feel me bare inside you? Hot pulses jetting up into your womb?"

The thought does make me a little weak in the knees, at least until I consider all the children that might follow. "You said you wanted to become a respectable businessman and move into the family mansion . . ."

The corner of his mouth lifts. "I'll take you with me, of course."

The idea makes me slightly ill. "And what would we do? Take the train into the city for work every day or be chauffeured by your driver?"

A flicker of confusion passes over his face. "You wouldn't have to work, Sophie. Not another day in your life."

My anxiety blossoms into full-blown panic. "What if I wanted to?"

"Why the devil would you want to? Why would anyone want to work if they didn't have to for money or the sake of appearance?"

My lips press together to hold back barbed words that nearly fly off my tongue. I take a deep breath and try to remain calm. "I don't plan to be a shopgirl forever and there are a great number of causes I care about."

"You've made that clear, *Comrade*. But as my wife, you'll need to be more careful about which ones you lend my name to."

I think of all the times he's indulged me with a wink and a nod. The reality of what he's suggesting sinks in with horrible clarity. He sees me as the kind of woman who will marry a man and become an extension of him, a possession he can control. Perhaps the spankings aroused him because he always thought of me as a child. I've let him think that. Until now, I enjoyed his mastery of me as love play. I've dismissed his Victorianism as quaint and charming. But maybe it was deadly earnest. Maybe it was a thing meant to transform me into a wife.

And if I become his wife, that's all I'll ever be.

How foolish I've been to believe desire wasn't dangerous to someone like me, someone who took precautions. Someone who doesn't care what society thinks. It never occurred to me that desire might be more dangerous to me than anyone else. "You shouldn't have put this on a card, Robert."

He looks shell-shocked. "Why not? You're not turning me down, are you?"

Tears fill my eyes. "I was never angling to land the most eligible bachelor in America. I'm my own person. I love you but that doesn't mean I want to be *Mrs. Robert Aster.*"

He takes me by the arms, as if trying to understand. "Is this because of Clara and Leo? I can't promise to cut them out of my life, Sophie, but I can promise you they won't be more than friends."

"Don't be silly. I'm crazy about Clara and Leo. I would never want to cut them out of our lives."

He brightens. "You wouldn't?"

"Of course not. Robert, I think I first fell in love with you when I realized you could find it in yourself to form such tender attachments to them, without regard to convention . . . but I should have taken a warning. You couldn't make your relationship with Clara and Leo fit into what was expected, so you left them. Well, you can't make me fit, either. I'm not a substitute for them that you can mold into a more convenient shape."

"You were never, ever a substitute, Sophie. Don't you know that I love you?"

"I want you to *respect* me and to respect yourself, too . . . and I don't think you do."

A look of pure pain flashes across his face. "Are you saying you don't want to be with me?"

The question makes me hiccup with bitter, near-hysterical laughter. "I want to be with you all the time. I want you more than I thought anyone could want another person. More than reason or good sense would allow, and that's the problem."

A hint of a smile returns to his lips. "I don't see how that's a problem."

"It's a problem because I'm not sure I like who I become with you."

His smile evaporates.

Then he pales. "I think I need to sit down." He reaches behind him and finds a delicately wrought iron chair, lowers himself onto it, straightens his hair, and gives me a look of pure devastation. "What the devil are you saying?"

"I've been telling myself all the things we do together are play. That when I bent over your knee for a spanking it was harmless. But maybe those fantasies should have stayed secret and then I'd never know this about myself. I'd never know how much I crave in the bedroom all the very same evils that I fight against outside of it."

Wiping the sweat from his brow with a monogrammed pocket square, he seems to get ahold of himself. Then he gingerly reaches for the card in my hand. "Let's forget this, Sophie. This clearly isn't the right time. Sometimes I forget how young you are. You haven't seen or done enough yet. We'll go back to the way it was until you're ready."

He's patronizing me now. Likely he always will. He knows how I feel about marriage; I told him from the start. The very first day I ever met him. But he obviously dismissed it, just like he's dismissed everything else I've had to say that didn't involve being bedded.

"Too late, Robert. You made the rules. Either I obey you or it's over."

He crumples the card. "We're not playing anymore, Sophie."

Tears slip down my cheeks. "But I'm afraid it *is* over."

He angers. "Why are you doing this? I *know* you want to be with me."

I'm grateful for the sensualist he's helped me discover inside myself but not enough to betray the woman I've always been and the woman I want to be. "You're right. I want to be with you but I also want to be someone people look up to one day. And I can't be both."

The words come out before I realize the extent of the damage they will do. My hands fly to my mouth as if I could catch what I've said and take it back. But I know that my words twist inside him with all the hurtful things his father has ever said over the years. With all his insecurities and perceived failures. Even now, he doesn't guard those angelic hazel eyes against me, so I can see the toll it takes.

He stands up, his face a mask of pain. "I see."

"Robert, wait," I say, as he walks to the door. "Robert!"

But he's gone.

I hate myself.

I hate myself for hurting him. I hate myself for wanting him. I hate myself for all the immoral thoughts that give me pleasure and for not knowing which part of myself is a fraud.

Am I the girl who loves strong hands holding her down or am I the girl who can hold herself up?

I tell myself that heartbreak is just a growing pain and that when I finally emerge from it, I'll be something different. Something better. But in the meantime, I can't even bear to be alone with myself.

I throw myself back into my causes, attending meetings at the Civics League every night. It's the hottest part of summer. Tempers are high in the city and people idle about on fire escapes in a state of overheated torpor, but I'm cold all the time. Day after day, a chill seeps into me and I feel like I'm never going to be warm again. Perhaps I've burned so hot with Robert that it's all ashes now, nothing left inside me but cold, hard reason.

I should be glad of it. I've always wanted to be that kind of no-nonsense woman who makes an impact on the world.

Irene and Ethel try to keep my spirits up but I cry myself to sleep at night, snuffling back my sobs underneath the blankets so I don't wake them. The days are even worse, because I spend them in the Aster Hotel, where everything reminds me of him, and everything is stamped with his name.

One afternoon, we get a shipment of peach-colored lingerie with rosettes for the display counter and I burst into tears, so violently sad that even Mrs. Mortimer pats me on the back and sends me home for the day.

It's two weeks before I see Robert again. I'm shakier now than I was the first time he summoned me to his office, and when I see him at his desk, piled high with papers and other evidence of diligence, I realize I have more reason to be. There's no dazzling smile for me, no witty repartee, no evidence of his boyish charm. Instead of a silver flask of liquor, he takes a gulp from a teacup and finishes signing his name to some paper before reluctantly meeting my eyes.

"Miss O'Brien," he says coolly, setting the tone for our reunion. "I wanted to return this to you."

He hands me my journal, fastened with twine. It's just a little book, but the weight of it seems too much to bear alone. It doesn't seem right that I should have it. When he took it, it was more mine than anything else in the world. But it's become ours now. And maybe it's so heavy because the end has been written.

I try to make him look at me. "Robert—"

"*Miss O'Brien*, I want you to know that I've read your list of the hotel staff's complaints and I found most of them to be reasonable, well-considered, and articulately presented. You are still a very per-suasive woman."

How can he compliment me when he is so obviously angry? A ray of hope warms my breast. "Then you're going to make changes here in the hotel?"

His mouth turns down at the corners. "No. You see my father owns this hotel. He always did. I'm merely a figurehead, put here to pretend I'm not a complete disgrace to the family . . . or to any woman who might find herself in my company. At any rate, the ambassador has heard rumor of a strike and you should know he's hired some men to intimidate the agitators in the coming weeks."

He's warning me. He's giving us a chance to strike, to act together before we're singled out. I don't know if he does it out of spite for his father or love for me. Either way, standing here, so close, unable to touch him—it's crushingly painful, and it's all I can do to banish the tears that spring to the corners of my eyes.

I thought I knew Robert, but what if he's a stranger to me? Straightening my spine, I ask a question that's been niggling at me. "What happened to Mr. Underwood? He wasn't on duty in the elevator when I came up and he ought to have been."

"I saw to it that he accepted a job elsewhere," Robert says, frostily. "Somewhere I won't have to look at him every day."

"But you swore to me that you wouldn't take any action against him when I told you that he was the one who knocked Gertie up. You gave your word."

"What do you think, Miss O'Brien? Do you think that I grabbed him by the lapels of his jacket and tossed him out? Because I wanted to. Trust me, I did. But for your sake, I secured him a promotion. I believe I've satisfied the requirements of honor."

"A promotion?"

Robert puts his pen down and leans back in his chair. "I don't know if you were aware, but Mr. Underwood is a married man. He has a family on the outskirts of the city. His travel to and from work takes up more hours of his day than is ideal. He harbors a secret dream of being a professional golfer. There's a green only a five-minute walk from his home. When I arranged for him to receive an offer of gainful employment at the country club, he seemed positively thrilled to accept it."

I blink. "How did you learn all that?"

"I pay attention to what people want and need. It's a skill I perfected in the war. The country club needs enthusiastic employees. Mr. Underwood obviously needs more time with his wife. It seemed an ideal situation."

Every sentence is clipped and professionally distant. And in each of those sentences is buried enormous hurt and a reflection of who he is. He thinks it's a skill, but he's wrong. His way of seeking out what people need and finding it for them is a talent. It's a gift. He saw into me, found what I wanted, and gave it to me.

It isn't his fault that what I want is so wrong in every way.

I can't even beg him to take me back, because a woman ought not beg a man for anything. "I suppose that's a very diplomatic way of handling everything," I say. "Thank you. Maybe you should reconsider going into politics . . . I think you'd be awfully good at it."

"I'm not going to live my life for my father."

"You're not living it for yourself, either, so why not?" I'm afraid this will be my last chance to ever speak so familiarly with him. He glares at me, but somehow I find the courage to go on. "When the ambassador says he wants you to make something of yourself, it doesn't have to be the plan he's mapped out for you or a rebellion against that plan, either."

"You're the last person I ever thought might defend him."

"I don't like his politics and I abhor his business practices, but he just wants his son to take advantage of the opportunities that he worked for. He's not so different than anybody's father that way. Where he went wrong is never telling you how proud of you he is, letting you think that you failed him because you didn't *kill* enough people. He should have understood what a true hero you are. That's why you love Leo Vanderberg. Because he *knows* the strength that's deep down inside you. He knows the hero that you are, and I know it, too."

Robert closes his eyes. "Don't, Sophie . . ."

"I'm so sorry for what I said when I turned down your proposal. I know how it sounded—I never meant it that way. I only meant to comment on *my* worth, not yours."

"*Your* worth?" he snaps. "You don't think I valued you? You were worth more to me than anything. More than my entire family's fortune."

The sentiment is powerful but I notice he speaks in the past tense and that he still doesn't understand. "I want my worth to be measured in more than money. I want to be measured by my actions, and not those in the bedroom."

There's a long silence and then he says, "The first time I ever loved a woman, I lost her because I didn't understand her. I thought I understood you, but I don't. And it's clear now that I never will."

"What don't you understand? Do you think every woman wants to be cosseted and—"

"Answer me this," he says, jabbing a finger in my direction. "Are you really so inflexibly devoted to the principle of nonconformity that you can't tolerate even a tiny bit of convention in your private affairs?"

"Marriage isn't a tiny thing. And I'd like to know how someone like *you* can break from what's expected of you in the bedroom, then resign yourself to a life as a traditional businessman with a conventional marriage just like the father you pretend to despise."

"Convention isn't always bad," he insists, without answering my question. "You *like* that I take charge."

"Only in one way, but I shouldn't, even then. I'm wrong to. The things I've exposed to you . . ."

"*Good Christ*, do you think you're the only one, Sophie? Do you think I was never terrified by what you bring out in me?"

My voice wobbles. "Then maybe neither of us is very good for the other, are we?"

CHAPTER

Ten

The next morning, I catch a glimpse of Clara in the lobby surrounded by an entourage of valets and porters carrying more shopping bags and hatboxes than any one woman should ever need. Having returned from her trip to Cape Cod, she's ornamented with a glamorous wide-brimmed hat topped with a wild puff of yellow flowers. She sweeps right past me, then stops, causing several members of the hotel staff to crash into one another.

"Sophie!" Clara kisses both my cheeks, but I realize that's just a show for the onlookers when she hisses. "So what's the idea giving Robert the icy mitt? He's crazy about you and you're breaking his heart. You've got him all balled up about—"

I turn away to hide sudden tears and shake my head, miserably. The estrangement with Robert is more than I can bear; I don't think I can take being bawled out by her, too.

"Oh, don't cry!" she says, pulling a handkerchief from somewhere inside the complicated folds of her dress. "I can't take it when anybody else cries because then I start to cry, too." She gives the handkerchief to me and I dab at the corners of my eyes, afraid I'm going to break down right here in the hotel with everyone watching.

"Let's duck into the ice cream shop and get away from the crowd," she says, and just like that, she abandons everything and everyone to usher me into a leather booth where I try valiantly to compose myself.

"Oh, Sophie, I was all set to blister your ears but good. But now I see that you're just as balled up as he is. I don't understand why! Is it my fault? Is it what we did? That was just a little harmless fun . . ."

"No," I say, sniffling into her gardenia-scented hanky. "It wasn't that. That was . . . a wonderful evening. It isn't you or Leo or Robert, or even the three of you together—"

"Oh, hell, we've had our good times but I can keep my paws off him. Robert's a swell fella, but he's not *my* fella. In the end, I swear to you, Leo's the only one for me . . ."

"No, I mean it. It isn't about the three of you. It's just that Robert is—"

"Rich and handsome? Witty and urbane? I can see how a girl might hesitate to *settle* for that . . ."

She's needling me. She doesn't have to tell me his virtues and in truth, she's only talking about the ones on the surface. The aspects of Robert I love most aren't obvious to most people. Like his kindness, his compassion, and his genuine interest in providing for people. "There's nothing wrong with Robert," I stoutly insist. "It's just that . . . he proposed marriage to me."

"The rat bastard!" she cries and every yellow flower on her hat shakes with merriment.

"You don't understand . . ."

She's still chuckling. "Oh, I probably understand better than most."

"I don't want to be tied to a stodgy old legacy or imprisoned by his family's precious reputation. I don't want to become a shadow of myself . . ."

"Do you think Leo keeps me in a castle tower?" Clara asks. "Trust me, every day with Ace is the berries. Marriage is what you make of it and anybody who tells you otherwise is selling snake oil."

"But I know what Robert wants to make of it. Deep down he's a traditionalist."

"Sophie, all he really wants is to be loved and cherished for exactly who he is and who he can be. That's all anybody wants."

I don't think I'll have the courage to explain, but Clara's the only person who might understand. "It's more than that—just the marriage proposal, I mean. Most men wouldn't encourage thoughts like I have . . . wouldn't goad me to do things in bed that I ought to be ashamed of. I love him for it, which means that there's nothing to stop me. And something's gotta stop me or I'm never gonna be anything but what I am right now. Just a shopgirl in a hotel boutique where men think it's cute that I like to read a book or two."

Clara tilts her head, her hat at a precarious angle. She stares at me a few moments, then reaches into her handbag and pulls out a pack of Lucky Strikes. She lights one, then waves down a waiter and says, "We'll have two scoops, please. Make mine chocolate. Sophie, what flavor's your favorite?"

"Strawberry," I murmur, craving any sweetness that might chase away the bitter.

When the waiter leaves, Clara asks, "Those reporters out there trying to get a glimpse of me through those windows are going to write about what flavor ice cream I ordered. What do you think it says about me that I like chocolate? Do you think it means I'm a pushover or a Dumb Dora?"

I'm not sure what she's getting at and I shake my head. "Neither . . ."

"Then it must mean that I'm a terrible actress or maybe it means that I can't make a good film."

"It just means that you like chocolate."

"Now you're on the trolley." She exhales, a spiral of smoke escaping from her ruby red lips. "My favorite flavor of ice cream doesn't have a damn thing to do with anything. And if I weren't famous, nobody would even care. I'd walk into a shop, make my order, eat my ice cream, and close the door behind me when I was done. It seems to me, that's what you oughtta do."

The waiter brings us two scoops, just like we asked for, and two spoons. "You really think it's that simple? That people can just do whatever they want in bed?"

"Sex is never simple. But everybody's got a favorite flavor. Doesn't matter if they're a sinner or a saint. So you like strawberry. So what? It's nobody's affair but your own. So eat it. Enjoy it. Then go be whoever you want to be. You're going places, with or without Robert Aster."

We don't say anything else for a while. I'm too lost in thought and by the time I'm ready to take a spoonful of my ice cream, Clara's already finished hers. "I better get a wiggle on or Leo will send out a scouting party for me . . ."

"Thanks," I say.

"We're headed back to Hollywood in the morning. Come and visit us sometime," she says, sliding out of the booth to give me a tight, affectionate embrace. "Oh, don't get nervous. It'll all be completely innocent. I just thought you'd like to see what it's like to make a film about Sacco and Vanzetti."

"That's so kind of you," I say, my throat tight with emotion, because I'm grateful for so much more than the invitation.

She smiles, dropping too much money onto the table. "Enjoy your ice cream."

And then, with a sashay of her hips, she's gone.

The next day, we strike.

We picket on the street in front of the hotel with hand-painted signs and placards. Bellboys and maids, kitchen staff and table waiters, shopgirls and florists, janitors and shoe-shine boys, Negro workers

332 · *Stephanie Draven*

and white workers. All of us dressed in our Sunday best and singing little slogans as the ambassador's driver pulls his breezer up front and the old man snarls from the backseat.

"You're all fired!" Old Mr. Aster shouts as the traffic backs up behind him and shrill whistles and horns sound from the street. "What's more, if you don't leave the premises immediately, I'll have you arrested for trespassing."

A ripple of fear passes down the line and I hear gasps and low murmurs even though I know every one of us prepared for this possibility. Flustered, I clutch the sign in my gloved hand as a gust of wind blows two pamphlets out of my pocket and into traffic. If I chase after the errant pages as they tumble down the street in front of the hotel, I won't have to face the ambassador. But if I don't, who will? "It's a public street, Mr. Aster," I say, putting steel into my voice. "Besides, you can't fire all of us. If you do, you won't have any way of running your hotel."

"Is that what you think, young lady? I could find a replacement for each and every one of you within a day."

"What about me?" The voice comes from down the street and everyone turns to look. I don't need to look, but I do. There Robert stands, dapper as ever in my favorite blue linen suit, the one that makes his eyes look greener and fits snug around his broad shoulders. "Can you find a replacement for me, Father?"

I'll give the old bastard credit for one thing: He hides his surprise, assessing the situation so swiftly that he doesn't miss a beat. "You'd be the easiest one to replace, Bobby!"

Robert shows a flash of teeth, a charming smile that almost disguises the feral anger underneath. Then he laughs. "You're probably right. You never needed me to run this place."

The confrontation between father and son is so personal it's painful to watch, but none of us can seem to turn away from it, least of all me. Of all the times to make a stand against his father, this seems like the worst moment Robert could choose. I'm proud of him, but also overcome with a desire to save him from this ugliness. "Robert, please . . ."

My voice is drowned out by the ambassador's fury. "This is all your fault, Robert," he says, waving his cane in our direction to encompass the entire picket line. "I put you in charge here and look what you've let happen. You're to blame."

Robert takes a few more steps towards his father, hands in his pockets, nodding his head. "You're absolutely right. If I'd run the place the way I wanted to, maybe the hotel staff wouldn't be so unhappy."

"Not another word, Robert," the ambassador says, fuming. "This isn't the time or place for this conversation. Get in the car."

"I'm not getting in the car and I'm not crossing this picket line."

"Your mother was always too soft with you," the old man fumes. "You were her baby so I let her spoil you. You've had everything handed to you."

Robert presses his lips together in grudging admission. "You're right yet again. Almost everything good I've got was a gift from you or somebody else. But there are a few things I've earned for myself, and one of them is standing right here."

At this, he makes a half turn to face me.

The ambassador looks befuddled. "Are you talking about this girl?"

"Yes, I am. Because you see, I think she loves me."

My hand goes to my mouth and the sign I'm holding in the other hand starts to flap. "Robert . . ."

"In fact, I think she loves the very things about me that you can't stand. And if I've won her love, it's something I did all by myself. Maybe the best thing I've ever done."

"I might have known you'd lose your head over some little chippy," the ambassador snarls.

Robert's head snaps in the ambassador's direction, his expression dark as a storm. "You're my father, so you get a warning. But only one. If you ever call her that again, I'm going to smash your teeth in."

334 • Stephanie Draven

His earnest threat of certain violence shocks me into a wide-eyed gasp. I don't know what to say. I don't know what to think. It's all madness.

Robert turns to face me again. "I'm not asking anything from you, Sophie. You don't even need see me again after today. I just need to know whether or not you still love me. Because I've been giving the matter some thought, and I've realized you're the smartest, bravest, kindest, sexiest woman I know. You're *it*. You've changed my whole life."

"Robert—"

"I sleep now, you know. Right through the night. And I don't need liquor to do it, either. I thought I couldn't sleep because I didn't know who I was; the truth is, I just didn't know what kind of man I wanted to be. Now I know, and that's because of you. And even if I've lost you, it'll all be worth it if I know you love me."

"Oh, Robert," I say, shaking my head, unable to say more.

"*Do you* still love me?" he asks again.

My heart leaps to my throat. "Of course I do!"

His smile is soft and soulful. "Then give me a sign to carry."

His father's voice booms over the passing cars. "Robert William Aster, I vow by the Almighty, if you carry a sign for these ungrateful reprobates, I'll disown you. I mean it. I'll cut you off without a penny."

Robert doesn't even glance over his shoulder. He's just stares into my eyes. "It'll be worth it."

"Robert, stop," I say, unwilling to be the cause of this kind of strife.

"Listen to her," the old man says. "All your life you've been a somebody. But you're nothing without the family fortune. You'll be a nobody."

"I don't want to be somebody. I just want to be good for something," Robert says, pushing an errant wisp of hair out of my eyes. "And for someone."

"That's it. You're cut off! You'll be a penniless beggar, that's what you'll be."

"I don't think so," Robert says.

"You're dreaming, my boy."

"Maybe." Robert takes the sign from my hands. "But at least I'll be able to sleep at night."

⁂

I'm dead on my feet when the sun finally sets.

"You need a break," Robert says, walking the picket line beside me in the sweltering heat. He glances at Hamilton, Irene, and Ethel arm in arm. "Your friends are willing to spell you."

My clothes cling to me like wet rags and my toes are blistered, so I'm in no position to argue. I go with Robert around the front of the hotel and he sits me at the edge of a fountain, pulling my shoes off, one by one. Bone weary, I dunk my toes into the water and let out a delirious sigh.

"Isn't that better, Miss O'Brien?" Robert asks with a tip of his hat.

"You're behaving suspiciously like a gentleman, Mr. Aster."

He laughs. "Touché, mademoiselle."

Looking at him in the glow of the streetlights, I ask, "Why did you join us today? Just what do you think you're doing?"

"I'm following your lead . . . I can do that, you know."

"No, you couldn't," I say, remembering the silk tie he broke in love play. "We tried that once."

"Just because I like you under me in a bed doesn't mean that's the way I want you out of it."

I swallow. "That's not how it sounded when you proposed."

"Well, I made a mess of that, didn't I?" He clears his throat, pulling his tie open so that both ends hang from his sweat-stained shirt collar. "So what was his name, the young coal miner who got you to agree to marry him?"

My eyes close and I see a flash of meadow flowers, but I can't remember his face anymore. "Quinn," I say softly, ashamed of myself. "But I never agreed to marry him. I know how I made it sound, but

I wasn't being honest. Quinn proposed, but I never said yes. It's just that when a boy dies, especially the way he did, you saint him in your heart. Then you can't very well admit that you ever had doubts. Not even to yourself. He becomes a way to fend men off. Because they'll believe you if you say you're a widow in spirit, but they won't believe you want to be your own woman."

"I'll believe it," Robert says. "If you'll let me."

"Just what is it you want me to let you do?"

He has to work himself up to an answer. He cups his hand, dips it in the fountain and splashes the water on his face, smoothing it into his hair with his fingers and letting it drip down the back of his neck. Then he turns to me and says, "I was furious with you, you know. Hundreds of women—literally, hundreds—have thrown themselves at me, trying to get me down on one knee. Yet, both times I've been ready to shackle myself to a woman, body and soul, I've been turned down. With Nora, I could chalk it up to follies of my youth. But you? I thought you ought to have been damned grateful for the offer. It stung my pride like the devil when you weren't."

"Do you really think—"

"Let me finish," he pleads with me. "Or I don't think I'll be able to get it all out. The truth is, I've always been good at figuring out what other people need and abysmal at taking stock of what I need. I've finally realized that I don't need your gratitude. I don't need my pride—though I'd like to keep a little of it—and I don't need marriage. I don't need my father's approval, or to impress society ladies in the tearoom, and I don't need any of a thousand things I was brought up to believe were important. What I need is you, in whatever capacity you'll have me."

"So you're saying you *don't* want to get married?"

"I'm saying we can live in sin and become the most notorious lovers in the city, if that's what makes you happy," he says, lifting my hand to his mouth and kissing my fingertips. "That's what I want, Sophie. To make you happy. That's all I've ever really wanted. Because making you happy makes me stand taller. It makes me steady and strong. It makes me at peace with myself in a way I've never been. So it's a selfish thing, really . . ."

His words chip away at the dark caverns in which my fears live and light breaks through. It's a blinding feeling, as if I'm seeing the world in vivid color for the first time. By god, I've been the greatest fool that ever lived. What he says is an echo of everything I feel for him. All those times, I wondered how I could be so filled with spiritual joy at the animal acts that gave us pleasure, I never considered the simple truth of it.

I love to make him happy. Making him happy makes me stronger and truer to myself. And that's how it ought to be between a man and a woman in love. In and out. Push and pull. Give and take.

That's something beautiful. Something I'd be a fool to deny. A single tear slips over my cheek and I put both hands over my heart, to keep it from bursting. "I love you, Robert Aster. I'll be yours if you'll be mine."

"I'm already yours," he says, his words a solemn vow in the night.

"Good thing, then," I sniffle. "Because neither of us can afford a wedding."

"Don't get too excited by the idea of our impoverishment, *Comrade*. I'm not penniless yet."

"You think your father will change his mind?"

"He might. If I run for political office, he won't want the Aster name diminished no matter which party backs me, but truthfully, I don't care what the ambassador does. I don't need his money the way he thinks I do."

"You've never been without money, Robert."

"I don't plan to ever be," he says, affronted. "You see, most soldiers need to live off their wages. I saved mine and invested it into a wildly successful little movie company with my business partners, the Vanderbergs. We've made a handsome profit so far. That's the beauty of unfettered capitalism for you, by the way . . ."

I laugh through my tears. "Are you trying to pick a fight with me, Mr. Aster?"

"Will it get your Irish temper up if I do?"

"It just might," I say, throwing my arms round his neck.

"Then I'd better cool you off!" he cries, falling back, dragging me with him. We hit the water with a splash and I yelp with laughter as droplets rain down on us from the fountain above. I try to drag myself up but he holds me against him under the spray until the rapture radiates through my whole being.

"C'mere," he says, leering. "I want to give you something new to write in your journal . . ."

He kisses me, heedless of passersby who point and stare. Grinning, I rest my hands on his soaked jacket where I feel something slightly crinkly in the pocket. "What's this?"

"Another card, but it's all wet and smeared now."

A thrill of excitement goes through me. "What did it say?"

He looks down at me sheepishly. "It said: *Love me forever.*"

My heart squeezes in my chest and I'm filled with joy.

Love me forever.

I know the rules. And this command is one I'm honored to obey.

AUTHOR'S NOTE

The Roaring Twenties were a time of sexual liberation, experimentation, and exploration. Having just won the vote, women were at the forefront of social causes and societal change. In spite of—or perhaps because of—Prohibition, the Twenties were boom times. Young women attended college, flocked to major cities to find work, and lived on their own in numbers never before seen in the history of the nation. Homosexuality was more public and more tolerated. Rules for dating changed. Nonmarital sex became common, and women began to demand and use birth control.

Flappers changed the world of business, fashion, politics, and popular entertainment. The Hays Code wouldn't be adopted and enforced until 1930, which meant major Hollywood films pushed the boundaries of propriety and gave the country some of its sexiest stars. (Clara Bow was one of them, and she served as an inspiration for me.)

In short, the Twenties were a period of social transition—one of those pivotal times in history when women took one step forward, before being shoved two steps back. And because flappers have more in common with women today than almost any generation since, I wanted to write about them.

For me, the beauty of using an historical backdrop in fiction is that you get to comment on the world today. That was certainly the case with this book. So while I spent more time studying the etymology of era-appropriate words and idioms than I did actually writing the stories, I've erred on the side of accessibility. The flavor of the Roaring Twenties is reflected in the dialogue and narrative, but an occasional anachronism crops up simply because it made a point or was too delicious to resist.

For reference, the stories in this book take place in 1928 and 1929 before the stock market crash that touched off the Great Depression. The exact chronology of the affairs involving Joe Kennedy, Gloria Swanson, William Randolph Hearst, Marion Davis, William S. Paley, and Louise Brooks have been fudged a bit but occurred roughly contemporaneously.

People from all walks of life came together to agitate for progressive change in the Twenties and, in many instances, African Americans led the way. At the same time, the era saw a resurgence of the Ku Klux Klan, inspired, in part, by the 1915 race-baiting incendiary film, *The Birth of a Nation*. Consequently, it was with some trepidation that I used the word *Negro*, which was polite vernacular at the time.

I want to make plain the fact that while Sophie, my working-class Irish heroine, is first seen encouraging a black coworker to participate in collective bargaining, this should not be taken to diminish the leading role in the social movements taken by African American women like Ida B. Wells, Amy Jaques Garvey, Mary McLeod Bethune, Mary Church Terrell, and others like them.